THE MIDNIGHT PRINCESS

KEIRA DOMINGUEZ

KLICKITAT CANYON

CONTENTS

For my husband

These books would not exist if I didn't sail my ship on the vast, fathomless sea of how much Nathan Dominguez loves his wife.*

*Also, babe, while we're here, is this a good time to remind you that Shaun White is not a floppy-haired, snowboarding slacker but an inspirational American athlete and entrepreneur?

1

ROYAL WEDDINGS

ALMA

"You look happy, *elskede*."

My uncle spins me around, and my dress, deep blue with a scattering of brilliant sequins across the skirt, swirls against my hips. Sleeveless and low-cut, I'm aware of how it frames the line of my shoulders and delicate collarbones, a daring look for a princess of Sondmark.

I give him a kiss and continue on my way, circulating throughout the ballroom, taking care of my mother's guests—a wide network of family and friends—smiling at their jokes and dancing when I must. I have a word with the band leader when the songs get depressing. No one is allowed to be famished or friendless on New Year's Eve. Not on my watch.

I'm halted in my course by Caroline. "The Crown Prince of Vorburg arrived, ma'am," she informs me as we step away from the loud music.

"Finally." My gaze arcs over the crowd. "Did he say what detained him?"

It's almost midnight, and even though his arrival was always going to be discreet, the man is hours late. I'm not impressed. The requirements of my royal position suffocate me as tightly as the corset bodice giving structure to this gown, but I'm still doing my duty.

"Snow in the mountains," Caroline answers. "We lodged him in the Tower Suite along with his aide, as you instructed, and communicated that Her Majesty will meet with him in the morning."

Check, check, check.

My mother's secretary melts into the background, and instead of running off to monitor the canapé situation, I take a glass of champagne offered by a passing footman. The queen's last assignment of the year has been discharged, and I've earned a rest. I down the liquid in two swallows, and the bubbles wrinkle my nose. It's a party, isn't it? Depositing the flute on a side table, I lift another from a tray, giving it the same quick treatment.

Everyone deserves a night off. Even me.

I wait to feel the heavy load of royal responsibility roll from my shoulders. The relief. The peace. I wait.

And wait.

Maybe a little more alcohol will solve it.

I chase an ever-retreating serenity to the bottom of the next glass and the next, but the champagne does more than jostle the Pandora's box of emotions I've kept padlocked for an entire week. It knocks the lid off, spilling the contents where anyone might see the betrayal, exhaustion, and pain.

As the clock nears midnight, I stand in the middle of the dance floor, and my cheeks burn hot. It would be nice to stand here and cry myself sick, but the horror of such a thing roars to life, its size and scope dwarfing every other emotion. I'm not supposed to have feelings. I shake my head, and my brain knocks against my skull with a bruising thud. I'm allowed to *have* feelings—just not allowed to show them.

A swirl of blue and red and yellow lights flash against my eyelids. I've never been drunk before, not even in college. At royal engagements, I've only ever sipped half glasses of champagne, nursing them along until the bubbles go flat.

This is not a comfortable sensation.

The room is stiflingly hot, and a burning pressure shifts from my eyes to my heart, affording a brief window of sobriety. *Get out before you disgrace yourself.*

Jolly good idea. Pressing a hand over a hiccup, I melt through a doorway into a narrow hall, following an instinct to find someplace cool and quiet.

Music follows me from the ballroom, a depressing pop ballad about the misery of meeting your ex in the boxed wine aisle of the grocery store on a snowy New Year's night. Instead of turning around to have another talk with the band leader, I speed up, brushing heavily against a potted fern, wandering blindly until I find myself at the orangery—a little-used room with fountains, rows of south-facing windows, and blue moonlight streaming through the glass.

As soon as I step across the threshold, the relief is immediate, and I let out a loud sigh of pleasure, the sound of it swallowed up in the soft shadows. This is perfect. There's no one here to ask questions about my engagement—about when stupid Pietor will be returning from his stupid charity trip to the other side of the stupid world. No aunt will tell me how lucky I am to have him or drop a gentle hint about wanting an early notification of the wedding date because she's spending spring on the Riviera and needs to have this nailed down so the jeweler knows what to take out of the vaults.

A tear slips down my cheek, and I wipe it away with a white-gloved hand. Surely it won't hurt to cry where no one can see.

I breathe slowly, deeply. No one in the palace will ask about the Italian bikini model Pietor had his hands all over because no one but my family knows about her yet. No one is going to congratulate me on the broken engagement and pronounce me well rid of my fiancé because no one knows about that, either.

No one is going to tell me that they thought I was the reliable one. That I've let down the family. That I'm causing trouble for the House of Wolffe. That will come later.

A distant bell chimes the last quarter hour of the year, and I shake my head to clear it, clapping my hands at my temples to make the clanging stop.

Am I sober enough to return to the party? A gust of cold air hits my bare shoulders and I shiver, peering into the dark shadows, past root-bound citrus trees in their ornate pots, their branches cringing against the high glass ceiling. Then one of the shadows moves.

"Who's there?" I call, half-convinced I imagined it.

A dark form unfolds from a bench.

"*Hej*," I yelp. I wait for an attack of manners, but inebriation hugs me like a massive marshmallow.

A man's voice offers a greeting. "*Witma*."

Oh, no. A Vorburgian. I'm not supposed to encounter one of those until morning when I'm capable of good posture and representing the Crown as a princess of the blood. Instead of feeling properly horrified, the alcohol has its way, and a laugh bubbles up my throat.

I tip my head, encountering the gray eyes of a stranger. "Hello?" I say, trying English.

"Hey." He smiles, the white of his teeth a contrast to the dark facial hair.

I take in his faded jeans and heavy-soled black boots, a leather and lambskin aviator jacket, and hair drawn back into a small loop. A few loose strands brush his jawline, and another pop of broken laughter escapes my lips. He doesn't look like my mother's secretary—neat, precise, fade-into-the-background Caroline. If this is who the Crown Prince of Vorburg has brought with him, we're going to murder them in trade negotiations.

"Too hot for a royal aide," I murmur.

"Excuse me?"

I'm sober enough to be deeply thankful my words were spoken in Sondish. I blink heavily. English, Alma. Speak English. "What are you doing here?"

I squint in confusion. My English is excellent but something about my phrasing seems off.

A smile touches his mouth. "Me and the stuffed shirt just arrived from Djolny. I thought I'd take a look around the palace before heading to bed."

My brows lift. Stuffed shirt? That's one way to refer to a future king. "You thought you'd go on a self-guided tour of a foreign palace? Were you going to poke your nose inside the linen closets, too?"

As soon as the words escape, I know they're the wrong ones. There's a diplomatic way a princess handles people who need to be put in their place, but I can't quite remember it.

He wanders closer, his booted feet scuffing the tiles, and shrugs his massive shoulders. "It's New Year's Eve. I couldn't settle down."

"You and me both," I laugh. "Nothing good happens on New Year's Eve."

Memories of last year cut through my brain fog like a ceremonial sword through a birthday cake. Memories of talking with Pietor in the drawing room, when we decided it was time for him to propose with his great-grandmother's opal. The sinking feeling that there would be no getting around the hideous, boil-shaped ring.

I glance down to my gloved hand. I remember Pietor's self-conscious laugh as he hitched up the leg of his tuxedo pants and went down on one knee during the New Year's ball—right in the center of the dance floor. How all eyes were on us. How we kissed at the stroke of midnight, congratulated by a crowd of family and well-wishers.

Everyone told us we were perfect for each other.

Were they wrong? Was everyone wrong? Tears threaten again, but as I stare into the warm gray eyes of the Vorburgian aide, the memories retreat until their echo is as soft as the music from the ballroom.

"What's not to like about New Year's Eve?" he asks. "I thought it was a time when anything was possible."

I snort—a sound I haven't made in twenty-five years. "It's a series of unreasonable expectations poured into shapewear and a party dress, capped off with a disappointing kiss at midnight. Who builds a holiday around the three pillars of"—I tick my fingers—"dashed hopes, crushing loneliness, and alcohol?"

He laughs, tipping his head back, exposing the strong column of his neck. My eyes widen, and a primitive thought shoots from the tiny part of my brain beyond the reach of rigid control. *He's beautiful.* Too wild and unkempt, but in the blue light of the moon, my fingers itch to touch him.

A flush spreads across my cheeks and down my throat. What is this? Attraction? I haven't allowed myself to feel that since before Pietor, at least. I get rid of it in the same way I'd send back an over-seasoned dish. No. No. Do not want.

But the unwelcome thought returns with surprising resilience. Strange. But if I can force myself to wear high heels for eight hours in a row and smile into the lens of every camera pointed at my face, I can control this.

"You were supposed to arrive hours ago," I say, gripping my hands together.

"There was snow coming through Elsum Forest," he answers, his voice rich and low. "We were crawling over the pass and had a flat tire."

Why is his American accent so flawless? My muddled brain gropes for an explanation. Maybe he's a dual citizen, washed out of the U.S. diplomatic corps, and the royal family got him cheap. I look for clues to support my thesis, but the alcohol has made me slow and ridiculous. I keep getting sidetracked by how pretty he is.

"I bet you're good in the middle of a blizzard. You look like you could rip apart tree trunks with your bare hands," I blurt, placing a hand against my chest and enunciating clearly. "As a trained Girl Tracker, I could light your fire."

He nods solemnly, but his eyes sparkle with laughter. "You could," he answers, tucking his hands into his back pockets. His eyes drift to my lips and across my shoulders, and I catch an unexpected flare of appreciation lighting his eyes. When was the last time I got a look like that? At least a year. Maybe two.

"This is your first time in Sondmark." The statement is a mess—half question, half declaration. I'm never this unfocused, but his eyes are gray.

"Yes. I'm touring the city tomorrow. What parts should I hit?"

I wander to the window, tapping against the pane. Remnants of the storm swirl around the palace grounds.

"Tourists go to the harbor. You can take selfies with the statue of Horst the Invader, and there's a cheese market where the workers wear folk costumes. They'll charge you double if you don't speak Sondish."

I'm exhausted by the effort of organizing my thoughts and reining my tongue. The air coming through the glass is cooling my skin, but I want more of it. I twist the handle and crack the long window a couple of centimeters, holding it against the gusts of wind.

"But?" He wanders to my side.

"But what?"

"But you think I shouldn't waste my time."

How does he know what I think? I put a palm to my flushed cheek. "The harbor is really nice," I insist. "Like a postcard."

"Postcards aren't real," he submits, his voice a soothing touch.

It's true. Handsel's oldest quarters are a thin façade of a Sondmark that doesn't exist anymore.

Cool air swirls around us. "Where else should I go?"

"Roslav Cathedral." I tap another pane to indicate the part of the old city miraculously untouched during the occupation. "You'll get to see the wooden throne of Harald Dragonslayer. It's where we hold coronations."

He turns his head. "And royal weddings?"

I clap my hand over his mouth, palm soft against his lips. "We must not speak of royal weddings."

I still for the space of several heartbeats, hearing the roar in my ears, registering a pressure in my chest. Gradually, the sensation shifts as his eyes hold mine. Warmth licks along my forearm and I snatch my hand back before it spreads.

"It's getting close to midnight," he says, looking out the windows, watching the yellow light spill from the ballroom. "You're missing the party."

"I'm not missing anything."

"No Sondish traditions? Am I giving you a year of bad luck by keeping you here instead of doing the chicken dance when the chimes strike twelve?"

"The Handsel Hustle," I say with a giggle.

His lips press into a smile, and he leans against the glass with one of his big shoulders. "What *do* you people do?"

You people. This man is no diplomat. "We fry dough and roll it in sugar—" I halt.

"And?"

I release the window latch. "There's a kiss to bring luck. And then we sing 'Wish You Health, Money, and Love.'"

"A kiss for luck? You have to get back in there for that."

Vede. Pieter again. My broken engagement again. Failing my mother again. I swallow away the tears, but the effort takes a toll. "I told you, New Year's kisses are always disappointing. Anyway, there's no one to kiss." There. I said it—the truth, even if it's to a stranger.

His gaze sharpens, and he gives me a slow smile. "No one?"

My stomach flutters, and I blink several times, wanting to parse out his meaning. I could if I were sharp, sober, and clear. But if I were those things, I'd be back in the ballroom, thirsty, humorless, and duty bound.

Beyond the glass, fireworks begin to burst over the city, anticipating the New Year by a few seconds. I emit a squeak of delight. The explosions set off more blasts until the whole valley comes alive with spiraling light, crackling booms, and screaming whistles. Farewell, demons of the old year.

"It's the wrong time," I remember.

He laughs. "Is there ever a wrong time for that?" he asks, nose almost to the glass. A shower of sparks blooms in his eyes.

My breath catches, and the distant crowd begins to count. "Ten, nine, eight..."

A loud boom cracks over the harbor, rattling the window panes. Massive fireworks shoot from the decks of naval vessels, lighting up the valley.

"Seven, six, five..."

The light in the orangery shifts from blue to crimson to gold, playing against the planes of his face. I'm caught in a spell, carried along by champagne bubbles, a whole city of lights, and a man who makes me want to curl around him.

"Four, three..."

I take a breath, surrendering to my most inarticulate, foolish wish. "I can't have bad luck all year."

With a low laugh, he tugs me close, steadying me with his hand, warming me through the thin material of my dress. His eyes dance. "You won't."

I lift my face. This is nothing more than a quick kiss to usher in the new year, but when his lips touch mine, I know I'm wrong. He feels it too. I sense it in the way his body suddenly quiets, every shuddering dial turned all the way down until he tilts his head, angling his mouth for something that lingers, a kiss that takes the last brittle straw of the old year and spins it into gold.

I lean into him, forgetting that I'm a princess for a moment, forgetting that I have responsibilities and a reputation. Promising to pay tomorrow for the indulgences of tonight.

He gathers me close, and wind tears the window open, swirling through the room, fluttering sheltered leaves, and tossing my skirts. Something wild has been let loose in the palace, shaking my root-bound self.

It's too early, I think. But the thought is pushed out by a warm thumb tracing the rim of my shoulder. No. There's no wrong time for this.

"Two, one!" The distant chimes ring but I don't hear the shout that pours from the ballroom. I want to push my fingers through his hair, but just as I lift my hand, he raises his head. A breath breaks from his mouth, and a smile plays on his lips.

My lungs catch, but sound rushes in on me. The guests are already halfway through the traditional song.

I take a large breath, eyes enormous. "That was—"

His voice is low, stunned. "Yeah."

2

HANDS OFF

JACOB

For one frozen second, as fireworks explode over the Handsel valley, the girl and I watch each other, light touching the soft curves of her face. A midnight kiss was not on my bingo card.

All the way through the forest, Karl was relentless about royal protocol and keeping to the timetable, every setback and delay making him more anxious. As soon as we arrived and were escorted to our suite, he became absorbed by a complicated skincare routine, and I slipped away, desperate for fresh air and two minutes of silence.

I'm a grown man. I wasn't going to get into trouble. I was going to keep my hands off the valuables.

I look down. One hand holds this girl around the waist. The other rests on her shoulder, our skin warmed by the contact as her scent fills the air.

What the hell just happened?

I open my mouth to ask, but her expression turns to one of surprise mixed with horror. She peels herself out of my arms and ducks around me, latching the window closed, extinguishing the wind with a flick of her wrist.

"Happy New Year," she murmurs, running away before I can say a word.

There's nothing to do but return to the suite, assure an anxious Karl that I haven't done anything to cause an international incident, and lie awake for hours, wondering when I'm going to see her again.

When morning comes, I wake to the familiar sounds of my alarm—the clashing drums and resonant, Viking vocals of Thorock—and throw an arm over my face.

"Welcome to Sondmark, Your Royal Highness."

I bite back the warning he'll only ignore. *Don't call me that.*

Karl shoves the drapes aside, his voice cutting me away from the illusion that I might be in the flat situated above my workshop on the outskirts of Djolny, nursing a cup of coffee and going over my accounts before the day's work. It cuts me away from the pretense that I'm still plain Jacob Gardner, dual citizen, a man who might have lived in Europe since he was thirteen but whose roots belong in Oregon.

I silence the music and grin into the crook of my elbow. No matter who I am, I've already had an unforgettable welcome. My mind retraces the curve of her back as she leaned into me, remembering her laughing eyes and the way she asked to be kissed.

But Karl won't quit fussing around the room, making pretentious adjustments suited to my new title. Finally, my feet hit the floor. "*Chol nia*, Karl. Can you give it a rest?"

"Never, sir. I took the liberty of setting my alarm an hour before your own. Your robe?" he asks, turning a sour smile on my pair of flannel pajama bottoms. He holds the robe open, but I scowl and snatch it out of his hands.

"My name is Jacob," I say, shrugging it over my shoulders.

Karl bows. I swear the *zekle* looks for reasons to do it. "Of course, sir."

A gust of wind rattles the windowpane and I wander over, bracing my hands on the frame to inspect my view. Handsel is a mix of modern skyscrapers, orderly rows of townhouses, and public squares. Parish churches with narrow, elegant steeples dot the valley floor, but the stony gray heft and flying buttresses of Roslav Cathedral dominate the center of town.

We can't talk about royal weddings.

I run a thumb along my lower lip and cover a smile.

"Sir?" Karl asks.

My hand drops, curling into a fist. "The nudists are going to freeze their toes off," I say, pointing at the whitecaps in the harbor. "It'll be a cold New Year's Day plunge."

My answer disguises my one, driving thought. Who is that girl, and how do I meet her again?

Karl clears his throat. "We don't have much time, sir," he says, opening a leather portfolio. "Your meeting with Her Majesty The Queen begins in little more than an hour. In that time, you'll need to have breakfast, shower, shave, and dress before we present ourselves."

"I'm not shaving." I'm surprised he hasn't brought in a barber to cut my hair, too. Karl thinks he'll wear me down with repeated asking. Never.

Even though I'm the crown prince of Vorburg, that's one decision I can still make.

My American mother, an otherwise sane woman, waged a battle in the Vorburgian courts, taking the better part of two decades, to have me acknowledged as King Otto's biological son. Her depositions and legal filings seemed a strange hobby—one that took up half the dining room table but required nothing more of me than a careless prick of the finger—until the sudden decision legally declaring me King Otto's child, a prince of the blood, and his only heir.

Who knows what Mom hoped for when she moved us to Vorburg and started all this? A house? Money? For my father to take an interest in his biological son? She couldn't have imagined a victory of this magnitude.

Legal or not, no royal command or parliamentary edict could've persuaded me to become the heir to a kingdom I only half belong to. But Mom cried when the verdict was read.

She doesn't cry for anything.

Karl takes a pen and strikes the item off his agenda. "If you're not shaving, we have more time to acquaint you with the situation in Sondmark. You are woefully unprepared for your meeting with Her Majesty."

"I had deadlines to meet," I remind him. "Clients I had to satisfy."

"A crown prince doesn't have clients." My aide pinches the bridge of his nose. It's not yet 8 AM and I've destroyed his patience. A new record.

"I appreciate that the king let me fulfill the outstanding orders. It's a shame I lost a finger." I hold my hand up, bending a knuckle. Karl blanches. I grin, unfolding the digit.

"Sir," he scolds. He can't be more than a year or two older than me, but he sounds like an old man meeting God, prepared with notes on how to order the universe. He clears his throat. "Her Majesty Queen Helena has reigned for over thirty years. She has one son and four daughters."

"Names?" I ask. I wonder if the girl from last night is someone like Karl—a royal aide, scurrying somewhere in the palace with a sheaf of papers and her own agenda. No. I can't imagine someone like Karl getting tipsy, even on New Year's Eve.

Karl holds up a tablet. "This is Crown Prince Noah. He's unmarried and hasn't had a serious relationship in several years. The queen will only approve of the right sort of consort." He swipes his finger. "Princess Ella. She's a bit of a rebel."

The picture shows a smiling girl with a curvy figure and a bright shock of curly red hair. I like her already.

Swipe. "Her twin is Princess Freja." This time, the girl is tall and slim, her hair straight, and her expression something out of a medieval triptych—the Virgin Mary slowly finishing her chapter while Gabriel the archangel waits impatiently in an adjoining room.

I look over my shoulder as I make the bed. "This is the one who eloped last week?"

Karl gives me an approving nod. The fact that Freja's wedding took place in a Vorburgian chapel sparked off a crisis between our countries. It's the reason I'm in Sondmark.

"She doesn't look like someone who would get carried away by emotion. Was he rich?"

"Hardly. I urge you not to say anything about the wedding to Her Majesty." Karl suggests. "Avoid the topic altogether unless she introduces it. The Sondish are easily irritated when it comes to Vorburg, and this needs a light touch."

I don't need a reminder about light touches from a man who has never attempted to inlay birch in a mahogany panel. Good craftsmanship requires precision. The palace, for instance— I glance to the ceiling, surprised to see that the round room is offset from the central spire by at least a foot. Careless. Well, my point still stands.

Karl swipes to yet another princess—young, very girl-next-door. "Princess Clara. She's dating a Navy officer."

"Her mother approved?" I ask, shaking the pillows in their cases.

"Unlikely. She's also currently suing the press for breach of privacy. Queen Helena has her hands full." Karl flips the cover closed.

"You said four daughters," I say, stretching my arms over my head with a huge yawn.

"Mm?" Karl clicks his tongue, scolding himself. "I got them out of order." Giving another swipe, he holds the tablet out.

I glance at the screen in a cursory way and feel the recognition in my body first—in the way my stomach tightens and my pulse pounds. That's her. I snatch the tablet out of his hands, fingers dragging across the screen and magnifying the image until I'm certain. Yes. That's her.

"Who is this?"

"Princess Alma." His answer is prompt, and even though I'm expecting it, the word 'princess' is like a jab to the gut, knocking the air from my lungs. "She's the eldest of the girls."

"Was this taken at an official event?" I snap.

Karl leans in. "Yes, the Monument Day observances last year."

The girl from last night is wearing a wide-brimmed hat and her face is covered in a veil, brown hair swept to the side in a knot. Her face is stiff and ceremonial. Her clothes are black and fit like a glove. Even her high-heeled shoes are perfectly aligned, each toe just kissing a line in the pavement.

I try to merge the images—the one on the screen and the one in my memory. The one who looks like she's carved out of marble and the one who stole my breath. I shake my head and toss the tablet on the bed. "What's her deal?"

"Deal?" he echoes, plucking it up.

"You said the queen has her hands full." I am working very hard to sound like I don't care. "What headaches does this one cause?" Does she wander the palace after a couple glasses of champagne, looking for strange men to cast under her spell?

Karl actually laughs. "Princess Alma is the perfect princess. The Foreign Office has intel on each member of the Sondish royal family, and this one has never stepped a toe out of line." He looks me over, his gaze lingering pointedly on my bedhead. "If you want to take any royal figure as your model for correct behavior, you would do well to choose her. Now, sir," Karl claps lightly, "we must respect the schedule."

I head to the shower, where the fittings are spacious and the water pressure is good. I'm jealous. The royal residence in Vorburg, Djolny Castle, has four ghosts and a time-traveling witch. As a proper fortress, it comes complete with fire-stained walls, narrow gates, stumble stairs, and thick parapets atop which my ancestors displayed the severed heads of their enemies. On one of my brief visits, the castle tried to kill me three times.

I lather and rinse, cutting the hot stream of water, and brace myself against the tiles. The girl last night kissed me. When I held her, she fit. In an ordinary world, Jacob Gardner would get her number. What's Crown Prince Jacob supposed to do?

I wonder what the chances are that the girl in that unreal photograph has a twin they hide in the attics and let out for parties. Maybe I should find an ax and start knocking down doors.

With a frown, I reach for a towel. No matter what organically-sourced, nitrogen-dense fertilizer Karl keeps shoveling about my titles and position, a princess is too rich for my blood.

"Seven minutes til eight," Karl calls through the door.

I speed through the basics of hygiene, pulling most of my hair back into a confining loop, and throw on some clothes, returning to the suite.

"You said you had a suit." Karl grips the back of a chair.

I look down at the blue suit, purchased from a secondhand shop for when I need something to wear at weddings and funerals. "This is a suit. It's a classic," I explain.

Karl inhales slowly. "From when? The Cold War?"

At least it's my own. During these last few weeks, I've been slow to accept my father's money. Slow to let his courtiers make me into someone I'm not.

Karl pulls a chair out, herding me to the breakfast table. "It's better than what you arrived in. We're incredibly lucky to get a second chance to make a first impression."

"It would have been fine."

Karl shudders. "You looked like an auto mechanic."

I snap the napkin out of its folds and toss it next to my plate. "One of us crossed a snowy mountain pass in leather-soled dress shoes. But sure, I'm the crazy one."

"You're the heir to the throne of Vorburg. I should have seen to our safety."

I glance at Karl's starched collar, the suit that whispers about inherited generational wealth, and the shine on his fingernails.

If I had waited for him to see to our safety, he would have died in the snow. I would have had to eat him.

Karl checks his wristwatch. "It's time for me to meet with the queen's secretary. You are to check your appearance before you leave that door. Your teeth. Your hair. Put on your suit coat and adjust your cuffs...such as they are."

"I've dressed myself before, Karl. Every day for thirty years." Nothing I say eases the tight, anxious look in his eyes.

"Teeth. Hair. You move in five minutes, sir," he says, setting a checklist at my elbow, along with an electric timer.

He gets in another bow before he goes, and I wolf down the eggs and sausage. I finish up by spreading cream on a bun, spooning a fat dollop of strawberry jam over the top. The jam slips, landing on the silk tie Karl conjured. It features the colors of Vorburg's national flag, white and green representing snow and forest.

"*Chol nia*." I swipe at it, spreading the mess. Now it looks like a deer has been shot and field dressed in the forest. I dip a napkin in a glass of water, blotting in what I imagine is the correct way. It is not.

The timer beeps insistently. I silence it, run a sucking tongue along the front of my teeth, scrape strands of hair away from my face, don my jacket, and rip the tie off my neck, wadding it into a pocket.

When I find Karl, he takes one glance at the state of my shirt and looks as though I wandered into his medieval village with open sores and a suspicious cough.

On the other hand, the queen's secretary, *Vrouw* Tiele, gives me a greeting and a brief nod, leading us into the administration wing. I shoot Karl a bland smile. *See? It's fine. No one is bothered.*

"I hope you rested well," she murmurs. "Her Majesty is looking forward to making your acquaintance."

A big, fat, diplomatic lie. After Princess Freja eloped in The Stranger's Parish, a chapel located in Handsel but on the grounds of the Vorburg embassy, my father pounced. Sondmark, our closest neighbor and oldest enemy, owed him a favor for the lapse in protocol. On my first mission as crown prince, I'm here to collect.

"We've got those Sondish *zekle* right where we want them," he said. "We have to press our advantage while they're swimming in humiliation. An elopement. Ha!" He clapped his hands, rubbing them together. "The queen's guts will be melting. She's going to wish you had never been born."

I gave him a cold smile. "It won't be the first time my existence represented an inconvenience for a European monarch."

My father, a stranger to shame, laughed at that.

When we halt in front of a pair of white and gold baroque doors, *Vrouw* Tiele flashes me a gentle smile before throwing them wide and announcing the title. His. Royal. Highness. Jacob. Crown. Prince. Of. Vorburg. Every word is a chisel, carving me into shape, each strike painful and gouging.

How can I live up to it? I can't. I enter the room like the queen of Sondmark is just another client employing me to build fitted bookshelves. I will be respectful, secure in the knowledge that I've spent long years of apprenticeship learning my craft.

Her penetrating blue eyes regard me as I cross the room, and with every step I am judged.

That's fine. It's good to know how it is right from the start. I'm an illegitimate son transformed by opaque legal processes into someone she has to condescend to notice. I'm a novelty—and not a welcome one. No necktie was ever going to hide these facts.

Queen Helena rises, and I bow. That's the one thing Karl managed to pound into my thick skull as we navigated into Handsel last night. "Royal heirs bow to reigning monarchs. It doesn't matter that she's not your queen or that you're in her home territory and that she's the host. She outranks you. You must bow."

The bow is awkward. I've performed two or three of them before this week, and every time I feel like I've wandered into a children's puppet show. Act One: The Whiskered Walrus pays his respects to the Queen of the Ocean.

"Would you care for tea?" she offers when we're seated. "Coffee?"

I grin—the wide American smile Karl disapproves of. "No, thanks. I just ate."

Her eyes flick to my shirtfront but she clasps her hands. "I understand you're new to royal life. How are you finding things?"

It's ridiculous to talk to the queen of Sondmark like we have anything in common. "I'm getting used to it."

"As you assume your new duties, we cannot help but feel that Sondmark, being such a close ally, should aid you in some way."

She uses soft generalities, but I'm a carpenter and know better than to let things rattle about, unsecured. "You know why my father sent me," I reply. I nod at the secretary sitting primly on the periphery of the room and smile. "I bet *Vrouw* Tiele has been busy making the logistics happen."

My blunt words bring a brief flash of irritation to the queen's eyes. "She has, indeed. I understand you need to get up to speed on royal protocol before the state visit." Her expression is polite, but I sense the control beneath it. "Twelve weeks between now and then. It's interesting that His Majesty should choose such a sensitive time to introduce his only son to Vorburg and the international community."

"That's King Otto, for you." I shrug away the implications of having a father who doesn't hesitate to use his son as a pawn.

The queen nods. "You will be placed in Prince Noah's former suite for the duration of your visit. Your aide will be lodged on the next floor up. This will enable you to come and go as you like, prepare your own meals, and have a degree of independence you will, no doubt, appreciate."

Stay clear of me and my family. The words might as well have been shot out of a cannon. *Vrouw* Tiele passes a binder of materials to Karl.

"Thank you," I say. "That's generous. I'm supposed to choose a tutor."

"Your choices are limited. Crown Prince Noah's schedule will be full in advance of the state visit. Princess Freja is still on her honeymoon."

I remember my father's advice, doled out in Djolny Castle as he perched on the edge of a squat chair, his shirtsleeves rolled to the elbow and a tumbler of vodka resting on his knee. It was the first time I met him after the legal decision. The first time I met him as his acknowledged son. His personal physician listened to his lungs with a stethoscope located and relocated across his back, the pink and white skin as wholesome as a freshly scrubbed baby.

"Disgustingly healthy," the doctor pronounced before rolling up his tools and leaving.

King Otto pushed his sleeves down, absent-mindedly slotting a cufflink through a hole. "I like the look of you," he said, eyes on his wrist. "You have a chance if you play your cards the right way in Sondmark. The middle girl wants out, and you might be the vehicle she's looking for. You could do far worse."

"Sir?" He's my king. I returned to Oregon during the summers and holidays, but Vorburg has been my home since I was 13. My father's picture was on the wall of every classroom and post office in the country. I couldn't forget. "Far worse for what?"

He looked up, his eyes suddenly sharp. "Marriage."

The word was a joke. It had to be. "I'm not looking for a wife."

"You damned well should be. You're my son if I say you're my son, but to my people," my father didn't pause as he delivered the rough verdict, "you're a bastard—a lowborn bastard. Get yourself a wife with an old title and a big tiara. Show her off and give us a bit of glamour. It'll go a long way to securing your place."

I realize now that he must have been talking about Ella, the rebel.

Queen Helena is trying to herd me in another direction. "Princess Clara has the lightest schedule and would be—"

The trouble with woodworking is that you can measure and plan and cut on the right side of the line and still have to bash the pieces together with a rubber mallet. Everyone knows I don't fit here, and in my mind's eye, I see the queen reaching for the tool that will bash me into her own plans.

I think of the last time I fit—slotting into position as softly as a kiss. My jaw hardens. "I'll take Alma."

3

SOOTHING ACTIONS

ALMA

I wake to the wreckage of a life blown completely off course. My head throbs, and I squint as weak winter light shafts across my face. Groaning, I retreat into my fluffy duvet to escape the hard blow of each fresh memory. All that champagne. The tears. The orangery. The man. *Stultes es*, the man. The kiss. Another groan wells from my chest, and I muffle it against a pillow. *Please be a dream. Please be a dream.*

I present myself in the Great Hall as punctually as ever, prepared to discharge the queen's first assignment of the year. Emotional breakdown notwithstanding, I can do this.

"You are in no condition to do this." Clara's matter-of-fact diagnosis comes with a wrestle for the clipboard. "I recognize a hangover when I see one. Go. Hydrate. Have a cracker," she commands, waving the complicated list of family members departing for Paris, London, parts of Germany, and select enclaves of North America. I've recorded everything. Destinations. Transportation. Departure times. Luggage items. Notable jewels to be checked out of the vaults. I haven't omitted one servant, pet, or child.

"Go," she prods. "The palace won't fall apart if you have a bad day. I've got this."

I should put up a fight—remind her of the time we temporarily mislaid the 3-year-old heir to the Margraviate of Dacsu-Angoes and nearly caused a succession crisis—but the checkerboard tiles are giving me vertigo.

I nod, kicking off a round of throbbing, and give her my best advice. "Check everything. Trust no one. Frisk the teens."

She gives me a crisp salute, and I retreat to the breakfast room to find Ella straddling the back of a Louis XV chair, her feet hooked around the elegant cabriole legs. She casts me a glance as I carry a cup of coffee into the dimmest corner of the room. "You look like a woman with regrets," she says, hunching over her laptop.

"I had a little too much to drink," I reply, picking my way carefully over each word.

"First time?"

"Yes," I groan into the black depths of the coffee.

"Don't be so hard on yourself. You've had one of the roughest weeks of your life. You're suffering the thousand natural shocks that flesh is heir to. I'm not surprised you hit the sauce."

I wince against the light. "You make it sound common."

Ella shrugs. "You're a person first and a princess second. A break-up is a break-up is a break-up. Stop trying to fight it, and surrender to the process."

I give the smallest, tightest laugh. "The process?"

She taps away on her keyboard. "You cry your eyes out until your face hurts, and when that stops, you'll think you've ascended to another astral plane—the one populated with all the Stoic philosophers. It's very 'Happiness isn't found in a man but in Virtue alone.' Then you'll go somewhere with an open bar..." She waves a hand at my hangover.

There's something reassuring about being on a well-trodden path with familiar checkpoints. I've always been a star student. Passing through the remaining phases should be easy.

"And then?"

"At some point you'll decide to get your groove back."

My brow furrows, and I want to take notes. "How?"

"The usual." Her eyes sparkle. "Dance clubs. Low-cut dresses. Making out with strangers. I, for one, can't wait."

Blood rushes to my face, and I grip the coffee cup with both hands. There was a dance, I was in a low-cut dress, and I kissed a stranger. I'm flying through these phases.

Memories of last night flicker against my eyelids. There was nothing soft about him except the way he held me. I recall the touch of his hands, and a shiver of desire works across my shoulders.

Dominanstid. I squeeze my eyes tight and count slowly in my head.

One, two, three...

It was the champagne. That feeling of intense attraction wasn't real, and when I open my eyes, I expect it—and this hangover, too, as long as I'm asking for the moon—to be gone.

...four, five, six...

It was the fireworks, whistling and booming, shaking the windows.

I can almost feel his lips.

"Alma?" Ella prods me.

My eyes snap open, and I blink against the lights. "I'm fine."

I am. I am fine. I take a small sip of coffee and grimace. It's little wonder I can't stop thinking about last night. The whole thing is appalling. I kissed someone who might take his story to the press. Stupid, stupid, stupid. I try to work out the best wording for an apology.

To: The Personal Aide of the Crown Prince of Vorburg

Concerning: The kiss I begged you for in the palace orangery

Dear Sir—

That's as far as I get before another groan escapes me.

Ella looks up, eyes narrowing, and I head off her inevitable questions. "How do you know so much about getting over a break-up? You haven't had a boyfriend in—"

"Don't start with me," she snaps.

I manage a smile. "What are you up to this morning?"

She tilts the screen around. "I'm updating my app for the state visit."

Ella is a princess, but she's also a computer genius. She's written an app that quizzes us on titles, modes of protocol, biographies, and faces—helping the royal family navigate tricky social situations with ease.

She taps the keys and grunts. "He may as well be a ghost."

"Who?"

"The new crown prince of Vorburg. News sources in Djolny don't have much more than a name—Jacob Gardner. King Otto locked down his heir as soon as the verdict was released because all we have is a street view image of his workshop, an extremely blurry photo of someone who might be him at a school reunion, and the barest biographical sketch from the lawsuit."

I lean over her shoulder. "Didn't he have to show up in court? I'm sure there were photographers."

Ella shakes her head. "He was an anonymous litigant, and the court case wasn't supposed to go anywhere. It was all done under his mother's name." Ella taps the keys and pulls up an old picture of a young woman in a sequined costume, her face made up for the stage, and another photo of an elegant middle-aged woman with ashy blond hair, exiting the courthouse in large sunglasses. "With their typical tact and generosity, the press call her *Ludivo Nerzka*—The Leggy Dancer. Her court case languished in dark judicial dungeons until, for reasons known only to himself, the king decided to let her win it."

Ella scrunches her nose. Her glasses slip, and she pushes them back. "The prince was supposed to arrive last night, but I've seen no sign of him."

I clear my throat. "He came. Late."

"Ooh! What does he look like? Does he have the Biron nose?" Ella shapes the air around her face, outlining the comically prominent feature inherited by a string of Vorburgian kings.

"I only met his aide," I say, a blush climbing up my neck.

Much about last night is hazy, but the details of that kiss are like a Lalique vase. They are clear, they are gorgeous, and they are going to cost me. *Vede,* I remember sighing against his lips and going in for more. I must have lost my mind.

A tingle travels up from my fingertips, and I frown. Returning the cup to the saucer, I think of several bracing, fortifying words that sound suspiciously like my mother. *You don't even know that man. His hair probably doesn't feel like anything special. It meant nothing.*

It has to mean nothing. If I developed an interest in such an unsuitable person, my mother would probably assemble a crisis management team.

My brother Noah would disapprove as well. I don't know when he became the Grand High Inquisitor of Royal Human Resource Irregularities, but he has taken to reminding us that it's not the Middle Ages. That royal secretaries and housekeepers can't be expected to live for us, and us alone. He'd say the aide and I didn't share a kiss. We shared a power imbalance, and I abused my side of it.

Ella leans toward me and puts the back of her hand against my cheek. "Are you all right? You should drink lots of fluids. It's the best way to get it out of your system."

I remember the kiss. There's not enough water in the North Sea for that.

A sound at the door jerks me to attention, and I see Mama's secretary, looking like she allows herself a single glass of sherry every Christmas Eve to toast the holiday. Calm. Sedate. I used to look like that.

"Good morning, Your Royal Highnesses." She bobs a curtsey.

Ella bucks her chin. "Hey, Caro."

Caroline's gaze shifts to me. "Her Majesty requests a moment of your time, ma'am."

"Are you in trouble?" Ella's laugh follows me out the door.

Caroline escorts me to my mother's too-bright sitting room. My eyes sting, and a sheen of perspiration washes over my neck and up my face. Thankfully, a curtsey is second nature and, when Mama offers her cheek, I lean in for a kiss.

"Good morning, Mama."

"Alma, may I present you to His Royal Highness, Crown Prince Jacob," she says in the Vorburgian way, *Yah-cup*, "and his aide, *Pane* Karl Nowak."

Aide? No, no, no. It's too soon for this. My heart spirals to my toes, dragging every bit of color from my face as I reroute vital functions to make it possible to appear regal and self-possessed. One breath. When I think I've just about got it, I turn, smile set, eyes darting away from the dangerous minefield that is the tall, semi-feral figure who looks like he escaped from his bedroom in the middle of a natural disaster. I fix my gaze on the reasonably-sized man with creased trousers, meticulous tailoring, and a nose that seems to have escaped the worst outcomes of the genetic lottery.

I make a curtsey and offer the crown prince my hand. "A pleasure, Your Royal Highness."

A bark of laughter escapes the Vorburgian giant, but I don't break my concentration.

"Ma'am," the prince says, hand at his throat.

I've already turned to the aide, who doesn't look anything like a Karl. "*Pane* Nowak, welcome to Sondmark." I extend my hand and he takes it, eyes dancing with laughter.

A flutter of panic stirs my sour stomach. *Stultes es,* why is he smiling? Has he snitched on me? Is the prime minister going to get a briefing?

"Alma." My head swivels at my mother's sharp command.

Her posture is terrifyingly correct, her lips pressed into a flat line. Mama always looks queenly, but when her irritation is ignited, she's the picture of Queen Ageltheld, standing over the body of her fallen king, holding the enemy back with a bloody sword. I can almost see the Wolffe family motto burned into the wall behind her. "Conquer, if you dare." Something has displeased her.

Karl smiles and I want to smile back, tracing my finger along the edge of his lip. I blink several times, trying to clear my throbbing headache through sheer force of will. He leans forward. "I'm Jacob."

"Pardon?" I must have lost twenty IQ points since yesterday, and I give his hand a desperate squeeze. *Help me.*

He looks over my head, an easy thing to do, and smiles at the queen. "I was brought up in the U.S. and prefer my mother's pronunciation."

It takes a second, but understanding hits like a nuclear warhead, rippling a path of destruction through my self-respect. *I'm Jacob.* This is the crown prince. I drunk-kissed the crown prince of Vorburg last night. If any more blood leaves my face, I'll be as transparent as one of those spindly, deep-sea creatures camouflaging itself from predators.

"*This* is Crown Prince Jacob. Jacob," Mama repeats. She looks at him. "Do you intend that to be your regnal name?"

"Regnal?" he says under his breath, brushing his thumb across my hand.

"The name you will rule under when you become the king," I murmur, hardly pausing to wonder why a midnight kiss should make it natural for him to ask the question of me or why I would supply the answer like a faithful vassal.

"Do sit," Mama says. I peel my hand from his and subside into a chair like I haven't made the biggest blunder since...since midnight.

"My father's health is excellent. Being a king is something I won't have to worry about for a long time," he tells my mother, taking a seat.

The conversation settles into the familiar pattern of royal audiences, and I withdraw into a support role, attempting to form an assessment of our guest. Nothing about this is ordinary. I laughed with him. I pressed my lips to his. I know that he smells like spice and fresh-cut wood. I know I want to push my fingers through his hair. I know how I'll fit if I step into his arms. *Perfectly.*

I shake my head and try to look at him through Mama's eyes. I note that Jacob is large enough to dwarf the chair on which he sits. He has pulled his long hair out of his face, confining it in a loop, but the loose strands brush along his jaw. He's not comfortable here. I see it in the way his hands tug his cuffs and run down the length of his lapel. Body language experts describe these as self-soothing actions, but even if he's out of his element, he's not being knocked on his heels by Mama's subtle disapproval, either.

Maybe he gets this quality from his father.

King Otto was exiled from Vorburg as a young man, and during the Cold War, he rallied the international community for support and intervention, broadcasting from secure locations in North America and the United Kingdom. He was tireless on behalf of his country, and they loved him for it.

When the occupation ended, he helicoptered into Djolny, leading a party in Liberation Square that didn't stop for a week. Few modern monarchs have suffered the loss of their throne and gone on to have such a sweeping, victorious reversal of fortune. In the course of decades, he became a living, breathing symbol of resistance. A national saint.

Placing a knuckle against my lips, I check a laugh. King Otto never lived like a saint.

During his exile, he cut a swath through Hollywood and never met a blonde he didn't like. He didn't have *amours*, the French press would say, only encounters—*irrésistible, clandestine.*

How much of the father is found in the son?

I glance at this hitherto anonymous litigant, and he tips his head almost imperceptibly. *Hey.* His eyes smile. Probably another skirt chaser.

I clear my throat and begin a calming litany. Monarchy is built on a history of strategic marriage alliances and established bloodlines. Now that armed rebellions and fratricidal stabbings are rare, the practice of primogeniture means the oldest child inherits the throne, making possible the peaceful transfer of power. Wars have been fought, entire religions schismed, by the single edict that no illegitimate child can rule. These essential truths were laid out to me as soon as I was old enough to realize that every park in Handsel contained one of my ancestors cast in bronze.

The litany is interrupted when Jacob, upsetter of divine law, catches me looking at him. He winks. Some feminine, adolescent reaction ripples through me, followed by a tardy bloom of disapproval.

My mother's voice sounds like it's coming from a long way off. "...happy to extend this personal favor to His Majesty. Princess Alma...Alma— " Mama repeats.

"My apologies," I blurt. Present.

Mama carries on, smoothing over my uncharacteristic lapse. "Princess Alma will act as your personal tutor, serving at my pleasure."

Alma? That's me.

The one, cold, shriveled kernel of comfort I harvested from my encounter last night was that I wouldn't have many reasons to cross the path of the man I kissed. I wouldn't even have to look him in the eye if the composition of my apology was precise enough.

I'm sorry for asking for a kiss.

I'm sorry for touching your neck.

I'm sorry for liking it so much.

I can lie.

"Everyday?" I say, the word squeezing through my narrow throat.

Mama's brow lifts. *Alma. Get yourself in hand.*

I scrub away every vestige of panic fighting for a piece of my voice. Taking a breath, I adjust my tone. "Everyday?"

"Weekdays," Mama says, as though her plan to foist him off on Clara hasn't been destroyed. She sounds friendly and conversational, but I'm not foolish enough to believe this is a request. "You'll have to work efficiently in the short time, and I'll have *Vrouw* Tiele redistribute your assignments among your sisters."

My heart thumps so violently that I wonder if I may have an undiagnosed medical condition. This man has seen me tipsy and undisciplined. He's been subjected to needy romantic advances I'll have to explain away as mere Sondish tradition. He knows what my breath smells like.

I nod, inhaling through my nose.

Jacob reaches over, placing his hand over mine, and a war breaks out in my chest. His touch is improper, but it feels so good. "Are you okay?"

I look into his warm gray eyes, coating my answer in the thinnest crust of ice. "I am well, thank you."

Mama glances between us, at our hands. "Perhaps you're worried about the wedding."

At Mama's words, I pull my hand away, tucking my hair back and straightening my spine. This is the moment she's decided to tell the world about my broken engagement? In front of the man I kissed last night?

He'll see what a disaster my life is.

I smooth my skirt and lace my fingers gently together. Soothing actions.

"Don't worry," Mama goes on, pinning me with her level gaze. *Bear up.* "You did the most important part by choosing the groom. We'll leave the planning to a team of professionals."

She makes it sound like I'm still engaged—that Pietor and I only have to choose the seasonal flower scheme and recessional music instead of sorting out how I'm going to get his monstrous ring back to him and move on with my life.

Mama keeps up her easy-going monologue, allowing me to get used to the idea before expecting me to take my part in this exchange. "You can certainly be spared from your wedding plans to perform such an important task for our close ally."

When Crown Prince Jacob speaks, it's a single word, bare as a stone. "Wedding?"

Sondmark and Vorburg have a well-documented history of sinking each other's ships over minor slights, and Mama's lie makes me look like I'm a cheat. This is bad.

Mama smiles. "I don't expect the engagement was big news in Vorburg. My daughter's fiancé is His Royal Highness Pietor, Hereditary Grand Duke of Himmelstein."

I can feel Jacob's eyes on me, but I can't correct my mother. I wouldn't dare.

Silence stretches, and then Jacob nods. "Thanks for giving me so much of your time, ma'am. I'm sure you have a busy day ahead." Though he's the guest, his royal position conferred through a judicial process instead of Divine right, he's in total command. "Are we good?"

4

— · —

RUNAWAY WAGON

ALMA

"Are we good?" Mama spits. She sails through Caroline's office and into her own. I follow like a tin can tied to a newlywed's bumper, my nerves jangling and battered.

"Clara was supposed to be his tutor." I venture.

The official reason was that my little sister has few official assignments, but I know my mother. Having Clara tutor the prince would mean that the crown prince would be looked after, Clara would discover less free time to spend with her Navy-hero boyfriend, and, in teaching best royal practices, my little sister might be moved to remember what constitutes proper behavior.

Mama stops abruptly. "Plans change." She lifts her queenly chin. "Putting up with that man is the price of Freja's hasty elopement, and he wants you. My options are limited."

He wants me. I shake my head imperceptibly. Not like that. The Crown Prince of Vorburg is sparring with Mama and I'm only a piece to be moved around the board as the game demands.

"Still, it presents an opportunity," Mama continues. "You can collect valuable information on the Vorburgian mind as we move forward with the trade negotiations."

Okay. This is the assignment. Turn Jacob Gardner into His Royal Highness Crown Prince Jacob, report significant findings to Mama, and spend day after day with a man who holds a deadly attraction for a significant part of my subconscious.

To get through the next three months, I'll just have to hit that part over the head with a shovel and bury it in a shallow grave. When King Otto's royal entourage rolls into town and attempts to soft-power their way into favorable trade conditions, I only hope the wind turbine industry appreciates my sacrifice.

Mama takes her seat behind her desk, leafing through parliamentary papers as she speaks, segmenting her attention like slices of an orange. "He is totally unsuited for royal life, but we can't afford to be in Vorburg's debt at this critical stage." She pauses, hands full. "Did you see his shirtfront?"

I am not expected to answer which is good because, grubby and water-stained as it was, it couldn't hide his muscled frame.

"If anyone can teach that man how to be a prince, I know you can." Mama signs a dispatch with her customary flourish. Helena R. Helena Regina. Helena the Queen. "Goodness knows you have your work cut out."

As it is spoken, so let it be done.

"May I understand why you gave him the impression that I'm engaged?"

Mama's pen stills but she doesn't look up. "Are you questioning my judgment, too?"

Too.

Like Clara. Like Freja. Like Ella always has. Like Noah was born to do. Like our father, who has surely earned the right. I'm not like them. Mama has rigid expectations but holds herself to the same high standard she sets for others. It's fair. It's motivated by love of country and love of family. I've always understood that.

Question her judgment? "No. Of course not."

On Christmas morning, I brought her the news that my fiancé had been photographed in a compromising situation with an Italian bikini model, the damning pictures texted to me by a friend of a friend. It had been a bad day to deliver bad news.

No one had slept a wink. Freja's elopement had just hit the papers, and the palace was in chaos. New drafts of Mama's Christmas speech to the nation were coming in every quarter hour, each taking a slightly different tone on my sister's rushed wedding. The queen was commanding a war room.

Mama looked at the pictures and cast her eyes to the ceiling. *Dominanstid.*

"Will you break it off?" she asked. Any other mother would have grabbed the nearest tennis racket, flown to Lijuela, and beaten the wayward fiancé to death. Or offered to. Mama's eyes were on the political implications for her country first and the personal feelings of her daughter second.

I nodded.

I blame Clara and Freja for my change of heart—for introducing possibilities I hadn't anticipated. For making my engagement to Pietor look as cheap as a plastic Christmas wreath next to a bough brought in from the forest with its sharp, bright scent, as heavy in my hands as any living thing. For looking so damned happy.

I watched Mama add my burden to the others she carried that morning, and guilt twisted my stomach. She returned the nod, decisive. "I need a few weeks of quiet surrounding the state visit. Freja's kicked a hornet's nest, and we'll be lucky to avoid a referendum about the monarchy, much less having her tossed out of the succession. Secure Pietor's cooperation," she directed, holding her hand over the phone receiver. Something in my face had her reaching for a box of tissues and plonking them down in front of me. She had been sympathetic but distracted. "Don't worry, Alma. I'll find someone more suitable."

With her words to Jacob, the plans have changed. I won't just have to be quiet about my relationship status. I'll have to wear the engagement ring on my finger and pretend to miss my fiancé, even within the walls of the palace. I release a breath slowly. There wasn't a speck of luck in that New Year's kiss.

"The important thing is that His Royal Highness needs to understand that you are strictly out-of-bounds," Mama continues. "Mark my words, King Otto is shopping for a royal bride."

"Bride?" My chin jerks.

She stabs a finger in the air. "If they handed that man the crown, he would lose it inside a week, but if they could frame him as Crown Prince Jacob, son-in-law to Her Majesty Queen Helena of Sondmark, he would not be so easily discarded."

Mama speaks of maneuvers, and I imagine Jacob and I facing one another across a chessboard. The black knight moving against the white rook. Vorburg and Sondmark. We cannot meet unless in battle—no hope of mutual victory.

Mama returns to her papers. "I will not be Otto's puppet."

"What is the king like?"

"Passionate and charismatic. But he's also a shameless womanizer and drinks like a fish."

"A bad king."

She puts her pen down and considers the question seriously. "Nothing as simple as that. He suits the national mood of Vorburg, reflecting their ideals of manhood and leadership. He led them through one of the darkest chapters in the country's history and embodied the heroism and resistance they needed to believe they themselves possessed."

"A good king."

Her hand seesaws, one of Père's mannerisms adopted over thirty years of marriage, and offers me a smile. "An effective king."

I accept her answer as one of the complicated moral calculations of leadership. "Will the crown prince stay in the Tower Suite?" I ask.

Mama raises a brow. "And host him for dinner every night? Heaven forbid. I put him in Noah's old rooms."

Noah's rooms? Maybe Mama has spent so much time mired in international politics that she forgot the palace floor plan. "Our private quarters are quite small. The suite has a shared sitting room and a kitchen."

Mama waves her hand. "You hardly use it."

When she finally excuses me, I execute a tight curtsey, depart the room, and run down the length of the hall, my brain jostling to an aching rhythm. *Vede, vede, vede.* Everything hurts, but I arrive at my suite in seconds, banging through the door, past the kitchenette, down the short hall, and into the shared sitting room.

It's not a mess, but my things are everywhere—a favorite paperback mystery, spine cracked, perches open on the arm of the sofa. My knitting, a craft I'm genuinely terrible at, spills out of a basket on the floor. A graphic hoodie, a Christmas gift from Ella reading "Beauty" on the front, "Beast" on the back, hangs over a chair. I cram these into a basket and get on my knees to reach under the coffee table for a fuzzy slipper. I'm so focused on my task that I don't register another presence until a pair of slip-on dress shoes one might generously describe as 'vegan leather' crowds my vision.

I yelp and scramble away, landing on my backside as the basket spills at our feet.

Crown Prince Jacob crouches down to eye level. "Hey."

Blood drains to my toes, but he picks up my things and scoops them into the basket—calmly, comfortably—and holds out his hand. What would a princess do? I scramble to my feet—gracefully, royally—and step away as far as I can, taking the basket from him. "Good morning, Your Royal Highness."

This formality amuses him. Though the man is in a suit, he has an aged, canvas duffle bag slung over his shoulder which he drops onto the table. "I thought this was my room."

Ignoring the fullness of his lips and the laughter in his eyes, I try to remember that the manufacturing sector of Sondmark needs me now. If my mission is to fix this man, I'm determined to see only his flaws.

Item One: He can't ask questions disguised as statements. As crown prince, his communication will have to be both diplomatic and direct.

Item Two: There will be no crouching over unsuspecting princesses. It's unsettling.

I place the basket on a side table, moving as though my knees and ankles are tied with invisible string.

"You are in the right place." I put my hand out and give him my best Alma-of-the-people smile—the one I employ when someone wants a selfie and their phone takes forever to get to the point. It's a smile that says, "I enjoy this. It is pleasant to us. In such a manner, I could sail into the eternal sunset forever."

As soon as he touches me, a frisson of attraction brushes every nerve and thousands of impressions queue for my notice.

I beckon a single safe thought forward to speak for them all. His skin is rough.

Item Three: Moisturize.

"It looks like your place," he says, glancing around.

I gesture, palm up, at Noah's door. "The rooms are adjoining. You will be there and I"—I sweep my hand around to gesture at my own door—"will be here. This area," I say, employing both hands, "isn't anything more than a common pass-through."

I must look like a first-class flight attendant performing a pre-flight safety check, and he grins.

Item Four: Fix the smile.

As a royal figure, he'll have to find one that is at once warm and faintly unapproachable. One that doesn't ignite the cotton fluff in my brain, lodge under my rib cage, and make me want to lean into him. Imagine an entire country full of women subjected to a smile like that on a regular basis.

"Are you going to show me where everything is?" he asks.

I lead him to the narrow galley kitchen, and he looks around, hands searching for the back pockets of his jeans. Finding the smoothness of a pair of suit pants, they drop to his sides.

"Housekeeping will stock the refrigerator for you and order any supplies you need," I cough, dragging my eyes away from the sight. "You'll be free to cook for yourself as much as you like. Your aide will have those details."

"We won't have to work out a schedule?"

"Schedule?" I ask, straightening a calendar.

"You cook from five to six on Tuesdays and Thursdays and I take Wednesdays at midnight under a gibbous moon and a rising tide—that kind of thing. Most roommates—"

"We're not roommates," I correct. "Think of this as a hallway. I don't use the kitchen. It's all yours."

"Really?" He touches an old birthday present from Clara with the tip of his finger, eyes dancing. It's a novelty coffee mug with a picture of me doing exaggerated Mick Jagger duck lips and a speech bubble that reads, "Hey. You. Get off of my crown."

"I get why you might want to avoid me," he says.

I back away several paces. "Why would I want to avoid you?"

His gaze holds mine too long to be innocent. *You know why.* But he places a hand on his chest. "Vorburg. I'm the enemy."

"Nonsense." I clear my throat and pivot, trying to avoid the temptation to be fidgety or apologetic. "If you have any questions, you only have to dial Housekeeping."

"Will they speak Vorburgian?"

I want to laugh. No one in Sondmark speaks Vorburgian on purpose. "Anyone in the palace who deals with foreign guests will have an excellent grasp of English."

He pauses to examine the door frame into his suite. Original Ostphalian era workmanship, the door is slightly rounded at the upper corners and comes to a gentle point at the top. He opens and shuts it several times to the accompanying sound of wood rubbing against wood.

"Does your room match mine?" he asks.

A rookie question. "In a 500-year-old palace, nothing matches. The walls aren't plumb, the corners aren't square. The best strategy is to adapt to it rather than expect it to adapt to us."

This is the reality of monarchy, Crown Prince Jacob. Let the lessons commence.

He leans up against the door jamb, legs crossed at the ankles.

"You didn't know who I was, did you?" he says. "Last night."

There it is. I look around the room—my own small kingdom. A deep sofa faces two wing chairs, and a fire crackles in the hearth. An old dollhouse sits on a raised platform next to a long bench stacked with mismatched feather pillows. In the tall casement windows, the aged glass hangs heavily in each diamond pane, distorting the light and images without.

The parkland beyond is snow-covered and peaceful, and I wish I were running the springy trails woven through the woods. You can run from almost anything.

Not this. The kiss can't be ignored, so it must be dealt with.

I square my shoulders. "I didn't know. I was not in my right mind, but even so, I was wrong to kiss you, no matter who you turned out to be. I'd like to apologize." There.

He frowns, looking as fierce as his Vor ancestors—minus the face tattoos and battle nudity—but he probably doesn't know how thorough my apologies can be. I've had training.

"I regret that you were caught up—" No, Alma. No passive voice. No euphemisms. "I regret kissing you. It was—"

Jacob bumps away from the door and plucks a bright pink sticky note off a wastepaper basket. "*Svet*," he says, holding it up. It's my own penmanship.

"Oh," I say, derailed, "that's 'garbage' in the Himmelstein dialect."

"Your fiancé is from Himmelstein."

I persevere. "I had no intention of kissing anyone—"

"Because you're engaged."

My mother does this, too—strips things down to their most essential essence, getting to the heart of the matter even when flunkies and courtiers want to wrap their monarch in a veil of fog.

I have to fall back on one of my mother's favorite sayings, *Never dwell, never tell,* but I hate it. He'll think Princess Alma is unfaithful. Disloyal. Reckless. My eyes close for a second but, when I open them, I am resolved.

"It was inexcusable," I say. "I wasn't careful of the amount of champagne I consumed—"

"Where's your ring?" His gaze slips to my finger.

I clasp my right hand over my left, and my stomach feels soft and sick. "Opals aren't meant to be worn everyday. They damage too easily."

"*Svet*," he repeats, leaning over the wastebasket, and pushes his thumb across the sticky strip. When he turns to me, the note slips off again, falling to the floor. "Is there more to your little speech?"

"Only that I sincerely ask for your forgiveness and want to assure you it will never happen again." I'm trying to sound sincere and self-contained, but I can't seem to relax.

He swallows. "Nothing to forgive. What about...what's his name? Pietor? Should I send him a text? Explain about the fireworks and the bad luck? He wouldn't have wanted you to have bad luck."

Thinking of Pietor makes me want to throw something. "He's fine." I strangle the impulse with well-modulated breathing. "You must be feeling tired from your journey, and I don't want to keep you from getting settled."

Jacob grins. "Are you going to teach me how to do that? Tell me to push off but make it seem like you're doing me a favor."

There's something infectious about his smiles. They make me want to return them, smiling with my whole chest, like a child with bunched cheeks and squinty eyes. I would look silly.

Before I can answer, our front door slams open, and my sister Ella comes bounding through. I step back, banging against the hard wall of Jacob's chest. He grips my elbows, keeping me on my feet and nearly enclosing me in his arms.

The contact is brief. Familiar.

"The prince is—" Ella skids to a stop and blinks up at Jacob. "—here," she finishes. Her hand shields the lower half of her face and to me she mouths, "Hot."

Jacob's laugh is unrestrained. "Call me Jacob," he says.

Ella's fingers prance together. "You're the crown prince of Vorburg."

He cups a hand around the back of his neck. "That's what they tell me."

"I have so many questions—"

I turn Ella and propel her from the room.

"His Royal Highness has unpacking to do," I say, slipping into my familiar role as big sister and law-giver. "There will be lots of time to get to know each other."

Out.

She spins out of my grasp. "Can I get a picture?"

Jacob glances at me over her head and pushes his hair back, loosening the loop. A fall of hair kisses his lips and my fingers curl into my palms. *Stultes es.* We'll have to fix that, too.

"Is that going to break a rule?" he asks.

His question relegates me to being a warden, and I register the soft pressure of disappointment. As with all emotions, it will pass if I ignore it. "She's not going to post it in public. Go ahead."

Jacob swipes Ella's phone, holding it at arm's length for a selfie as he angles her within the frame. She perches behind him on her tiptoes, hands resting on his shoulder. For the app, she'll cut herself out of the profile picture.

"Good?" he asks.

She examines the picture and makes a sound at the back of her throat. "My hair's doing its thing today."

"It looks great, Your..." His brow lifts. "...Majesty?"

My sister laughs. "Not in this country. You can call me Ella. I'm across the landing and two doors down on the right. Come find me when you need a break. We can fire up *Runaway Wagon* to blow off steam. You play?"

Runaway Wagon is a racing video game. The medieval wagons are heaped with vegetables, the load tipping precariously as the player pilots the goods down the mountain course and into a market town, avoiding competition-adverse trade guilds and wealth-redistributing bandit gangs. Such are the morsels of information one can glean from Ella, simply by osmosis.

"Doesn't everyone?" Jacob holds up a fist and Ella gives it a bump.

Watching them, I register a pang of jealousy. Two whole minutes and they already know how to be friends. With me, he is tense, watchful. I wish—but no. I bite the edge of my lip. Everyone in my family wishes they had Ella's easy touch with strangers.

"All right. I won't keep you," Ella says, giving a tiny salute.

Jacob stares at the empty doorway, scratching his neck. "She did it, too—took off and made it sound like a personal favor." He turns to me and drops his hand. "Do you want to come over and help me figure out the shower knobs?"

"Another time. I'm sure you have a lot to do," I say.

He shakes his head, a smile tucking one cheek. "It's like a superpower." He grabs his duffel bag and heads to his suite. I watch the effortless play of his muscles across his back with the tingly sensation of standing on the edge of a cliff, gusts of wind rocking me on my feet.

"You look like you hit it off with Ella," I call, almost desperate. "It's not too late to request a different tutor."

He tosses the bag into his room and gives me a long, penetrating look.

"Pass."

5

—·—

MASSIVE ROCK

JACOB

Karl drags my duffel bag to the ironing board. "They have me staying in separate quarters, Your Royal Highness," he says, frowning at the ceiling.

My stomach tightens. My new title produces the same reaction as a small-town bully with a baseball bat standing too near the Coke machine—it's a risk to be assessed, a gauntlet to be run. I wonder if I'll ever get used to it.

When Karl unzips the duffel bag, his face spasms. At least life holds these little joys.

"Sir," he says, lifting the flannel coat I wear in the shop, which has holes everywhere. Tiny shavings of sawdust sprinkle on the rug. "For what occasion did you anticipate the need for this?"

"A gentleman is always prepared for every occasion." I don't think Karl appreciates hearing one of his little kernels of wisdom echoed back to him.

He continues his task, and I duck into the common area, picked clean of any signs of a princess save for a few bright pink sticky notes clinging lifelessly to a picture frame, a light switch, a vase. These are a reminder that however long our paths run on parallel tracks, they won't intersect.

Chol. She should have said something. She should have been wearing her ring. She should have stayed safely in the ballroom where I never would have seen her. She should have been kissing her fiancé, and I should have been disappointing Karl.

I run my hand through my hair, gathering it into my fist. *Chol nia.* This little dream, this delusion, lasted less than twelve hours. She explained herself—about the champagne and the mistake—with an apology so watertight, I could launch it into the ocean. I'm not entitled to feel betrayed or to ask her what in the hell she was thinking, playing with a heart she found in the wild.

What began is over already. I should be thankful I escaped without any damage.

I make my way to the small kitchen, opening and shutting cabinets, finding basic cooking instruments and dishes. In the compact refrigerator, Alma's few things are circumscribed on the top shelf, leftovers stacked neatly in matching glass dishes.

A note indicates my things, supplied by some palace servant—a carton of eggs and a container of milk, a few fresh vegetables, cheese, and a hummus dip. I pick up a small glass jar with a gold foil lid, stamped with a word I sound out: "Pan-ke-druss." Peeling the lid back, I sample the thick, gray, contents with a knuckle.

Gagging, I turn the sink on, plunging my cupped hand under the tap and taking several long swallows. What is wrong with these people? My father, his ministers, and history warned me that relations with Sondmark would be hostile, but I expected a grace period before an attempt to poison me.

"Karl," I call, returning to my room. The ancient door shudders as I close it.

"Sir?" Karl enters from the closet, a thick wood hanger hooked over his forefinger. Hanging from it is a faded graphic t-shirt.

I close my eyes. "Have you been ironing the t-shirts again?"

"It's my responsibility to make sure you represent the monarchy well." He points to a photo of King Otto he placed on the bedside table. Exhaling tightly, I move past him, grabbing a pair of jeans and shirt.

He shouts through the firmly closed closet door. "Sir, does this mean I'll have a chance to work on your suit?"

He sounds so damned hopeful. Tugging my t-shirt down, I glance at the heap of clothes on the floor with a nagging sense of guilt. I drape the limp blue polyester over the ironing board, placing the white-ish shirt with the graying collar next to it—not helpful but suggesting a certain willingness to be so. I throw on my jacket and jam my wallet into my back pocket.

"Sir?" Karl says, when I return. It's impressive how much mileage he can get from the word.

"I'm going out to get a feel for the city."

"Advance work for the state visit. Excellent." He reaches for his phone. "I'll notify palace security."

"No, no," I turn my collar up. "No one knows who I am. Not for twelve more weeks."

I escape The Summer Palace, a building which can't decide if it's a fairytale castle or an armed fortress. Traditional guards in deep red uniforms emblazoned with the dragon of Sondmark in gold thread keep watch in a frigid wind, feathered caps ruffling as they stand at attention in front of the impressive main gate. Those are for show. The iron bollards, well-armed security officers, and surveillance cameras are the real deal.

At the top of the hill, I catch a Ryde and it drops me in the heart of the tourist district near candy-colored shops and upscale restaurants ringing the harbor. Expensive. Inauthentic. Just as she'd said. Or I'd understood. I pause a moment to wonder what she'd say now that it's midday and the champagne has burned off. I shove my hands into my pockets. She'd sound like a chamber of commerce brochure, but some part of me believes that no matter what she said, I'd know what she wanted to say.

Heading inland, I circle the park at the center of an expensive square and watch a man in tasseled loafers exit a townhouse.

"Historically speaking, markets in western Europe won't stabilize until—" He slips into a waiting black town car, off to shape international monetary policy.

On narrow, ordinary streets, there are no tourists, only signs of everyday living—a local bakery, a parish church, a corner shop where I buy a plain white candle—but in every window facing the street, curtains are drawn back, granting a peek into a world of inviting wintertime warmth complete with fairy lights and colorful pillows. The Sondish like to present these little pictures, but they seem fake. When things get too much, I bet they retreat to a washroom and scream into the decorative hand towels.

Turning west, I discover a park where old men have gathered, wearing soft berets and heavy scarves, speaking a language that seems to be some blend of Italian and Spanish, their breath and laughter mixing in the piercing cold.

When the sun sets, when I have more memories of Sondmark than the upturned face of a girl reaching for a kiss, I return to the palace, grateful for cold ears and a red nose. I push through the common room door to find Karl waiting next to a sturdy gateleg table in the sitting room. He greets me with a bow.

"Knock it off," I mutter, but there's no heat in it.

He pulls out a chair and I frown at it. He frowns back. I drop into the chair, and he smiles. "I've prepared a dinner of French onion and beef stew, Your Royal Highness, with a side of—"

I can't do this for the next three months. "I'm more than capable of looking after myself." I tap the spoon on the bowl. "Don't you have some Sondish interests to subvert? Some sleeper cells to contact?"

Karl's brows tent. "It's never a good time to jest about covert operations, sir."

"Too soon?" His mouth pinches, and I laugh. "All right, here's the deal. You bow and scrape from nine to five, but I need to turn off the royal protocol at the end of the day."

"There is no on or off for a crown prince," he insists. "You *are* the crown prince."

Not yet, I'm not. While at the Summer Palace, I exist in limbo, in a kind of workshop situated between the virgin forest and the ancient castle. I've been sawn away from my roots, fighting and straining as I fell, only to be carted to a mill. I'm full of knots and raw edges and the marks of the saw. There's no telling what I'll become. What I'm certain of is that Karl can force these honorifics on me, he can iron my t-shirts and serve my dinner, but it hasn't made me a crown prince yet.

"I'll text you when I'm coming down for lessons," I say. "You can pick up my laundry and leave it outside. Otherwise, I'm on my own."

He leaves, possibly offended, but I can't let him be the one to decide how much of Jacob Gardner remains when this is all over. If that means I'm in charge of the care and washing of my original Zombie NaBombie t-shirt, so be it. When I do my dishes, a podcast about bronze age societies plays over the Paige device. I'm content to hold on to these normal things.

I treat the rest of the night like I'm in my flat back home. Using the candle, I apply wax to the door frame, eliminating one nuisance. I call my mom. She laughs when I describe Karl traveling in wintertime conditions. I lay out my carving tools and scroll through my phone, looking for a project. When I climb into bed, wind shakes the windows. Just before I lose consciousness, I remember what I've been trying to forget.

Alma. I have to stop thinking of her, and I make a resolution. She's just another one of these uptight royals. I won't like her. I'll keep my hands to myself. I'll keep my thoughts away from that kiss.

That's the plan. Remember who I am. Forget the princess.

When morning comes, I grab some fruit from the kitchen and my suit from a hook outside the front door. I brush my teeth, spitting my toothpaste out to repeat my name in the mirror three times like one of those games meant to conjure a vengeful ghost. *Jacob Gardner. Jacob Gardner. Jacob Gardner.*

I don't meet the princess until Karl escorts me to my lessons in a drawing room on the main floor. This is going to be an ordinary occurrence. I'll see her every morning for hours. The sooner I can make peace with these facts, the faster I'll build up an immunity to being around her. I look deeply, exposing myself to the highest dose, wanting to get it over with. She's wearing close-fitting slacks and a high-necked sweater that drapes over her curves and brushes the underside of her jaw.

I wait to feel nothing.

"Morning," I say, still waiting.

She smiles—a Handsel harbor smile, tidy and meant for show. "Good morning, Your Royal Highness." She greets me in English. "I trust you had a good night's sleep."

She pushes nutbrown hair away from her face, and I barely register the greeting for the massive rock on her left finger.

"*Chol*, is this the ring?" I ask.

She doesn't glance down. "That's it."

Forgetting my resolutions, I hold my hand out. She rests her fingers lightly in the center of my palm. The stone is the same color as the bitter white milk found in a dandelion stem and the fittings look ancient, curling over the rounded corners of the gem like a pair of venomous fangs. I brush my thumb over its face, and it slips to one side.

"Used?"

She takes a shocked breath. "Heirloom. It's eco-conscious."

It's ugly, is what it is.

She withdraws her hand and indicates a couple of chairs for Karl and me, offering refreshments.

Karl sets a thick packet of material on the coffee table. "His Majesty King Otto wished to supply you with all the pertinent details, ma'am."

No. I intercept the binder and ruffle the pages containing testimonials from former teachers, several pages of photos, the financial details of my bespoke woodworking business, the results of several clean drug tests, and a whole section about my mother.

I give Karl a cold smile.

"You won't be needing these," I say, isolating the pages about my mom. I rip them out, slipping them into my pocket before spinning the binder back to Alma. "Who are you working for, Karl?"

My one-man sleeper cell gives me a bland smile. "Vorburg. Of course."

Alma opens the book and runs her finger along a line of text. "His Royal Highness Crown Prince Jacob, formerly known as Jacob Gardner, is half-American," she reads. "Born in Blackberry, Oregon to Ms. Tiffani Fawn Gardner—"

"She doesn't have anything to do with this," I cut in.

Alma holds her finger in place and looks up. "She is the mother of the next king of Vorburg," she says, stating a fact I haven't come to terms with. Mom doesn't care about all that. "We are your team. If protecting her privacy is important to you, we can plan for that, but to do so, we need a full picture of what we're dealing with in order to smooth your transition into royal life."

Her words are stripped of judgment, but she has a notepad next to her teacup. Even upside down, I can read the bullet points. *How to hold his tongue. How to enter a room. When to touch.* She's already aware of my shortcomings.

She gives a crisp nod. "Shall we proceed, sir?"

"Jacob."

"Hmm?"

"Jacob." I give her a slow smile, liking the way my name has thrown her off balance. "You're on Team Jacob."

Her cheeks wash pink, but when she turns to the next tab in the binder, she's in command again. "You attended Little Duckies Preschool and Blackberry Elementary." The sheer volume of information this skims over is impressive. "Then you enrolled at Skip Middle School."

Does Karl's dossier tell her about how Blackberry Elementary doesn't feed into Skip Middle? About how I moved up to my grandparents' property on the Nehalem River when Mom had her cancer treatments in Portland, spent my summers fishing and building leaky boats out of scrap lumber, and my winters in grandpa's single-wide tool shed inspecting dozens of mixed nuts containers from the food warehouse that he'd repurposed to hold random keys, flange head screws, eye bolts, and wads of bungee cords. How I can still hear the blended sounds of rain beating on the roof of the trailer, the AM radio crackling in the background, and the scrape of a carving tool.

"The next record is your enrollment at the Royal Academy of Vorburg at the age of fourteen."

Another vast store of information is buried in the white space between the black lines.

She picks up a pen, touching the tip lightly to the page. Her eyes meet mine, and I feel the powerful drag of attraction. I wait for it to pass.

"How is your Vorburgian accent?"

I grin. "Karl?"

My aide clears his throat. "It's quite good, actually. Not perfect. It's most noticeable in the sound of his soft H and how he flattens some vowels. His vocabulary is as extensive as mine, however."

Alma makes a notation.

"Not quite that extensive," I correct, tipping my chair back on two legs. Alma watches the angle and makes another note. I tip a little farther. "Karl calls me all kinds of names I don't understand."

"Sir." It's as close as Karl will come to scolding me in mixed company. He turns to the princess. "I said it wouldn't do to get a reputation for being *tovorny*—recalcitrant," he supplies for her benefit. He glances at me. "It means—"

"Obstinate toward authority. I know what that means in English."

"It will have to be perfect in less than three months," Alma directs. "Perhaps you could make that your priority, *Pane* Nowak? It must be absolutely flawless and include idioms, slang, and humor." She adds a bullet point on her notepad.

Alma's brow lifts when she reads over my transcripts from the Royal Academy of Vorburg, discovering a failing mark in History of the Early Middle Ages.

"How versed are you in Vorburgian history and the history of northern Europe?"

Her pen is ready to record and repair.

"I think it's pretty good." Grandpa still listens to AM radio in his woodshop, but I listen to audiobooks and podcasts, mostly nonfiction topics ranging from history to classical literature to economics.

She looks at me with serious eyes. She kissed me. The memory intrudes when I don't ask for it. "Want to test me?"

Her lips, I know how soft, purse. "Royalty isn't a pop quiz. Do you—" A knock on the door interrupts her.

She calls out in Sondish and conducts a brief exchange. It's like I'm hearing the language for the first time. Textbooks will tell you that Sondish is a cousin of English with a higher degree of throatiness. From Princess Alma's mouth, it's strong and nimble. I wonder what it sounds like when she's whispering in the dark.

"The Royal Academy of Vorburg is one of the most academically rigorous private schools on the continent," she says, interrupting my thoughts. "They don't typically accept transfers from Skip Middle School."

Karl spins the explanation. "Even before the confirmation of Crown Prince Jacob's royal parentage, His Majesty concerned himself with his heir."

I watch the slight lift of Alma's brow, an expression on the edge of a smile. She sees right through Karl's public relations, and when she looks at me, I start answering a question she hasn't even asked.

"My mother reappeared in His Majesty's life with compelling evidence of my identity. When faced with the...reality of my existence and the potential disaster it constituted, he threw money at us. Quite a lot. You can call my father a lot of things, but you can't call him cheap."

She nods. "Your grades weren't outstanding, but given that you were a graduate of the Royal Academy, you could have gone almost anywhere."

Again, I feel the question rather than hear it. Nice royal girls take you right to the edge of a cliff and wait until casting yourself over the edge seems like your own idea.

"I didn't go just *anywhere*. I apprenticed at Appe and Sons for more than eight years. I worked hard to master my craft and learn the business. Within the world of restoration carpentry and bespoke furnishings, it's a name that commands respect."

Not with Karl, though. "He also attended École Sciences."

I shake my head. "Half a semester hardly qualifies—"

Alma makes a note. "That helps."

6

LITTLE DUCKIES

ALMA

Crown Prince Jacob's academic record is bad, and there's no use hiding it. These things always have a way of getting out, whispered from ear to ear until they're splashed across the front page of some tabloid.

"Idiot Prince Picked as Vorburg Heir"

"Six Times Crown Prince Jacob Misused the Past Perfect Tense: Term Papers Uncovered"

"Dolt on the Throne"

They're easy to imagine.

I skim through the binder, picking out more damning details. Each time, my stomach drops like a child's toy, bouncing down the stairs to the dungeon.

There were three suspensions in four years for unruly conduct. At sixteen he was involved in a fistfight with the heir to a powerful petroleum magnate. I double check the name. *Vede.* Young Jacob Gardner aimed high. I leaf through the documentation showing that, behind the scenes, King Otto settled the dental bills and had his lawyers bribe everyone down to the school janitor's third cousin to sign non-disclosure agreements.

It won't matter. These things always have a way of getting out.

I'm not afraid of this biography, as such, but I know how this world works. Jacob doesn't have an unimpeachable pedigree to back him up. The people of Vorburg aren't acquainted with his character and have no reason to extend grace when he falls short of perfection.

He will have one shot to introduce himself. Our job, though he doesn't know it yet, will be to cobble together a story strong enough to weather the damning details. He has to control the narrative from the moment he steps onto the global stage.

Our midday meal reveals an appalling number of things he has yet to learn. He puts his elbows on the table, leaning forward when he speaks. He talks with his hands and devours his meal quickly, prowling the room in a restless fashion while his aide and I finish at a more civilized pace. In the afternoon, I turn to a tab marked 'Legal Issues and Citations' and release a relieved breath when I find there's not much there. A speeding citation for a motorcycle. A dispute involving his business and an aristocratic estate, settled by a small claims procedure for 10,000 *polskas*. He won that one.

Once he enters adulthood, the dossier gets thinner, and Jacob seems to fade out of the official record. I stare at the page as though doing so will conjure a fully realized human man.

A hand drops over the paper, and I blink, focusing on the nicks and scars over his skin.

"Excuse me," I say, raising my gaze, "for allowing my attention to wander. Now—"

He flips his hand and knocks his knuckles against the page. "No worries. It's hard sitting still all day."

He tells me this like he knows a secret. My secret. About how hard I have to work to dampen every fidget and suppress every twitch. How I have to run every day, the sound of my sneakers absorbed by the dense forest floor, to present the picture of a calm princess. How he sees the invisible waters which rush through me, alive and bracing.

"Of course," I say, closing the binder with a snap. "You must want to rest."

He gets to his feet and stretches, rolling his neck. "I don't like school rooms. Maybe you caught that from the binder."

I did, where it was buried in records from Little Duckies room aides and the Early Intervention specialist assigned by the school district. "Student has little interest in completing non-preferred tasks..." "Alternate accommodations must be devised for the pre-cooperative child..."

"Are you up for a walk?" he asks.

I glance out the window, where downy flakes drift from the sky. "It's snowing."

His mouth pulls into a lopsided smile—endearing for a man his size. "You're a Sondish princess. I thought the frozen tundra was your natural habitat."

Conveying facts is safe. "Sondmark is in a temperate deciduous biome."

"Temperate? Sounds perfect for a walk." Jacob's smile sharpens. I realize the trap only after it's sprung. No matter what the academic record indicates, I can't afford to underestimate him.

We meet on the top steps of the back garden after I've donned a fur-lined winter parka and thick-soled boots. "Is *Pane* Nowak coming?" I ask, ignoring the miracle of Jacob's appearance—the perfect fit of the lambswool coat, and the dark knitted cap covering his head. I note that his bare neck is a strong contrast to the white wool.

My examination of him, I tell myself, has everything to do with my mission. The crown prince doesn't look inconvenient, difficult, or pre-cooperative. Instead, as the snowflakes drift between us, I get a stupid, fluttery feeling that he looks confident and commanding. He looks like a king.

Jacob adjusts his gloves, sending me a sidelong glance. "Karl refuses to be seen in anything that doesn't go with Oxford dress shoes."

Maybe Jacob only looks royal because he's abandoned the ill-fitting blue suit and Vorburg-themed tie. Maybe that's all it is, because his shoulders are too broad and his hands are too big. His nose, I allow, is aristocratic, but it's got an endearing jog in the bridge where it's been broken. I wonder if it's a souvenir from that kid in the fourth form.

I swallow hard and look away, vexed that I keep wandering from the kind of cool, clinical observations I can pass along to my mother.

"Shall we?" I say.

We set off, skirting a stand of spreading oaks planted during the bloody reign of Frederick IV. A wide swing hangs from a thick branch of one of the knotty giants, and I brush the snow from the seat as I pass. We have just twelve weeks to accomplish an impossible task.

"What?" he prods, breaking through my thoughts. Our breath, exhaled in the sharp cold, condenses into fog.

"If I have any hope of helping you, I have to know every detail from that binder."

He sniffs in the cold and tips his chin up. "I know what people say about my mother's hair and her name and the fact that she never went to college. You think I'm supposed to be fine with the name-calling now that the source is my father?"

I take a few steps, my boots breaking through the crust of snow. Sooner or later, he has to trust me with this. "I don't know your mother, but I do know that she stood in the same arena as a monarch for over a decade. That takes perseverance."

He shoves his hands into his pockets. "Yeah. She has that."

"What else?"

For a long while, the only sounds are a soft wind and the steady crunch of footfalls. This is his sore spot. The press will find it. They always do.

"She was the youngest," he says.

I don't ask questions. I wait.

"She didn't want to live on a farm, which is funny," he adds, "because now half her flat is potted plants."

"I'm terrible at keeping plants alive," I offer. This is more information than I've released to the public in five years. He drags a branch and lets it spring away, dropping a fall of snow. A smile touches his mouth. He knows what I'm doing. Making a trade.

He plucks his lip with a row of teeth. "What do you already know?"

Because I don't walk into new situations without as much preparation as possible, I know that Tiffani Fawn Gardner dropped out of school and ran off to L.A. when she was seventeen, eventually landing a few USO tours as a little of everything—singer, dancer, comedian.

"Just an outline." I don't fool myself into thinking that's the full picture.

He shrugs and picks up an acorn, flinging it back into the woods. "Then you'll know that she met my father in West Germany, right before the tanks rolled out of Vorburg."

I nod.

"They didn't have more than a couple of days together." That, I didn't know.

"Nine months later, I was born in Blackberry," he concludes. The meat of his story has been picked clean, but I wonder if the dancer loved the king. I wonder if she was scared. I wonder how her parents welcomed the prodigal. Gently, I hope. Dozens of questions beg to be asked, but Jacob, I remind myself, is a job. I only need to know the essentials.

"She managed an apartment complex, I understand." I reach into my memories of sharing an apartment with schoolmates at Harvard and dropping into the office to report maintenance issues and pick up packages. "Was that so she could have you close by?"

He nods. "She snaked out drains with a baby on her back." That's not a fact the press have uncovered. "When I started preschool, she put me on the back of her bike."

"Little Duckies." It's impossible to say the name without wanting to pick daisies and fingerpaint.

He smiles, and I feel a measure of relief. I don't want this to be torture. "I had a thing for Teacher Teresa."

His beard catches snowflakes, and his cheek, pink in the cold, tucks. I can't afford to be derailed by the way he smiles—an odd combination of something new and something very old. A freckled young boy and a mountain god with a long memory. The smiles are potent, pulling at the edges of the official princess, threatening to unravel her. "Your grandparents lived in Skip."

"A little town about thirty minutes into the mountains. Do you want to know what they thought of us?"

I do, and it has nothing to do with making him ready to be a king.

"They offered to take us both when I was born. I don't think they thought she could stick it out on her own."

"But she did." The outline fleshes out.

"With lots of babysitting and the occasional hundred-dollar-bill falling from my grandpa's pocket when we needed it most," he murmurs, filling in the picture still further.

He describes his mother as independent and brave. She would have to be to fight a king, absorbing every slander the press could throw at her for more than a decade to put her son in line for the throne. How much of the mother is found in the son?

Our steps take us to the point of the palace grounds, and we watch the fluttering white-tipped waves rolling across the ocean below for a few moments before turning back.

"Now it's your turn," he says.

"Pardon?"

"I told you about my life."

A shiver of horror brushes through my veins, but I give a polite smile. "I won't be giving you a test about me."

He reaches out, catching a snowflake on his hand—an innocent gesture. "In order to be satisfied..." he says, closing his palm. I watch the microexpressions on his face in fascination, and my boots fumble in the snow. He steadies me. "We both have to give a little. That's the miracle of capitalism. I tell you about my long-standing passion for a room aide at Little Duckies, and you tell me..."

He coaxes me like we're simple creatures who met by accident. Like we're not both operating under a commission from our respective monarchs. There's a guilelessness about it, and

I laugh because it hurts my throat to keep it back. "What do you want to know? I've got all kinds of stories about the palace ghosts. Or do you want to know about the jewel vault?"

The last of my laughter evaporates in the winter air, and his chin bucks toward my left hand. "Tell me about your fiancé."

I take a drag of oxygen and my lungs burn with the cold. I'm prepared to recite an amusing family anecdote about Frederich the Wary—how he gave a crazed speech to parliament carrying his wife's severed head in a bag. I am not prepared to let him see a millimeter more of Princess Alma than I have to. I shuffle through a store of information and lay the facts down like face cards.

"Pietor is thirty-five. He was educated at the University of Amsterdam and is the Hereditary Grand Duke of Himmelstein."

Jacob nudges me with his shoulder. *That was nothing.* "What's the Hereditary part mean?"

"It means he's the heir—the crown prince, just as you are."

"I told you I was a love child, conceived at a U.S. Air Force base. I'm not sure how you're going to beat that." I haven't come close.

"Pietor's been in Lijuela for several months on a humanitarian mission—plastics prevention and ecological clean-ups." My words are spare and careful, conveying none of the aggravation of wasted years or the certainty that I'm disappointing my mother.

Our walk brings us to a slight rise, and Jacob moves ahead, kicking steps into the slope with his large boots. He jogs to the top, and placing my footsteps in his, I follow him up the bank.

"Your fiancé does humanitarian work? That's very...righteous," he says. "You must miss him."

Miss him? That *would* be a confession worth making. Now that it's all over, I realize I never missed Pietor. I missed having a fiancé at my side when the press was pestering me about the wedding date or when Parliament was running him through the vetting process, but I never allowed the actual man he is to take up more space in my life than an appointment on my calendar.

I stride forward.

"When does he return?" Jacob asks, gaining my side.

I want to break into a run. I could probably lose him in the forest. "I'm not at liberty to say, but thank you for your interest."

He chuckles, the low rumble of laughter shaking my insides. "What?"

"You just told me to back the hell off. Is that what this training is going to be about? Learning more inventive ways to be antisocial? Sign me up."

I will not laugh. "I did no such thing."

"Far be it for me to contradict a lady," he retorts, his tone dry.

My lips twitch. He is a man difficult to hold at arm's length, and I contemplate the next three months with foreboding. It's easy to imagine that he will storm past my boundaries if they're too rigid. Perhaps flexibility is the wiser tactic.

I click my tongue and let him see an actual emotion. Exasperation. "I have to teach you how to hold a conversation because you're not doing it correctly. You ignore the rules which govern polite society, ask more than you have any right to, and give out way too much."

"I'm in your hands." He holds his arms wide, wide enough for me to step into them. I'm shocked to realize that my feet want to carry me forward. Is this what the old pirate explorers felt when a new discovery rose into view? There are, I am finding, parts of myself that were hiding past the rim of the horizon all this time.

I retreat a fraction. "We have to get back," I say, touching my cold nose with the back of my wrist. "You've given me your deepest Little Duckies secrets, but you're scheduled to practice your accent with your aide."

Jacob groans, his face pointed to the sky, the scruff of his beard beyond carefully groomed boundaries.

"Alma—I can call you Alma?"

I go hot and cold. "What if I don't want you to call me Alma? What am I supposed to say? What if a hundred telephoto lenses and civilian cell phone cameras are picking it up?"

Jacob pivots and walks backward, hands stuffed into his jacket. If scripted royal protocol is my second nature, this easiness is his—the careless, powerful way his body takes up space and the way his eyes never leave my face. I don't think he even knows he's flirting.

"Don't you like it when I call you Alma?"

I do.

Vede.

I do. He says my name like someone who hasn't heard of the Duchy of Lowenwald or watched me swear allegiance to the Sondish constitution on national TV. He says it like someone who ran into me at the bookstore with a scone on a plate and a copy of *The Contentments of Saint Olav* under his arm. Like someone I made out with once.

I clutch my hands together. "Whether I like it is not the point. What if I really don't?"

"It sounds like you do want me to call you Alma."

I give a little ground to this aggravating man. "You may use my given name, when appropriate."

"Thanks, Alma. And?"

"And what?"

"You're going to call me Jacob, right?"

I tilt my head. "Do you notice the way I am not presuming anything?"

"You have to call me Jacob," he says, missing my point so thoroughly that I want to get his eyes checked. "It'll be weird if you don't."

"My mother is a cousin to half the crowned heads of Europe, and their pet name for her is Lenni. They share memories of summer vacations at the Hunting Lodge every August. Personal letters she receives begin, '*Meine liebste* Lenni' but the official ones coming from the same source don't even use the word 'you.' It's always, 'In honor of Her Majesty's 55th birthday...'

or 'We were heartened to hear of Her Majesty's visit to affected areas...' It would be best if I didn't use your name," I say.

"Why?" he asks. He couldn't possibly take my word for it.

"Even as unignorable as you are, there will be times when you have to disappear into your royal role. Formality will allow you to do that."

"We're alone, Alma." He looks left toward the valley and right toward the forest, wreathed in low clouds. "We don't need to disappear."

I reach for a better explanation, finding it in the number of traditional handicraft workshops I've toured. "Look, you were a woodworker."

"Am." He frowns. "I am a woodworker."

No, he's not. Even if he doesn't realize it yet, that life is over. I slip a glove from my hand. "The way you asked to use my name is like picking up splinters when you don't have to."

I gesture for his hand and he places it in mine, palm upturned between us. I run slow repeating motions over his skin, back toward his wrist. "*Call me Jacob. Pass the water. You don't mind me doing this, right?* Talking like this is like sanding across the grain."

He gives a satisfying shudder.

"Now listen to this." My hand reverses, running slow, easy passes in my direction. "*My name is Jacob. You're welcome to use it when you feel comfortable. May I trouble you for a glass of water?*"

He's finally understanding, but it comes with a price. My breathing is uneven, and every pass brings the sensation of fire up my arm. "Do you hear the difference?"

His fingers curl around my hand. "What I hear is that when I do it your way—"

"The royal way."

"—I don't get what I want."

In his grip, I feel a ridge of calluses at the base of each finger and scrapes across the palm. I trace the scar curving over the knuckle of his thumb and turn our hands over to explore further.

The absence of sound—even of breathing—penetrates my consciousness. I tug my hand away and walk toward the safety of the palace. "Tomorrow, we have to begin moisturizing your skin."

That evening, I elect to have dinner in my mother's apartment, and she asks for my thoughts on this strange half-royal creature we're incubating until the state visit. I tell her about his language proficiency. I hold the secret of my attraction for him, hiding in my careful palms. At the end of the night, I retreat to the gym.

Clara is on the stationary bike, texting on her phone, and Ella is on the floor with a manga spread out under her chin. I miss the sight of Freja doing some dumbbell lunges in the corner, ignoring us while she blasts Puccini through her earbuds.

"How bad was he?" Ella asks, turning a page and shifting into another yoga position.

"Nothing to report," I say, beginning my warm-up.

"Why do all my sisters lie to my face?" Ella grunts, shaking her hair out of her face.

Clara rolls her eyes. "*Stultes es*, get over yourself. Freja's wedding wasn't personal."

Ella crashes to the ground, a sheen of sweat on her face. "We shared a womb. Of course it's personal."

"We can't make the stroopwafel twice," I cut in. What's done is done.

I sacrifice myself for familial peace. "Would it interest you to know that the Crown Prince of Vorburg is a walking diplomatic disaster?" I turn the treadmill to my preferred settings and pick up my pace, visualizing my royal duties hailing me from the palace grounds, flat-footed and dithering, while I speed away.

Clara joins my peace project. "Ooh, do tell. What's he like?"

"I thought he was nice," Ella says. "Big and nice. He'll do fine."

I dig into my stride, springing off the balls of my feet, pacing myself. Ella's words could describe a well-kept lawn, not a man who brings every nerve to attention when he walks into a room. "Nice isn't going to help him become a crown prince," I say. "He doesn't care about titles. He doesn't think I have anything to teach him. I'm not even sure he wants to be here."

"You sound like one of the guys from *Five Minutes to Marry*. You know," Clara's voice drops into a gruff impression of a reality show bro, brows comically tented. "I just want to make sure she's here for the right reasons."

Ella laughs but my thoughts catch on the memory of Jacob kicking the snow into steps. *Big and nice.* There are other words I could use to describe the crown prince.

Obstinate.

Hot.

I close my eyes tight. The number of times I caught myself checking him out today... Too many. I steady myself on the bars of the treadmill, sweeping the mental image almost all the way out of my head. I can blame Pietor and our broken engagement for this. Nature abhors a vacuum.

I glare in the general direction of Lijuela, south, southwest. If I were still firmly engaged, I would be thinking of Jacob as an inconvenience with a jam stain on his shirt, figuring out ways to solve him, not thinking, "Take it off. Let me pop it in the laundry while you wait."

My sisters glance at each other and I school my expression. "If he were a civilian I met on a walkabout, he wouldn't make any kind of impression." Every word is a lie.

"As things stand, the gulf between Jacob Gardner and The Future Monarch of the Entire Country of Vorburg is wide. I have to construct a big enough trebuchet to fling him across the gap," I say.

Clara laughs, never failing to be amused by medieval siege engines, and Ella hops on the treadmill next to mine.

"It'll be all right. He sounds like me."

What is meant to be a bit of encouragement makes me uneasy. Ella's commitment to being the perfect princess is nonexistent. She only gets away with it because with four other children to choose from, Mama can deploy her strategically. Vorburg has but one king and one prince.

Clara hops from the bike and joins us.

"I just have to break through his resistance," I resolve.

"I was resistant, too, but I'm just as royal as you are," Ella says. "I'm just not like the rest of you."

"How's that?" Clara asks.

"Insufferable." Ella makes a face of disgust.

Clara is distracted by a text, and Ella's eyes meet mine in the mirror. "Our ancestors split skulls to get on the throne. They weren't philosopher-kings," she reminds me. "There's room for all kinds of royals in this world. Let Jacob be Jacob."

7

BOILING PITCH

JACOB

Karl hovers at the door of the tiny kitchen, a dry-cleaning bag hooked over one finger.

"Hang the suit over the door and go," I say, reaching up to tighten a cabinet screw with my multipurpose tool.

"*Vrouw* Tiele sent me your schedule. She used bullet points and a color-coded calendar."

"What's that smile for?" I ask, swinging the door back and forth. I make another adjustment to perfect the alignment.

"She's wonderfully organized," Karl admits, the tips of his ears lifting. "We'll be going over state visit details this morning. Her Royal Highness would like to see you in the Chevres drawing room to begin learning the Fundamentals of Eating."

This is Little Duckies all over again. "I know how to eat." I snap the tool closed. In the few days I've been here, I haven't seen so much as Alma's heel rounding the corner of our suite. "It's insulting. The pride of Vorburg won't stand for it." Karl will back me up.

He doesn't. "Eating in public is a different matter, sir." His eyes start at my bare feet and continue up, his expression sour. "I'll leave you to change."

I glance down, brushing the back of my hand over my 'Johnny *Flamen* Marr' concert t-shirt, and carry the dry-cleaning bag into the sitting room. Even after having been washed and pressed each day, the cheap materials of the suit remind me of 70s era imitation wood paneling. No one is mistaking it for the good stuff.

Ever since the verdict came down, the king has been trying to make up for the fact that I grew up wearing hand-me-downs from my cousins and looked forward to Mac & Cheese Surprise—a dish requiring Mom to slice hotdogs into the boxed noodles—every Friday night. But he's trying to pay off a debt that can't be wiped out, attempting to erase the things that shaped me into the man I am.

A distant timer sounds, Karl's warning that I can't commit the Sondish sin of keeping people waiting. I should be out the door now.

I shuck my jeans and jump into the suit pants, buttoning them at the waist. Jeans get tossed against my bedroom door to land in a crumpled heap at its base. Quickly, but with all due care for the bangers he produced, I peel off my vintage concert tee, draping it over the arm of the sofa, and thrust my arms into the sleeves of my dress shirt, the starched material flying around me as I locate the buttons.

I hear a tiny squeak and see Alma spinning quickly around. She hits a side table and steadies it. "I didn't know you were still here," she breathes. "I came— It's fine. I didn't see anything."

I glance down to make sure I'm not actually flashing her. The pants hang off my hips but the barn door, as my grandma would say, is closed. Maybe she's never seen abs.

"I'm sorry," she repeats, talking to the front door. "I should have knocked or something."

With a grin, I fasten the buttons. "I shouldn't be changing out here," I say. "Okay, done. You can turn around."

She does, but a flush climbs up her neck, and she averts her eyes as I shove the dress shirt into the waistband, forward and back. I breathe out a silent expletive. I'm not allowed to find an engaged girl—scheduled to walk down the nave of Roslav Cathedral to wed an ecological saint while the entire world looks on—cute.

Eyes fixed on the ceiling beams, her repentance plays on a loop. "I'm sorry. So sorry."

I lean forward, hands gripping the back of the couch. The stiff neck of my shirt gapes open. "I haven't seen you come through here. I was beginning to think you had a secret passageway."

"Not in this room," she says, leaving open the possibility of secret passageways in other rooms. She chances a glance at me and inhales sharply, biting her lip. "I was...I was getting my notebook. I forgot it." She points to her suite. "I'll get it now."

She shoots through the opening almost as soon as she cracks the door. I take the tie from the hanger, gather my clothes into my bedroom, and begin the process of retying the *zeklen* thing until the front finally hangs where it's supposed to.

I hear her door open, and I shout from the other room, "I'll be down in a second."

"No hurry," she calls.

My tie is properly mangled.

At seven minutes past the hour, I present myself in the Chevres drawing room to a princess who looks like she spent the morning leafing through the pages of a book on etiquette instead of checking me out. But I know what I saw.

"Good morning," Alma says, her hands folded in her lap. Surrounded by so much properness, I savor the memory of the blush on her neck and the telltale intake of breath. "Have you been moisturizing?"

Not even once. "Didn't get to it."

"You may do so now."

She hands over a bottle. I'm used to knowing where my pennies go. Mom taught me early how to calculate the cost per unit, which is why I buy my lotion in large, medicinal containers. I squeeze enough out to adequately cover a dried lentil, glancing up to gauge her approval.

Alma watches my hands and frowns. "We need to be methodical as we tackle your lessons." She reaches blindly for the table but frowns more deeply as I rub in the lotion. "I prepared a syllabus—" Something snaps and she abandons her prepared remarks. "Here." She waves for the bottle.

I hand it over and she squirts a circle of lotion the size of a copper *polska* into her palm. "Hands, please."

"It's going to be wasted on me," I say, obeying her.

"Every morning and night," she explains, working the solution into my skin, rubbing each of the calluses, spreading her thumbs over my palm, holding my rough hand between her small ones. "You can't skip even once."

She switches hands, giving the same thorough treatment to the other, and I silently watch her bent head. This is nothing. No more than when she caught me changing. I was laughing then. I look away now, picking up the faint scent of sandalwood and flowers. This lotion isn't an olfactory throat-punch. It's too expensive.

"Morning and night?" I repeat.

Her fingers still, and I fight the impulse to hold on. She pulls away, wiping her hands on a cloth. Maybe she thinks of me as a bear wandering through the halls of the palace, sniffing the suits of armor. Dangerous.

Alma clicks the bottle closed and hands it over, along with the syllabus, in command of herself again.

I scan the headings. Food, Dressing, Public Manners... "We're not going to spend any time on Naps, Taking Turns, and Going Potty?"

Her brow lifts.

"This is basic stuff. Do we really have to spend a whole week on food?" I fiddle with a button, and she glances away. "I know how to eat."

Her smile allows that I might have a passing acquaintance with a small-town buffet and sneeze guard. "The most complex protocol has to do with food. We will only scratch the surface in a week, but it's a solid beginning."

The daily schedule sketches out a similar routine: wake up, have breakfast, meet with Karl to discuss my father's expectations or the events surrounding the state visit. Next comes five or six hours with Alma as she drills me in the most basic elements of royal life. In the late afternoon, I'll study the Vorburgian language and the richness of its history.

I grunt. Karl's going to have to work hard, hand-waving the fact that most of my ancestors were raiders, warlords, and murderers.

"Is there any time for me?" I ask, suffocated by the inflexibility of these lessons—the way they feel like hard yellow plastic, the kind from the game I played in my grandmother's front room when we raced to place odd shapes into specific slots before the heart-slapping buzz of the timer and the sudden, jack-in-the-box pop of the board.

"I don't understand the question," she answers. "Every minute of the schedule has been designed for your needs."

I drop the pages to the table. It's pointless to fight when we don't speak the same language.

Shortly before midday, a servant rolls in a cart of food, setting out two elaborate table settings and uncovering a series of complicated dishes. My stomach rumbles as soon as the scent reaches my nose, but I don't recognize anything as satisfying as a piece of fried chicken or scoop of mashed potatoes. Instead, each plate has spears of vegetation jutting upward or unnaturally round deposits of semi-solid substances. There are fiddly bits.

"We're supposed to eat this?" I ask.

"Not yet, you're not." Alma smiles and turns to the maid. "I'll be serving. Thank you, Sibela." Alma flicks me a glance. "First we'll run through a state dinner simulation."

"It'll be cold by then."

"That's correct. We begin with walking in."

She positions me on her left, as though the rumbling stomach had never been. I offer her my elbow but she lifts my arm, running her hands along it, setting it in a level plane

I tense from the contact, hating it in precisely the same way I hate the hunger gnawing at me when food is within easy reach. She pulls back. "My apologies. I should have asked."

I rub a hand over my heart, pushing away the tightness. "You have my permission to manhandle, when necessary."

She rests light fingers over the back of my hand.

"Will you be wearing gloves again?" I ask.

Again. I don't mean anything by it, but the word—and the memory it calls—buffets against us like a sudden gust of wind, the kind that makes you correct the steering wheel and say, half-praying, "Almost home."

She straightens her shoulders, and I smile. Alma's going to start monologuing.

"The British monarchy do not touch when they do this in London. They simply walk into the room in pairs. Sondmark, in contrast, is old-fashioned. Every royal house in Europe has a slightly different protocol, and it will be your duty in the coming years to learn it, relying on trusted advisors. They want to make Vorburg look good."

"Not me?"

"You and Vorburg are the same thing. You give the state a human form."

I glance at a long mirror, taking in my rumpled suit and scuffed shoe, comparing it to the woman wearing pearl earrings and the kind of sweater you can't throw into the wash with a pair of jeans. On the surface, there's no way I can measure up, but my thoughts complicate when I think of the stammering, blush-pink girl from this morning. We're not so different.

When I finally conquer the mechanics of sitting at a table—to be done after the monarch sits and with the aid of a footman—we move on to the actual food.

"This is *Sole Bonne Femme*," she says, offering an ice-cold filet of fish resting atop a swirl of frigid cream sauce. She sets it down. As my hand halts over the array of cutlery, she holds her breath in anticipation of my choice.

"Correct," she whispers when I pick up a fork. "What goes in your other hand?" It takes me three tries to select the notched knife, and when I do, she reaches forward, adjusting my grip on the utensils, hands cupping mine, fingers gently molding them into position. *Twelve weeks.* Heat pours through my veins, and when she retreats, my hands go slack, the silverware clattering against the china.

"Again," she prompts.

"Like this?" I ask.

Her hands return, and with them comes a slow and familiar eruption of warmth spreading from my palms and up my arms as she corrects me. *Chol nia, Jacob.* She's engaged. I grip the utensil more firmly.

"Too tight," she says, reaching again.

"I've got it," I insist, forcing myself to relax.

She shows me how to slice through a wedge of Sondish pie with a quick, decisive stroke, instead of wiggling my fork against china. I make more mistakes. She catches every one, bending over my plate, breath on my skin as she instructs me on each point. If I could be perfect, I might escape this torture.

"The good news," she assures me, "is that no one expects you to eat much at a state banquet. If you don't know how to tackle a dish, you might discreetly observe your dinner companion or move the food around enough to be polite."

"I'll starve."

She gives me a side-eye. "A crown prince will never starve. I suggest you eat something at the palace when you can let your guard down."

I lean back in the dining chair. "I don't understand the fuss. Food is for eating."

A crease tucks her cheek. "One of your kings was poisoned over dinner."

"A rival to the throne?"

"It was his wife's lover."

I catch a brief smile and match it. "No one will care if I make mistakes. They'll accept that I'm not perfect."

"That's where you're wrong. Your public face has to be flawless. If it is, you can protect your most precious commodity."

"What's that?"

"The life you have when no one is looking. Whenever you're walking a rope line or in a friendly interview, you can be tempted to disclose personal details," she goes on. "But once a piece of information is given away, there's no getting it back. It'll show up in tabloid articles written after you die. It'll shape the narrative about your character and reign. A good rule to live by is that you are a fortress, and you don't drop the drawbridge for just anybody."

I grin. "Should I keep a cauldron of pitch boiling over the fire?"

She glows with an approving aura. "Ideally."

"How long before you dropped the drawbridge with your fiancé?" I regret the question as soon as it leaves my mouth.

Her eyes flicker. "Every relationship you form will be different."

I prop my elbow on the table. "You just did it," I say.

"Hmm?"

"You dodged that question. I was too direct, again?"

I swear she's relieved. "It's good that you recognize it."

"Who do you let in?" Boiling pitch wobbles on its stand. "I mean, who should I let in?" Alma likes it when I give her a chance to tell me how to behave.

"*Whom*. Your oldest school friends and your family are the safest."

"No can do, boss. I don't have siblings, I've never known my father, and I can't think of a topic my oldest friends would rather talk about less than the unbearable burdens of wealth and privilege."

She bites her lip even though she wants to laugh. "You'll find your people."

"I have."

The clock chimes, and Alma begins gathering her things. "Hmm?"

I made it through another day, torn between wanting to slam myself behind a door and pour cold water over my head, and wanting to stay as close to her as I am now. "You can be my people."

She stands abruptly. "I'm neither an old friend nor family."

"True." I stuff my hands into my pockets. "But you're not going to run off to the tabloids if you find out I sleep in one-piece winter flannels," I say, following her to the door.

Her eyes dance in a way that makes me want to go through each map and atlas in the palace, defacing every sign of Himmelstein.

"Stop," she says. Then, as though her better judgment has succumbed to a beating, she asks, "*Do* you sleep in one-piece flannel underwear?"

I click my tongue. "Wouldn't you like to know. That question was far too direct, Your Royal Highness."

Her lips twitch until, finally, she laughs. In the space of a single heartbeat, we shift from unwilling tutor and difficult student to something that might be strong enough to bear the weight of trust.

"Stop avoiding your sitting room." I exhale, leaning back against the doorway. "I feel like I chased you out."

She lifts her hand, hovering a slim finger over the wavy edge of my blue suit. "We have to address your clothes," she says, scooting past me and jogging out of easy reach.

I wave, and she shakes her head but waves back. A flash of white on her hand warns me away.

Alma is engaged. I can't forget.

8

TIARA WOBBLES

ALMA

The reception hall of the Vorburg Embassy is packed. I hold a stilted conversation with their Minister of Technological Cooperation, nodding politely when she talks about low-level hardware incompatibilities.

"I couldn't plug my curling wand in at the hotel without bringing along an adapter. Imagine, our capitals are 130 kilometers apart, but it's like visiting an alien planet."

I laugh, but the Cold War mentality remains entrenched in Sondmark. I have traveled north, west, and south, but I've never been east to Djolny.

Minister Chezna glances at the ornate ceremonial doors leading off to the tiny chapel Freja eloped in a mere fortnight ago. She doesn't dare bring it up. None of us do.

"Sondmark and Himmelstein have the same specifications for electrical outlets," she says, committing to her throughline. "You must be pleased. When you get married, nothing has to change at all."

"Nothing," I nod.

I take a sip of champagne, trying to look my best in a Were-wolf's Girlfriend dress. A difficult task. The ruffles around the neck, cuffs, and hem manage to be both droopy and shiny. The designer leaned hard into a "harvesting the wheat but in a discotheque" aesthetic, and it's the perfect day-to-night outfit for young, sensible lady farmers.

Ordinarily, I could count on a few days of backlash for look-ing ridiculous in public, but it's going to take more than a bad dress to do that because the tone of Freja's news cover-age has neatly shifted in the last couple days, away from the near universal acclaim she received when she got married. These days, journalists write some version of, "But, you know, Princess Alma is the one doing it the correct way—getting parliamentary approval, allowing her future husband to be carefully vetted. Who is this foreigner with whom Freja entangled herself? What alliances does he have? Isn't Princess Freja's forfeiture of her place in the line of succession a reasonable price for flouting the rules? I'm simply asking questions."

My dinner companion is an old friend, and we catch up between courses and toasts. I nod along with half a mind, the other half wondering where Jacob is. Mama handed him over like a knapsack of rocks, commanding me to polish them. That must be why I carry the thought of him everywhere, even to parties where he has no business being.

He must enjoy his relative freedom. Without paparazzi stalk-ing him down the pavement, he can wander the streets of

Handsel, an anonymous figure in the winter crowds. He's free until Monday, when he'll return to my corrections and drills, the endless reminders about forms of address.

With every attempt to civilize him, he asks, "Why?" The question shakes the foundations of every assumption upon which I've built my life. Why does it matter if we drape our napkins in our lap? Why don't we just shake hands with a foreign monarch? Why does my title matter? Why does all this make me someone worth bowing to?

Still, the barbarian is making progress.

"Alma?"

My friend gives the tiniest prod. I return an apologetic smile and shake my head, wishing that, just once, I got to come to these things in a ponytail and stretchy athleisure instead of this sparkly, doleful gown, chandelier earrings, and the Lowenwald diamond kokoshnik. It's the heaviest tiara among the royal jewels allotted to the princesses—and the one most often relegated to me. None of my younger sisters will tolerate the glittering sunburst, unwilling to put up with the splitting headache that comes with the weight of that much splendor. I see them around the room, laughing with other guests, at ease because I'm the one carrying the burden.

A hairpin shifts suddenly, digging into the soft flesh of my head. An hour into the tedious Vorburgian speeches and the dull irritation has become a sharp pain, radiating from the spot and settling behind one of my eyes, throbbing wickedly. I maintain a serene façade, my eyes fixed on the speaker rather than the hands of the clock as the seconds tick by.

At the night's end, we return through a gauntlet of flashing cameras and shouted questions. *Is Princess Freja leaving the royal family?* Only when the Rolls Royce delivers our party back to the Summer Palace do I allow myself the luxury of releasing a breath.

Ella glances at Clara as she leads the way up the staircase. I see the concern. "Anyone want to come to my suite? We could watch *Fieldnotes from a Teen Queen* and take a drink every time the characters breach protocol."

Though exhausted, I smile. "We'd be plastered before the makeover."

The movie is dumb and tropey, but I never get tired of the scene when the Alabama beauty queen learns she's the long-lost monarch of a fictional island nation in the Mediterranean. Her starchy aide cures her from an addiction to bedazzled ball gowns, fake eyelashes, and overabundant spray tan by taking her to a vintage Dior exhibit.

If only it was as simple to turn Jacob into a crown prince.

"I've got an early engagement tomorrow," Clara says, whipping her phone out. "As long as we don't really make it a drinking game, I'm in." She taps the screen at lightning speed. "Let me cancel with Max."

I cover her phone. "If I don't get to sleep, I won't be worth anything. Honestly, I'm planning to go right to bed."

My sisters exchange another look, worried about me and doing a bad job of hiding it.

I turn to my suite, leaning heavily against the wall when I hear their doors shut. I slip fingers under the frame of the tiara to find momentary relief.

"Alma?" a low voice calls.

The pain comes roaring back when my hand drops. I straighten my spine and arrange my face. "Jacob."

Vede. I haven't spoken his name until now, even if that's who he is in my mind. He *Alma*s me at every turn, but I haven't budged, keeping this thin crust of ice between us.

The Sondish have a saying about thin crusts of ice, posted on a sign at every canal-crossing in the city. *Begeert um Ees an dem falsh Sigheit so geb.* Beware of ice and the false security it offers.

My chin tightens with the effort to appear normal. He can't possibly see it in this light. "Good evening. I hope you had a pleasant day."

He falls into step with me, hands in his jean pockets. "I took a car and ran out to the ruins at Felslot."

The castle, besieged by the Vors and left half razed, sits on a broad, grassy plain. Even in the summer, the wind, unbroken by hills and mountains, scours across the landscape. In January, it would be frigid. I blink heavily against the pain and keep my question short. "Climb to the top?"

"I ran up with a Vorburgian flag and claimed it again," Jacob says, his smile uneven. "It's mine now." He gives my shoulder a bump and looks me over, lifting his brow. "That's quite a dress."

"We need to work on that," I breathe, trying to sound mildly amused instead of on the verge of passing out. I just need to last until I'm safely in my own room.

"What?" Another shoulder bump. The contact is soft, but a shaft of pain lances behind my eyes.

I gather the edges of a smile. "Your diplomacy. Amateur hour. You hate the dress."

"I don't hate the girl in it," he smiles, and then it drains away. His gaze sharpens as I pass him in the doorway. "What's wrong?"

Vede. "I'm a little tired."

"Is it the crown?"

"Tiara." I add to the list of things he doesn't know. "The queen's dresser will be around in a few minutes to pick it up." I glide carefully up the narrow hall to my private door and put a hand to my hair. The hand-shakes. In this light, he won't see.

He does see.

Without a word, he pushes through the door of my room and presses me into a chair.

"Pain relief tablets?"

"Second drawer." I gesture to the bathroom, unable to claw myself out of the well of agony dragging at my temples. With eyes screwed tightly shut, I breathe deeply, slowly. This will pass. It always does.

A glass of water is pressed into one hand, a couple of tablets dropped in the other.

"Drink," he commands, standing over me until I do. Jacob sounds like a crown prince—steeped in privilege and used to being obeyed.

I tip my head back, and the weight of the tiara shifts, dragging a whimper from my throat. I press my lips together, but tears gather in my eyes. He's got to go. I have to get him out of here before I fall apart. Before I can form the words, Jacob moves behind me. I feel his hands on my hair.

I reach to stop him, and our fingers touch, tangle, pause. A tear slips down my cheek, and silence fills the room for the space of five heartbeats.

"I'll be careful."

I can't even talk, but I drop my hand.

"This is something I should learn," he says, voice resonant and soothing, placing me back on my pedestal as his tutor. His second pass at diplomacy is better than his first. "Won't my wife wear one of these things?"

"Amber," I whisper. His fingers dig into the thick coils of hair, and I grip the edges of my seat.

He withdraws a hairpin and drops it on a side table, bringing a tiny measure of relief. "What about amber?"

His question keeps me talking. "Vorburg has the richest amber deposits on the North Sea. Unless your father sold them off, the crown jewels include a whole parure in amber." More hairpins scatter on the table, and I sigh, leaning into his hands.

"Parure. I don't know that word."

I like how he never pretends.

"Tiara, earrings, necklace..." I answer, allowing myself to believe that I really am teaching him something he has to know, that I'm not at his mercy. "A matching set. No one has seen them in decades."

"Mm."

He extracts another pin, and the tiara wobbles. I brace it as he discovers more anchors, brushing my neck and the tips of my ears, sending tiny electric shocks along my veins. When he lifts the tiara free, I hear a knock.

"That will be Mama's dresser," I say, standing reflexively.

"No, you don't." Jacob eases me back into my seat, hand clasping the back of my neck, almost circling it, his index finger sinking into my hair. "This is the box?" he asks, touching the tooled leather case.

When I nod, he fits the tiara inside, and I hand him the earrings. Technically, this box shouldn't leave my hands, but the tablets haven't kicked in.

"I'm coming back," he says with a voice well-suited to demanding answers and calling for decisive action. The list of his virtues is growing longer. There was almost nothing in that column last week. "Change into something comfortable."

I hear the low-voiced conversation at the front door and duck into the closet. Sliding the Werewolf's Girlfriend onto a padded hanger and my high heels into a fitted cubby, I glance at my nightgown. Rich honey-colored satin cut on the bias, paired with a deep neckline outlined in delicate lace trim. It's not the only one. Every nightgown I own screams, "I'm an obscenely rich widow living in Monaco for tax reasons and willing to allow a gigolo to attempt to seduce me out of my fortune."

Every *flamen* gown has a matching robe. All flamboyant. I groan and slide the hangers around, looking for anything that communicates, "I'm a prudent public servant who would know to tie her fortune up in a diversified stock portfolio and carefully vetted real estate investments".

At the back of my closet, I unearth a pair of basic joggers and an old Harvard sweatshirt. It will have to do.

Jacob's voice, muffled through the door, finds me. "She inspected the box twice and told me to tell you that if you ever let them out of your sight again, you're getting the Cyclops."

I yank the pants on and juggle the shirt, looking for the way in.

"Cyclops?" he adds.

"Clara's tiara," I explain, tugging the sweatshirt over my hips. I ease the door open. "It's got a big rock in the middle that looks like an eyeball."

When he gets a look at my outfit, he gives a low, teasing whistle.

I return a quelling smile. "Thank you," I say, guiding him out of my room. I'm acutely aware of the stack of lumpy winter hats next to my knitting basket, the pile of papers scattered across my desk, and a novel, *Death by Plum Flummery*, on my bedside table. If he sees any more of me, I'll have to kill him.

It would not be the first time an extrajudicial assassination of a foreign prince happened on the grounds of the Summer Palace.

Jacob turns quickly, and my hands land against his chest. Even a piercing headache can't override the unwanted wish to slip and keep slipping until I'm in his arms. *Vede*, Alma, no. This princess of Sondmark would never do such a thing—betray the trust of her queen, drop her defenses in the face of an enemy, want something she can't have.

"Let me," he says, voice low. He moves into my space, and I have enough sense—just enough—to move away. I keep moving until the backs of my knees hit a chair, and I sit down with a plop. "I'll do the hair, too," he says.

"You don't have to," I breathe, but I'm tired and his hands are already working another set of hair pins out, and this feels so good. I close my eyes.

The painkillers hit when he's halfway through, the medicine slowly unweaving the band of pain over my brow and temples, and I let out a sigh.

"Say what you like about the Old World," he murmurs, "but you don't get over-the-counter painkillers like that in the U.S."

A braid slips loose, and he works the translucent rubber band from the end. His thumb presses into the plait, deconstructing it from the bottom up, the rippling hair holding its shape.

The tips of his fingers explore another coil, his brows gather, and he tips my head to the light. "Why is this so complicated?"

he asks, running a finger along the roots of my hair. Each time a section moves, it feels like a bruise.

"I need to look good from every angle."

"You're in pain."

"I'm impatient." I tap his hand, resting gently on my head, fingers tangled in my hair.

He tips my face up so we're eye to eye, even if upside down. His gaze flicks to my lips and away, leaving my stomach in knots.

"Is it worth it?"

I don't think of the pain as a choice. It's a natural consequence of the life I lead—as inevitable as the ghastly Werewolf's Girlfriend frock, chosen simply because the designer is Sondish. I blink against the weight of Jacob's undivided attention and imagine how easy it would be to stretch up so slightly, touching my lips to his. I swallow, tipping my head forward.

"Are you going to finish?"

Monday will come. Once this is all over and he returns to his room, we can forget everything and return to the way things were. I'm sure of it. I've read fairy tales. When princesses fall asleep, magical, impossible things happen.

He holds a lock of hair in front of my face. "I like this color."

I tuck the strand back. "It's just brown."

"So is mine." He's silent for a second and then grips my shoulder. "We're not cousins, are we?"

I choke on a laugh. "What has *Pane* Nowak been teaching you about the history of Vorburg?"

"He started with Ulek the Bear carrying a house on his back, hibernating in the Lyste Hills, and having villages spring up between his paws. We've made it to the reign of Piasa III." He sets his jaw. "Give it to me quick. Are we family?"

I indulge a seed of mischief. "Almost everyone belonging to a European royal line is family." His face falls, and I want to snap a picture for Pietor. *This man ogled me. He touched my hair. He doesn't want to be my cousin.*

Thank heaven, he's not my cousin.

"Our families only intermarried once, but that was almost 500 years ago. The union produced no children."

He releases a relieved breath and drags a stool over, setting it before me, knees bracketing mine as he continues his work on the tiny anchoring braids near my brow, essential for keeping the tiara in place.

"We share a common border," he says, the pink tip of his tongue appearing as he concentrates. "Surely, we gave you a princess or two, out of pity."

"We gave *you* a princess out of pity."

When he works the plait free, I tip forward, steadying myself with a hand to his chest. I lift it away, my fingers curling softly.

"Was it a happy marriage?" he asks, interrupting a tiny mental crisis.

He poses strange questions. "It was a medieval marriage, entered into for the benefit of nearly everyone except the two parties most concerned. It sparked off the War of the Amber Cross."

"But were they happy?" he persists.

It didn't matter if they were. "Sondmark took its princess back. Scholars have nothing to say about the relative happiness or unhappiness of the couple."

He resumes his work. "What does Alma say?"

I have a soft spot for that princess, though I've never said so out loud to anyone. "Sondmark had to keep her locked in a tower for the rest of her life, and Vorburg never stopped trying to get her back. Scholars might be blind to the implications, but I'm not." I lift my shoulders. What that princess felt shouldn't matter. What I think about it shouldn't matter, either. "And that's why these trade negotiations are such a big deal. They will give our countries a chance to settle the old grudge."

"That was 500 years ago. How can we possibly still—"

He doesn't get us, but he has to. "Do you like football?" I ask.

"Soccer football or American football?" Jacob pulls down the last of my hair. My head is tender and sore, but I gasp when he plunges his fingers in the mass and massages my scalp.

Gritting my teeth, I force my voice to remain even. "Heretic. There's only one kind of football when you're in line to rule a European kingdom, and you are required to love it."

He grunts a laugh. "I was a baseball kid."

I make a noise of disgust, choked off when his hands slip, fingers above my ears, palms hovering against my cheeks. I've never been touched like this. Not once.

"The grudge is alive and well. When the Dragons play the Djolny Vipers, the fans sing this song called 'No Second Princess,'" I tell him.

"Ouch." He repositions my head, reaching over the crown. "It's just as well you're engaged, then. There's no danger of accidentally falling in love with you."

I smile as I stare at our knees. It wobbles. I don't have to pretend when no one is looking.

"You shouldn't get ideas about my sisters, either," I say when I'm sure I can speak.

"I don't have ideas about your sisters. Is this good?" he asks, rubbing the muscles at the nape of my neck.

I'm shaking. "It's good."

9

— · —

FROG SOUP

JACOB

"Into bed," I say, dropping my hands and looking down and up and everywhere.

She chuckles, the sound of it digging into my mind the way my grandfather turns the soil over in his garden. Easy. Effortless. Preparing the ground to plant carrots or cabbages.

"I have to brush my teeth, floss, take off all this makeup..."

"Moisturize."

We say the word at the same time, the beginnings of a secret language only we speak. Meeting her eyes, I tell myself, for the thousandth time, that she's engaged. I can't belong in the corner of her mind the way she already belongs in mine.

"Then bed," I murmur, backing from the room and pushing through the door.

After I turn out the lights in my own room, I spend the night wondering what the hell kind of boundaries we just crossed. Undoing her hair. Talking. Handing her a couple of tablets and a glass of water. It was twenty minutes, give or take, and she didn't tell me her life story. We just talked.

I wake before dawn, reaching for my phone and rubbing my eyes. My ears pick out the restless groaning of ancient beams and flooring. Alma is up, too.

I peel back the covers, open the door, and wait. Pink sticky notes dot the room, and the ornate dollhouse is firmly closed. Our no-man's-land is deserted, but I watch the slow turn of Alma's door handle and how she tiptoes through the narrow opening. I grin. She's in a ponytail, wearing the old Harvard sweatshirt from last night and a pair of electric blue running shorts over black leggings. There are a pair of trainers in one hand and a sticker-covered water flask in the other. She pivots carefully and halts, mouthing what I'd bet are panicked Sondish swear words when the old building responds to her shifting weight. Her door swings gently ajar, exhaling a long creak.

I cross my arms and tilt my head, watching her lodge the trainers under the other arm and carefully pull her door shut. This isn't the face of a woman going for a jog. It's the face of a woman bent on redrawing smart boundaries, stringing barbed wire and hammering pickets into the ground.

Good. I need all the help I can get.

Alma relaxes her death grip on the handle and straightens. The line of her shoulders looks self-satisfied—the way mine must appear when I measure once and make the right cut anyway. When the room is bathed in perfect silence, I softly clear my throat.

She flails and lets out a squeak, dropping the tumbler with a metallic crash. It rolls in my direction, drunkenly following the irregularities of a centuries-old floor until it comes to rest against my bare foot. I scoop it up, reading the stickers, and my cheek tucks with a smile.

Among the trophies of past marathons, she's got an anthropomorphic pastry sticker that reads "Donut Give Up," and a zombie, his clothes in rags and flesh rotting off his face, is captioned "Run For Your Life."

She bends over to pull on the trainers. "I'm headed out for a jog."

"Into the city?"

She jerks the laces tight and shakes her head. "Into the woods." I hand over the flask, and she clasps it over her stomach in a nervous habit she would never let me get away with. "Thank you for your help last night. My head feels better."

I want to tell her to hydrate, to watch out for roots and patches of ice, to take her hair down if she starts getting a headache. "Sure," I say, scratching my neck.

She watches me for a long moment and turns, setting her ponytail swinging. "Thanks again."

When she disappears into the hall, I release a breath. "Anytime."

Since it's Sunday, I drive down to church, slipping into a pew of Roslav Cathedral as the service begins. Though I don't understand a word, I follow the order of service in a program prepared for English-speaking tourists. The Sondish rites are similar to the Vorburgian ones, and my mind wanders to Alma, sitting on a chair last night, a leg tucked under her, head tipped back to look up at me. My ears redden and not only because the cathedral is colder than an ice box.

I set my jaw. This wouldn't keep happening if I could see her as engaged. When Pietor returns, I'll have Alma set me up with a friend and give me lessons in royal dating. Maybe we'll sit on the floor of our common room to play a game of *Mangos from Mangos* and I'll see her nestled against her fiancé, trading glances, and speaking their own private language.

Maybe then I'll finally get it through my thick skull that she's taken.

As the song of a boys' choir fills the cathedral, I shift in the narrow bench, trying to get comfortable. An impossible job. *Oma* Gardner used to say that the harder the pew, the stronger the doctrine, and if this is so, these Sondish Lutherans are near heaven. The long, stone-set aisle is flanked by rows and rows of wooden seats, the walls and columns a contrast of creamy white and butter yellow. There is nothing to distract me from piety except the thought of Alma who, if royal news websites and Pixy influencers can be trusted, will walk down this very aisle on her wedding day.

When he finishes, the Sondish priest sends us away with words which even I understand. Peace be with you.

It's a fragile peace, but I hold onto it until Monday morning when I enter the Chevres drawing room. Alma's hair is tied back in a thin, black bow, exposing her neck and ears—all the places my hands have already been—and when she stands, I shutter my eyes. She asked me to greet her formally from now on, using her title but bowing as though she were a queen.

I advance. "Good morning, Your Royal Highness." I take her hand and bow. It's like using a router jig, I've decided. I'm following a course already laid out, limited in my choices but protected from my own stupidity by that fact. Follow the guide, and I won't screw up.

She clears her throat and glances down.

"You held my hand too long," she says, tugging out of my clasp. "The press will have their stopwatches out."

My brow furrows. "I'm not the king."

My precious spring blossom, her expression seems to say, and she begins to leaf through the day's materials. "You'll be an unknown element, so everything you do, especially at the beginning, will be taken as a clue about your character. To the Sondish press, you're a foreigner, and they'll want to see if you are about to cause an international incident. They're rooting for that outcome, actually." She places a finger against a page and begins to trace her progress through a paragraph. "They'll sell more papers if you do. A young, good-looking bachelor is a goldmine."

Her words banish any hope of peace.

Alma continues to leaf through a stack of notes and extracts a magazine, tossing it on the table. The sound restarts my brain, and I focus on the image of Crown Prince Noah staring from the cover of Businessman's Quarterly.

Shoving my hands into my pockets, I hunch over it like it's a table full of volatile bomb-making materials. Noah has a slick, dark suit, a square jawline, and tanned skin, under a headline that reads, "The Prince: Sondmark's Visionary Answer to Economic Progress, Politics, and the Past". *Chol.* The man looks serious and impatient—like he has too much on his hands to be dealing with the petty trivialities of a photoshoot, but also like he can't help the way he looks in a suit.

I plow a hand through my hair. Noah is everything I'm not—educated, polished, at ease—and the idea that we have the same title is a joke. He doesn't have to work to be a crown prince. He just is.

Alma leans close, and my attention scatters. "His position," she says, "allows him to shine a light on some of the meatiest topics facing the country, but it also means that questions about the succession are fair game. His dating life is a matter of national interest. Yours is too, until you're safely married. The spotlight will be intense."

It's not what I expected when I agreed to the job. Even knowing that King Otto was my father, I never had much interest in the royalty thing. I was hard at work building my business. The role of the monarchy in Vorburg—lumbering coaches and military reviews, a few times a year—seemed peripheral.

I thumb through the magazine article, which features Noah in a variety of settings. The prince in his office. The prince in a hardhat, touring a recycling plant. The prince in his garden with a dog of some indeterminate breed. There are quotes about "the long-term fiscal outlook" and how "reuse makes as much economic sense as it does environmental." He doesn't sound useless and peripheral.

I slap the magazine on the table. "That's what a thousand years of strategic breeding gets you."

Alma flips through the pages, landing on Noah in the stables wearing a moth-eaten sweater and muddy boots. He carries himself in the careless way only people with serious money can.

"What do you mean?" she asks, sliding her gaze all over me.

"I wasn't strategic. I was a failure of birth control," I grumble, feeling like the bear emblazoned on the flag of Vorburg. "It's ridiculous to make leadership decisions based on biology."

"More silly than holding an election and having less than half the country insist that the results were impacted by the weather in key constituencies?" Alma takes a seat and picks up a photo of the queen on a side table. "The prime minister and parliamentarians grapple for votes, but the queen is beyond partisanship. She represents her people in a way no mere politician could hope to."

Alma sounds like those online lecturers, holding a clicker and telling warm anecdotes set to a slide show. I include the wrap-up she hasn't. "...so thank you for coming to my BIL Talk."

Her smile includes a wince. "Did I get carried away talking about constitutional monarchy?"

I love it when she's carried away. "You've almost convinced me to disregard my deep affection for representative democracy," I tell her.

"Almost?" She rubs the backs of her fingertips lightly against her blouse and examines her nails. She blows gently on them, casting me a look of innocent triumph. "I'm losing my touch."

Alma would be so proud if she guessed how many feelings I'm covering up right now. I grip the table. "You can't beat the Blackberry Fourth of July parade, musicals about our Founding Fathers, and the ease of mail-in voting."

Her smile disappears. "You vote?"

"Always."

Alma's teeth fret her lip, and I crouch in front of her. "Why are you making that face? I thought that would finally be something I'm doing right. You know, 'Flosses regularly, sings along to the hymns, does his civic duty.'"

"Voting is good." She shakes her head like it isn't. "Your father's ministers will have an official position on your citizenship and how you exercise it."

I drop my head and swear fluently in a language she can't understand.

My grandma tells a story about a frog being boiled slowly in a pot. I got into these royal waters when it was cool, but the longer I'm here, the more it smells like frog soup.

"Jacob," she whispers, touching my shoulder.

I lift my eyes. "How many things do they expect me to change? I'm American. I'm Vorburgian. Dual citizenship is a thing in the year of our Lord twenty—"

"It isn't for a crowned head of state." She runs the tip of her tongue across her lip. "My grandmother went into labor with my uncle when she was on a state visit. Very unexpected. The host government had to designate the hospital room as extraterritorial so that he wouldn't be born a citizen. He wasn't even the heir."

"What calamity will befall us if I cast a vote in Oregon's third congressional district?"

She shrugs, lips pulling in apology. "Loyalties can't be divided. Something always wins out."

My fist drums lightly, restrained but rhythmic. "I'm here, aren't I? I turned over my financial records to the government and shuttered my business. Doesn't this look like I'm making this my top priority?"

The silence stretches, and I rake my hair back under her steady, critical gaze.

Finally, she clears her throat and looks back to her notes. "Do you want a real answer?"

I nod.

"We need to consider the message you're sending."

Understanding Alma is complicated by her royal politeness. "You mean my clothes?"

"Among other things."

"I'm wearing a suit." It wrinkles when you look at it wrong. "Isn't this what you want?"

Her mouth pulls. "It doesn't matter what I want. It's about what your position demands. Every decision you make about your appearance tells a story."

A knock sounds at the door and, without needing to be told, I straighten and pivot away like we're double agents, passing state secrets.

She makes them wait until she's collected herself, sharpening the edges of her princessness again. "Enter," she calls.

Caroline holds the door, and Karl slides a box of binders onto the table I'm slouching against. (The Basics of Posture isn't on the syllabus until next week.) I read the spines of each as they're unpacked. Royal Men of Vorburg, Contemporary Royal Men, Influential European Men.

Every road was always going to lead to these binders. "They couldn't leave me alone, could they?"

Alma's tongue clicks. "Don't be a baby. You know and I know that this"—she points a finger up and down and up my frame—"isn't going to cut it. It says you think this whole thing is superficial and not worth bothering about."

"Bravo, Your Royal Highness," Karl interjects with a slow clap.

"It's no time to start a war," Caroline says, dipping into a curtsey and dragging him from the room. "Do ring if you need anything more. Sir. Ma'am."

Alma and I are left with only the company of an ornate mantel clock announcing its presence with a soft tick, tick, tick.

"I'm bothering," I grit out.

"Don't lie to me. You look like you're having as much fun as someone facing a government firing squad."

"Is this supposed to be fun?"

Alma sighs, leaning back. She's tired and letting me see it. "Why are you here?"

I could give her the truth but the whole of it is too big to swallow in one sitting. So I give her something small and easy to digest. "Once upon a time, a mommy and daddy didn't love each other even a little."

"Jacob," she scolds. But her eyes dance.

10

MYSTERY SURGEON

JACOB

"You're giving me a make-over," I say, when we've leafed through the binders for more than an hour. "What is this? *Fieldnotes of a Teen Queen?*"

"You know it?" Delight washes over her face before she assumes a more businesslike tone. "We have to bring your exterior presentation into visual alignment with your new job title." Her hands weave through the air, eventually forming a straight line.

I cross my arms and stand squarely in front of her. "It's a make-over."

"It's no different than giving you a hard hat to operate a fork-lift," she insists, chin lifting in an obstinate angle. "It's necessary for the job."

"Are you pleased with your blue-collar analogy?"

Her eyes sparkle. "A little."

I look away. This is dangerous. It was fine when the princess was trapped behind a dense thicket of royal manners but now the thicket is thinning. Narrow paths open up, rabbit trails that may lead anywhere. What would I do with a princess if I caught her?

Alma has been banging on about diplomacy for days, and some of it must be sinking in because I keep telling myself that having the future Hereditary Grand Duchess of Himmelstein as a friend will be good for Vorburg. A friend.

The thought of friendship sours my mood.

"If Vorburg needs me to be their crown prince so badly, they should take me as I am. No one's going to buy this," I say, waving a hand up and down my heavy frame, "as crown prince material, no matter what you put on my back. I'll always look like a bear, and nothing in these binders will convince me otherwise."

She closes the distance between us. "All right Jacob, I give up."

She's too close, and every inch she claims, the more I struggle to think straight. "You're saying I get to keep this suit?" I don't even want the suit.

Her cheek tucks. "Oh, no. We'll burn that suit."

"Burning synthetics? What will your fiancé say about the smoke cloud?" I drag her impossible-to-remember engagement between us, waving it like the hugest red flag in all the land.

The smile disappears and she swallows. "Let's leave the binders and drive around Handsel. Maybe I can get you to accept the benefits of cohesive visual messaging."

Alma sounds like she's delivering a presentation on third quarter earnings, but the possibility of getting out of the palace wakes me up like my grandpa's retired hunting dog when he jangles the keys.

"Can I change?" I ask.

"Be my guest."

I charge up to my room, tearing off my tie and loosening the top button on my shirt like a superhero racing off to an elevated train disaster. Reaching for a pair of jeans, a soft-worn t-shirt, and my leather coat is automatic, and it's only when I'm lacing the boots that my mind wanders back to New Year's Eve. This is what I was wearing.

I tug the laces tight and return to the Great Hall, jogging down the stairs. Alma emerges from the admin wing with a trench coat slung over one arm looking, as she often does, buttoned up and hot.

Taking the coat, I hold it out while she tucks herself inside, scoops her ponytail from the collar, and belts it neatly around her waist. I step back, giving her a whistle.

"You have to stop whistling," she corrects with a slight shake of her head. "Pretend you don't even know how."

"I look like I'm hunting for Handsel's best biker bar, and you look like you're on your way to an economic forum."

"You don't whistle at people going to economic forums." She glances at me, but her gaze bounces away. "I'm driving you around until you start understanding the secret language of people's clothes."

I understand hers. In order to silence it, I cast my eyes to the ceiling, flinching away from the faces looking down. The palace is like a jump-scare. In Blackberry, art is a single landscape print over a sofa, a thrifted seascape in the half-bath, or a culturally insensitive buffalo painted on velvet. It doesn't loom and intrude.

"Ready?" she asks.

"After you."

I fall in line, following her through the back corridors of the palace, watching the swing of her hair. When we come to a side door, she fishes keys off a hook and pushes through it. The January sun is blinding, and the wet pavement steams under its steady glare.

"This one." She steers me toward a silver Mercedes sedan. A nondescript blue Fiio occupies the space next to it with a bright orange Mini Cooper in the stall beyond.

"All the money in the world and you didn't spring for a red sports car?" I ask, getting the door for her. She maneuvers into her seat, and I catch a scent of flowers before I close the door with a firm click. I take a deep, bracing breath before I walk around the car and slide in next to her.

"Being famous is a fulltime job," she says as the car adjusts itself to her seat and mirror settings. I swear I hear her mutter 'Ella' before firing up the engine and backing out. "In a few months, you'll see the point of being incognito when you can."

We pause at the security gate while she answers a series of questions determining whether she needs a security detail. They land on 'not' and in a quarter of an hour, we enter the forecourt of a hospital, slotting between a battered BMW and a bank of electric bikes.

"Welcome to St Leofdag's, where we're going to play a game called Mystery Surgeon." She grips the steering wheel and leans forward, light touching the soft lines of her face. "We're going to pretend you have an inflamed gallbladder and you have to choose someone to operate based strictly on appearances."

Her. I choose her. Alma looks like she's been turning in the extra credit since kindergarten.

Without warning, heat tips through my veins and I shift with the restless need to exit the car, slap my coat to the ground, and get some air. I thought this energy I've been bottling up since I met her was an ordinary, if unusually strong, male reaction to an attractive woman. It's not personal. Nearly every male is gifted with these kinds of reactions about the time he gets his first skull hoodie and a graphing calculator. It's juvenile. It's nothing.

I scratch my neck. This isn't nothing. I always liked the smartest girls in class with the straightest braids and the neatest pencil cases. Alma is my type.

Chol nia.

I have a thing for a princess from the wrong country. She has a fiancé, and it's her mission to change everything about me. Awesome. Brilliant life choices, Jacob.

"Jacob," she prompts.

What am I supposed to do now? I do the only thing a man can do when he's being thrown around an emotional mosh pit. I adapt the strategy of those Greeks who could stand uncomplainingly in the face of a hailstorm of arrows and certain death. I stare through the windscreen.

"That guy," I say, pointing to a pair of people mounting the front steps. "The shorter one."

"Why not the other? Tell me quickly. Don't think too hard."

To run away from my thoughts, I start making observations. "He looks like a *zeklen*—" I cough. "Sorry, like he's full of himself."

"Why? Give me details."

"That hair, for one. He doesn't have one person in his life telling him how stupid he looks. He's doing a lot of finger stabbing."

"Good. Anything else?"

"The suit is shiny, and the stripes are..." I don't know. I only know I hate it. "I don't trust that guy."

"What about the other one?"

"He's got fun socks and there's a strap around his leg, so we know he rode his bike in," I say, warming to my subject. "He thinks about the planet, and he's got a family."

Alma leans over, resting her hand on my door. Her ponytail brushes my neck as she tries to get a better view, and I stare hard at the ring on her finger until she shifts back.

"How do you know?"

I swallow. "No one wears that tie unless it's a gift from a child. If there are people who put their lives in his hands, I guess I can. He's the one that'll get a crack at the gallbladder."

What the hell? I like this game.

"What did we learn, Jacob?"

"Nothing about how they would actually handle gallbladders."

My reward is a smile, half-hidden, but it's enough to keep me hard at work for the better part of an hour. When the light begins to change, she drives us to the wharf, scoring a prime spot next to the promenade. A bitterly cold wind blows off the ocean, bringing low clouds, and scattering all but the most hardy tourists. A statue of Horst the Invader dominates the harbor.

"Your ancestor looks..." How to put this in the most diplomatic way? "Like he's on the cover of one of those sexy books from the 80s," I say, pointing at the choppy seas slapping up his muscled calves. "The ones they leave at the laundromat in a basket."

Alma chokes on a giggle. "Thanks to a few surviving accounts, we know that's what he actually wore—fitted trousers and a leather tunic. Horst was a lover *and* a fighter." She winks. "Either way, he came to slay."

I shake my head to keep the grin from completely taking over. "I'm embarrassed for you right now. Your ancestors are cringing. Is there a sponsor I can call? Maybe the royal family of Motovia could stage an intervention."

She elbows me, and I grunt.

"I like his braids," I allow, holding a lock of my hair between us. "Mine is almost long enough. Could my makeover—"

She reaches to the back of my head and grabs a fistful of hair, tugging it, lifting my chin. A gust of wind shakes the car. "We're here to people-watch."

Our glances catch and hold. In the second before self-consciousness breaks through, before we can remember that we don't fit or that a mountain of 'shoulds' and 'supposed-tos' divide us, my mind plays out a million different ways to love her.

I imagine pulling her into my arms, the sound of the ocean muffled against the glass of the windows. I see myself checking my phone after a session in my workshop, earmuffs perched up on my forehead while I scroll for her text. I can see myself stretching out on the grass and pressing a kiss against her neck in some park back in Djolny.

Alma blinks, and the moment is gone. Her hand works out of my hair, and she retreats into another hemisphere, maybe the one where her fiancé is.

"Sorry." The word is hardly audible. "This game is called Captain of the Guard. You're going to pick one." She takes several slow breaths and looks out the window like she's waiting for her own hailstorm of arrows.

I scan the harbor and pause on a group of students taking selfies, each using the magic of forced perspective to look like they're picking Horst up by his head.

"Quickly," Alma urges, herding me away from introspection. "It's cheating if you wait for someone to break out in tae kwon do."

"The girl in the heavy pea coat. She's the only one prepared for the weather," I explain, ticking off my observations. "She's got heavy boots and one of those cross-body bags to keep her hands free for the martial arts."

"Her friend is bigger," Alma pushes back, pointing to the student balancing along the sea wall.

I snort. "He's wearing canvas shoes without socks. In Sondmark. In January. If I take him on a black-ops mission, he'll probably fall over and shoot me in the back."

"Black ops?" she laughs. "What kind of crown prince do you expect to be?" Her smile disappears too fast.

By early afternoon, the slow plink of rain turns into a downpour, chasing the last tourists into the safety of cafes and hotels. We turn back to the palace, winding through the quiet streets of Handsel, when a string of lights blurs the raindrops on the windscreen.

"Stop," I say, pointing to the small bistro with a black and white striped awning and a sign with gold letters. La Baiser Chaleureux. Against swishing wiper blades, the small-paned windows glow with light. "There was a line around the block when I came here last, and I couldn't spare the time. Hungry?"

"Not really." Alma shakes her head. She's lying.

"Breakfast was hours ago. What did you eat?"

"Jacob," she reproves, as though it could ever be a punishment to hear my name on her lips. "I told you not to ask personal questions."

I shake my head. The line on when I'm supposed to treat Alma formally has been shifting with the tide. "Hot gluten, Alma. Hot." I lean against the dashboard, peering into the gloom. "The place is deserted. You can lecture me on comportment the entire time."

She plucks her lip with her teeth and cuts the engine. We run through the rain, and I hold the door for her, shaking out the umbrella.

"Stop being impressed at basic manners," I whisper, catching the look on her face as she passes.

"*Weelkomme*," a voice calls.

An old man with a crisp white hat is situated behind the counter. As soon as he sees the princess, he stumbles off his stool and doffs his cap, performing a deep bow. Alma doesn't wave him off or protest. She simply moves forward with a smile as warm as the air fogging up the glass.

"What a lovely establishment you have," she says. "Everything looks delicious."

She flicks me a glance. *Taking notes?*

"What do you recommend?" she asks, leaning over the colorful display case. The owner, delirious with pride, takes her on a tour, and Alma holds my elbow, willing me to relax. We make our choices, but the proprietor fills a box with assorted pastries and Alma promises to share them with her sisters.

"May I offer you something to drink?" he asks.

"Espresso," she answers.

He turns to me. "Hot chocolate."

Alma swallows a smile.

"Let a man have his hot chocolate," I say, commandeering a booth. I may not have enjoyed being hauled off to Europe when I was a kid, but it has its points. Here, you can get thick bittersweet chocolate served in an atmosphere of marble and glass, brass fixtures, and rich wallpaper. It's almost a religious experience.

I inhale the aroma before taking a sip. "All right, Alma. You win."

Alma's brow lifts, and I raise the porcelain cup, full of thick chocolate and topped with a dollop of whipped cream. "Appearances matter." I grin into my cup. "If I ordered hot chocolate in Blackberry, the waitress would bring me a mug of hot water and a packet she smacked twice on the counter to get the powder to settle."

Alma resists the urge to gloat, instead tearing off a piece of croissant and popping it into her mouth. "You don't look like a hot chocolate man."

I lean back in the booth and lift my shoulder. "I guess you can't judge a book by its cover."

11

GRUMPY CINDERELLA

ALMA

Cocoa-dusted whipped cream kisses his lower lip. I brush my mouth to signal him but he furrows his brow in confusion. I touch my mouth again and his eyes shift to my lips, lingering on them. A flush, brought on by simple sugars and concentrated Italian caffeine, rises up my neck.

"You have a spot of—" I tap my mouth.

"Ah," he says. A row of even white teeth pluck at the lip, rolling them until it's gone. "Did I get it?"

I nod, wiping my hands. My whole soul gropes blindly for a copy of *Timeless Manners for the Modern Royal*.

The problem that has lurked and hovered in the shadows for the last weeks has returned. Mama taught me to shine a bright light on any difficulty, but I've hesitated, afraid of what I'll see.

"Dragons shrink when you face them," she used to say. "You just have to be brave enough to do it." Such were the bedtime stories of Queen Helena.

I can't wait any longer. I have to look at it while it's small enough to be vanquished.

The truth is...*stultes es*. Think it, Alma.

The truth is that the problem is bigger than a kiss. Whenever I'm around Jacob, the peaceful horizon I could once count on begins to tilt. When he smiles or grumps or even breathes near me, I feel myself slip off my axis. I clench my hands under the table.

The way to solve this problem is to exhibit more control. That's what Mama would say. I school my expression. I don't let myself look at him. I breathe ordinary color back into my cheeks. I think about how out of place he would be at a royal banquet and how it's my job to fix his manners.

The dragon withdraws to the shadows.

"When eating in public—" I begin.

The bell over the door jangles, and a lavender-haired girl with elaborate make-up and a massive pink hair bow bursts through the door, her cell phone mounted on the end of a selfie stick. "No line," she crows, spinning with her back to the display case.

Vede.

I flinch and Jacob covers my hand. *What?*

My eyes widen. *Danger.*

It's a Pixy influencer. We see these people at royal engagements—have learned to lean in for selfies or smile politely as a phone is thrust into our faces. Panic brushes my spine. I promised the head of palace security that I wouldn't get out of the car—promised him with the earnest heart of a princess who knows the stakes—but here I am with no security detail in the company of the secret crown prince of Vorburg.

So? Jacob gives a half shrug.

Do you know how big the international incident is that I'm about to cause?

Stultes es. Stultes ES. This is what comes of improvising. I imagine Mama laying into me at a family meeting. "Great are the misfortunes of the House of Wolffe to have such princesses," she'll say.

Though the influencer is prattling on in Sondish, her purpose must be clear, even to Jacob. "The Warm Kiss," she enunciates in English, providing a translation of the name of the establishment. If it's bad to be caught, it's worse to be caught trying not to be caught. I have to get out of here, but I'm frozen.

Jacob squeezes my hand. "Stay on my left," he whispers. He gives me a pointed look, collects the box of pastries, holding it near his head, and hauls me to my feet, enveloping me in the smell of earthy aftershave and aged leather.

The dragon is back.

Jacob shields me with his bulk as we cross the checkerboard floor, passing the influencer spinning in whimsical abandon. At the door, he gathers me into the crook of his shoulder and bundles me through in one swift motion. He thrusts the box into my hands, raises the umbrella, and we run through the rain. Misty air seems to sizzle against my feverish skin, but I fly over the cobblestones. We made it. *Dominanstid,* we made it.

He bundles me into the car, arm flung over my head as he guides me in. Laughing, he slides into the passenger seat, shaking his fingers through his hair. Flecks of cold rain hit the backs of my hands. I grip the wheel and breathe deeply, eyes trained on the gold-lettered sign. *The Warm Kiss.*

I promised Nils Helmut—looked him straight in the eye as I delivered a predictable, bland itinerary and assured him I could be trusted. Instead of letting me loose in the city, the head of palace security should have tackled me as a threat to the peace of the nation and tasered me in the neck.

"That was almost a disaster," I say.

"Almost a disaster means it wasn't a disaster." Jacob's smile tips up on one side, inviting me to see the joke.

I can't. "You're the crown prince of a semi-hostile government. If you'd been found roving all over Handsel with me, the novelty of it would have been every headline tomorrow, impacting trade negotiations, your first impression on the global stage, and my reputation."

"Your reputation," he murmurs. "We wouldn't want to ruin that." Jacob clicks the seatbelt in place and glances over. His mouth softens. "There was no way to plan for that."

I put the car in gear and ease into the road. "That's no excuse. I'm supposed to plan for the unexpected." I peer through the rain-lashed windscreen to the blurry lights of the palace on the hill.

"You're supposed to be superhuman?"

"I'm supposed to know my job. I froze in there." *Vede.* He didn't.

Once we arrive at the Summer Palace, I hand him over to Karl.

"Accents and idioms, today," Karl informs us. "We'll spend the next few hours talking."

Jacob glances over his shoulder as he follows his aide, hands tented in supplication. I can't help it when my lips twitch. I nod him onward, having no doubt he'll understand the textures and nuances of the message. *Don't be a baby.*

My smile disappears with him, and I retreat to my room, sinking onto the bed to stare hard at the wall. My mother was wrong, and this is a bad time to find that out.

When I was a child, I believed my mother saw everything and everyone, her unblinking stare uncovering injustice, comforting the downtrodden, and encircling her kingdom in a warm maternal gaze. I could rely on her to take care of me and *be* careful of me, to know my best interests even better than I do. My trust in her judgment has become the foundation of every choice I make.

But she's wrong about dragons. It would have been better if I hadn't looked at this one. I remember the weight of Jacob's hand in the narrow point of my waist. How he recognized the threat posed by the girl with lavender hair and acted. How I forgot everything when he held my hand and pulled me into the rain. He wasn't dangerous when I didn't know—when I was determined not to know—that I like him.

Like him. I snort. The old Sondish saying is more accurate. *Our roots tangle.*

It's not love but it's not nothing. I'm a princess at the mouth of a cave, holding a quivering lantern, unwilling to delve deeper. The part I see is too much already.

I sigh and scrub my face in my hands, but when my thoughts refuse to shift, I reach for my knitting, finding a rhythm in the task, and try to work out a paradox.

Mama sees everything, but she didn't see Jacob coming.

It's a long night, but when I step through the doors of the Chevres drawing room the next morning, I carry a renewed resolve to do my best for my student, my motherland, and my mother. The silver lining is that, thanks to yesterday's field trip, I seem to have convinced Jacob of the importance of the clothes he wears—an excellent redoubt from which to bomb the rest of his resistance.

Hearing his step at the door, I try to steel myself and fail. Even in an ill-fitting suit, Jacob catches me off guard.

He performs the greeting smoothly but his eyes narrow as he straightens. "Something wrong?"

Yes. Something is wrong. I was up half the night thinking about how sorry I am that Jacob Gardner is the crown prince of Vorburg. How that means there's no way he'll ever kiss me again.

Karl taps on the door, escorting a stocky man with impeccable tailoring. Getting his name required issuing a diplomatic license plate on specious grounds for one man, rubber-stamping a passport for another, and dangling before a third the promise of a favor to be redeemed at a later date.

I turn to Jacob. "Allow me to introduce you to Mr. Tumwater," I say. "He's the best-kept secret in London."

"Secret?" Jacob echoes.

Karl looks serious. "Never give out the name of your tailor, sir."

I smile. "Together with your aide, he will guide you through the process of expressing your personal style."

"He'll be my fairy godmother." Jacob bites his lip. Worried fingers play with the lapel of his suit, and I want to thread my hand though the crook of his elbow.

As the morning passes, our anxious Cinderella becomes grumpy. "I told you, just put me in whatever everyone else is wearing," Jacob says, glaring at the swatches of seemingly indistinguishable gray fabric the tailor flings over his shoulder. "It's just a suit, Karl."

I rub my temples. "How can you say that when you've been wearing the clothing equivalent of a single-use plastic bag?" At this moment, I would kill to be laying the cornerstone of a community recreation center with a little bronze trowel instead of fighting a Vorburgian bear.

Jacob flings the swatches back and crouches in front of my chair. "I'm never going to be—" His gaze sharpens, and he pauses, pouring a glass of water and pressing it into my hands.

I take a long swallow, instantly refreshed, as he continues his protest. "Your brother is a crown prince. He looks fine. Ergo, get me a couple of what he's wearing, and we call it a day."

Karl pinches the bridge of his nose, and Caroline enters, bearing a tray of light refreshments.

I look over Jacob's shoulder, conscious of his nearness—how his arms are braced against my chair and what it must look like. I take another sip of water, maintaining my posture, ignoring him but fitting neatly within the half-circle of his arms. "Caroline, how soon can you bring me a collection of pictures of Prince Noah? I need him in a variety of suits."

"I have them ready now, ma'am."

That's Caroline. A total professional.

Jacob thrusts himself away, and a television emerges from a sleek modern console. Tapping the screen of her tablet, Caroline's personal ThumTac account pops up on the larger screen with boards titled Family Gifts, Coastal Granny, and Noah.

Noah? I never imagined Caroline using his name. She knows the proper codes of conduct—the titles and the courtesies, the two paces she must follow behind Mama. That's one of the things the queen appreciates most. Caroline knows her place. The heir to the throne would be the last person on earth to make her forget it.

Intense stillness comes over Caroline until her chosen page loads. "This is at the Ragnar Prize banquet," she says, speaking matter-of-factly.

The photo was taken the same year I met Pietor. I can see my pale pink gown in the background—the tiara and sashes, the aged astrophysicist who escorted me into the room. Pietor, with his white shirt front and ramrod posture, was a perfect match. I swallow back a knot of humiliation.

"That's a tuxedo," Jacob says, raising his arms like a ref dispensing double yellow cards. "I'll take one of those."

Caught in a whirlwind of exasperation, I shoot from my chair and flick his forehead. He catches my hand, and we stand stock still—his brow arched, my eyes blinking. I don't know which of us is more surprised.

I should be thinking of how assaulting Vorburg's next head of state will impact bilateral investment or the Strategic Coastal Partnership proposal, but I keep forgetting that he isn't just Jacob.

I keep forgetting that I'm Her Royal Highness Princess Alma. That we haven't known each other forever. That he's not someone I should touch without the permission of an ambassador.

I lift my chin. "I'm—"

He rubs his forehead and drops my hand. "Don't you dare apologize."

My cheeks burn, but I nod, gesturing to the screen. "Noah favors Italian-made suits with lighter material and a sleek silhouette. He's got the build for it."

The words are clinical, but halfway through this explanation I realize I'm staring at Jacob, running my eyes along the breadth of his shoulders. I jerk my gaze away, giving Caroline a blind nod. *Carry on.*

Caroline pulls up a few more photos of Noah in suits, and Karl points out the unstructured shoulder, high buttons, and tapered waist. These are paparazzi shots, and in all of them, a tall, slim model, dressed in startling high-end fashion, completes the picture.

"Are these recent?" Jacob asks Caroline

"Most of them within the last few months, sir."

Jacob cocks his head. "Does your brother have commitment issues?"

"We are not going to discuss His Royal Highness's private life," I warn.

The clock on the mantel chimes the hour, Caroline bundles the others off to find refreshment, and Jacob braces his arms against the table.

British tailoring. That's what he should wear. The image of him—properly suited with his expressive face and silky hair—walks into my mind. No pinstripes or flashiness, just substantial materials with a few well-considered touches. Supple pocket squares, rich gold cufflinks. Double breasted? I associate double breasted suits with old aristocrats and Slavic crime lords, but I can picture him in them easily.

"You have to participate," I scowl, dropping my guard now that there are no witnesses. "Do you want to look like Horst wading out of the harbor?"

"Do *you* want me to look like Horst wading out of the harbor?"

He's too close. My hand forms into a fist and I uncurl it, turning to a stack of magazines and leafing through pages like my life depends on it.

Jacob perches against the table, his shoulder brushing mine, as calm as I am agitated. He's too close.

"Does he trade them out every week?"

"Mm?" I manage.

He points at a collage of Noah and his dinner companions, and I incline my cheek to him, sensing the precise border beyond which are consequences I can't control.

"A week isn't even long enough to find out what kind of books they like," he says.

Did Pietor ever know about my cozy mysteries? About how some of them come with recipes in the back and how I've tried a few? No. Once we decided we would suit, our conversations covered timing and logistics. When he told me he liked tropical locations, I went immediately into itinerary mode, asking Uncle Georg for the use of his private island for our honeymoon.

"Maybe he likes variety," I counter, stacking stacks into new stacks.

"One awkward first date after another. That's not variety." He shoves his hands into his pockets.

"No? What is?"

His voice is easy, but I hear how careful he's being with his words. He can't hide the effort. Not from me. "Being with someone through every season, the good and the bad, the young and the old, in sickness and in health."

He isn't looking at the screen anymore, and the words sink into the narrow space between us, only the ragged remnant making landfall against my ears. Running the boat up the shore. Palms against the sand. Kissing the ground.

I can't like him. I can't. But even as I think it, I see the two paths opened up before me. One is well-paved and marked with reflective signposts to pleasant, predictable destinations. The other leads to a dark forest where apple-cheeked little children meet witches and get baked into pies.

I hold a stack of papers like a breastplate, and the dark unknown of the forest path dances on the edge of my vision. "Who would have tagged King Otto's son as matrimony's bravest soldier?"

Vede. I regret the careless words as soon as I say them.

He lifts a shoulder like it doesn't matter. The shrug is a lie. "You always want what you never had."

12

FIRST GENTLEMAN

ALMA

The afternoon brings more disputations. Jacob fights us about shoe fastenings, metal finishes, and sweater vests. He glowers at Karl, his patience as thin as the dense, dry bread we serve with tea. "Do I look like a sweater vest guy?"

I like this man, and I don't want to. The feeling is like a tiny colony in a new territory, and my only hope is that influenza or a bad winter or hostile natives will wipe it out. In the meantime, the unwelcome emotion doesn't stop me from rolling my eyes. I like him, but Jacob Gardner is an obstinate pain in the neck.

I conduct a swift online search and find a British footballer, beard neatly trimmed, checked shirt under a sweater vest open at the throat, sleeves pulled up his tattooed forearms. The image is intensely masculine, showcasing the way a sweater vest can be a classic way to introduce color, texture, and pattern in less-formal settings. I hand over the tablet and go up on my tip toes, directing his attention over his shoulder.

"Is this that soccer player?" Jacob asks.

"Football," I correct, reaching around him. I zoom in on the picture with the push of my fingers, feeling my pulse leap, noting it like a scientist clicking her pen. "You could get away with something quite fitted." Our eyes meet, and I pin on a coaxing smile. "This decision could single-handedly revive the dwindling sheep breeds of northern Europe. You might even save the economy of the Vorburgian Isles."

His chin tips up and away, an uneven, unwilling smile on his face. "I'll try *one*."

I flash Karl a look of triumph, and the aide sends Jacob a glower. "Her Royal Highness says try it, you try it. I say try it—"

Mr. Tumwater digs into his notions box and hands me a slim leather notebook. "I'll measure, and you'll stand next to me and record."

I've been measured thousands of times and know exactly what it entails. The idea of weaving myself around Jacob makes my knees soft. "I don't want to mess it up."

"Write what I tell you," he says, dismissing my concern.

I position myself near the crown prince. I can do this. I can. I once faked enthusiasm for the workings of the internal combustion engine because I had a crush on a boy in the fifth form. I can certainly fake being bored by this task. Piece of cake.

"Take your jacket off," the tailor instructs.

Jacob shrugs out of it and turns, folding the article over the arm of a chair like a boxer draping his robe over the ropes. His shoulders roll under the synthetic cloth, the fabric straining over his bulk when he places his hands on his hips.

I'm pale in the effort to command my pulse, my color, my thoughts. "His shirt has too much material around his waist," I blurt.

Karl joins us, his expression critical. "I noticed that."

I train my eyes on the rest of the shirt, cataloging its deficiencies. It's worn and creased. Though recently laundered, the white of it is no longer that of new snow, freshly fallen. This snow has seen smokestacks and industrialization, possibly a curry dinner.

"We'll begin with the neck," Mr. Tumwater instructs.

The tailor measures his arms, shoulders, and chest, speaking quietly as he asks me to record, occasionally asking me to hold the end of his tape. This close to Jacob, I try to imagine we're measuring a piece of furniture for placement in a dorm room, but as with Napoleon marching into Russia, some endeavors are doomed to fail. I press the back of a hand against my cheek, fanning slightly when Mr. Tumwater adjusts the placement of the tape.

"This is how you find the natural waist," the tailor tells me. I set my jaw and follow him around to the front. "Bend to the side, sir." Jacob bends and Mr. Tumwater guides my hand to the furrow, friendly and educational.

"Can you find the other side?" he asks, taking the notebook. He steps back and I square up in front of our subject.

It should be nothing. It should be like dissecting a clam, identifying the parts from a reference guide. I feel my way to the narrow point on his other side and wonder how Mr. Tumwater will reduce this poetry to numbers and notations—something mathematical and scientific. "Here?" I whisper.

"Excellent, ma'am," the tailor says when I step back. He passes the tape around Jacob, reading and reporting the centimeters. I scribble them into the book, knowing I can't transmit any of this information to Mama.

He's high-waisted and long-limbed. I know the way his broad shoulders taper and that his right arm is a fraction longer than the other. I know that his breathing checks when I stand close. Mama doesn't need to know any of this.

By the time Mr. Tumwater takes the little book from my hand, my skin is hot and cold. Freja would give me a cookie. Ella would tell me to build a pillow fort and take to my bed. Clara would ask me how I've managed to get away with groping a man for the good of the country.

Karl orders one tuxedo, several sport coats, and two suits—one in blue wool and the other in charcoal gray—to test the fit before further adjustments. For his casual clothes, we decide on classic chinos and slim fitted button-down shirts. No skinny jeans. This decision was reached after a protracted argument about the width of his shoulders during which I did more touching than was strictly necessary.

"I'll compile a list of ready-to-wear options for your approval, ma'am," Karl says, packing away our materials. He turns to Jacob. "I'll meet you in your suite for our lessons, sir."

"Not tonight." The words leap from my mouth. Caroline glances up.

I know how little time we have. I know how perfect he has to be before we cast him onto the world. I know. I know. But he's tired. I can see it around his eyes and in the way he kneads the back of his neck.

"This is enough for today."

Karl pinches his lips. "I hoped to start explaining historical pronunciation shifts and the Exceptional Consonant Stretch."

I cannot leave the crown prince to such a fate. "Tomorrow," I say.

"As you like." Karl gives a curt nod and lifts a box from Caroline's arms, following her up the hall.

There's something about the way he does it that makes me ask, "Is she in for an evening of linguistic history?"

"He's not that nice to anyone," Jacob observes.

He lifts my work bag from my shoulder and opens the door, ushering me from the room. A strange fact, probably gleaned from one of those nature documentaries narrated by Daavi Drikkidorp, slips into my consciousness. Sea walruses can return to a beach filled with ten thousand other sea walruses and know by scent and sound the one sea walrus who belongs to them. It's a miracle, that kind of connection. I thought it was. But I could close my eyes right now and know exactly who I'm walking with, know the sound of his step, and know how to keep pace at his side.

I let myself feel the exhilaration of danger for a moment—of standing in too-deep water and having a wave strike me on the back, pushing me off my toes. Sooner or later, I have to return to the shore, soaked to the skin.

When we enter the Great Hall, Clara speeds past us, fastening an earring and racing to the foot of the stairs, balanced on impossibly high heels.

"Where are you headed?" I ask, using English for Jacob's benefit.

"*Hej.*" She looks at Jacob, head tipped to the side. "Is Alma being merciless?"

He smiles. "You look good."

My little sister sparkles when she's happy. Today, she's lit up like one of the chandeliers in the ballroom. "Max's commanding officer and his wife invited us to dinner. How do I actually look, Alma?" Clara spins, showing off her narrow cigarette pants, silk blouse, and crisp blazer. "If you tell me to change, I absolutely will."

"Perfect," I say. She darts away and we mount the stairs. "Why is it perfect?" I ask.

"I thought I was getting a break." He raises his hands above his head in a stretch and the shirt untucks a little, exposing a narrow band of taut muscle. I dig my fingernails into my palm.

Jacob continues, blind to the havoc he leaves in his wake. "If she goes to one of those shoeless houses, her pants won't be dragging on the ground. It looks pulled together"—a phrase I taught him today—"but not intimidating?"

I nod approvingly. "Why is intimidating not a goal?"

His shoulder bumps mine and a shock of electricity rocks through my stomach. "We're not on the clock anymore."

"Civilian," I taunt. "Royals are always on the clock. It's the price we pay for gilded chair rails and bronze statuary."

In our suite, housekeeping has come and gone, leaving a single lamp lit, casting much of the common room in darkness. We've had our fill of each other today and need a rest. That's what I tell myself as I reach for my bag. He shifts it into his other hand.

"What are you doing for dinner?" he asks. "Are you eating with your mother again, or do you have to get done up?"

I've spent the whole day answering distracting, obstinate questions like, "What psychopath named this color oxblood?" I don't hesitate to answer him now.

"Housekeeping left a plate of veggies and hummus in the fridge. I'll add some cheese and nuts."

It won't satisfy my appetite, but I can't eat at my mother's table where the *coq au vin* arrives with a side of geopolitics and a reminder to keep my eye on our Vorburgian guest. If I was honest about how well I'm keeping my eyes on Jacob, she might start a war.

"That's not enough," he says.

"It's enough for me."

As if on cue, my stomach gurgles.

Jacob grins. "Change into something comfortable. I'll make you an omelet."

I'm too famished to turn him down. "You cook?"

I hear a low chuckle. "Some of us didn't grow up in a palace." He hands me the bag and walks backward, luring me with promises of a hot meal on a cold night. "Go change. I've got mushrooms, ham, peppers, an avocado…"

"An avocado in Sondmark?" I laugh. "In January? How rich is your father?"

He ducks into his room, calling across the divide. "You can share some of your fancy cheese."

I throw on a pair of leggings and the Harvard sweatshirt, and return to the kitchen, clutching my Gruyère and Fontina, when he appears in the doorway.

He's wearing another one of his concert t-shirts, this time featuring a man with a wild cloud of hair, his lips a smear of red lipstick and thick eyeliner apparently applied by one of those captive elephants who do art for charity.

The shirt must have been laundered hundreds of times because the neck is slightly stretched out and the material is soft, hugging his chest like an emotional support koala.

He reaches over my head for a couple plates and I lean out of his way, backing into the counter, hands gripping the edge.

"That's an old shirt," I observe. Purchased before he had all these muscles.

"Vintage. Original. Rare." He grins. "I thought you were good at diplomacy." He fires up a burner and reaches for more ingredients.

"Can I help?" I ask.

He sets a grater in front of me. "Two cups of cheese."

I click my tongue several times. "You'll get 500 grams, and you'll like it."

We work quietly, my ear trained on his progress—the crack of the eggs, the shake of the seasonings, and the whisk working through the mixture followed by the gentle sizzle when it's poured into the skillet. The album title stretches in neat copperplate across his chest.

Jacob clears his throat. My eyes snap closed.

"Do you play?" I manage, nodding at his shirt. "Guitar or anything?"

He leans on the counter and crosses his ankles. "Enough to impress the ladies."

I don't want to hear about ladies. "How much is that?"

He squints an eye. "Two and a half verses of 'Escalator to Limbo.'"

I snort. "Let me guess, when the key change comes you have to tune your guitar."

"I'm that dedicated to the craft." He palms his chest, mock-serious.

I tear my eyes away from his chest in time to see his expression change. It's nothing special, this look he gives me. Nothing more than a lingering gaze on my eyes and mouth. But my slow, hormone-addled brain shifts into overdrive, delivering a clear, lightning-fast translation of its meaning.

Jacob likes me, too.

I don't want to know. No, that's not quite true. I *can't* know. So I turn on the tap of the sink and start washing a bowl, waiting for this forbidden knowledge to swirl down the drain with the last of the bubbles.

"Here," he says, taking the bowl, brushing his fingers with mine, and drying it with a dishcloth. We linger in this state of potent awareness for several moments until he clears his throat. "I'm not very musical. I just like music."

"What kind of music is that?" I fling the question at him, doing my part to keep realizations at bay.

"You don't know The Antidote? Come on." He tosses the cloth down and drops into an off-tune bass.

I want you

Can't have you

A better man would know better

"I played this on a continuous loop through most of seventh grade because Anna Melanson started going out with my best friend," he says, plucking the shirt away from his body.

I laugh because the alternative is horrifying. "Was their breakup super satisfying?"

"They have three kids and run a successful heating and cooling business." He turns the omelet with the flick of his wrist, and the smells make my mouth water. "I think she's going to run for mayor in the next election."

I laugh. "You could have been the First Gentleman of Blackberry instead of a lousy crown prince."

"Right?"

When he's in this mood, I think I could ask him a question—*the* question—and get a real answer. He loves his grandparents and his home in Blackberry. He's uninterested in leading a European country and living in a castle. As far as I can tell, he'd be content to handcraft furniture for the rest of his life. As much information as his dossier contains, this is the blank page at the heart of it. Why did he agree to become the crown prince?

"What do you want for toppings?" he asks, closing the door on complicated questions.

"Anything."

"Not anything. What if I put on canned tuna, creamed corn, and yams? You're fine?"

"I'm fine."

He sets the spatula down. "Nobody likes everything."

When I don't answer, Jacob heaps a generous amount of grated cheese, diced peppers, and ham onto one side of the omelet, flips it, and makes a rustic half-moon. It's going to be delicious.

Every day I look for ways to protect him when he assumes the role he wasn't born for. Though we're not on the clock, I can't afford to ignore it when he gives me an opening. "Have you ever tried mämmi?"

He grunts, tipping the omelet onto a plate. A quick swipe of a dishcloth and the pan is ready for his spinach and avocado omelet. "What is that? A Scandi metal band?"

"Food. It's gritty and sticky, and some people say it looks like paving tar. The Finns serve it around Easter to, I don't know, remind themselves of the inevitability of death and the hope of the resurrection. Motovia has a dish—it's a loaf of bread with herring poked into it, like a helmet with fish spikes. It's the stuff of nightmares."

I smile when he grimaces. "You can't make that face when people present you with their treasured national dishes, Jacob."

"Be real, boss," he says, handing me a fork. "You've never been grossed out?" He carves a large bite out of his omelet and pops it into his mouth.

"I've been grossed out. No one unaccustomed to them looks at a dish of boiled silkworms and thinks about how edible and delicious they'll be. But I managed to swallow down a few pods, and no one guessed my feelings."

"So you lied," he says, gray eyes twinkling.

The word stings. "I showed manners. Consideration. Poise. I thought you were trying to get better at diplomacy," I answer, taking a golden bite oozing with rich cheese, tender ham, and bright peppers. My eyes drift closed for a second as I savor the taste. This is heaven. I don't have to pretend.

He clears his throat. "Do you always have to hide what you feel?"

"Welcome to royal life." I blow gently on my fork. "You have to choke down lots of things you hate."

13

GELATINOUS OOZE

JACOB

In the morning, she starts in, almost before I've finished my bow.

"You have to learn to eat foods you don't like."

"Is this about the Finnish paving tar?" My nose wrinkles, and she points at my face.

"See? That. We can't have that. We have to address it," she declares, "or the press is going to eat you alive." Her voice drops. "I can't let that happen."

"You think that's going to tip the scale? My expression? We can clean up my beard and these clothes and maybe even make me smile like a *zekle* all the time, but I've got problems before I even walk through the door."

"What problems?" she snaps. "We can solve the problems. I'm not going to give anyone a reason to talk down to you."

I shake my head, shoving my hands into my pockets. "They'll eat me alive no matter what I do. I'm an American bastard—"

"Stop it," Alma shouts, pounding the table with the flat of her hand. When the last echoes of it die away, she closes her eyes. "That is the last time I hear you speak of yourself that way."

I shrug. "I don't care what anyone says about me."

She takes a long drag of air. "Of course you do. This thing"—her hand waves to my tired suit and my loose posture—"is part of who you are. It's casual, it's American, but it's also an act."

I could say a few things about her smooth hair and perfect makeup. "I've never tried to hide who I am."

Her jaw sets. "You're smart, Jacob. You figured out that when people were being dismissive about your abilities or your speech or your mother"—I tense—"you wouldn't play their game. You'd rather flip over the game board than give them the satisfaction of beating you."

"Did you get that from the dossier?" I grit out. "What else do you think you know about me?"

"I know you're loyal. I know your family and your home mean everything. You don't want the people you love to think you've outgrown them."

"Are you a fortune teller, Alma?" I ask, shifting under her close examination. "Am I having my stars read? Is failure supposed to bring shame on the House of Gardner? It won't fly. I have a great uncle who died in a shootout after robbing a bank. My cousin owns a junkyard."

She shakes my arm. "Stop it. Just admit you're getting good at this—the forms of address, making a proper bow, the correct way to eat peas—when you're hardly even trying. Think of how good you could be if you *tried*."

As refined and royal as Alma is, she's a dog with a bone. There's no wrestling her out of an idea once she's fixed on it, and soon she adds another element to our routine each evening—the preparing and consuming of culinary abominations from around the world.

She's still engaged. I tell myself that I'm not enjoying it too much. It's a lie.

Over the course of several nights, we eat cheese with live insect larvae, pickled seal flippers, and a kind of fish that, if prepared improperly, will lead to a sudden, violent death.

"You can't be serious," I told her one night over a dish of gelatinous ooze. "I thought we were going to try things like haggis and cheese in a can."

"Haggis is delicious." She scooted the dish closer. "I've sincerely eaten every one of these things on diplomatic missions for my mother."

I prodded the ooze. "Have you ever wondered if people hate Sondmark and this is their way to make sure you never come back?"

She propped her chin on her fists. "Dig in, Jacob."

The way she says my name is what keeps me doing this, night after night. Every second we spend together, I have to act like I'm not interested, like her nearness means nothing, like I wouldn't crawl over broken glass if she asked me to.

When it's my turn to offer her a dish, I start simple, bringing Alma a container of raw pickled herring. She takes one look and smiles. "I'll dish them up."

I get a fire started in the fireplace, bending low to blow the embers into life, and wander around the sitting room, picking off the remaining sticky notes—vocabulary lessons which remind me of the man whose country and language she's forcing herself to adopt—and toss them into the fire.

The frustration of her engagement feels like an ache in the palms of my hands, and I open a folder containing translations of select human interest columns from the Sondish news outlets to distract myself.

Over the last weeks, I've learned that the press is divided about the wisdom of Princess Clara's lawsuit. Prince Noah receives generally positive coverage except from the *Daily Worker*, whose columnists refer to him as "an inherently exploitative product of monarcho-capitalistic hierarchies."

Princess Ella is a favorite, but the image the press has is one of their own creation, cobbled together from her candid photos and off-the-cuff remarks. The press is eking every bit of newsprint from Princess Freja's elopement that they can, running constant photos of the newlyweds touring some of Florence's best museums or wandering through markets.

I slide the folder onto the coffee table and crouch in front of the dollhouse. Alma's upcoming marriage to Pietor is discussed in the press with a breathless disregard for named sources. An anonymous vendor claims they've set a June wedding date. A "close friend" suggests the groom's conservationism will play a major role in the smallest details—locally sourced and seasonal flowers, organic elderberry cake, and bee-friendly seed packets given as favors.

All this royal nonsense should be a joke, but I'm not laughing. I hate Pietor. Even if he adopted stray puppies and donated a quarter of his income to rewilding the countryside, I'd still hate him.

Alma carries a tray in from the kitchen, gently negotiating the furniture, clad in a soft sweater and dark slacks.

I look away, training my eyes on the dollhouse. Focusing on it like I'm charged with its restoration, trying to forget my reaction to her. The roofline is a mix of craggy medieval crenelations and delicate French turrets. The face of it marries Ostphalian timber framing and stone, more harmonious than the actual palace, which meanders without order along the headland. These craftsmen cut away anything which couldn't be contained within the sharp confines of a childish rectangle.

"Ready?" she asks.

I take a breath before I turn my head, bracing myself. "Can I open this?"

"Sure." She scoots around the coffee table, and I unfold from the crouch, taking the tray and setting it down. Our fingers brush. I scrub the sensation away on my jeans.

"There's nothing to see. All the accessories are packed away and stuffed inside," she continues, nodding to the dollhouse.

"Why did you put it in here if you're just going to keep it closed up?" Other people forget to put things away, get careless or lazy. Not Alma. If she carves out room in her life for a thing, it matters.

She shrugs like it doesn't. "It was just taking up space in the nursery. It was a gift from the government of Schwascle when we hosted them for a state visit."

I trace a finger along the ridgeline. "You played with it?"

She busies herself, loading up a plate with the Vorburgian delicacy. Her nose doesn't even wrinkle at the scent of pickled herring when she hands it over.

"Yes. Our British governess taught us to handle priceless things in a careful manner." My ability to distract her with questions about the dollhouse is a sign she might not be whole-heartedly looking forward to her meal.

Going to the dollhouse, she swings the front panel wide. I expected magic. I expected the inside to match the richness of the exterior. Instead, more than a dozen ornate rooms are packed to the ceilings with paper-wrapped parcels.

"But?" She doesn't like my questions, but she doesn't lecture me every time I ask one anymore.

She lifts a shoulder. "We were five little kids. It was fragile. No matter how disciplined we were, pieces broke. That's what hap-pens when something is not just for show." Her nose scrunches in memory. "There used to be a rocking-horse. I wasn't careful enough, and it broke," she says, pointing to one of the highest rooms. The nursery.

"Didn't you fix it?"

"I wouldn't know how to fix it." She nudges my shoulder, the light touch disturbing my calm surface. "Time for dinner," she says, serving herself.

"That's an...elegant portion." I cock my brow and heap my plate.

She quickly finishes a thin sliver of pickled herring while I demolish mine and ask for seconds. The fact that she hasn't gagged even once is disappointing, but returning the tray to the kitchen, I see the remains of the fish, lying in a row.

"Well, well, well."

Alma brushes by me to scrape the dishes. "It's not the right season," she insists, filling the sink with hot water and suds. Pushing her sleeves to her elbows, she slips her engagement ring onto the counter and dons pink rubber gloves, scrubbing vigorously. Hair has worked out of her bun, and pieces of it are sticking to her skin, damp in a cloud of steam. I imagine bracing my hands on either side of her waist, pushing the hair off her neck, and following it with a kiss.

I hate Pietor.

I try to do the thing she's trying to teach me—to carjack my human emotions, stuff them in the trunk, and drive them off a high bridge. It's the memory of my grandma smacking my knuckles with a wooden spoon that convinces me to keep my hands to myself.

"Those herring are too lean," she explains, attempting to sound rational. She's adorable, and she's failing. "They're not in season."

"My people eat pickled herring year-round," I say, looking up at the ceiling, crowded in this tiny kitchen. There's nowhere else to be. I grab a towel, wiping the counters and the top of the fridge where Housekeeping has already been. "And the whole point was to eat pickled herring like a Vorburgian."

"You don't eat them like this until May," she counters, the words high-pitched, desperate. "They don't get fat until the North Sea gets warmer. Did you know that the custom started during the reign of—of...?" Her words trail off and she swipes the back of her wrist on her forehead, leaving behind a trail of soap.

"Eating raw herring is an established culinary tradition," I say, brushing a thumb across her brow.

"It's a dare that got out of hand," she snaps. Alma clamps her lips together and plunges her hands into the sink. "You'll be expected to take the first bite of the new catch when you're king—right off the boat. They'll like you even more if you carve it up with your own knife."

"I already do that," I say, reaching around her. I pinch the tail of a herring and drag it through onion and dill. "I'd never even seen this kind of fish until my first term at the Royal Academy."

Alma sees what I'm not saying. "What happened?"

"Kind of gruesome," I warn her. "On my first day of school, a group of boys—the best blood in Vorburg, so I was told—held me down and stuffed my mouth full of the stuff."

Her brows lower in a snap and her eyes flash. "You had bullies?" The memory is too old to sting, but at her look, I fear for their lives.

"Not much," I grin. "Anyway, the joke was on them. Pickled herring is the best."

Sondmark doesn't agree. They're too civilized for the raw, lightly brined delicacy, plucked straight from a fishmonger's cart and eaten on the spot. Even when they eat it for good luck, they shudder.

"You've got to try it the Vorburgian way," I insist.

Her nostrils flare. "Fine."

"You should be glad they're so skinny," I say. "There's less to consume."

With a strained expression, she draws a gloved finger down her neck, pushing the hair back. Her tongue darts between her teeth, moistening dry lips.

"You first," she says.

Easy. Raising the herring above my head, I tilt my chin back and lower the fish to take a salty bite. I lock eyes with Alma—a taunting, rounding-the-bases, home run celebration—as I swallow. Then I catch something she wouldn't want me to see.

Attraction.

She blinks, the flash is gone, and she lifts her chin like a baby bird. "Ah," she prods, and the sound has me positioning the fish above her mouth. As it nears, her nose wrinkles. She closes her eyes and sways.

I steady her, snaking an arm around her waist. Her pink rubber gloves lift slightly, suspended at her side, but she doesn't push me away. It hurts to draw air.

"That face would get you tossed out of the country," I breathe.

"Hurry, hurry, hurry," she says, a fisted glove drumming lightly on my arm.

"Here goes."

She takes a stingy bite, holding it in the well of her mouth. "Ah, aw, eh," she breathes, gagging it down, punctuating each chew with a miserable moan. She clutches my shirt front with her gloves and burrows in my arms.

A laugh rumbles through my chest. "You're going to have to work on your game-face before I let you loose at the St Jusuf's Day festivities."

"*Vede*," she gasps, "How do you do it?" She rips a glove off and holds the back of her wrist to her mouth, gagging against my shirt. I don't mind. "Is St Jusuf's for singles? No one is going to want to kiss this mouth ever again."

I give another laugh, trying to break up the incredible tightness of my chest. "The tradition is that you're supposed to kiss someone who just ate some, too."

The words are out of my mouth before I've thought them through. The realization hits both of us at the same time, and we freeze, my hand on her waist, closer even than we were on that midnight.

I'm afraid there aren't enough wooden spoons in the world to keep me from reaching for what I want. I draw a breath, but before I can move, there's a tap on the door and someone clearing his throat.

"*Chol nia*, Karl," I grit out.

I look up but the man at the door isn't Karl. The stranger's light brown hair is streaked with blond highlights, his skin has a deep, nutty tan, and his shiny half-boots look fit for grinding the faces of the poor.

"I don't know who Karl is," he drawls, waves of European nobility sheeting off an enormous forehead, "but I know my fiancée when I see her." His gaze flicks pointedly to my arm.

Alma wiggles in my tight grip, a flush on her cheeks.

"Pietor."

14

USUAL STYLE

ALMA

Jacob's arm tightens around my waist, and my breathing becomes erratic. Hauled up against his chest, I want to forget that Pietor exists.

"Alma," Pietor snaps.

I toss the gloves on the counter, jam his engagement ring onto my finger, and drag myself out of Jacob's arms.

I dredge up a smile. "This is a surprise."

"I see that, darling," Pietor answers, not sparing me a glance as he stares down Jacob.

The testosterone standoff ignites something within me. My cheating ex-fiancé is supposed to be in another country, making love to his causes and any adjacent models. Instead, he's here, littering hollow endearments like trash along a shoreline.

I lean up to kiss him, exhaling the brine of the North Sea into his face, and he lurches back, throwing an arm across his mouth. A fun geographical fact is that Himmelstein is completely land-locked. They have lots of root vegetables, but not a lot of pickled herring.

He thrusts me away, nostrils flaring. "Darling," he grinds out, "I'll wait in the sitting room while you tidy yourself."

I look over to see Jacob lounging easily against our kitchen counter. He's been like a sponge this month, absorbing the astonishing amount of information I've thrown at him, filing it away for later use. I know that intent, sharp-eyed look. He's absorbing now.

"Don't mind me," he says, flipping a hand towel over his shoulder. "I'll just be in my room."

Not happening. The old Ostphalian door is nowhere near thick enough for my peace of mind.

"We'll go downstairs," I say, gripping Pietor by the arm. The arm is muscled, no doubt hardened by weeks at sea in a high-tech rowboat, plying his oar to the other side of the world. I wish he'd kept rowing.

Halfway out the door, Jacob halts me with a question, a mischievous light dancing in his eyes. "You want me to wash up after us?"

"*Zekle*," I hiss.

His low laugh follows me from the door and when I catch up to Pietor, my color is high.

My official fiancé tucks my hand through the crook of his elbow. "He's washing up after the both of you? You wasted no time finding companionship," he says. "He's rougher than your usual style."

A Sondish princess is supposed to be precise and modest, representing the monarchy as the queen wishes and making room for her to participate in the vital work of governance. I imagine the headlines if I were to push him down the stairs. "Usual style?" I murmur. "I can't hope to achieve the numbers you have."

"You're not *still* upset?"

We enter an anteroom used to house cloaks and hats when Mama throws a ball. How fitting. The engagement between Pietor and I has been a similarly serviceable article, tailored to fit the monarchy.

Mama placed him next to me at the Ragnar Prize banquet, and our conversation found its way to his recent trip to the Arctic to bring awareness to organic pollutants building up in the fatty tissue of Arctic animals.

Between the mushroom-wrapped veal and the apple sorbet, we discreetly bent over his phone, scrolling through his Pixy feed: Pietor crouching next to a harp seal. Pietor standing on a glacier. Pietor's beard covered in ice, his blue eyes gazing brilliantly at the camera.

He ticked all the boxes. He was titled, serious about global issues, philanthropic, and aristocrat-handsome—the kind of handsome which balances out the risks of the Hapsburg chin and potential for genetic blood-diseases with the likelihood of obscene wealth and access to heirloom jewels.

Given the long history of Sondish monarchs, I never expected a happily-ever-after, but as long as our union never included being bricked up in an abandoned monastery by a husband-king in the grip of syphilitic madness, I thought I could handle it.

While some of my old classmates dreamed of finding love and others of being a first wife with an ironclad prenup, I aimed for a good working partnership with a man who would never make me ashamed to hold my head up in public. Mama and Père, as fractured as they are now, have that.

I look at the man who once held my future in his careless hands.

"Your family has been in the news," he says, leaning against the mantel. "Clara is fighting in the courts. Freja ran off with an immigrant." He lifts a lazy brow.

"My sisters are no longer your concern," I cut him off.

He plucks at the folds of his pocket square. "As long as you wear my ring, they are. Your mother is going to find herself with a referendum on the monarchy if she doesn't take care."

"Leave my mother out of this," I warn. "I ask only that you keep our break-up discreet until after the state visit. Consider it your debt for the mess you caused."

"I caused? I was doing conservation work for an impoverished nation while my fiancée has been running around with a man who looks like he has a promising future in waste management." Pietor pulls an exaggerated yikes face, the tendons of his neck pulling. "What a headline that would be."

My veins run with the blood of warrior queens, and when I hear Pietor threatening exposure, my reaction is violent, gut-deep, and nothing to do with protecting my family from scandal.

Don't touch Jacob.

I am close to ripping a medieval weapon off the wall, dragging the tip across these marble floors, and pressing it to his neck. Pietor is playing on dangerous ground.

I close my eyes and hear the voice of my old nanny, Poppy Fforde-Hughes. *What does a princess do? She uses her words.*

I breathe, guiding Pietor away from the topic of Jacob. "Those pictures were innocent?"

Pietor shuffles away from the mantel. "Gabriella, who is a noted humanitarian, by the way, was covered in sand. I was trying to be a gentleman."

"Yes. I could tell by the way your tongue was down her throat."

Pietor's eyes sparkle. "One might begin to think you were jealous."

I enunciate clearly. "Only if one was an idiot."

Pietor turns to the mirror above the fireplace, brushing aside the hair with the back of a pinkie. "My...extracurricular activities are no reason to break it off." He tips his head and looks at me through the mirror. "You once called this a suitable arrangement. That's one thing I've always admired about you—that you don't tell yourself fairy tales. I trust that once your ego has recovered, our sensible Alma will return. You'll agree with me that it's best to keep things as they are."

"No." It's a complete sentence.

Pietor lifts a hand. "It's not so simple. Our engagement has been a godsend to my country."

The Grand Duchy of Himmelstein isn't merely land. It's a corporation, of sorts, funneling vast amounts of wealth via high-end holiday homes, farming, residential and commercial rents, and even a prison, into the pockets of its CEO, Rolf, the Grand Duke of Himmelstein. Pietor, as his heir, is being groomed to take over these holdings.

"Himmelstein is doing well," I say. Mama and a fleet of accountants made sure of that.

He shrugs. "You never know when you'll get a bad harvest or a pandemic. Since our engagement, banks have been lining up to offer low-interest loans—perfect seed money to fuel long-term investments and diversify our portfolio. It's not good business to break things off at this critical stage, Alma."

"It's good business for me."

"Is it, though?" He chuckles. "These trade talks between Sondmark and Vorburg are at a vulnerable point. Didn't you almost go to war over mackerel?"

"Scallops," I snap.

He gives a mocking half-bow. "You don't need the distraction of a broken engagement."

"This is why we asked for your silence until the talks are concluded."

Pietor tips his head. "You need more than my silence. I came through Queen Magda International Airport, and by tomorrow morning, the whole country will know I'm back. If I'm not seen at your side, playing the doting fiancé, I don't give us more than a couple of weeks before we start showing up as blind items. Three before people start conjuring conspiracy theories. Neither of us can afford for news to leak."

I hate that Pietor is right. If our break-up gets ugly—if he goes public about my mysterious 'companion' and I lob a volley about Our Sainted Lady of the Lip Fillers—my mother will be sidelined during the negotiations, and they will be left in the care of her bumbling, offensive prime minister. Everything I care about will be damaged. *My queen. Sondmark. Jacob.*

I shake my head and make a correction. *Sondmark's indispensable ties to Vorburg.* Those will be damaged.

My mother would negotiate her way out of this mess, and I'm not her daughter for nothing. "What do you want?"

A light leaps in Pietor's eyes. "If I can't have you back"—a brow lifts but his delusion receives no encouragement—"I need us to appear as a happy couple. We'll do press interviews, gala appearances...the usual. In order to reassure investors and bankers, I can't have any tapering off."

What will it cost me, being at Pietor's side, behaving as though I'm in love with him? Pretending. I release a slow breath. If I can make this deal, it would be one less thing Mama has to handle.

"You can carry on with the trash collector in private," Pietor offers.

My head snaps up. "You drag him into this and the deal is off," I say, surprising myself. Every negotiation has deal-breakers, but they should be few and confined only to the most vital things. How did Jacob become mine?

"Excellent," Pietor answers, passing me on his way to the door. "I'll be in contact soon."

I'm restless when I return to the suite. The kitchen is pristine, and I flick off the lights. The worst thing about Pietor is that I'm a conservationist at heart, striving to leave no trace when I visit forests and nature preserves. It's one of the facets that drew me to him. But seeing him again makes me want to dump industrial waste into the watersheds and burn a mountain of tires.

I flick the light on and off several needless times.

I climb into bed and work on knitting, churning out the tightest, stabbiest stitches while the winter wind roars outside. An hour later, I throw the homeliest knitted cap anyone has ever produced into a basket and punch my pillows, no closer to rest. It'll have to be the gym.

On my way, I pass Ella returning from an evening engagement. Her dress is a cocktail gown in floaty forest green with tiny scattered flecks of gold, so carefully appropriate that I'm immediately suspicious.

I look closer and see that the specks are Seongan characters. "Sneaky," I conclude.

Ella gives me a too-innocent expression. "What could you possibly mean?"

I'm not in the mood for games. "Getting the fashion press to do your dirty work."

They'll mention Seong in their coverage, and Pixy will add an auto link to every social media post, steering donations to relief agencies working to alleviate the Seongan Crisis. My little sister's hands will be clean from the charge of interfering in international affairs.

"What did Mama say?"

Ella dimples. "We were on public roads before she gave me a proper inspection. I offered to wiggle out of the dress in the back seat of the Rolls. I can't think why she said no."

She reaches for her phone. "You okay? It's late for the gym," she murmurs, typing something out.

I'm not giving an answer to the top of her head.

She looks up and tips the phone. "Sorry, it's Marc. He's in Seong, just updating me on conditions."

Ella drops the phone to her side, eyes lingering on my face. "Hey, come obliterate a few demons with me, sometime, if you're feeling stressed," she says. "It won't make you as sweaty as a run."

I dredge up a smile. "Will do."

Will never do.

I jog down another level to the gym and push through the door, halting abruptly on a squeak of sound. Jacob has come before me and, damp with sweat, he is in the process of pulling off his shirt. I gape at a figure that looks like Michelangelo's half-carved Atlas, arms raised and bound in rock, tearing out of the stone prison.

We have a copy of it in the palace sculpture garden, and I've gotten used to sliding my eyes over it, hardly registering the details. In the split second before Jacob emerges from the fabric and I am expected to slide my eyes over him without registering his details, I trace the muscled arms crossed over his head. I follow the trail of dark chest hair, tapering down to his stomach.

The current fashion is for men to look like hairless Egyptian cats, innocent of experience, lost, in need of mothering and a home cooked meal. I, however, have an appreciation for the classics.

"Alma."

The door bangs against my backside, scooting me into the room.

"Hello," I say, crossing to the treadmill. "I thought you were studying."

"I thought you were with your fiancé."

I appreciate the reminder. Pietor will keep me from throwing myself at Jacob.

Jacob tosses his shirt aside, unselfconscious, and wanders closer, hooking his hands over a pull-up bar, watching me power up the machine. I keep my face averted, but the whole *flamen* gym is made of mirrors, and his chest is like one of those paintings where the eyes follow you around the room.

"You lift weights?" I ask. My eyes flick to his face but catch on the muscle outlining his shoulder.

"Among other things."

I tap the buttons of the treadmill, increasing the speed to something that demands my attention.

"You're a runner," he says.

"Guilty."

This is good. It reminds me that Jacob and I are nothing alike. It won't be hard to forget him when he's gone. I'll run all the time.

"Does he run with you? Your fiancé?"

"Sometimes," I say. Pietor tried to run with me once. He threw up and claimed it was food poisoning.

Jacob swings lightly on the bar, wrists close together. I want to push my fingers through his unruly hair, so I train my eyes on a bright orange yoga ball.

"Did you miss him?" he asks.

I never missed him a day. I take a squirt of water and swallow.

"He was doing charity work."

15

CLEAN SHAVEN

JACOB

Alma's stride lengthens. Her gym clothes, a loose wicking tank top and pair of cropped shorts, are those of a serious athlete. Her shoulders are strong, her legs are long. I catch myself looking and jerk my eyes to her face.

My mother didn't raise a gym creeper.

"Charity work is great. I asked if you missed him."

She scowls and my chest tightens. Her polite, royal demeanor chips off around me like bad plasterwork. I want to slide a finger under the ragged edge and hurry along the destruction. Some days, I want to start an earthquake.

"If a person doesn't answer a question, you should find a better one." She maintains her form even as she delivers the lesson.

"Not the boss of me," I mutter.

"What?" she asks.

I lift my voice. "I have to agree."

She nods but gives me a side-eye. I pull my hair back, raking my fingers through the roots until it's secured in a band. I move to the treadmill, flick a towel over the handrail, and return to the puzzle which drove me down to the gym at this hour.

Alma didn't miss her fiancé.

I know what I saw. She was in my arms, the memory of that midnight kiss crowding us together. When Pietor spoke her name—barked it like a foreman halting a workplace safety violation—her expression withdrew, packed up as neatly as a toolbox.

My jaw sets.

He was out of the country for six months on his expedition to save the world. The globe, stubbornly unsaved, turns on, indifferent to a man rowing across an ocean in a dinghy.

He's tan and sleek, but I met his type every day at the Royal Academy. They walk around with a face full of old money, the question, "Do you know who my father is?" never out of reach. If you peer into the depths of their soul, you discover it's not such a great distance to the pebbly bottom.

These things are forgivable.

What isn't is how he didn't miss Alma.

It's not that I needed him to look at her like a carved saint in a church—eyes upturned, gazing into heaven, soft hands touching in prayer, a look I'm afraid I could wear too easily. But he needed to cross some lesser threshold to keep my contempt at bay. Relief. Longing. Pulling her into his arms no matter who was watching.

If I hadn't seen Alma in six months, I would have kissed her so hard it would have shifted the earth's axis. It would have solved climate change. Maybe even had a go at world peace.

Pietor grimaced.

"So, pickled herring," I say. "Ten out of ten? You're serving it at the wedding?"

She smiles. "I have to improve before the state visit."

"If I can do Pankedruss, you can do herring."

"You said Pankedruss tasted like a crime scene," she says, flying through these miles, her pace eclipsing mine.

Her nose crinkles with silent laughter and I tip my head up, looking at the ceiling. How? How did he stay away for six months?

"You all right?" she asks.

"Mm. I'll get used to the death yogurt if you come around on the herring. Do we have a deal?"

She reaches over and bumps my knuckles. "Deal."

I last another mile, male pride holding me up by the back of the neck for most of it.

"How long can you run?" I ask when I've had enough. My chest is heaving, and bracing my feet apart, I punch the hexagonal "STOP" button and wipe my face on a towel. Hair brushes along my jawline. I can barely speak.

"How long do I have to run?" She gives me a lopsided smile. "Between eight and fifteen kilometers."

I work out the conversion. "Between five and ten miles."

Her eyes widen. "Jacob. You were a bespoke furniture maker—"

"I *am* a bespoke furniture maker."

"You used the metric system every day."

I hop off the treadmill and lift a pair of dumbbells, curling them slowly from the elbow, one at a time. "Not if I could help it. Metric is cold."

"Cold like the vacuum of space where everything is measured properly by international scientists using the metric system?" she asks, half laughing, totally appalled.

I glance up, catch her watching me in the mirror, and begin using exceptionally good form. "Try telling a fairy tale using kilometers. You'll bore yourself to death."

"Speaking of death," she says, her strides lithe, "do you ask your doctors to prescribe vital medications by the pennyweight?"

I look down, hiding a grin.

"You've lived in northern Europe almost twenty years," she says, hitting some keys and turning her speed down to a brisk walk. Lightly sweating, she tips her chin, taking a swallow of water.

She belongs to someone else, but try telling my hands that. Try telling my eyes. She only has to walk into a room, and attraction sparks along my nervous system. To what end? Alma went to Harvard, and I went to trade school. I shuttered my business, and I'm giving up my anonymity to step into the monarchy. I'd be a fool to throw my heart after them, too.

But Alma stretches, rolling her neck and shoulders, and my mind becomes like the smooth surface of an egg.

She halts her machine. "If you haven't learned to think in metric, you're doing it on purpose."

I rack my weights. "I can't help it that the metric side of a measuring tape looks like a government oversight committee."

"And the other side is—?"

"A mysterious rollercoaster of mythic potency and manly valor."

Alma laughs and throws me a towel. I trap it against my chest, hand to my heart.

I scrub it over my skin and tug on my shirt, reaching the door before she does. She walks through, careful not to brush against me. "Sorry for throwing things," she murmurs.

When she walks up the dim hallway, I watch her, dragging a hand around the back of my neck. "Anytime."

Sleep doesn't come. In the morning, I talk with my father, a stilted conversation with too many dead ends. I text my mother.

When I jog to the drawing room, I throw myself into Alma's routine, glad to get back to the lessons—to churn through the days until I'm gone and she's behind me.

At midday, we're facing off on opposite sides of the circular table while Caroline and Karl confer over lesson plans and Mr. Tumwater works some fabric pieces with long white stitches. All of them are pointedly out of the line of fire.

"You have to do it," Alma insists.

"I don't *have* to do anything," I counter, arms braced against the table.

"You're going to look silly if you don't."

"Do I look silly now?"

Her lips clamp tightly, and she gives me a look that would have a lesser man calling for the scissors. "Caroline," she says, shaking with how much she wants to scream, "show us the kings and prince consorts of Europe."

Caroline leaps into action and fills the screen with more than a dozen men in ordered rows. They resemble high school shop teachers, lined up like this, posing for the school yearbook. Some are tall. Some are taller. Many have clean-shaven faces and close-cropped hair. Some attempted to camouflage the way their chins drift into their necks by growing a sharp line of facial hair, giving their faces depth and topographical interest.

Some of the monarchs are in military uniforms. Some of them are in the kind of casual clothes you can afford to buy when nothing casual is expected of you. No one is headed out to dig up the septic tank. None of them look like an overgrown bear.

"What do you see in the physical appearance of these men, Jacob?"

"Inbreeding," I snap.

"Jacob." She grinds my name through gritted teeth. "Why are you being so obstinate?"

"Let me have my hair, Alma."

"Sir," Karl picks his way forward, glancing between us, fingertips tented. "Her Royal Highness knows the enormous effort it will take to turn you into the kind of crown prince Vorburg can be proud of." The glance he gives me is one of misgiving. My suit is still the same one he's been coaxing back to life each night. He must doubt we've made any progress. "If your hair distracts from your ability to inhabit your role, it must be sacrificed."

"Shedding every aspect of what makes you interesting is no way to go through life, Karl."

The little clock on the mantel chimes the hour, and Caroline takes my aide by the elbow, gesturing for the tailor to follow. "Time for lunch. We'll leave you to your candid discussion."

Alma nods but doesn't take her eyes off me.

"Look," I say, rapping the screen with the back of a knuckle. "Bald, bald, bald, bald. Do you know what they would give to have this hair?" I tug one of the locks forward, holding it between my fingertips.

In a moment of weakness, I allowed Alma to work my hair loose. She got me into a chair and raked her fingers from my temples to the nape of my neck before my self-protective instincts were roused and I started fighting back.

Her eyes flick to the ends of my hair, and her teeth tug gently at her lower lip.

"A fortune." I clear my throat. "They'd give a fortune." I give her a coaxing, diplomatic smile. "I'm my own man, Alma. You wouldn't want to erase my shadows and textures."

"A monarchy has no interest in your shadows and textures." She joins me at the screen, touching each photo with a different set of priorities. "A monarchy needs you to be tidy, unexceptional, neutral, clean, conservative, professional, businesslike."

She missed one. I touch the corner of a photo. "This one is God's literal messenger to a fallen world. Do you want me to be that too?"

"Jacob." Her eyes close briefly and her long lashes brush the tops of her cheeks. She looks tired. Where is her fiancé to drag her away from babysitting a stubborn prince? "We are not glib about the pope."

"Alma," I say, closing the distance between us, feeling the air shiver. "In the life before this one, I worried about workplace safety, bidding for contracts, and making payroll. I'm the only royal here with the experience of starting my own business, therefore," I hit her with irrefutable logic, "*my* hair is businesslike."

She looks up, and I feel a tremor race through my veins. In making my point, I've gotten too close. *Chol nia*, if I were Pietor walking into this room, I'd punch my teeth in.

Her hand starts for my hair, and my stomach tightens.

Her fingers curl into her palm, and she backs away. "This isn't finished."

16

AMBER TIARA

ALMA

It's the queen's birthday. Not the official one in June when half the country waves flags, dances in the streets, and finds a military man to make out with. Mama's real birthday is at the end of January when the ice on the roads has frozen into hard sheets and only the people who love her best risk the trip to the Summer Palace to take part in the celebration.

Pietor is not one of her loved ones, but nevertheless, he stands in the corner, scrolling through his phone. Photographers are shivering at the gates of the palace, snapping pictures of grand jewels and couture gowns as the guests drive through, hoping to turn such meager crumbs into a story. For the sake of national peace, one of those stories has to be "Pietor and Alma, Together A gain".

Ella and Clara accept this, but they haven't let him near me all night.

I stand with *Tante* Ann-Margrethe, taking a flute of champagne for her when Mama's housekeeper Una passes them around. Clara performs the same service for her godmother, Lady Grete, who looks around in vacant delight before downing the glass in one swallow.

Freja's absence is like a sinkhole we're trying to tiptoe around.

Pictures appear in the press—heartbreakingly ordinary pictures of Freja and her husband in an Italian market choosing oranges, of them walking hand in hand with a bunch of flowers. In every photo, she wears vintage Chanel sunglasses and wide palazzo pants. Though she doesn't perform for strangers or paparazzi, her happiness is tangible. The pair keep reaching for each other, brushing fingertips, shoulders, waists.

She is with us in spirit, she writes, the card propped among the floral tributes on the sideboard. That doesn't feel true. My sister, no longer revolving around Mama's sun, has performed a one-woman celestial revolt.

Could I have done the same in her place? When I planned to marry Pietor, it never entered my mind to truly leave Mama. Consider the concerns of Himmelstein? Yes. Learn a new language? Yes. Prioritize anything over my family and the crown? Never.

Caroline rings a small bell, nodding at the footmen to dim the lights, and a video montage is then projected onto a wall, filling the room with pictures and film clips of Mama's childhood—riding ponies next to her father, being chased around the garden by her mother. The young princess trying—failing—to smash a champagne bottle against a ship, the bank of dignitaries stunned into inaction. The laughter in the room is tinged with nostalgia.

During a brief clip of Mama walking down the aisle on the arm of her Pavian groom, the room falls into silence. Her steps are resolute, and her face is like war as she forces herself to fulfill the terms of the marriage contract signed by two kings—one dead, the other deposed. The sounds of the protests shook the walls of Roslav Cathedral while she made her vows, they say.

The new queen did her duty, though she had no love for her future husband. The young prince had fled his war-torn country with nothing but his title. When I was a girl, I could listen to that story for hours because I knew how it turned out. Happily ever after.

I watch the shadows moving over my mother's face as she watches the montage. What emerged from Mama's loyalty to the crown and steadfast defense of the nation was good, the story went. It's a lesson I hoped to repeat with Pietor but the problem is that it's all gone to hell. Their marriage has been wrecked by the same duty to the crown that started it off.

When the montage concludes, the lights come on. Père, standing on the opposite end of the room from Mama, raises his glass. "Helena. May your harvest be a good one," he says, toasting her a happy birthday in the Sondish way.

I catch Clara's uncompromising expression over the rim of my champagne flute. She gives her head a micro shake. I can all but hear her make a solemn vow. *No arranged marriage for me.* Never.

Tante Ann-Margrethe tugs on my skirts. "What is it?" I ask, slipping into a chair. My great-aunt smells of cigarette smoke beneath the Dior perfume.

"Are they still being stupid?" she asks, twitching her finger between my parents. "No, don't bother answering that. I can see they are."

"Not stupid," I say, in a rare mood to talk to someone who's seen seven decades of scandal wash under the bridge. "They're hurt. Père is still angry that he wasn't allowed to attend his father's funeral. He refuses to see that her hands were tied."

Tante Ann-Margrethe snorts. "Still your mother's daughter. Don't cast her in the role of a helpless damsel, *elskede*. It doesn't suit. She's never been a woman who lacked resources to do what she really wanted to do. Your father knows that, and you'd do well to remember it, too." She touches my face to soften the sting. "Your mother made a blunder. She ought to own up to it."

I bristle at the uncompromising judgement. "A number of factors led to—"

Tante Ann-Margrethe cuts me off, adjusting her fur stole. "You can't turn the people you love into pawns. You can't run roughshod over their happiness or their suffering. Not if it's really love."

She makes it sound simple. My great-aunt shakes off the sentimental mood, taps me on the knee, and asks, her voice raspy, "When is your wedding? Don't even think of giving me nonsense you couldn't even peddle to the press."

I flick a glance at Pietor, in deep conversation to Uncle Georg, and give her a serene smile. "I wouldn't think of giving you nonsense."

My silence stretches.

"*Tsch.*" The sound is scornful, and the meaning is clear. My generation is hopeless.

Ella leads a cohort of rowdy younger guests off to the billiard room, and I spend the evening circulating, seeing to the comfort of the older ones. In a lull, I approach my mother, wishing her a happy birthday. The paper crown on her head manages to look regal, and she gives me a kiss on the cheek.

"You're doing well," she says. Her praise fails to warm me.

At the stroke of eleven, I walk Pietor to the Great Hall. Music emanates from the family wing as we wait for his car to be brought around, and I gaze at our reflection in the tall mirrors. From a distance, we look like a pair of lovers saying a long goodbye.

"I have an interview with *The Sun Rises on Himmelstein* next week, and I'd like you to be there," he tells me. "We can pre-record the segment in my hotel suite. I'll have my secretary be in touch."

I nod. This is just business.

"Your uncle told me about that man I saw in your suite." My nerves shiver to attention as Pietor brushes his lapel. "They'll let anybody be a crown prince, these days."

"They let you." I pivot sharply, gathering my skirts, and make for my suite.

Before I even make it to the sitting room, I hear Jacob's English carried through the door, unregulated by any sense that he might be overheard.

"I am," he says, speaking over the phone. "It's fine. No, it's not like the Royal Academy. For one thing, no one is trying to stuff my head into the toilet. No, I'm kidding."

I slip off my slingbacks and creep forward, taking a path to my door that would appear random to a cat burglar or anyone who hadn't walked these creaking floorboards every day for eight years.

"I'm not lying. Mom. Mom. Honestly." I open my door, my heart thrumming softly in my throat. Jacob oiled these hinges last week, and I don't have to worry he'll hear me.

"I'm not sure you'll recognize me when I come back," he goes on. "I'm not sure *I'll* recognize me. I've learned that every natural instinct I have is wrong, but I've also learned three ways to tie a tie. Yeah. Mid-March. His Royal *Zekle*— What? I'm a grown— *Oma* wouldn't even know what it means," he protests. But he murmurs an apology. "His Majesty the King wants me back for a couple of weeks before we do the state visit."

"No, the food is fine. They don't like herring." I think I hear a grin in his voice. "Well, nothing tastes like your food." He laughs. "No, no, no. Don't send them. Mom. Honestly. I'm hanging up now. It's late. Yeah. Love you. Mom. Mom. Mom. I have to go."

When I thought about the kind of woman who could single-handedly turn her child into the next king of Vorburg, I pictured someone with a cell phone surgically attached to her hand and a team of aestheticians working on fine lines and wrinkles. The more I've come to know Jacob—his work ethic, his sturdy sense of right and wrong—the more I assumed he was embarrassed of her. I thought that's what he was trying to hide when he ripped the pages from the dossier.

I was wrong. The affection between them is palpable, even through a heavy door and a phone line.

I hear his floorboards shift and I dart through my door, catching the corner of an occasional table with my dress. A lamp totters and my desperate attempt to right it sends us both banging to the floor in a loud crash.

"Alma." I hear his muffled shout.

Vede.

"It was a ghost," I call, Wolffe family shorthand for, "It's nothing. Don't come."

But Jacob doesn't know about Celine of Anjou, whose husband caught her *in flagrante delicto* with a Danish philosopher. She's a restless spirit and we blame things on her all the time.

Jacob bursts through the door, breathing hard, and takes in the lamp and lack of blood. He sags against the doorframe, pushing a hand through his hair.

"Alma."

An inevitable concert t-shirt skims his stomach like the wing of a bird over a peaceful lake, and I flop back, sinking in acres of tulle, clamping my eyes shut. Jacob, filling out American denim in the way he does, is too much for my delicate constitution.

He rights the table and the lamp, setting the squashed lamp-shade over the bulb like a hat. Then he reaches for my hands and hauls me to my feet. "Are you okay?" he asks, turning me around by the shoulders to perform an inspection. He leaves fire everywhere he touches and I shrug out of his grasp before my ball gown goes up in flames.

"It's nothing." I take a step back into a chair and sit down with a thump.

"I didn't realize you were in here," he says. "I wouldn't have been so loud."

"No bother," I answer, reaching for the clasp of my necklace, fumbling for the catch.

"Nice party?"

I feel like a bubble of glass emerging from a hot furnace—malleable around him in a way a princess should never be. I can't tell him the truth, so I coat something bland in frosting and hope he doesn't know the difference.

"It's an ordinary birthday party. Paper buntings and a cake."

For such a big man, his smiles are soft. "Candles and ice cream, too?" he asks, standing behind me. He pushes my hands aside and finds the clasp of the necklace, fingers brushing sensitive skin. When it's undone, he lets go, and it slides into my palm.

"It's January."

He shakes his head. "There's never a wrong time for ice cream," he says, settling onto the bench at the end of my bed.

I should shoo him out of here on the principle that Vorburg should not have such easy access to Sondmark, but part of me wants to crawl onto my bed, bare feet tucked up under my skirts, and talk about my day with someone who actually wants to know about it.

A memory surfaces from last spring. I had pulled up to a crosswalk while a primary school was having an animal parade, and I watched five-year-olds march past with homemade masks and tails tucked into the back waistbands of their trousers, singing a song about piglets as their teachers herded them out of traffic. I laughed the whole day, but when Pietor had asked me what I'd done, I dropped a few names of government ministers I'd met with. Even then I was editing myself for him, holding back the best part.

I don't have to protect anything from Jacob. I swallow thickly and stare at my reflection, wondering where this certainty came from.

He knocks my knee with the back of his hand. "What else? Was your fiancé there?"

I want to tell him about Clara's hard, determined expression and the way Caroline, failing to read the room, chose too many photos of Mama and Père looking at one another like people who had produced five children, open to the imminent possibility of producing a sixth.

"I'm getting ready for bed," I say.

He lifts his hand. *Be my guest.*

"Okay," I surrender. "Let me change first."

I sweep off to my changing room, immediately filled with regret for not asking him to get my zipper started. But that would have been foolish in the same way that walking a tightrope over a venomous snake pit is foolish, I think, wrestling it open.

When I return, I'm wearing one of my full-length satin nightgowns, the blue robe billowing behind me as I walk.

His lounging posture jerks to attention. "What's this?"

"This is what I sleep in." I lift a challenging brow. "This is my room. If you're not leaving, I'm not digging up some sweats just to make you feel comfortable."

"I'm not mad." He raises his palms but looks away. "Tell me about the party."

I reach for the make-up remover. "We toasted the queen with champagne."

"Drinking again?" he tuts.

I fire a cotton swab at his head, and he bats it away with a grin.

"You were talking to your mother, weren't you?" I go on offense.

"She couldn't sleep," he says, satisfying the spirit of interest haunting the room.

I appear to be engrossed by the process of removing my eyeliner. He picks up a pile of knitting, puts his hand into a hat, and turns it this way and that, seeing the flaws.

"She lives in Vorburg—a small flat off Liberation Square."

"That sounds nice."

"It is nice. It's just large enough to host her book club." His smile shifts.

"An English book club?"

He nods. "Mom can manage most of the Vorburgian vocabulary, but tenses and syntax are a mystery. You should see her try to buy lemons. She's a menace." I laugh and hear a low, answering chuckle.

I catch his eye in the reflection. "She sounds nice."

His expression sobers. "She is nice."

I turn my head when the windowpanes shake in the wind. Jacob reaches forward, a light touch at the lobe of my ear and along my neck, and a shiver brushes against my skin that might be me or him.

"You're missing an earring," he says, lightly guiding my head to tilt the other way. The chandelier of stones brushes my cheek. "I'll find it."

He crouches, running his hand along the patterned rug until he discovers the back and then the long earring, resting under a table skirt. From a kneel, he holds them to me in his palm, the lamplight flashing along each facet. This is nothing like the last time a man presented me with jewelry from this position. Even in my memory it feels like something that happened to a stranger.

"Do you like this kind of thing?" he asks. "Or do you wear it because you're expected to?"

He lays the earring on my palm, and I place it in the case. "I like that it has centuries of meaning, and feeling connected to the people who wore it."

I begin to work a solution into my skin, turning pink and shiny. "Vorburg has some of the best jewels in Europe."

"Do we?" He reaches for my cozy mystery and smiles, cupping a hand behind his head. The hem of his t-shirt lifts a few centimeters, and I perch tingling fingertips on a tube of hyaluronic acid, not even giving my inner voice the satisfaction of reading me a lecture about decorum and hot, foreign future heads of state. I'm starting to go deaf to her.

I clear my throat. "Vorburg's Viking raiders never saw a monastery they didn't plunder. And of course, you've got all that amber."

He finds my bookmark and starts reading. "Miss Pendragon inspected the doilies scattered around the tearoom to discover patterns of skulls and daggers dripping with poison in each one. Macabre, certainly, but the handiwork was extraordinary..."

I should stop him. Maybe give him a copy of *Timeless Manners for the Modern Royal* to round out his education. But his reading voice is perfect, and I slide into bed, pick up my much-abused knitting, and stab out a few rows while he unfolds the mystery. A storm batters the stone walls of the palace, but I am perfectly content.

He turns a page, his voice soft and drowsy. "My wife will wear an amber tiara?" He places a finger to mark his spot and closes his eyes.

I let myself look at him, watching the gentle rise and fall of his chest.

My own tiara is intimidating and regal, but the amber tiara is romantic—five wreaths of diamonds in a looping wildflower pattern. Within each loop hangs a golden drop of amber, salvaged from the original crown given to the bride who traveled from Sondmark all those centuries ago.

I nod, though he can't see it. "Diamonds and amber." A vision of Jacob putting it into the care of his future wife hits me like a wave. "Take care not to fall in love with a blonde," I say. A cloud slides over the moon, deepening the shadows in the room.

I yawn and yawn again. His reading continues, and the knitting slips from my hands. He takes it from me and arranges a blanket up to my chin.

"I won't," he murmurs, brushing dark hair from my face.

17

PEOPLE PERSON

JACOB

Though we never talk about it, we begin to gravitate to the common room. She'll have materials relating to one of her patronages spread out on the coffee table, and I'll bring my dinner over, nurse a beer, and read through packets of obscure Vorburgian history prepared by Karl.

I'm never told to push off. She never scurries away. While the small fire in the grate warms the side of my face and the winter wind howls, we hardly leave each other alone.

We talk about everything but this.

On a Saturday morning in early February, I wander out of my room, determined to eat three bites of Pankedruss, wondering if the day will come when I ever look forward to it. Heavy clouds crowd against the windows, and I stretch hugely, scratching my stomach.

When I open my eyes, Alma is standing in her doorway, looking up at the ceiling like I am working on her last nerve.

I'd ask her why, but her hat is decorated with a huge flower, and the brim is tilted at a sexy angle.

I emit a low, teasing whistle, and Alma laughs, tucking her handbag under her arm. She tilts her head at an even sexier angle, trying to put on an earring.

"Where are you headed?" I ask, pulling up the camera feature on my phone so she can use it as a mirror.

She tilts her head the other direction, and I revise my thesis. This angle is also sexy.

"An old friend is getting married a few hours south. We have to set out early."

I feel for my back pocket with the top of my phone, sliding it in. Wanting to talk to Alma is bigger than how much I don't want to talk about weddings with Alma.

"Another royal?"

"*Adel.* That's what we call the hereditary noble houses in Sondmark."

"Are they combining their lands and wealth like you and Pietor?" I have to turn her wedding into a joke, or I'll say something I mean too much.

Her smile falters but she moves on. "The bride is a primary school teacher for one of my cousin's daughters. My brother set them up."

"I thought he didn't do commitment."

"For other people, he does." Alma looks uneasy. I open my mouth to offer her a glass of water or bite of Pankedruss when a knock sounds on the door.

"Coming," she calls, skirt twirling against her legs as she turns.

That'll be Noah.

It's Pietor.

He spots me over her shoulder, and I flex my hand. Leaning forward, he gives Alma a brief kiss. "Ready, darling?"

"Mm," she says, giving me a brief, polite smile before she goes.

The feeling of wanting a fight sticks to me throughout the day. In the afternoon, Karl brings me my limp suit, fresh from dry cleaning, and demands to see my wardrobe.

"Have you even tried on your new clothes?" he asks.

I lead him to the closet where they hang in garment bags and Karl emits a noise of frustration and despair.

"What are you waiting for?" he asks. "An embossed invitation?"

Thanks to weeks of fittings and endless instruction covering everything from the history of the bone button to the innovations of the canoe pocket, I realize the clothes are going to be nicer than anything I've ever worn before.

"New clothes, new man," Mom used to say when we went shopping for back-to-school things at the department store in Blackberry. A twenty-four pack of pencils would sit in the cart next to stiff, dark jeans.

I cross my arms. "I don't get why we're trying to dress this up. We won't fool anyone."

Karl inhales through his narrow nostrils. "No, no, no…sir. You don't get to have an existential kick-up now. Are you the crown prince of Vorburg?" he asks.

"By some cosmic joke, I am."

"That's it, then."

"I didn't know what I was getting into," I counter.

Karl rips the plastic from the hangers and begins arranging the items by color and type. He lifts a blue suit and gives the hanger a shake. "This is your destiny," he declares. "Figure it out."

"Figure it out? A master craftsman taught me how to do carpentry. Where's the illegitimate crown prince who is going to teach me how to do *this*?"

"You have Princess Alma," he counters.

"I don't *have* Princess Alma," I roar.

I don't have her. My chest rises and falls with the enormity of it. I don't have her, and I don't want anyone else.

Karl looks at me for a long time. "Wear the clothes," he says, "sir."

That evening, after a solitary meal eaten standing up in front of the fridge, I retreat to the gym and scroll through a roughly translated Sondish gossip site for news of Alma's day.

PAPZ has already posted several still images and a short video clip of her and Pietor attending the wedding. When she walks on the short path from the parking area to the small Lutheran church, she has her Sondish wedding handbag in a tight grip, the opal ring front and center.

In the video, Himmelstein fusses with his lapels, wobbling the umbrella over their heads. Alma has to skip to keep beneath it.

The contrast between her and her sister—the one on the honeymoon—couldn't be more stark. Not once has the camera caught Pietor glancing at her, touching her arm or elbow. Sliding his arm around her waist to keep her close under the beating rain.

In one article, the PAPZ headline reads, "Pietor Got Jacked: Elegant Princess Alma arrives at the wedding of Count Aloysius Fogh van den Schackenborg and *Vrouw* Laura Fisker with fit fiancé."

I descend into a plank position, forearms resting along the rubber mat, phone stopwatch counting off the seconds. The phone rings, and I tap my ear bud.

"My son and heir." My father's gravelly voice booms through the tiny speaker.

My jaw sets. "Your Majesty, how good of you to call."

He doesn't regard the distance I've placed between us. "Have you talked to Tiffani?"

"You mean my mother? Yes. She calls her son from time to time."

"What do you mean?" he barks. "I call my son. I'm calling him now."

"Is there something you wanted?"

My relationship with His Majesty King Otto of Vorburg is cool. He doesn't mind that, he tells me. A number of Vorburgian kings seized the throne from their fathers. Drawing and quartering them in the aftermath was a family tradition. We're doing fine.

The king cuts to the chase. "Karl reports that you're not wearing the clothes they made for you. He says you're fighting them every step of the way."

My grandma would sit Karl on the bottom step of her staircase for being such a loathsome tattletale.

"I'm doing everything that's being asked of me." I've spent hours familiarizing myself with the fussiness of royal protocol. The bowing. The forms of address. The endless practice that has me mirroring every gesture Alma makes, watching her move, feeling it drive me insane.

"You haven't cut your hair, son."

"I'm not cutting my hair, sir."

The old man growls. "You want to look like a girl?"

I look down at my muscled thighs, the sweaty tank top, and work-callused hands.

"You'll look like a fool when you take your place on the world stage," he barks.

This is rich coming from a man as gaffe-prone as my father. There's video footage of him on stage at a music festival, wearing a dress shirt and tie, pumping his arms like the wheels of a locomotive. It's one of the most famous GIFs in the world, and people use it when they want to specify precisely how drunk they got last night.

"Since when does Vorburg submit to Sondmark?" I ask.

A pause. I can almost visualize the internal wrestling. In the end, national pride wins out over the need to make his son obey. "I like to hear it. Give those *zeklen* Sondish royals a taste of Vorburgian will." His approval is like a dead sun. It doesn't warm me. "Have you made any progress with any of the princesses? You chose the engaged one to be your tutor." He releases a pungent curse. "This is no way to get married."

I can't talk about Alma and how she's taken.

"What do you know about getting married?" I don't know much, but I do know that the only way to deal with my father is to stand my ground and fight.

"Cut it, Jacob," he bites, his tone a throwback to when his country had an empire.

Vorburgian power came without respect for what Alma would call propriety. I remember a lesson from Karl about a Vorburgian queen, blessing her husband's mistress on her deathbed and meeting his bastards, blessing them each in turn. She's hailed as a saint, but so is her faithless husband. There is no contradiction in the Vorburgian mind. Few of my ancestors understood anything about keeping one woman happy.

My Gardner forefathers were different. Carving civilization out of the wilderness is all they knew. Along the staircase in my grandparents' house, generations of them, Scotsmen and Germans with full mustaches and piercing eyes stare into the camera from the bosom of a large family.

My mind goes to Alma, dressed for a wedding, the brim of her hat revealing her mouth and the curve of a cheek, skipping after her fiancé in the rain like she didn't matter and didn't expect to matter. I swallow past the knot in my throat.

"Wear the clothes. Make us proud," my father says.

"Yes, sir," I say, finishing the call.

He's not going to let this question of a bride go, but royal or not, I can't change my nature. I have to love my wife. Gardner men do. Maybe it's an idea which isn't useful for the life I've accepted. Maybe Karl would say I am thinking like a peasant. Maybe Alma considers it middle-class or simple. But I can't choose my wife strategically. It's not how I'm made.

I return to my suite, change, and return to the hall, not even hiding the fact that I'm waiting for her. If Pietor comes, I'll have sense.

I lean against the wall, releasing a breath when she mounts the stairs with her sisters. Clara peels away to her suite, but Ella sends me a wave.

Alma stops in front of our door, looking at me across the width of the hall. "What are you doing out here?"

"Waiting for you, boss." I can't tell her the truth—that I can't stop thinking about her—but I can't lie either. I bump away from the wall.

"It's late."

I hear the slam of a door and hurrying footsteps. Clara, having already changed, sprints down the hall, fishing her keys out of her purse. When the commotion passes, I look at Alma. Her lips are pressed together.

"It's late," I say.

"Max sails this week," she explains, opening the door.

I follow her into our suite and flip the light on in the kitchen. I wait for Alma to hustle me out, almost hoping she'll go so far as to place her palms against my back. She'll tell me that she's tired and doesn't want to talk.

Alma unfastens her coat. "Heat up a kettle, will you?"

She heads to her room. Grinning, I open and shut cupboard doors, watching the steam rise from the kettle. I call to her, "What kind of tea?"

"No caffeine at this hour," she says, returning. She looks at the tea caddy over my shoulder, bracing her hands on the backs of my arms. This room is tiny. All I have to do is turn around.

"No caffeine it is," I say, scooping the loose-leaf chamomile into an infuser.

I pour the hot water and feel her soft breath against my neck, warming the skin. Setting the kettle down with a thump, I put a lid on the infuser and escape her light grasp.

"My father called," I say, gripping both counters, trying not to notice that she looks as good in a pair of boxy silk pajamas as she did in the wedding clothes. Her hair is down, her make up hastily scrubbed off. There's a dark line she missed on the rim of one eye. It doesn't matter.

In this buttoned-up two-piece pajama set, she's even more covered up than she was before. It doesn't matter. My hands ball into fists. There's nothing to do while we wait for the tea to steep.

Alma takes a chocolate digestive, nibbling along the edge. "Do you get along?" she asks.

I trace the rim of the counter with my thumb. "I thought we weren't supposed to ask questions. I thought we were supposed to go through life as vanilla robots."

"Robots don't have flavors." She smiles, playing with one of the buttons on her top. "I withdraw the question."

"I've met my father in person twice. The first time was when he opened a new wing at the Royal Academy. He'd come to glance over his bastard whose school fees he was paying."

"Jacob." My name is a whisper—gently admonishing.

"The second time, he called me to Djolny Castle to congratulate me on a successful legal campaign." I remember the exact words. "That's when he told me I'd be learning the family trade and that he was shipping me off to Sondmark."

Alma plucks her lip with her teeth.

"You have a question?" I ask.

No response. I release a breath and run a hand through my hair. "You have my permission to ask."

"Why didn't he just teach you himself?"

"Can I be honest?"

She nods. "Always."

"My father is a people person, not a...*person* person. Crowds love him, and he'll go down the line, shaking every hand and kissing every baby in Vorburg." Watching him do it is like watching a master woodcarver coax concentric circles of water and the half-submerged form of a sea otter from an inanimate object. If you let your eyes relax, you can almost believe it's the real thing.

"But if he'd married my mom, I don't think he would have known what to do with either of us. For now, he just wants me to find a wife."

Her brow lifts, and I want to kiss the curve of it, to have her lips press into my neck. To go beyond the scope of our assignments. Wouldn't my father love that. My blood goes hot and cold.

"He actually told you so?"

"He suggested I get Ella to mentor me." I nod, pouring out two cups of tea. Handing hers over, I lean against the counter at her side. "I know. It's crazy."

She blows on the surface of the liquid and gives a low laugh. "Not at all. He's being strategic, and you had to go and choose the engaged princess. Your father must be furious." She bumps my shoulder, setting off a wave of electricity that rolls through my veins but never breaks. "Ella's not dating anyone at the moment, and you get along. I could set you up if you—"

I raise my eyes to the ceiling. This girl will be the death of me. "Don't. It's not why I'm here."

She gives another light laugh. "Good thing, because—who would have thought?—Sondmark is running out of princess-es." Her mouth sobers, and she takes a swallow of tea.

"How have you done it? Find someone when you're ham-pered by the, uh..."

"Massive generational wealth? Sense of entitlement? Burden of rule?" Her eyes dance. "Clara practically threw herself at Max's feet, and if he wanted to back out, I don't think she'd let him. She tells us that being in the military makes it easier for him to understand things like constraints on his time and how he's supposed to behave in public."

"And Freja?" I sip slowly, cooling the liquid with my breath.

"Oskar wants nothing to do with royalty, and we haven't sorted out how he'll fit into the institution because they moved too fast for us to figure it out." She taps her cup and gives me the kind of smile where I know her throat hurts. "Can I be honest?"

My stomach tightens, but I clink my mug on hers. "Always."

"My mother never would have figured it out if Freja had waited. Like the goddess she is, my sister acted first and let the chips fall where they may."

Is this my by-the-book princess?

"They look happy," I say.

"They'd better be." She looks into her mug, eyes unfocused. "It's going to get rough before it gets better."

"How did Alma find Prince Charming?" I ask, trying to lighten the mood. I don't want to hear the answer, but it serves me right, being attracted to a woman who belongs to someone else.

Attracted?

Sure.

This will be my punishment.

Alma takes a gulp of tea. "You have to understand that my mother was brought up in the old days, when marriage alliances were worked out decades before they were executed. Even after the Pavian monarchy was toppled by a dictator, she fulfilled the marriage contract with King Zeren's second son."

"Your father?"

She nods. What does all this ancient history have to do with her and Pietor?

"She has spreadsheets maintained by Caroline, filled with eligible partners who know the rules of operating in a monarchy. You know," she says, like I might actually know, "heads of friendly nations, men who don't need the money, people from an impeccable bloodline... everyone gets a ranking."

Her cheeks flush as she gets into her story, using words like *bloodline* and *eligible*. They're foreign to me. She dips her head, a curtain of dark hair falling between us, and my chest feels like it's caught in a vice grip turned tighter and tighter. A question forms, but I can't dislodge it.

Alma's eyes dart to my face and away. This is not one of those times I can be trusted to draw my own conclusions. I have to ask.

"Are you talking about an arranged marriage?"

I'm right. I know I'm right. *Chol nia, Alma.* My heart hammers in my chest. I can't be right. She wouldn't throw herself away like that. She wouldn't try to make me understand and agree. As different as we are on the surface, underneath we're the same. Same loyalty to our family, same seriousness when we approach our jobs, same way we have to be with each other.

I scrub my face, praying I'm wrong.

She shakes the hair away and exhales. "That's it. Pietor was top of the list."

18

At Last

ALMA

It's a false spring. The weather warms, and I run the wood-
land trails. There's no danger of seeing Jacob. When he looks
at me now, I feel the disappointment he's too well-mannered to
express.

Well-mannered. My old nanny used to say that manners were
just a way to show people you cared about them, and instead of
instilling this essential truth, I drilled him in the pale shadow of
protocol.

I do press events with Pietor. We attend concerts and plays
when I have no official duties, and Ella pins his photo to a dart
board in the games room.

One morning, as my family comes and goes from breakfast, I
leaf through the papers. In one, my sister's new husband frowns
at the paparazzi jostling Freja as they approach their flat, his arm
protectively outflung. Media training would have helped him.
We're supposed to walk steadily forward, expression impassive,

no hunching over or blocking the flash photography. Bore them to death. That's the way to survive the spotlight.

Oskar wouldn't know that, and even if he did, the picture is innocuous. It's the headline we have to fear. *Royal Pressure: Pavi Lashes Out Amid Succession Row.*

The palace response will be temperate. There will be no pointing out that Oskar didn't "lash out" and that talks of Freja's place in the line of succession are premature. The best Mama can do is congratulate the couple and ask for privacy.

I pick up *The Daily Missive.* Old acquaintances have emerged to tell the 'real story' of Oskar's life, like rats scurrying off a ship to spread disease. Stories about how he didn't talk much in primary school. How he lives in a Pavian 'enclave.' How Pavians are tightly connected, helping each other into positions of influence. The text of the article posits that Père, a Pavian when all is said and done, had a hand in their match.

More than thirty years of walking faithfully two steps behind Mama, and the press still can't grasp Père's intense loyalty.

On an opposite page, Pietor and I provide the perfect counterpoint. My face has been airbrushed beyond all recognition, my smile brilliant and gleaming. The graphic designer cropped the distance between our bodies so that it looks like Pietor stands protectively in front of me, absorbing the attention and taking the snapping cameras all in stride. A masterclass in media management by HRH Pietor, Hereditary Grand Duke of Himmelstein.

Ella flops into a chair across the table, craning her neck to read the headlines.

"*Neer* Velasquez and Freja are coming for tea," she says, pouring out a cup of coffee.

"I didn't see it on my agenda," I say, pulling my phone out and checking the calendar.

"Just with Mama. She invited the traitor as soon as they got back from the honeymoon."

Traitor? I sigh. "Ella, stop it. Freja has her own life to live."

Ella balls one of the newspapers into a wad and shoots it into the wastebasket. "That philosophy is a little New Age for you, isn't it? Right along with finger cymbals, deep meditation, and hemp pants." She strikes a sloppy half lotus and rolls her eyes. "Living our own life. There's only so much of that we get to do, is what I thought."

Ella is having a proper tantrum, but I can't blame her for being upset. If anyone paved the way for veering off the proscribed royal path and running into an oncoming elopement, it was her.

Pietor would never have tempted me to do such a thing.

Memories spark up my mind. Jacob waiting up for me. Jacob in the tiny kitchen, getting tea. Jacob glancing over. *Can I be honest?*

Warmth floods my chest, and I run from it. "Freja's marriage wasn't a personal slight to you," I remind Ella. "None of us were invited."

The look Ella sends me is enough to ignite a riverbed. "It was the most important day of her life, and she couldn't be bothered to ring her twin."

When I make my way to the Chevres drawing room, I think of what Freja did, of what I would have done in her place, of the lessons I should take. The one that would upset my life the least is that I can't let anything matter to me as much as she let Oskar matter to her.

I'm leafing through the daily schedule when the door opens. Jacob delivers his correct greeting and I hardly glance up, it's so expected.

"Today we'll cover titles," I say, reaching for a notebook.

"That's it?" he asks.

I glance up, down, and up again. In the time it takes for an entire worldview to be overthrown, I scramble to my feet.

"The crown prince, at last," Karl whispers, coming closer to inspect the tailor's work.

The ensemble is simple and unfinished. Jacob has no watch or cufflinks, the pocket square is stuffed carelessly at his breast, and his tie is a basic half-Windsor. But the jacket skims his shoulders, framing them in luxury and quiet authority. Genius. I want to give Mr. Tumwater a royal commendation and name a Navy ship in his honor. I want to commission a bronze statue of him to stand in Liberation Square, scissors held aloft, measuring tape curling to his toes. What he's done with Jacob—

Jacob suffers through our inspection, eyes closed, mouth in a grim line, annoyed that we're making such a fuss, and I move around the back where the breadth of his shoulders is lovingly accentuated. Karl's examination is more technical, and when he lifts the vent of Jacob's jacket to check the drape, I bite my lip.

Expensive wool suiting falls away from what I am convinced is the most commendable backside in northern Europe. In future, government ministers will take credit for Vorburg's soaring GDP and boom in tourism, ascribing the successes to financial policies or forward-thinking legislation. No one will chalk it down to the cut of a pair of trousers and the new crown prince wearing them.

Karl lifts his brow, and I give him a look of exquisite distress, shaking my hand and wrist—the universal signal for, *The tailor did a nice job. So hot. Literally burning the palace down.*

Jacob, still determined not to look at us, clears his throat. "Well?"

Stuffing the screaming fangirl into a box, I move to his front, squaring up to him in a brisk and businesslike way, and brush his shoulders. I straighten the knot of his tie, gaze trained on how the blindingly white dress shirt looks against his strong neck. My hands halt and my heartbeat is deafening.

His eyes snap open.

"This is a good start." I toss my hair and step beyond his reach with joints that feel tight and uncoordinated. "Ready to begin?"

I work like a demon, walking us through the titles held by early Germanic tribes and carried into the formation of the Holy Roman Empire, throwing so many conquering warlords and notable historical events at him that there's no time for my mind—or my eyes—to wander. The honorifics—defunct, ceremonial, or existent—carry a dizzying array of meanings and significance, and I drill into each one.

"I'm just saying that 'pretender to the French throne' is an embarrassing title," he argues. We've been working for hours, and my stamina is waning.

"It's not exactly a title."

"If it gets attached to someone's name every time someone talks about them, it's a title."

"Score one for Vorburg," I mutter.

He laughs and stretches his arms wide, his back a curve. His jacket moves with him, sitting snugly against his neck. Karl departed ages ago, leaving me alone with this new creature, His Royal Highness Jacob, Crown Prince of Vorburg, and I let my eyes linger on him while he moves, trying to make sense of the transformation.

"Time for lunch," he says, running a hand over his flat stomach. "Hungry?"

He holds out a hand for me, an unconscious courtesy, and I walk silently beside him, trying not to stare.

As we near the Great Hall, we hear Ella's roar. "Take the cat if that's all you came for."

She lifts a basket from Caroline and thrusts it in Freja's hands, striding off in a thundercloud of furious muttering. Smit seems unphased, but the commotion draws my brother from his office. Striding past us wearing a severe, quelling expression, he scatters footmen to the secret recesses of the palace.

I move swiftly to smooth the awkwardness and kiss Freja's cheek. "You look gorgeous," I say, holding her at arm's length. "Marriage suits you."

My sister, faintly puzzled by the emotions of lesser mortals, gestures in the direction of Ella's flounce. "Has she been like this the whole time?"

This is exactly what she's been like the whole time, but I shake my head. "You know Ella. If she was really mad, she would have rehomed the cat," I say. Freja doesn't need to carry the burden of our sister's anger.

Freja reaches a hand to the man standing behind her, bringing him to her side. "This is Oskar. You've met, once or twice, I think."

She introduces him around. His bows are stiff but correct, and he holds my sister's hand without self-consciousness. They can't stay, she tells me. The cat has taken umbrage to the basket.

"Next time," I echo, waving them away.

I turn to find Noah towering over Caroline. "Show me your arm."

No one has ever dared ignore that commanding tone, and Caroline's habitually calm face is strained. "It's nothing," she says, holding her sleeve where blood has spotted the cream silk. "Smit didn't take kindly to his basket."

"We have to see to it," he insists. "Caro—"

"Your Royal Highness," she cuts him off, "I refuse to bleed all over the Great Hall."

Her resistance surprises me, but Karl solves the dispute by waving a plastic first aid kit. "No need to interrupt your work, sir, for such a trivial matter," he says in a half bow. "I'll see to *Vrouw* Tiele's care."

He whisks her off to an anteroom—the one dedicated to coats and ex-fiancés. Jacob wanders to my side and bumps my elbow. *See? Karl likes her.*

Frowning, Noah drops his hand, sliding it into his pocket. "How are you getting on with your training?" he asks Jacob, the question pitched nicely between official inquiry and friendly curiosity.

Jacob tips his chin. "Alma is trying to accomplish the impossible."

Noah flashes a smile, the one which has broken hearts across the globe. "On my first international assignment, I threw up in a dignitary's lap. I had spent the afternoon running around the beaches with my best friend and got heat exhaustion. My mother threatened to consign me to a dungeon until I could be trusted to hydrate and use sunscreen. You'll do fine."

"He doesn't remind anyone of that story," I say, when we've made our way to our suite.

Jacob dispenses with his jacket and pulls the shirtsleeves to his elbows. I rummage through the refrigerator and toss him a can of berrybeer. He pops the tab and hands it to me. I toss him the other one. "He must like what he sees."

"My father would tell me to exploit that," he admits. "He called me this morning—"

"You shouldn't be telling me this," I remind him.

I remind me. Sondmark and Vorburg are ancient enemies, no matter the rosy picture Mama wants to paint at the state visit. We shouldn't expose our vulnerabilities.

He nods. "Did you ever mess up as badly as your brother?" he asks, swallowing down the beverage.

Jacob has worked hard. He deserves this. Fishing my phone out, I pull up my library of GIFs, clicking on the extended one with the charging Hispaniolan galliwasp on live television.

"This is a gaffe?" he points at the screen. "Your face barely moved when it scuttled up your leg."

"It's the first impression anyone gets when they google Sondmark. The Minister of Tourism produces a report every year, and there I am."

"Do you have a problem with animals running at you, or is it a reptile thing?"

"Anything with scales." I shudder. "Anything that slithers or has moist skin."

He dries his hands on a cloth and grins. "His Majesty says I have to make myself marriageable."

"You won't have a problem with that." I fill a plate with odds and ends, shifting around the tiny space as Jacob reaches for some chicken. A hard knot forms in my throat. "Your father already has lists of brides he would approve of, I'm sure. You could probably ask Karl."

Jacob picks up a drumstick. "My father isn't in any position to tell me who to marry," he says.

"Whom." I correct without thinking.

"You have to stop doing that," he whispers, leaning against the counter.

Yes. We're off the clock. He must get tired of the constant correction. I step back, tugging the neck of my jumper. "You were saying?"

"Whom do you think I should marry?"

My brain shorts. "Who." I register my mistake as soon as the word leaves my mouth. It isn't fair. I was looking into his eyes, English is my second language, and I want to kiss him so badly.

His eyes dart to my lips. Though I've worked a miracle these past weeks, turning him into a nearly-civilized picture of modern royalty, the façade slips away. He's the same man in the jeans and leather jacket I met last month. He'd still kiss me if I asked him to.

Jacob takes a bite of chicken and wipes his mouth. "He can suggest until he's blue in the face, but I won't pick someone my father chooses for me."

This topic hurts in several ways at once and I dredge up a smile. "If you're already thinking about the succession, your metamorphosis into a royal prince is nearing completion. Do you want help finding a bride?" I scoot quickly past him to the relative safety of the hall. *Please, not that.* I've made numberless sacrifices as a princess of Sondmark, but I can't do that.

He follows me to the sitting room. "Will I need help? Has a title made me unmarriageable?"

If he only knew the number of women about to throw themselves at his feet, he wouldn't say such stupid things. I picture them as a mob, running at him in a thundering stampede.

"Not unmarriageable. But you'll need to be careful when you select her."

"Careful? How can you be careful when you love someone?" His brow tents.

"If you want to protect her—" *Her*. She'll be some basic tiara-chaser with a set of pearls and a megawatt smile. She'll have picked the right schools and adopted the right attitudes, training for this like some women train for gold medals. I hate her already. "If you want to protect her from being torn apart in the press and from feeling that she can never possibly measure up to her position, you'll have to be careful. This life isn't for everyone. You have to make a thoughtful choice."

He wolfs down a spinach quiche and talks around his bites. "That's dumb. Love just happens. It doesn't have anything to do with how suitable someone is."

My 'have you ever cracked open a history book' expression flashes. "My father was one of very few royal men of his generation. It wasn't an accident he was introduced at precisely the time my mother came of age or that their parents hammered out a mutually beneficial agreement with ironclad legal protections. When they married, there was a shared sense of commitment and duty. Love came later."

I thank Jacob for his silence—for pretending that's the end of the story when he must have picked up enough palace gossip to know all is not well between my parents.

He rakes a hand through his hair. "You'd gamble on a thing like that?"

The question is like water pooling at my foundations, slowly wearing down the limestone, eroding the soil.

"Marriage is always a gamble," I explain, shoring myself up.

He stretches his legs out and tips his head back, closing his eyes for a catnap before I march him through a long afternoon of European titles in the wake of the Cold War. I'm tired too, but when he's not looking at me, it's as though my hands go slack and the dozens of balls I'm juggling drop silently to the carpet.

Light plays against Jacob's face, and his eyes shift under the lids.

"Wouldn't being in love increase the odds of a successful marriage?" he asks, voice drowsy. He swallows. "Wasn't it a relief when you fell in love with Pietor?"

Stretching my arm out, I lean my head against the back of the sofa, and the voices in my head quiet. I am perfectly content to watch him drift on the edge of sleep. Words press against my lips.

I never loved Pietor.

19

Misfit Toys

JACOB

Alma likes the suits. All it takes is a dozen palace mirrors and the application of simple geometry to work it out. But when I look up, she frowns at her notes or glances over a map of Vorburg. Still, it's there. The way her eyes return to me makes it easy to adjust to these tailored jackets and close-fitting shirts.

If I cared less, I could make it a joke between us, peacocking around the drawing room.

If I thought this attraction could become something more, I'd be looking for my next move.

There are no next moves.

As my frustration grows, she wears the ring that isn't meant to be worn every day, twisting it on her finger.

Mom calls. She reminds me to send something to my grandpa for his birthday and tells me about the latest book her club is reading. "Basia made the choice, and you know what she likes. Trauma, trauma, trauma."

I laugh but want to ask her why she did this to me. I was happy with my life. Busy, anyway. Now everything I want feels just out of reach.

I work out in the gym, hoping Alma will find me. She never does, though I run into Clara and Ella. The exercise leaves me restless. *Oma* would say that there are only so many weights a man can lift before his brain starts turning into oatmeal. "There are fences to mend and holes to dig," she would say. "Go do something useful."

How useful can I be in a palace? I discover an answer one drizzly afternoon. My lessons finish early so that Alma can attend an official function, and I prowl through the halls, coming across a man working in a pair of coveralls, painstakingly replacing a length of crown molding.

Following him through an exterior door, he bends to remove protective booties, revealing shoes covered with paint and streaks of glue, a sure sign that he is one of my people. His English is bad, and my Sondish is worse, but we manage to work out that I want him to take me to his shop, and he leads me to a wide barn-like structure, bright and snug against the foul weather.

Crossing the threshold, I hear the harsh whirr of a bandsaw, and my blood pressure settles as gently as a sigh. That's it. I tip my head and close my eyes. That's the stuff. The air is fragrant with the smell of sawdust, metallic shavings, and the sharp tang of epoxy. Wood is sorted in slots along one wall according to type and size. Is this heaven?

Benn—we have exchanged names by now—gives me a look I take to mean, "Is this what you wanted to see?"

I place a palm against my chest. You're the best, Benn.

"Workshop?" I say, slowing it down.

He nods. "Workshop," he repeats, giving me a tour using the International Language of Power Tools.

I run my hand along a radial arm saw with a metal housing that looks ancient enough to have witnessed the early days of the Cold War. Benn whistles and draws a bead with his hand. "It still cuts true, huh?" I murmur. I like it. I like all of it.

Touch grass, the kids say. Go get yourself out of your head. I shake off Karl as often as possible, working through this attraction I have for Alma. I still see her every day, but now I have an outlet.

For the first time, I have hope that I'll survive this.

The palace restoration team treats me with extreme politeness until I scroll through a collection of my builds on my phone. Then they put me to work carving a length of molding with traditional methods—hand planes, chisels, and gouges—vital communication coming through a translation app and simple demonstrations. We fall into a pattern.

One night, as I make my way back from the shop, I catch Alma returning from an engagement with Pietor. I stop, watching them from the shadows as Alma removes her coat, revealing a dark dress that sparkles in the low light. He doesn't even look. *Chol*, what an idiot. Without a word, she strides across the black and white tiles.

She spent the whole day tutoring and then went to a second shift, throwing herself into uncomfortable clothes and making careful conversation.

Pietor just let her walk away. I would've kissed her. At least.

A voice of reason echoes in my head. Maybe they said good-bye in the car. I rub a hand across my sour stomach and Pietor calls to her, halting her on the lower treads with words I can't pick out. She doesn't turn, only lifts her chin and gives him the edge of her cheek as she makes a reply.

Something is off.

Even without a secret passageway, I beat her to the suite so that when she enters, I can wander from my room and look surprised to see her. "Did you eat?" I ask. These events are not for food, she's told me again and again. You're not supposed to actually enjoy anything.

"Not much." She hardly lifts her eyes.

"I'll make up a plate. Come get it when you're ready."

She doesn't want to say yes, but she's tired, no matter that her dress skims her curves like a second skin.

"I'll try some more Pankedruss," I coax, a heroic sacrifice at this hour. "Five tries. I might like it this time."

She gives a small smile, and I take myself off to the kitchen, wondering what I'm doing. Alma's problems are her own. If anyone has the right to help her handle them, it's Pietor.

When she returns, she curls up on the couch. Her face is scrubbed, and her hair is brushed back from her pale face. I love it all the more because she doesn't look this way for anyone else.

The smell of death hovers in the air as I set the tray down. Five attempts? What was I thinking?

She picks up a cracker and drags it through the gray goo with a smile that makes it suddenly worth it. "It's a vehicle, Jacob. Think of it like queso," she urges.

I swipe the cracker from her. "What did queso ever do to you?" I shove it into my mouth and throw back a swallow of water.

"One," she counts, cupping her hand and rubbing a thumb over the back of it. The look of strain isn't gone but it has retreated. "Just four more to go."

I exhale. "Give me a second while I stare into the abyss of eternity and contemplate the purpose of suffering."

"Such a baby," she laughs, sinking into the cushions while I prowl around, scrubbing my tongue with a napkin. She begins to nibble on the nuts and cheese.

I return, as I often do, to the dollhouse. Avoiding the staircase with its broken banister, I reach into the nursery to unwrap a set of tin soldiers. A woven fire screen. A table and chairs. A birdcage. A birthday cake. A rocking horse comes apart in my hands, and I grunt.

"I'm sorry—"

"That's the one I broke. Just wrap it back up."

"You want to wrap it up and hope for magic? That won't fix it." I turn to find her leaning over my shoulder.

Her brow furrows. She's close enough to kiss. "Isn't it better to leave it tucked safely away than to make a mistake trying to repair it?"

Is that what she thinks? "You said it's not a museum piece."

"It isn't," she insists.

"So stop treating it like one. If it's meant to be handled, you're going to break things. It won't hurt you to have a few misfit toys."

I run a light finger along the tiny stair railing of the make-believe palace. My toys were indestructible—plastic superheroes, mostly, and a basket of die-cast cars in my grandpa's shop. It's another reminder that Alma and I are nothing alike.

These days, I need all the reminders I can get. I push the thought further. I thought that after I'd learned a few things about bowing and dressing, I'd feel more like a prince, but I don't. All these weeks of training have only taught me how much I fall short.

A more unhelpful thought follows. *She can teach me.*

Alma, engaged and out of reach, looks up. "Fix things that break. Got it. I appreciate the professional advice from a bespoke furniture maker. Thanks for the consultation."

"The first one is free." I retreat, setting the crumpled parcel on the coffee table. "Two," I announce, taking a second drag of the Sondish death yogurt. "Three," I mumble around the bite. "Four." I breathe hard through my mouth. Best not to get my nose involved.

"Take your time," she laughs, settling down next to me and reaching for a handful of pistachios. "You need to savor the misery."

"Is this a professional consultation from a royal princess?"

Her eyes dance. "The first one is free."

20

Let's Go

ALMA

Pietor has been playing the part of the doting fiancé. The problem is that he's playing it too well.

Our segment runs on *The Sun Rises on Himmelstein*. He charmed the entire grand duchy by holding my hand the entire time and calling me 'A', excusing himself to the interviewer. "It's a little pet name I devised between us. She calls me 'P.'"

"And when may we expect your happy event?" the host asked, her alarmingly shaped eyebrows rising in expectation.

That's when my solid grasp of the Himmelstein dialect suddenly failed me. I brushed through the rest of the interview without committing to any date.

We attend an event at the Grousehof, a former royal palace which houses the Sondish parliament, and he tucks me gently into the Mercedes at the end of the night. The pictures will make the newspapers. They'll be folded next to the morning coffee and fresh rolls brought to the breakfast tables of northern Europe's most influential bankers who will then, it is supposed, find it in their hearts to extend a more generous line of credit to the grand duchy.

Himmelstein won't be the only ones to benefit from all this. Sondmark needs the appearance of Pietor and I as a happy couple, too. The trade negotiations with Vorburg have gotten tangled up with an obscure boundary dispute over a tiny island, sparking off a wave of protests. Queen Helena has her work cut out, trying to control the narrative. The last thing she needs is to be sidelined because another Sondish princess is in the press for the wrong reasons.

I inhale slowly. This lie serves me.

Me. I look out on streets slick with rain and release a bitter breath. The lie we're telling serves Sondmark. Not me. Maybe for the first time in my life, I feel the difference.

Pietor enters from his side of the car and takes my hand. I would once have seen this as a promising gesture, but now I remove it before we travel even a block from the Grousehof.

"You're being childish," he says. Hair falls over his forehead, and he herds it back into place with the scoop of a hand.

I train my eyes on the rows of tidy townhouses and brightly lit cafes, at the people meeting for drinks and a leisurely meal. No one else is making romantic decisions based on GDP and access to rare earth metals.

"We were an excellent team back there," Pietor says, adjusting the length of his cuffs. Checking them. Adjusting some more with a frown. "You backed me up nicely. Himmelstein will be left in the cold if some of those trade provisions go forward."

Maybe he's forgotten that I read the financial news as well as anyone. Himmelstein isn't hurting. "You have a point?"

"We're a relatively small economy, and when Sondmark sneezes, Himmelstein gets the flu. While these negotiations might erase some tariffs and ease commerce with Vorburg, the grand duchy will have to tamp down populist anxiety. We don't have a seaport. Our alliances mean everything, and instead of backing us into a corner, I wish you would join us. Himmelstein could use a princess like you."

I wonder if Pietor always spoke that way—advancing his own interests, indifferent to mine.

"You'll turn my head with talk like that."

"I wish I could. Think of us—Alma and Pietor, Sondmark and Himmelstein. Like Supernuss and wafer cookies, we go together."

"Supernuss is disgusting," I say. This opinion puts me out of step with the vast majority of Europeans, but the chocolate spread has never improved a crepe.

"We need you, Alma," he says.

I tell him that there's no need to see me through the palace doors.

When I return to the suite, a light shines from under Jacob's door, and his low murmur emanates from within. I check my watch. Midnight in Sondmark would be...mid-afternoon in Blackberry. He's talking to his grandparents. I wish I could push into the room and say hi to them over his shoulder. Maybe introduce myself as Alma—just Alma.

When did I become so hopelessly naïve?

I enter my room and think how wise Pietor is to try to win me back. Himmelstein isn't struggling, but the grand duchy is small. His alliance with me—with Sondmark—has been a diplomatic and economic coup. I can't blame him. I'd done as much research as he had, when we agreed on the engagement. It was the responsible thing to do. But amidst these concerns about monetary policy and tariffs, Clara and Freja have been merely happy.

I take down my hair and begin removing my make-up. What good is happiness? I blink away gathering tears and look at my reflection, the smudged eyeliner and streak of brow pencil blurring my features.

When I was a young girl, my mother read me her coronation oath, going over each word so I understood the covenant she'd made with God and her people. "It means that while I live, I live for Sondmark. It's a tremendous burden."

"Can I carry it for you?" I asked.

She smiled. "I have to carry it, but you may help me do so."

We pantomimed another oath, perfectly tailored for the narrow shoulders of a serious-minded young princess. I would be my queen's right hand and defender of our nation. It's a vow I've never regretted, but I can almost hear Jacob's voice in the back of my head. "Vow. Like a nun?"

He wouldn't understand that kind of vow, but he would understand loyalty.

I wipe the lipstick from my mouth. My sisters are merely happy, but in a sense, they've cut themselves off from the path of duty, from performing a vital role for their country, and from laying everything down for the people of Sondmark.

I accept their choice. I won't be jealous of it.

My sleep is fitful, and it's early when I make my way to the breakfast room, nodding politely when a maid tucks the newspapers next to my place setting. Pouring out a cup of coffee, I glance over the headlines of *The Holy Pelican*. "Vorburg Proposes 2% Drop in Agricultural Tariffs." Mama will be pleased. "*Neerheid* van Heyden Gives Firsthand Account of Seong Crisis." Marc, my brother's oldest friend, has been on the ground for several months, monitoring the situation in his mother's homeland.

I make a mental reminder to tell Jacob that *Neerheid* is Sondish for 'Lord' and turn the paper, scanning the headlines under the fold. "Royal Wedding Date Leaked, Waiting on Palace Confirmation."

I stand and hastily spread out the paper so I don't mistake a single word, murmuring in panicked fits and starts. "Palace spokespeople were unreachable Friday evening as news leaked on Pixy...an account specializing in sustainable, organic, non-dairy, free-range baked goods...September 20th..."

This isn't a tabloid, but Sondmark's most reputable news organization. My mouth dries up. The breakfast attendant is calmly arranging the table settings, blind to the fact that the bars of my royal cage are clanging shut. There ought to be a button, a bellpull, or an old air raid klaxon I can ring to get everyone out of bed and downstairs now.

I clear my throat and the maid looks up. "Yes, ma'am?"

"Has Her Majesty had breakfast yet?" My skin feels mottled and itchy.

"Came and went half an hour ago," she says. "She's preparing for a luncheon at the embassy."

Vede. Vede, vede, vede. My phone flashes and I leap on it. It's a text from Caroline.

Her Majesty expects you to stay out of the spotlight today as the palace considers a response.

"Excuse me." I nod my way out of the room, donning a tight jacket of anxiety, the buttons going from my neck to my knees. I don't need to worry. Mama is in charge. I'm fine. This is fine. The first order of business is to get to my suite. I race to the Great Hall and up the stairs.

"Alma!" Clara calls, chasing after me.

Vede.

"I'm fine," I tell her. She doesn't listen. Instead, she grabs my elbow, dragging me into my sitting room.

"Sure you are," she says, dumping me onto the sofa. "Is there any truth to it?" she asks. "Did you agree to marry—"

I dig my fingernails into the soft flesh of her arm and tip my chin at Jacob's door. *Shh.* But there's no need to take such care. We can hear him singing in the shower, offkey as ever.

"I'm not marrying Pietor," I hiss. Never. "I don't know how this got out."

"I think you should—"

Her words are interrupted with a loud bang, bang, bang on the exterior door. Before I can answer it, Ella charges through, coming at me with her phone extended. "The account is called @EarthCakes." She turns the phone and reads the logo. "'Composting responsibly since 2004. Sustainable. Delicious.' Doubt it," she mutters. "The comments are all over the place—"

I snatch the phone and scroll through, eyes darting back and forth over the lines of text.

@royalsroyalsroyals Squee!! I'm setting the date! Let's get that #HimmelsteinHottie to the altar!

@højpumpkinspicecoffee Alma has waited long enough! Have a watch-party invite list growing. Planning the cocktails. Sourcing my vegan leather wedding handbag now!!!11!!

@trashpandaprincess Lighting a candle and waiting on word from the palace. #toogoodforhim #hewaxeshisbackhair

Not everyone is so sure the wedding date is set. I take some comfort in that.

"There is a whole *flamen* crowd of photographers at the palace gates," Ella says. I feel like a wild animal backed into a corner, and she holds her arms out. "Bring it in. Princesses assemble."

We close up, an unpickable knot of princesses. I miss Freja's light touch, but at least, I'm not alone. We breathe in and out until Clara gives me a squeeze.

"You'll go crazy if you stay cooped up in the palace all day," she says, fishing a set of keys out of her pocket. "You should go to Max's cottage. Take a few hours, pack a picnic lunch, and watch a football match." She eyes me closely. "The press has been barred from the nature preserve since the lawsuit, so you'll have some privacy. But if you leave muddy footprints, Max won't let me hear the end of it."

I shake my head. "Nice offer, but how am I supposed to get past the photographers?"

I hear the clearing of a throat. Three heads pop up, all eyes on Jacob, too late to register the absence of off-key singing and the sound of water.

It's Saturday. Jacob ignored my dress code in favor of a pair of low-slung jeans and a classic white t-shirt straining across his chest. He ruffles his hair with a towel. "I can bust you out of here if you give me a minute to brush my teeth."

He disappears, and three heads dip into a huddle.

"Is he as hot as I think he is?" Clara asks. "Max broke my ability to gauge these things."

"Not my type," Ella says, flicking me a glance, "but I don't think Alma would kick him out for buttering his bread with a fish knife."

I pinch her and our heads conk against one another. We each rub the spot. "I have an ex-fiancé still haunting the palace. It's too soon to be noticing hotness."

Clara looks at Ella and giggles. "It's too soon, she says."

Ella offers a bland smile. "Hotness should text Caroline and make an appointment."

"I don't have feelings for him," I insist, my voice tight. He could walk in at any second.

As if on cue, Jacob pops his head around the door, his hand gripping his damp hair, bicep flexing. My sisters turn away, biting their lips. "Meet me out front in an hour," he says.

"The photographers—"

"No problem. I can get a vehicle they wouldn't ever suspect you'd use. I'll text Caroline."

Ella snorts.

Precisely an hour later, I emerge from my suite holding a knapsack stuffed with supplies, passing footmen whose glances linger on me with unusual interest. My thumb pushes the opal ring on my finger.

Skipping down the palace steps, I find a large box truck blocking the driveway, the engine idling. I wait for the moment that it pulls away to reveal Jacob leaning against a sleek motorcycle. That's his style. Instead, he hops out of the cab of the truck.

"What's this?"

"Your getaway car. I can drive us through the gates while you hide in the back."

"I dressed for a motorcycle." Sort of. I'm wearing dark washed denim, stiff and tailored, as well as ankle boots with sensible heels. I imagined us shooting past the palace gates, my hair tucked under a dark helmet, arms around Jacob's waist for safety. The press would never suspect uptight Princess Alma on the back of one of those.

He reaches for my hand, helping me scramble in through the passenger seat. "I wouldn't risk you," he says. My stomach dips. "It's winter. There's all kinds of debris and icy patches on the roads and the weather might turn. I want you safe."

I step over tools to crouch in the back between a pair of steel-toed work boots and an empty rubbish bin.

"Do you know where you're going?"

He chuckles, glancing at me in the rearview mirror, and pulls away. A deep rumble shakes the truck, lightyears from the engineered elegance of a Bentley.

At the gatehouse he stops, speaking briefly with Nils Helmut to reiterate the plan. "We'll have an unmarked car follow you to the cottage and stay at the end of the drive until you're ready to return." Nils lifts his voice, tinged with a laugh. "I hope your cargo isn't damaged."

We proceed slowly through the gates and I shrink from the commotion of the crowd.

"We're through," he says, picking up speed.

"Can I get out now?" I ask every five minutes until we bump down the rough track leading to Max's cottage.

Jacob's answer is always the same. "Stop distracting me."

When he cuts the engine, I unfold myself from the crouch, each joint screaming from such rough treatment. Tripping through the work supplies, I slither into the front seat, dropping out of the truck and into Jacob's arms.

Fog, rolling from the lake, wreaths us in dewy air. I'm supposed to be able to find refuge out here, to escape from the watchful curiosity of palace flunkies and a waiting press, but Jacob's eyes trace my face, lashes dipping as his gaze drops to my mouth.

"Do you have the key?" I breathe.

He tips his chin up. "You have the key."

Oh. Right. I untangle myself from his arms and lead him up the path to a modest stone building covered in crisp white and black paint. We push through the door, and from the narrow entryway, I see a small kitchen on the other side of the main room.

It's more simple and rustic than I imagined, but Max's furniture, some of the pieces decades old, makes a cozy, accidental harmony. There are signs of him and Clara in a few snapshots on the mantel and a favorite blanket folded neatly over the battered sofa. It's as tidy as a pin.

When Jacob stretches, he fills half the room. "Do you think Max would mind if I claimed the cottage for Vorburg?"

"I'd like to see you try," I say, heading to the kitchen. "He has access to actual cannons."

I begin to unpack while he prowls around every centimeter of the house. "You'll be my secret weapon. We could share the spoils of war," he promises, disappearing up the stairs.

"There's only one room, though," he reports on his return. "So we'll have to flip for the bed."

"Hmm?" My cheeks flush, and I open the fridge to soak up the cool air.

"When we move in," he explains. "I'm too big for the couch."

He stands over me, one hand on the fridge door, the other on the counter. Reaching in, he grabs a bottle of juice and I scoot backward. Out of the frying pan and into the fire. The horde of press was a minor inconvenience compared to the danger of spending a whole day doing nothing with Jacob.

"I'm not hungry," I say. "I need some fresh air."

He grabs his jacket. "I'll come with you."

We walk along the shoreline, hardly more than an overgrown track. He goes ahead of me, pointing out obstacles, and I stare at the center of his back, wondering how long I can keep up the pretense that preparing him to take his place as the heir to the kingdom of Vorburg is just a job. It hasn't been just a job in weeks. Every day I wrap him up in history, protocol, comportment, and the thin tissue of etiquette, praying it will be enough to protect him when the time comes.

We walk until the wind picks up and return for lunch. It's simple fare—sandwiches and sliced fruit. I haven't snuck in any death-yogurt, and he hasn't brought along pickled herring, but every swallow is as awkward as a first date, our knees brushing under the tiny table.

After we wash up, Jacob finds a record from The Antidote in Max's collection. "The best one," he says, slipping it from its protective sleeve. The needle drops, and the opening strains of "Monday, I'm Falling For You" play through the speakers. "Do you dance?" he asks.

That's one more thing he'll have to know, at least a little. The melody is slow, and I map a simple two-step over the beat. "I can teach you—"

But he pulls me into his arms and guides me around the small space, more skillful than simply swaying to a beat, a satisfied smile tucking his cheek. At first, I hold my back stiff and my shoulders level, trying to make myself believe this is a diplomatic reception and I've been paired with a foreign minister. Trying to get it out of my mind that I've never been held like this.

His hand drops across my back, pressing the small of it, leading me with an easy self-assurance, and stealing the words from my throat. I want—

We complete a circle and my body curves to fit his shape. The difference in my limbs feels like suddenly surrendering to a current, rolling onto my back to stare up at the starry sky, hardly conscious of the dangers downstream. I could live like this forever.

I miss a step and he steadies me with one easy motion, smiling when my shoulders straighten. *Vede.* What if I never feel this way again? What if the perfect husband Mama produces from her list never makes me forget I'm a princess?

"Where did you learn how to do this?" I ask, forcing myself to swim against the current again, struggling against the dance and the cottage and the man I never want to be without.

"My mom was a dancer. Don't you remember?"

Of course. The notes of the song die away, and I peel myself out of his arms, avoiding his gaze. I lift the needle on the record player. He bends over the hearth and lays a fire, working in silence. "I approve of him," he says, at last.

"Of whom?"

"Your sister's boyfriend. I assume everyone is freaking out about Max."

I don't even think about holding my answer back. "A little. He's not what we expected."

Jacob's hands still. "He's got great taste in music. A bit old school, but nobody who has that album collection just wants to play around." He lights the tinder and nurses the fire until it catches.

Returning to the sofa, he digs into my bag, removing the paperback, and hands me the knitting.

"Go ahead," he says, plucking out the bookmark and opening to my spot. "I'll read to you. We're still on the adventures of Miss Pendragon?"

"It's a series," I say, sorting out my yarn. I hold up the ball, looking for somewhere to put it, and he places it in his lap.

His voice drops into a warm cadence as he begins. "It was the third murder in a month. One was forgivable. Two was a tragedy. Three meant it was time for Agatha Pendragon to postpone the Tea and Rummage Sale in Support of Rural Midwife Retention at the Women's Institute to catch the scoundrel. The vicar would be cross."

I knit to the sounds of the clicking needles, the irregular pop of the fire, and his resonant voice until he puts the book down, slides more deeply into the sofa, and watches me.

I keep up a regular pace, dropping more stitches than usual.

"Does this happen a lot?" he asks.

Never. No one else—

"The siege of reporters at the palace gates," he clarifies.

The sofa is crowded with the two of us. "A wedding date is big news."

"The palace hasn't confirmed it." He holds the ball of yarn in a loose grip.

I don't want to lie. Instead, I search for a clean, discrete piece of truth to give him. "Mama doesn't like to have her hand forced."

The real answer is that we're damned if we refute it—all but inviting the press to discover that Pietor and I are on rocky ground and that their interest is justified—and damned if we don't. I'm sure this leak wasn't an accident.

It's Pietor. He likes his deal—marrying into the Sondish royal family and getting all the economic benefits which naturally accrue when your mother-in-law owns a sizable portion of the North Sea. There's no way one of his assistants accidently called an organic, high-end bakery and floated openings on a particular day just for, as Ella might say, funsies.

His move was meant to trap me—trap Sondmark—into going forward with this marriage or at least offering Himmelstein concrete cover for a much longer stretch of time.

"You've had a long engagement," Jacob says, switching on the television, navigating to an exhibition soccer game between Vorburg and Sondmark. The teams are playing in a sunny southern latitude, and the score is nil-nil. I'm thankful for any distraction and put aside my knitting.

"Not so long," I murmur, watching Mallok make a cross in front of the goal. Kepler barely misses the connection, and the goalie makes a long throw as the team retreats.

Jacob glances at me. "In September the weather will be chancy."

I tiptoe carefully around a falsehood. "The whole family shifts their August holiday for September weddings. It's not so long to wait. Americans regularly have engagements lasting a year."

Jacob grabs my knees and hauls me 90 degrees to face him. A thread of frustration tightens between us.

"Royal timelines don't work like that," he says, his voice low, scraping along the side of my neck. "It's maybe six months between an official announcement and the actual royal wedding."

I force a smile. "You've been doing research?" Emotions crowd against the bridge of my nose and behind my eyes while I make room for false ones that slip through, as thin as water. "If you're prepared to think about marriage, I could ask Caroline to draw up a preliminary list."

It's supposed to sound like I'm teasing him, but my throat hurts too much to get it right.

He frowns. "You've been engaged for more than a year already."

He pursues his point, but I skirt away. "It's a shame you won't let your father arrange a match for you." The words are lighthearted, but my heart hurts.

The noise from the television escalates, and I catch the replay. Vorburg's left striker sank a football into the back of the net like our keeper's hands were made of air. The Sondish crowd starts singing an old, rowdy folk song, drowning out the celebration of the visitors.

One Sondish princess, but not one more.

Beg for our treasure and raid our shores

Shake your swords and beat your shields

No second princess we ever yield

I choke out a bitter laugh, and Jacob's brows lower. "What are they singing?"

I give a rough translation. "It's a friendly reminder that we'll surrender a goal here and there, but you'll never get another princess."

The thread of frustration snaps, and he gets up and heads to the kitchen, clattering against the coffee table. I cup my neck and feel blood pounding through my veins.

"That's one thing I'll never understand about you people. There you are, living your lives, watching a football game..." He returns with a plate, a packet placed in the center. His tone is light, but there is bitter irritation around the edges. "You'll fight to the death over something that happened in the Middle Ages."

Unfolding a wax paper wrapper, I uncover a brownie and give it a sniff. Mint. My favorite pairing. I love mint and chocolate.

"We're nothing without our binding grudges." I take a bite and then another. My sweet tooth is almost never satisfied. I pay for treats like some sinner saving up for indulgences, but when these hit my bloodstream, all thought of denying myself disappears. "Where did you get this?" I ask, holding the remains of an edge piece between my fingers. Saving the best until last.

"My mom made them. She sent them over in the diplomatic pouch."

That's maybe the best use the diplomatic pouch has ever been put to. "I'm sure Sondmark has brownies somewhere." I pop the remaining piece into my mouth and kiss the crumbs off the pad of my thumb. Just one. I don't need more than a little taste.

"Sondmark doesn't have these brownies. Anyway, she sent them because she's sorry I'm homesick."

"Homesick for Vorburg?"

He lifts his eyes. *Think again, boss.*

"Have another one," Jacob says, offering the plate when Vorburg denies another Sondish goal. "It'll make you feel better."

I never get seconds. I hardly allow myself firsts. When I take it, he hides a smile.

Sondmark loses the game. Despite the song, the team surrendered more than one goal to the hated enemy.

Dusk begins to settle beyond the windows, and we pack up. He extinguishes the fire and cleans the grate. I take some paper wipes, dampened with tap water, and erase our footprints as far as the tiny entryway of the cottage. We stand there, too close in the confined space, and look around the refuge.

"It's like we were never here," I say, hand on the light switch. I bite my bottom lip.

Vede. I can't go back. Pietor will be there. My mother and her expectations that I'll handle this the perfect way will be there. I've spent a lifetime practicing self-denial and doing the right thing. This is just one more day. But the days stretch into the future, and I can't see any hope of rest.

A gust of wind shakes the cottage. "Alma." Jacob's fingers tangle with mine. His smile is gone. "We have to talk."

I look up, and my breath catches. I know what he's going to say. I've been running but not fast enough to evade the conversation that started in the orangery when a simple New Year's kiss turned into something more. If he speaks, a line will be crossed, and we can never go back.

I shake my head. "I can't."

He pulls me into his arms, and I stiffen. He releases a shuddering breath, which shakes through my frame, easing the tension between my shoulders. "I'm not trying to change your mind. You just look like you need a hug."

I burrow into him and try to forget the press waiting for a response, forget that I'm bound to my ex-fiancé for heaven knows how long. Forget that I've not belonged to myself for even longer.

I don't know when I start crying, but I feel his hands stroking my back and the low, soothing noises he makes.

I wrap my arms around him. I was doing everything right—carefully considering every step before I took it. In choosing the spreadsheet instead of trusting my gut or heart or whatever lesser organ seized the steering wheel, I would make my future foolproof. No mistakes. No missteps.

A bitter laugh chokes out. I've been on the wrong road this whole time.

Vede. The waste of it.

I feel feverish, like a seed before it breaks the husk and sends out its first shoots. A shiver works its way up my back, and Jacob chuckles.

"Cold?" His arms tighten like he's never going to let me be cold. I close my eyes and enjoy it for a moment. I pretend it's uncomplicated. Pretend it's friendly. Pretend it can last.

It's none of those things.

My eyes are red-rimmed, and I sniff, shaking my head.

"Ready to go back?" he asks.

He looks at me and seems to hear all the things I wish and cannot say. His fingertips brush the side of my face. His hand takes mine.

"Let's get you home safe."

21

MILLION MONKEYS

JACOB

Alma hasn't checked her phone once. She hasn't excused herself to the upstairs bedroom to carry on a low-voiced conversation with Pietor as they work it out together. She's been with me the whole day.

"Let's get you home safe," I say.

She nods, but I don't release her. For a second, I keep her folded against me, her strong arms around my waist, and the cottage door, lightly rattling in the wind, at my back.

I kiss the top of her head and pull away.

We return the same way we came. I wave to the security detail at the head of the drive and bounce onto the main road, grinning when she complains about being thrown around.

At the palace, she slithers through the gap between the front seats almost as soon as I stop. "Thank you," she breathes.

Alma hops out the door and heads to her mother's quarters, and I drive the truck around to the workshop and spend several hours working alone. I eat dinner alone. My session in the gym I spend alone.

At the end of the night, I hear her soft-footed return. Punching a pillow into shape, I stare hard at the door that divides us, willing her to tap on it, to whisper an invitation to talk.

I roll to my back, covering my face in goose down, emitting a frustrated, barely audible growl.

I glare at the door, and my gaze sharpens until I can trace the rough and sinuous grain of wood. Giving sleep up for lost, I reach for my phone.

"Is the offer to game still open?" I text.

Princess Ella responds immediately. "Of course. What's your poison?"

"I need to explode some reptiles."

"Console or PC?"

"Console."

clown emoji "Come on over, old man."

It's nearly one in the morning, but I do.

"You're up late," she says, greeting me at the door wearing flannel pajamas and a silk robe that trails behind her.

This is the future my father wanted to sign me up for, and I grin as I follow her. There's that saying about how, if you put a million monkeys in a room for a million years, they'll bang out the complete works of Shakespeare. Anything is possible given enough time. But as I slip into a gaming chair, I already know that an attraction between me and Princess Ella was never going to happen.

Not that she's not cute. She's cute. She's just not for me. Not bossy enough. Not calm as falling snow. Not watching me every second my head is turned. From the way she's cueing up the game without giving me more than a cursory glance, I'm not her type either.

We begin a joint operation on Turtle Doom, taking a few minutes to accustom ourselves to the controls. She makes an easy companion, undemanding, answering a steady stream of my questions. How much time do you all spend together? Do these tiara events ever get easier? Do you really like Pankedruss or is it the Great Sondish Lie?

I ask another question and try to make it sound like all the others.

"Why does your family still go in for arranged marriages?"

Ella gives a disgruntled laugh. "Here's the dark secret of the House of Wolffe. Her Majesty doesn't take risks."

My brows lift even as my fingers execute a complex sequence, navigating my fighter through an intergalactic wormhole. "She single-handedly forged the North Sea Confederation in her thirties."

You don't have to be interested in royals to know that.

Ella shoots me a glance. "Yeah, but she took the throne very young. Her father had just died, and she had to bear the weight of a nation on her shoulders." This statement doesn't elicit a skeptical lift of my brow the way it might have a month ago. "Fulfilling the marriage contract with Pavieau gave her stability and support."

A doom turtle holds an electrified bow staff to my throat, and I throw him off into a chasm, imagining the punchable face of Alma's fiancé as he falls.

"Nice," Ella murmurs. "Your father strong-armed his way into being the one to select the head of an emerging democratic coalition when the communists left Vorburg. He's lucky it worked, but Queen Helena is about the diplomatic approach. It took her a decade to apply the soft power that made the North Sea Confederation possible, executing a million trades and concessions instead of stretching her neck under the blade."

I grunt a laugh. A guillotine is not one of my grandma's plausible metaphors.

"So that's what it is for Alma and Pietor? They're a sure thing?"

I wipe a sweaty palm against my jeans, and Ella glances over. I set my jaw, blazing through a defensive position, sending turtle shells ricocheting around the space. She nestles into her chair and puts her slippered feet up on a cushion. Training her eyes on the screen, she racks up an impressive body count.

"When I was at Stanford, I'd go to these Thanksgiving celebrations where maybe the mom didn't want to do the matching paper plates thing, but she's hosting a princess and thinks she's got to be fancy. Then she runs out of matching cutlery, and all the stores are closed. So the top of the table has a matching set of dishes, and it looks great. But by the time you get to the foot, there's a fork she picked up at the church potluck, the oversized serving spoon, and a butter knife that's spent half its life getting chewed up in the garbage disposal."

I grunt a laugh. "You've described every Thanksgiving of my life."

"Well, that's how it's been for my mother as we've grown up and become independent people. We are an increasingly disappointing series of attempts to present the right picture. Some of us don't match. Some of us refuse to."

I wouldn't match the queen's perfect picture. The thought hurts, and I rub the heel of my hand over my chest, grimacing. Maybe this is indigestion. Maybe I've got heart valve cancer. "Your mom doesn't seem too mad about Freja getting married."

Ella gets attacked during a raid on a desert planet—a bad biome for turtles, I would have thought—and fails to account for her flank. A stupid mistake. She respawns in an abandoned village. "Everyone knows you can't tell Freja what to do. She's a laggy controller. Press the buttons all you like, but don't expect her to do what you want."

"Clara isn't in an arranged relationship." If it can happen for one sister, maybe—

Ella laughs. "Nobody expected Max. Not even Clara."

"And you? Are you going to try to present the perfect picture?"

Her smile is too bright to be real. "I'm an adult woman playing video games and living in her mother's house. I don't have anything figured out."

"How about Noah?"

"Noah is a *schpelt*." My brows narrow and she explains. "The nicest translation is that he's the kind of man who thinks women are as interchangeable as plastic interlocking bricks. There is no way Mama's going to risk the succession on his good judgment. I bet she's got some secret lab somewhere with rows and rows of cryogenically frozen princesses, all lined up for him to make his selection."

I swallow away the thickness in my throat. "Alma and Noah get arranged marriages, The younger two don't. You could go either way. Why not scrap the whole system?" The controller goes slack in my hands until she elbows me.

"Dude, turtles on your left." Ella withholds her answer until my head is back in the game. "You can't dismantle a system you're invested in."

"Alma's invested?" My hands are hot and cold.

She gives me a look, and I swear there's pity in it. I swear she knows. "Alma has never disappointed our mother."

"Never?" I murmur, knowing very well what the implications of that are. The queen is a reflection of her people. What is it the crowd sang at the football match? *One Sondish princess but not one more.* Even if her daughter wasn't already engaged, Her Majesty wouldn't want Alma to get involved with a Vorburgian nobody, even if he is a prince.

I push the thought away.

Ella stretches. Her eyes are apologetic. "Alma doesn't like risk any more than Mama does. She's got to be certain about something before she makes a leap."

Her words are unequivocal. Uncompromising. Tough luck. Move along. I get it. *Chol*, how transparent have I been?

"It's a ridiculous way to live. I won't let my father arrange my marriage."

She shrugs. "Easy to say you wouldn't bend to pressure when you've never felt it on your back." She delivers this morsel of wisdom as she methodically obliterates a boss in a complicated series of jumps and flips.

We rest through a cutscene.

"So, who can we expect to be the next crown princess of Vorburg? What's your type?"

I give a mirthless grunt. "Taken."

I train my eyes on the screen, intent on hacking apart marauding turtles. Ella's gaze bores into my skull. Finally, she performs a hard pivot.

"What did Alma say about the leak?"

"She said she'll handle it."

I return to the suite, pausing by Alma's door and moving on. When morning comes, I shower and dress in a dark suit, doing my best with the tie. By the time I make my way to the administrative offices, it's late.

The hallway is full of aides and secretaries striding with purposeful steps in every direction. Tablets are displayed, cellphones are hovered over. I see Alma coming from the end of the corridor, and I stop in her path, waiting for her to see me. It comes so late that she has to go up on her toes to stop herself from bumping into my chest. I steady her with a light touch, and she steps back.

She's wearing the ring, touching the tiny top button of her blouse. Not undoing it. Just letting her finger slide off the little pearl over and over. Flick. Flick.

Yesterday she slipped into my arms like she belonged there.

"Do you want to do this today?" I ask. I'll run away with her again. I'll do it every day, if she wants.

Her lashes flicker. "No reason to cancel."

No one disturbs us all morning. Mr. Tumwater messages us about the tuxedo but plans to stay in the workroom. Karl is monitoring the chaotic creation of the palace's official response before it's pushed out onto an unsuspecting public. Taking notes, I expect. Vorburg is a relative backwater while Sondmark is in the big leagues.

I play along with Alma, pretending not to notice that everyone has lost their minds. I want to make a joke about how catastrophic the situation is. Compare it to nuclear war, a second invasion from the east, or the crack-up of international superstars Lars and Bianca. I observe her pinched, white face, and hold my tongue.

Around noon, Caroline taps on the door and enters, giving her customary curtsey. "I have the response, Ma'am." Handing over the paper, she waits while Alma scans the text.

Finally, Alma nods. "Good. Send it out."

Caroline takes off and Alma chafes her arms. "Back to our lessons."

"You're not going to tell me what it says?"

She lifts a shoulder and puts on a newsreader's voice. "In planning for an event of this magnitude, there are many variables. Some of them have yet to be resolved. Her Royal Highness appreciates the interest and warm wishes of our citizens, etc., etc. Final plans will be communicated through official channels. Now," she wraps up, switching over to her usual tone, "we need to return to history. Where were we?"

"We're still on the War of the Amber Cross," I supply. "Why are we going over it in such detail? I know the bare bones."

She loves putting me right. "Because we hate you for it, and you hate us. You have to know why so you don't stumble into any tripwires."

Alma's phone vibrates and her eyes dart to the screen, lower lip caught between her teeth. The official response has been released, prompting a flood of personal texts.

"It's going to be fine," I say.

"Of course it is." She touches the top button, finger flicking off the top.

"You can be upset. I don't mind."

She closes her eyes, her breath hitches, and she drops her head. Maybe she needed permission.

"Hey." I kneel at her side, and run long passes between her shoulder blades. "Just breathe."

She stills under my hand.

"The initial skirmish in the War of the Amber Cross was just the crown prince's personal guard attacking his wife's kidnappers on the route back to Handsel," I say, already knowing how she'll respond to the word choice.

"You can't call them kidnappers," she corrects. "Sondmark considers it a rescue. Don't make that mistake into a hot mic."

"All right. The princess barely...escaped with her life."

The Vorburg account is raw, full of grief and rage and, being Vorburg, full of specific ways to enact vengeance. The crown prince writing to his father about how the princess had been stolen in the forest near their castle isn't a polite, distant read full of "My lady wife" this and "We were beset upon" that. It's all, "I will tear the flesh from their bones with my teeth. Blood will rain down their fortress walls until the return of my woman."

"How did they get from a few soldiers to Leif SobeIsen charging through the East Gate with more mounted cavalry than the world has ever witnessed?" I ask.

Alma whispers. "He couldn't let her go."

The phone continues to vibrate. She tenses, and I turn it off, silencing the notifications.

"Do you know how amber is harvested in Vorburg?" I ask. She accepts this digression as a natural consequence of trying to teach me anything. "Storms come, churning up the petrified forests under the North Sea, and you go down to the seashore in bright orange rain gear and stand in the howling wind and pounding surf with a wide shrimp net, scooping through the breaking waves, looking for treasure, tossing back the dregs. The worst storms give the best rewards."

"Are you trying to make me feel better?" Her voice levels out, and her muscles relax under my hand.

"Is it working?" I grin, kneading the tendons in her neck. I won't be here always. She'll have Pietor and the royal apparatus to fall back on.

What should be a comforting thought isn't. Other than her sisters, I haven't seen any support for Alma as a human being, only for her position. Dozens of people are wearing themselves out today to make sure the palace looks good.

Alma worries about me—about how I might fall on my face as soon as I assume my public role. In the beginning, everything she taught was about protecting me from that humiliation. But somewhere in the last few weeks, I sense a shift. Now she wants to protect me from being hurt.

It's my turn to be worried about her.

"Do you know what else about amber?" I ask.

"Hmm?"

"It's full of twigs, bugs, moss." I lift my hand until it hovers above her hair. She won't feel this. "It's a mess and I love it."

22

TURNING SPINDLES

ALMA

Freja slips into her chair at the long conference table as though she hasn't shaken the very core of the monarchy. She's wearing a vintage wrap dress and a satisfied look on her face. Even her skin has a faint tan. Freja regrets nothing.

I kiss her cheek as I pass, and she squeezes the hand I rest on her shoulder. Noah is early, as he always is.

"Welcome home," he tells her. "You look well."

Caroline takes Freja's heavy coat, bearing it off to a cloakroom, and I watch Noah's hand cup the back of his neck. His eyes slide away from our sister, idly following the secretary as she departs. Freja has unsettled us all.

When Caroline returns, she lays agendas at each place, reaching around us as she goes. Noah frowns as Caroline leans over his shoulder, straightening the packet with a snap, and allowing for her quick retreat.

Okay? I ask.

It's nothing. His eyes scan my face. *You?*

I nod. *Nothing.*

He slides a small tin of hard candy across the table, and I catch it. Wild berry. My favorite.

It was just the two of us before the twins showed up and demanded the lion's share of attention. By nature, we're both workhorses, putting our heads down and getting on with our public roles. Of course, his definition of that has stretched to include nosy magazine profiles titled "Crown Princess Roulette" next to thumbnail-sized photos of an entire page of models he's taken out in the last year.

My brother knows how discrete I've been. He knows this flurry of speculation and gossip about my wedding is my worst nightmare. He knows that when I nod and pretend like it's nothing, it's something.

With a smile, I pop a small candy into my mouth. *Thanks.*

Clara appears, swinging her leather portfolio. She hugs Freja from the back, kissing her face over and over. Smiling, Freja peels her off. When our youngest sister slips into her chair, I pass her the keys to Max's cottage. "Thank you. I really needed that."

"Anytime."

"Why is there a flotation fob on the keys to a house?" I ask.

"You never know when you'll fall in the water." She looks impossibly innocent.

Père and Ella arrive at the same time, and Père's effusive greeting—pulling Freja into his arms, calling her *donnina*, and kissing her cheeks—provides cover for Ella's pointed silence. I absorb these details and feel the strange sensation of wanting to share them with someone.

My cheeks flush with the specificity of the feeling. I want to share them with Jacob. I grip a pen by both ends, rolling it in my fingers, trying to erase the thought. Jacob isn't family.

Even my family doesn't get my whole self. Noah gets the piece of me that speaks honestly about my mother. My younger sisters get the piece that comforts and cajoles them into accepting the limits of our lives. Père receives the slice of Alma who can enjoy the present moment. Mama takes the piece who considers the future.

Any given thought can be shopped around to half a dozen people, but I don't want to shop with Jacob. I want to give him the keys to my mind palace and have him poke around wherever he likes, slipping records out of their sleeves, digging through the leftovers in the kitchen, stretching out on the sofa and pulling me against him—

The pen clatters from my fingertips.

Mama enters, and I scramble to my feet.

"Good morning." She glances down the table, and we take our seats again. "I'm pleased to see everyone gathered for this news. I met with Prime Minister Torbald yesterday," she begins. "He informs me that following the state visit next month, a bill will be introduced in Parliament to strip Freja from the succession."

She drops this information and Ella leaps from her chair. "That slug-faced *vailys*. He can't—"

Mama silences and seats her with a raised hand. "He can, and he will."

"It's only a number," Freja says, but her lips are pale. "It's not like I would be run out of the family. It's just that you won't be able to give me throw pillows and hats with the number 4 printed on them. I could pass them on to Clara."

"Don't," Clara snaps. Our littlest sister is the only one whose position in the line of succession would move up. Her eyes shine with unshed tears, and I bet she's biting the inside of her cheek—a habit she's trying to break.

Noah tents his fingers on a notebook. "The prime minister is flexing his muscles because we represent a threat to his power. If he wins, this move could easily lead to more substantial acts of aggression." He glances at Freja. "Does your position matter to you?"

Her smile wobbles. "I spent months trading on my title to get citizens of Sondmark into The National Museum last year. Being Her Royal Highness Princess Freja has some definite perks."

"Freja, do take this seriously," I say, wondering how she can look so calm about the prospect of her entire identity being ripped away.

Ella is merely outraged, her emotions simple and smooth. "Perks? You call the privileges and requirements of our life *perks*?" Mama raises a hand, but Ella raises her voice, too far gone to stop. "We serve the people of Sondmark. That's the deal our stupid, short-sighted ancestors made when they took the crown. The people need us to anchor this country so some blowhard whipping up popular sentiment doesn't push us into the ocean."

She begins slapping the table, pounding out a rhythm, her words a freight train. "We wear the clothes and the tiaras and contract loveless marriages and *barely* eat the food because we're here to serve. The perks don't matter. The duty does. Otherwise, this is all a racket."

The room echoes with her explosive fury. Have any of us escaped without shrapnel wounds? Not me. Mama contracted one of those loveless marriages. I have too.

"That's enough," Mama commands, lifting her voice. Ella flops into her seat, and Mama pins her with a look. "Comport yourself. Now," she pivots, "my office will work to mitigate the consequences of this hasty marriage..."

For the remainder of the meeting, family peace is a group project. We fill one another's gaps, we answer when we're spoken to. Even Ella accepts her list of engagements with none of her usual protests, likely a silent message to her twin. *See? I'm being royal.*

As soon as Mama concludes the meeting, Ella darts away, and Freja watches her go with a sigh, her mouth set. When Caroline returns the coat, Freja digs into her bag. "You're invited to our house party," she says, passing around envelopes.

I slip my finger under the wax seal, drawing the card from the envelope.

"Freja—" I gasp.

"Oskar did them," she beams. In a pair of exquisite miniature portraits, the newlyweds face one another in separate gilded frames. But what might have been a stiff, formal arrangement is made endearing by his arm reaching out of his frame to hand her a cookie.

"It says, "Plus one." Clara holds up her card. She looks around the room. "We're not invited all together...we're invited as separate people. Like, I am a person, and I can bring whomever I want to?"

Mama's displeasure electrifies the air.

"Yes." Freja's answer is blithe. We say she never notices undercurrents, but maybe it's more accurate to say she doesn't care about them. "We can't fit very many people into our flat, so it will be some of Oskar's aunties and uncles, my immediate family, and their special guests." She smiles at Clara as she adds this last bit.

"Let me RSVP right now. I'm bringing Max."

Mama clears her throat—as though Max is an unfortunately situated piece of chicken she can't dislodge. "Is it safe?" she asks, running her fingers over the uneven surface of Freja's scrolling calligraphy and Oskar's hand-painted art. "We won't fall through the floor?"

"We'll weigh the guests at the door," Freja replies.

Mama gives a cool smile. "Your father and I are honored to be your guests."

Freja nods. "Excellent. Oh, Mama. His Majesty King Giles extends his warmth and greetings."

"When did you see Uncle Giles?" I breathe.

"On our honeymoon. Mama suggested a visit since we were so close."

"Pavieau?" Père shouts. "You sent our daughter to Pavieau?"

Our father grips Freja's hand, but we are all in a similar state of shock. The only place we ever meet Père's family is in Switzerland, carefully away from the spotlight.

The cords of Mama's neck tighten. "It was merely a suggestion." She swallows and strides off, Caroline in her wake.

Awkward silence grips the room, and then Père stalks toward Mama's office.

Clara watches him go. It's a topic too serious to gossip lightly about, and when she returns to the subject of the party, we follow. "You aren't going to bring a Chanel model, Noah. You can't."

He bops her on the head with his invitation. "Who said I was?"

She slips out of his reach and gathers her things. "You should bring Caroline. She's practically family."

In a blink, he goes from teasing big brother to our future king. "I will not bring *Vrouw* Tiele. She has her own life beyond being at our mother's beck and call."

Karl has been practically vibrating in her presence these last weeks—like a Venus flytrap waiting for the soft brush of an insect's wing—and I stifle a laugh. "That's for sure."

"What's that supposed to mean?" he snaps. He shakes his head. "Forget it."

My family disperses and I tap out a message on my phone. *Where are you?*

In seconds, Jacob sends me a picture of a pile of sawdust. That's all. Just the picture. There are 93,000 square meters of palace. Is he breaking one of them?

I grab a coat and find a footman. Palace staff are trained to fade into the background, no more remarkable than an 18th century vase, until needed, and this one starts when I fetch up next to him.

He bows, "May I help you, Your Royal Highness?"

"*Hej.*" I pull out my phone and tilt the screen. "Do you possibly know where this is?"

He cranes his neck. "That looks like the restoration workshop, ma'am."

His directions are simple, but the afternoon is cold. Snow flurries swirl across my path, and I keep my head bent against the low clouds and dark skies. When I arrive at my destination, I find Jacob in the shop, bent over a whirring machine, guiding a metal tool down a length of spinning wood. Tiny flecks of sawdust fly back over his wrist, catching on his skin and hair, and a grimy radio picks up a BBC broadcast, the show hosted by an earnest, lisping historian discussing the Suez Canal.

I don't know much about tools, but I've been on enough factory floors—wearing protective hair nets and unnaturally clean overalls—to know this is not the time for a surprise. I perch on a stool and wait until the machine comes to a rest. He reaches for a caliper, taking a measurement, but when his hands drop to his hips, I ask, "How did you get here?"

He's wearing a quilted flannel coat that has seen better days over a t-shirt and jeans. He looks like a professional woodworker, but I also see a crown prince. The outlines of each blur together in the warm light.

Jacob turns down the radio. "You found me."

I think I'll always find him.

He leans back against his bench and crosses his ankles. "A carpenter returns to his natural habitat." This comes with one of his grins.

Vorburg is lucky to have him for the rest of his life.

"What are you making?" I ask.

He turns, his arms braced along the workbench, and gives me a nod, inviting me to inspect. I crowd into him, almost touching. Not quite.

"Do you know what this is?" he asks, turning his head nearly into mine. We take a breath. His gaze shifts.

"Some kind of lathe?"

He nods. "Can you tell what I'm turning?"

The palace has a number of projects going at any one time, and I attempt to place the small piece of wood in the context of a massive royal residence. It looks like a decorative matchstick.

I run a light finger over the wood, feeling the ridges. "Wait." I twist my head, getting a vertical orientation, inadvertently bumping him aside with my hip. My eyes close for a brief second while I mark time, waiting for the sensation to roll through me and recede.

There are thermal springs in Sondmark, places where groundwater comes into contact with magma-heated rock. Pools that steam all winter long and keep the snow at bay are natural wonders in these cold northern latitudes. Touching him is like finding one of those after a frigid, wind-scoured hike.

"Are these spindles?" Under the precisely turned piece of wood lies a graveyard of splintered attempts.

Despite the blazing light, it's so cold I can see our breath. I hold mine, trying not to give myself away. I feel a jumble of words—Sondish and English and French and German and Spanish and Pavian and Seongan—wrestle in my brain. "Oh. These are the spindles from the staircase in the dollhouse."

So many failed attempts.

"Alma—"

Vede. His gaze roves across my face and I stumble backward, red-faced and awkward. I perch on a stool. Maybe I can breathe if he stays exactly where he is. Maybe I can pretend that this is a friendly gesture.

"It's nice of you to think of replacing them." Nice. It isn't nice. Nice is a bottle of wine and a scented candle for your hostess. This is time and thought and talent. I've never received a gift like this.

"I'll have to show it to my mother. She'll appreciate it." She won't. Mama has probably forgotten we ever owned a dollhouse. "Maybe she'll even set it up in one of the public rooms for display." With every word, I create distance between me and the dollhouse, dismissing the years I loved it. Waving aside all the times I crouched in front of it, unable to bring myself to unwrap the pieces because I believed the brokenness would only travel in one direction. To more brokenness. Never to repair.

His hand closes on the spindle, and he nods.

"We just had a family meeting," I say, reaching for some way to erase the solemn, guarded look on his face.

"Oh?"

It's on my tongue to tell him everything, but he sorts his tools, sweeping away the mess. I have to remember myself.

"Freja's having a house party. I can bring anyone I want."

"Pietor?"

I wasn't thinking of Pietor. I never think of Pietor.

"He has business in Himmelstein." It might be true. "I thought this would be a good opportunity to take your clothes for a test drive."

He holds his paint-daubed flannel coat open. "These?"

"The new ones. You have to learn how to move in them, in public."

"Oh. An assignment." He shoves a hand into his pocket. "Sure."

23

— · —

GOOD NUNNERIES

JACOB

"Vest or no vest?" I call through the connecting door.

"I told you," she replies, "use your best judgment. Dressing for the party is tricky. It's a private event, but it will also be full of royals. I want to see what you think is appropriate."

"Are you laughing at me?" I respond, scratching my neck at the closet full of clothes—the old Jacob pushed to the side.

In other circumstances, they would be enough to last me through the end of my natural life, but Karl tells me I'll be spending my whole stipend each quarter because it wouldn't do to have the country see me in the same leather belt too many times.

"Jacob?" she prods.

My hand hovers over the ties. No tie, I decide. The party is not formal. "I'm ready."

Her muted voice is doubtful. "Let me see."

"Don't you trust me?"

I hear a low laugh as I swing the door open. I take a drag of air, and even without a tie, my throat is suddenly tight. Alma is wearing a black dress, not too short, not too long, and her hair is pulled to the side, exposing the line of her neck. I want to nuzzle into it and find out what she smells like up close.

I want to tell her that it's insane to throw herself away on Pietor, a man who wouldn't cut down a forest of briars or fight off a dragon to be next to her. My eyes flick to her hand. No ring.

She takes in my appearance, and her eyes dance. "I want you to explain the reasoning behind this look." I've gotten it wrong somehow, but I don't care because she's gorgeous when she laughs.

I pick up one of my feet. "I'm wearing boots because it's snowing."

She brushes past me, the air stirring with the scent of flowers. "Are you going on a hike? No. Also, this is a Pavian party, which always means there's always a risk of dancing. Boots off."

I sit on the edge of my bed and tug the laces, dropping the black boots with a thump.

"Socks, too," she says, rummaging in the closet and glancing over her shoulder. "Those are too thick to wear with dress shoes. Tell me about the shirt."

"A white shirt goes everywhere?" I say, wandering to her side.

She leans away for a critical look, tugging the seams at my waist. "Technically, yes, but it's sending it into formal territory. Remember, Oskar's relations will be there too, and we want to blend."

"I don't blend," I say, undoing the buttons on my shirt. The only place I look remotely at home is in the shop or back in Blackberry.

I tug the hem out of my waistband and peel the shirt off my shoulders with a grin. "Why is it that everytime you see my virile, hairy chest, you're struck dumb?"

"I'm not going to dignify that with a response." The words are cool but her cheeks are flushed. She hands me a striped Oxford, her face averted, and I shrug it on, doing it up one button at a time.

"Pants?" I ask.

"Don't you dare," she snaps.

I pull on dark dress socks, slipping into leather shoes the color of cherry wood, double-knotting them for security. She hands me the waistcoat that goes along with the suit pants, and after I do up the buttons, she brushes my hands away. I stand stock still, as she slips a button from the hole. The pink on her cheeks has traveled as far as the tips of her ears. "Leave the bottom button undone." Her chin lifts but her eyes don't. "Always."

Taking a breath, she crosses the room, returning to hold rolled ties near my chin. "This one with a Windsor knot," she says, handing me one of her choices.

"I only know half-Windsor." Every boy who ever sat in a church pew with *Oma* Gardner was expected to know a half-Windsor. "Anyway, won't it be too formal?"

"I love it when you listen to me." She grins, forgetting the distance she's placed between us over the last several days, blind to the danger of being kissed. "It's got polka dots. Think of it like making a trade—you've got a formal Windsor but in a playful pattern. You have to get the balance just right."

She turns up my collar and lays the tie against my neck, adjusting the length and weaving the fabric this way and that. She fumbles and retreats a step—right up against the closet door.

I catch her waist. "Careful."

We're as close as we were that night in the orangery, but this time I know she's bossy and straight-laced. Knits badly and blushes. This time, though, I know she's not free. When she cinches the tie, I step back and check myself in the mirror. "Good?" I ask.

She only nods.

"That's nice," I say, pointing at her black dress. My compliment is the understatement of the century. Alma looks like every dream I never knew I had. "What is it?"

"Vintage Sergei San Martin," she says. "It's Freja's favorite designer."

That's one more factor I haven't considered when choosing my clothes. "It's like I'm playing checkers and you're playing inter-dimensional chess."

Her smile flashes, and I let my eyes drop, skimming along the outline of her figure. The sleeves extend just beyond the soft bend of her elbow. "You look good." Her lashes flicker. If she were mine, this would be my cue to take her in my arms.

"Get on the bed," she commands.

"What?"

"Get your mind out of the gutter, Jacob."

She pushes me, and I fall back, propping myself up on my elbows, curious to see how events unfold. Her gaze has a dangerous weight—like a running saw with faulty safeguards.

"Your shoelaces are appalling," she says. She pivots a chair into position and guides my foot to the seat. I'm at Little Duckies again.

She doesn't waste her time with instruction, only pulls apart the knots I learned in kindergarten and does them up. The bows no longer look thick and stubby but lay flat, the loops dripping with money.

"What's that?"

"A Parisian knot."

I tilt the shoe back and forth. "How do you know all this stuff?"

"I've had a lifetime to learn." Her gaze drifts from my eyes to my waistcoat and back again. "Don't be hard on yourself."

"Should I do it this way every time?"

Alma shakes her head. "There are lots of ways I didn't even think to teach you." She moves around the room, tidying up the mess, tucking neckties away, and straightening my shoes. *Opa* does this sort of thing for *Oma*, coming after her in the kitchen after she gets breakfast on, wiping down the counters and cleaning the cast iron skillet. Like the afternoon turkeys crossing at the end of the drive, it is a sign that all is well in their little world.

A wave of longing knocks the words from my chest. "You don't have to get married," I say, as if it's as simple as exchanging one tie for another. Hard pressure builds in my lungs.

"If you come to Vorburg, I'll make you my master and I can be your apprentice," I say, using the familiar language of tradesmen. Her hand goes to her finger, twisting an invisible ring, and the room shivers with the words I haven't spoken. *You could be my girl. I could be your man.*

Alma's face is pale, but she forces a smile. "And spark off another war between our people?"

One Sondish princess, but not one more. She knows what I want. She has to. And she thinks the idea of us is impossible.

I sit up, hands braced behind me. "I'd go to war for you."

She stands at the dresser and closes a drawer with a snap. "Thank goodness it won't come to that." The sound she makes isn't a laugh, but it tries to be. "I'll be downstairs when you're ready." Alma is always running.

We drive across town. Ella sits in the front seat with the security detail, keeping up a steady stream of conversation and filling me in with just enough family gossip to keep me from making a massive idiot of myself.

"And of course, Clara has been dying to introduce Max to our parents, but there hasn't been any kind of precedent for these things," she explains.

"No precedent for meeting the parents?" Alma sits silently at my side. I want to reach for her hand in the darkness, lacing our fingers together.

"Not one. Every royal spouse before Oskar was hand-selected by committee. There's no guidance in *The Red Book* about princesses who step out of line."

Alma clears her throat. "That's not quite true. The section added by Frederick the III has an annotated list of good nunneries to pack them off to."

I try to imagine the committee that would select me. Anti-monarchists bent on sabotage. "Your father was selected by committee?"

"Even him. The King's Privy Council locked Sondmark and Pavieau in such a marriage contract that not even the rise of a military dictatorship could undo it."

I rub my hand across my midsection. "Your mother still sacrificed herself to it?" I must sound like a peasant.

"They're a strong partnership," Alma answers.

Ella snorts.

When we reach Freja's flat, I touch the knot of my tie. Alma brushes my hand away. "Trust me," she whispers. "Ready?"

Oskar is at home in his suit in a way I'll never be, but I remind myself that a sledgehammer isn't a precision screwdriver. Each tool has its uses.

We get along using his broken English and the few snippets of Sondish I've picked up. He drapes an arm casually around Freja's waist, and when she shifts, he catches her fingers. The papers have turned brutal in the last weeks, implying he's as much a disaster for the royal family as an oil spill—grasping for citizenship, access, and a leg up in society. Even in such a short time, it's obvious that Oskar's goals are far simpler and more elemental. He can't be without his wife.

Alma introduces me around the room as Jacob Gardner, skating over questions about my identity and translating when necessary. Eventually, she finds us a couple of chairs in a corner, and we wait for the arrival of Her Majesty.

When she comes, music and conversation grind to a halt. "To your feet," Alma whispers, rising with everyone in the room.

The queen receives the greetings of her hosts, and Alma grips my forearm, leaning into me. Throughout the tense byplay, I don't need her to tell me that Oskar has the protocol exactly right. The proper depth to the bow—for a monarch *and* for a mother-in-law. I understand the set Sondish phrases. *Your Majesty. Honored. Home.* It's so different from my own awkward, infrequent interactions with the queen as I travel to and from the Chevres drawing room.

She makes a remark in Sondish, and the room erupts into laughter. Something is loosed among the guests. It's like unclamping a delicate piece of woodwork, holding my breath that it'll maintain its shape, and discovering that it has.

"What was that she said?" I ask, turning my head slightly, almost meeting Alma's lips in a kiss.

She jerks slightly and finds my ear. I cover her hand as she leans into me. "She told him he carried away a treasure—like a true Sondish Viking. But look"—her grip on my arm tightens—"here comes Clara."

The youngest princess weaves through the crowd, intent on intercepting her mother, who is being introduced to every Pavian in Handsel. The lieutenant commander follows in her wake.

"He didn't stuff himself into a suit," I grumble. "Why couldn't I have worn a sweater?"

The party has grown louder, and Alma, smelling like a garden in full sun, has to practically wrap herself around me to hold a conversation. I hear her low laugh. "Because you always look like you're about to be overcome by a frenzy of lumberjacking."

Max Andersen looks like a man who sorts his kitchen implements by color and type. Even in his collared shirt and sweater, he looks capable of calling in an airstrike.

When Max bows, the queen nods. A few words—lost in the noise of the crowd—are exchanged. When Her Majesty moves on, Clara goes up on her tiptoes and kisses Max on the lips. The kiss lingers a little too long, and he has to pull her off him. But he looks satisfied, and they exchange a fistbump.

I fill a plate of food for Alma, content to watch the party as she explains the nuances. An hour in, the lights dim, and the Pavians cheer. Ella is perched on the sofa in her party dress, and several men pick it up and carry it to the wall as she laughs.

Freja comes to check on us. "Ella doesn't look murderous anymore. Will you do me up?" she asks her sister, scooping her hair to the side and turning around. "This button keeps coming loose."

"I thought this was what husbands were for." Alma's fingers are nimble.

Princess Freja gives an arch smile as she goes. "It's the opposite of what they're for."

Oskar pulls his wife into a dance, and on the opposite side of the room, one of his uncles invites the queen to take the floor. Alma's breath catches.

"What—" I begin, but Alma grips my forearm and claps a hand over her mouth.

Alma's father, Prince Matteo, stands on the edge of the dance floor, arms crossed, eyes pinned on his wife. He allows the couple exactly two turns before tapping the man on his shoulder and cutting in.

We watch the queen and her consort move around the floor to slow music. There isn't a sliver of light between them and the song ends before he lets her go. Guests applaud, and Alma releases a long breath.

"You look like you could use something to drink," I say, heading to the kitchen where I find Freja at the sink, rinsing out a cup.

"Prince Jacob—"

I shake my head. "Jacob."

She smiles. "It was good of you to come. We haven't seen much of the family this winter, but I want to thank you for standing by my sister at this time," she says.

I shrug. I don't pretend to understand the rules about elopement and the succession. "No problem. I'm sure it's been rough."

"More than rough." She places the cup on a drying rack and wipes her hands. "Alma tells very few people when she's suffering."

"Suffering?" I repeat. Freja has lost me, but I understand this isn't unusual with her.

"She feels pressure to do everything correctly. You've seen that?" Freja asks, opening the refrigerator and emerging with a platter of sliced fruit.

I'd have to be blind if I didn't.

"She's the oldest daughter." Freja peels away the cover. "She took care of her little sisters and was our example for how to behave. But when she needs help, she doesn't want to be a burden. Nonsense."

"Yes," I agree.

"It's bad enough now, having to see Pietor all the time, but it's going to get worse," Freja says. "The press will be terrible when they find out about the broken engagement."

"What?" My sharp question cuts through the princess's soft monologue. Finally, something concrete.

"You know what the press is—" she continues.

"Not that." My heart is charging in my chest and I can't get enough air. "The engagement. It's broken?"

Freja looks startled—like a prisoner digging her way to freedom and emerging into the warden's walled garden. "Oh," she says, going pale. "Oh."

The door at my back swings on its hinge, and Freja, fretting her teeth along her lip, tilts her head around mine. "Dearest. Best. Most precious one. Is your broken engagement *not* common knowledge in the palace?"

Dearest. Best. Alma. "I beg your pardon," I say. I damn near bow.

Every trace of the crown prince vanishes, and in one ferocious movement, I drag Alma from the kitchen and down the hall. We burst through the door of the flat, and I lean over the railing, looking down the three flights of stairs, and opt for the small alcove tucked between a window and the door, under a glowing green sign that reads "No exit."

I want answers now.

24

NARROW DIVIDE

ALMA

A seam of frigid air leaks around the window, stirring the valance. It should be a relief after the overheated flat, but it sharpens my senses, making it impossible to escape from an awareness of Jacob, standing over me in the dark.

Vede. The pretense of my engagement was a thick wall, reminding me of my position and dignity, keeping me from crossing boundaries and throwing myself at this man. Some days it was the only thing. Now that it's gone, we stare at one other across a narrow divide.

A song in Freja's flat ends, and another one begins—passionate and slow and Pavian. I need bracing Sondish clarity at this time of night. A rowdy polka to make us laugh.

My eyes meet Jacob's, and I brace myself for what's coming. Every trace of the crown prince I've taught him to be has vanished, replaced by something wild and untamed that has been there all along.

"You knew," he says, his voice hoarse. "You knew I wanted you."

I sway on my feet. I was ready to be called a liar. I wasn't ready for this.

Deep grooves bracket his mouth. "Why didn't you tell me about Pietor?"

I could never be afraid of him, but I'm terrified of this talk. Terrified that he'll see what I feel. Terrified of how many people I would disappoint and how many problems it would cause. Terrified of how far this might go.

Maybe Jacob doesn't see how far, but I do. It's not too late to go back to what we were before. I shake my head, "You didn't need to know."

"Alma," he growls, like the roar of Ulek the bear. "Don't pretend with me."

I dig through a collection of set expressions and practiced phrases, praying for one which will send him back to the party feeling like he had it wrong but that I haven't wronged him.

The longer I search, the more frantic I become. Wearing my royal persona used to be as easy as a knight in his armor, but I feel the clang and pinch of each piece as it's unbuckled and cast aside. When Jacob is around, the heaviness of chain mail is lifted from my shoulders, and I am vulnerable.

The thought sends a shaft of panic through me. "That's a personal question."

Jacob's face is stern and unbending. He narrows the distance between us. "Are you engaged?"

I swallow a knot in my throat, and press my palms flat against the door at my back. "What does the news say?"

The air shifts. I train my eyes on the tiny dots in his tie, and his voice drops as he braces his hands on either side of my head, looking at me straight on. "What's the truth?"

There isn't enough room between us for evasion.

I run my tongue over dry, unsteady lips, and music from the flat weaves through my veins. He's so close and he smells so good and I'm so tired of running. I lift my eyes, dismantling the last of my defenses. "I broke it off at Christmas. When—"

In a heartbeat, the distance between us vanishes. His mouth is on mine, hot, hungry, and demanding a response. I kiss him back, crushing rich wool suiting in my fists, and working my way closer as a not insignificant number of my brain cells go up in flames.

Finally. *Finally.*

Cradled between a door and a future king, I can't slow my pace. Jacob brushes his fingers along my neck, thumb resting in the hollow behind my ear, fitting me to him piece by piece. With every kiss, we mend the damage I caused by a lifetime of living like a miser, doling out affection one thin penny at a time.

His arm circles my waist, pulling me up to my toes, and his chest rises and falls under my hands. I feel every broken breath and some distant voice—some distant Alma—tells me it's too soon. That's what they'll say if anyone ever finds out about this. They'll say Jacob is a rebound.

I sigh against his lips.

There isn't room for a crowd of judgmental strangers—not my mother, her prime minister, or members of esteemed financial institutions—on this tiny landing. Just us.

He lifts his head, and I wait for second thoughts to run up on me like a tide. But I dance away, out of their reach, pulling his head down, kissing him, breathing in his scent again.

"Alma." His voice is husky. He sags against the door, and when he straightens his hands band my wrists. He pulls away, settling against the far wall, a tuck in his cheek.

I walk into his arms because creating distance is stupid when we don't have to. I can't think—I don't want to think—but I know I belong there. He folds me close and strokes my back with a shaking hand.

"Why didn't you tell me?" he asks.

I look up. "No one was supposed to know. Just family."

His cold fingers trace a path down the back of my arm, and I shiver. He rests his cheek on my hair. "Couldn't you see—"

"I didn't think it would matter," I say.

He gives my shoulders a light shake. *It matters.*

"You were going back to Vorburg. You weren't supposed to be"—I search for a word—"*you.*"

"You weren't supposed to be you, either," he laughs. Jacob lowers his head, mouth sinking against mine for a quick kiss. This is why he had to know. Because we've wanted to do this for weeks. Because every time he looks at me, I see it, and every time I look at him, I am undone.

He lifts his head a fraction and rubs the back of his hand against my cheek. "I deserved to know you weren't engaged."

My brain cells are fighting for their lives. "Pietor and I are still engaged as far as *The Holy Pelican* and *PAPZ* and *Sondmark Sports Fishing Monthly* knows. We have to be."

His hand checks and his eyes blaze. "The hell you do."

As much as I want to stay here, he has to understand. As I step out of his arms, the cold night air beyond the glass envelops me, and I shiver.

"We have to be officially engaged for a few more months while Sondmark and Himmelstein wrap up trade negotiations with Vorburg. Everything is in a delicate position, and there are a million ways to cause offense or be caught up in a news cycle." I reach for his hand, willing him to understand. "Even the smallest things can put the negotiations in jeopardy."

"Smallest things?" The line of his mouth is grim, and he gives our handclasp a light swing.

Does he imagine that I think this is small? Admitting to myself that I want this man is a rebellion. Admitting it to him is a revolution. There isn't anything small about it, but he steps away, bracing himself against the stair railing.

"Where does that leave us?"

I shiver again, feeling all the frustration of running on a treadmill, flying over ground but never going anywhere. I look around the landing—at the 'No exit' sign over our heads, glowing green. "I'm right where I want to be."

He looks up. "In a dimly lit hall where we have to worry about someone coming through the door or up the stairs?"

This spot of ground has been heaven. "For now."

Jacob takes a deep breath. He touches my face with a gentle hand, and I sway toward his arms.

"No." The word is firm, unequivocal.

I drop to my heels with a thud. "Pardon?"

"You can let everyone think you're engaged. That's your choice. You have your reasons, maybe, but I'm not fifteen." His eyes are sad but he speaks too clearly to be misunderstood. "I don't sneak."

I flinch at the word. What does he expect of me? "This isn't sneaking. This is discretion."

I hear a scrape, and he turns his head quickly. I pull myself together, and run a thumb across my lips, hoping the kisses don't show, reaching for an excuse. *I needed air. It's cooler here. We're discussing the state visit.* Anything to ward off suspicion.

Jacob exhales—abrupt, jagged—and looks down. He swings his shoe, and I hear the source of the sound. When he looks at me, his smile is apologetic, but there is heartbreak in his eyes. He reaches for me, touches a spot on my neck, and my pulse jumps raggedly under his thumb. His hand slips down my arm, catching mine. "This is sneaking."

"My sister," I say, tipping my chin toward the flat, "ran off to get married. I'm happy for her, but her right to the succession is being debated within government circles already." If he can't understand, it's because he's new at being royal. He's never had every action devoured by the public and picked clean. I have to make him see.

"My other sister has embarked on the unprecedented action of taking a member of the press to court because her private life was treated like clickbait. My family has sacrificed and bled for Sondmark for eight hundred years, Jacob. I can't just—"

"I know." He grips my hand like he'll never let it go. "I know. I don't have an eight-hundred-year-old reason."

"Then why?" I'm afraid of the answer, and I feel like I did when I was a child, crushing a rocking horse under my careless step. Like I should have known better. My voice is raw, vulnerable in a way I don't let anyone see. "Did I misread this? Is it nothing to you?"

He gathers my hands together, holding them between his, the answer as soft as midnight. "I spent my life being someone my father had to hide." He's not fighting. I almost wish he was. "I want this—all of it—but I can't be your secret."

I register the words and my eyes sting. I don't tell myself fairy tales. The responsibilities I feel for my family and my country are in direct conflict with his needs. No number of suspicious beans, magical godmothers, or anthropomorphic mice are going to make them disappear.

The chill off the window makes my teeth clench.

"We have to get back to the party," he says, voice gentle.

I blink. I'm supposed to have the right answers for every problem, but I don't know what to do now except follow his lead.

We return to the flat and meet Freja pacing the hall. Jacob gives her a brisk nod as he passes, but she catches my arm.

Her brows are drawn in worry. "I'm so sorry. You have to forgive me. You're together all the time, and I saw how friendly you were with each other. I thought he was someone you trusted."

I look into my sweet sister's face and hate her just a little bit. I hate her for not seeing that he's more to me than that. I hate that I'm hiding it so well. I hate that she managed to carry off a whole *flamen* wedding without telling the people who love her best. I know she knows how to keep her mouth shut. "You should get back to your guests," I say. "It's nothing."

But I stand on the edge of the party, watching Noah in a game of "Spicy Pepper" with some of Oskar's cousins, Ella in deep conversation with a man introduced as Uncle Timo, Max and Clara leaning against the bookshelves whispering, Freja and Oskar ignoring everyone as they sway to the music, and my parents presenting a polite face to the world. These are my people, but for the first time in my life, I want to scooch my chair over and add one more seat to this tight circle.

What I feel for Jacob is not nothing.

25

Performance Review

JACOB

The rest of the night is hell.

Alma emerges from the kitchen, her cheeks pale and drawn. I turn away before I give into the temptation to carry her into the landing and say I changed my mind, tripping over the words, and get back to the kissing.

Instead, I rope Max into a conversation about his cottage and the kind of sport fishing he goes in for. He offers to have me up again, but I can never go back there with Alma. I don't trust myself with her in that much seclusion. Oskar wanders into our circle and presses cold drinks into our hands, content with not saying much.

A dark dress catches the edge of my vision, and I grip the glass. There's a famous story about a Scandinavian ship, the largest of its kind, sailing from the harbor on its maiden voyage. The crowds were waving, and the ship-builders were still slapping each other on the backs over their excellent craftsmanship when it abruptly sank. It never made it out of the harbor.

Ella taps my shoulder. "Alma has a headache."

I look over the room. "Where is she? Can I get her some water?"

She lifts her brow. "She's having security run her home, but she'll send the car back for us."

Alma doesn't bail on events just because she has a headache. I give a tight nod and return to my drink.

The week that follows is a test of my resolve. I am polite and professional. The tutoring sessions hum with activity as we cover royal procedure and diplomacy. Karl is puzzled when he catches me being too obedient. Alma is the Alma I met weeks ago—rigid and careful. The difference now is that I see the effort underneath.

I do the only thing I can do to ease her burdens. I force myself to absorb every scrap of information she imparts and learn every lesson she has to teach. She is polite, but there is frustration in the line of her shoulders and the way her eyes linger. The toll this takes on me is that this is hell—knowing she wants me and that my stupid pride is the only thing keeping us apart.

She continues to be seen with Pietor.

One morning, she drives me in a golf cart to a large garage with rows of vintage Bentleys and several Mercedes. She's wearing a blazer and slacks, and as usual, I can't stop checking her out.

"Today we'll be working on cars—exiting, entering, and security protocols," she says, parking the cart out of the way. She greets Nils Helmut with a warm smile.

"I know how to get out of a car," I tell her, forgetting my resolve to be easy.

"Oh?" She gestures toward a customized Mercedes town car, parked sideways in a wide-open area. "Show me."

The head of palace security watches us behind dark glasses, and I feel self-conscious when I enter, dragging the door closed. "Now get out," she calls, voice muffled through the thick glass.

I hop out and slam the door, jogging over to her.

"Wrong," she chirps. I swear she enjoys it.

"I got out of the car." The air between us crackles with all the things we've said and done, all the things we'd like to do. Even as we fall into the familiar pattern of teacher and student, there are new layers.

"Would you show him, Nils?" she asks the security officer. He points two fingers in a pattern between me and two orange cones on the other side of the parking stall.

"Those represent the 'entrance' of whatever event you're arriving at," he says, "which makes this the most dangerous stretch of ground, from a security standpoint. We can secure that"—he points at the car like he's deploying soldiers through a strategic pathway—"and the venue. We've got bomb-sniffing dogs and security perimeters to lock it down. This"—his fingers sketch an outline of the concrete—"has more variables. When you follow the protocols, you give your team a better chance of keeping you safe."

"This isn't about you," Alma tells me. "You're not Jacob who runs a business. You're the heir to the throne—the representation of the state made manifest in your blood. If anyone injures you, they've injured more than a man." She lifts her brows, deadly serious. *Got it?*

I love you. I shake my head. *Got it.*

"Watch me." She takes my place in the backseat of the car and emerges from the opening in one smooth movement and sweeps forward. "Don't go on a walkabout unless you've cleared it with your security first. Security doesn't like surprises."

Nils closes the door and nods along. I can imagine him putting a teenaged Alma through the same paces, forcing her to recite his words like a litany. *Security doesn't like surprises.*

I nod, taking my place next to the car. "Get out, shut the door, proceed to the venue."

"No."

"I messed up already?" She laughs, which is the first one of those I've heard in days. My heart stumbles, and I grin. I can't help it. "I thought I wanted to be a man of the people."

"The merits of being a man of the people are debatable, but the reason you can't shut the door is because they lock when they're closed."

"That seems dangerous."

"Nils?" she prompts. Grabbing a heavy wrench, she bangs it against a metal work table. *Pop, pop, pop.*

At the sound, I freeze. Nils moves fast, shoving me up against the car, shoving my head down as he fumbles for the handle, yanking on it several times. Time slows to a crawl, and all the while, Alma keeps hitting the table.

After a few frantic seconds, Nils relaxes and I straighten, pushing a hand through my hair and smoothing my tie with an unconscious gesture.

"*Chol nia*, what was that?"

She throws the wrench down with a clatter. "That was the sound of shots fired. In the event of a real-life emergency, having a closed door wastes precious seconds. If something happens, the safest place is to bundle you back into the car and speed you to a safe place. Your security can't waste precious seconds trying to get the door open."

"Has that ever happened to you?" The thought makes my blood turn to ice.

Her neck tightens, and she picks up the wrench, returning it to its home. "Historically, Sondmark hasn't had a lot of assassination attempts. The nineteenth century was different, of course. Anarchists were always blowing up carriages or knifing grand duchesses on holiday."

She's not looking at me, and her lips are dry as she continues. "Vorburg has had a worse time, I think—"

Doesn't she know I know when she's hiding? I cut her off, pinning Nils with my gaze. "Has she ever had her security compromised?"

He nods. "A few times. The one that taught us the most happened more than a decade ago. A union strike got out of hand, and we were lucky no one had a gun. One of them made it into the car."

"He got right out again," Alma rushes, bundling the memory away.

I pin Nils with a look.

"Because she ordered the driver out of the car and refused to take the assailant to the palace." He glances at Alma. "Nerves of steel, that one."

She shakes her head. "Thank you very much, Nils. I'll take it from here."

The head of security jogs off, and Alma steers me to the Mercedes. A flame ignites at her touch.

She pushes me onto the seat, hands braced on the roof and the door, trapping me with her frame. I want to wrap my arms around her waist and pull her inside, to make a little trouble in the backseat of a car like a couple of kids.

"Jacob." Her voice snaps me out of my thoughts. "You have to remember the security implications of getting out of a car. No matter what flourishes I add next, don't forget that Nils already taught you the only thing you have to know. If you always do what your security team says, you'll be in good hands."

Her eyes are intent, and I nod. "Do what they say," I repeat. "I won't forget."

"Good. Now I'll help you with the aesthetics."

"I have an aesthetics problem?" I hold her eyes. This has been the most difficult week of my life, and I can't stop wanting her.

"Stop it," she whispers. For a second, I see how weak she is for me.

Alma clears her throat. "Most of your paparazzi shots will be as you cover this stretch of ground. Get it right, and you'll be in control of the press rather than them being in control of you. Now..." She pushes me deeper into the car and wedges herself in the narrow space between me and the door she closes behind her. The dark interior of the Mercedes feels like a cave at twilight, embers dying in the fire. No one can see through these windows. It would take so little to bend my head.

She catches my expression and tilts her chin, exposing the column of her neck.

"Stop it," I whisper.

Her lashes flicker in triumph but she hasn't forgotten that I'm here to get an education. "You won't have a skirt to manage, so it's relatively straightforward. The trick is to be simple and direct," her hand touches my knee, and I grip the leather seat, trying not to go deaf and blind with wanting her.

"Try not to twist too much as you exit," she continues. "Left leg out, straighten, followed by the right. Fasten your suit button—" Her lips twitch.

"What?"

"That's the picture they'll post, if you get it right—you buttoning up your suit."

"Why?"

She lifts a shoulder. "It makes you all look like medieval knights, snapping their helmets down and charging the dread host with blood and vengeance at the end of your lance."

"Is this a good thing?"

Again, she smiles, and it gives way to stupid laughter. That kiss released something we can't lock back up. I want her. She wants me. We can't unknow it.

"All right," she breathes, reaching for the door handle. I watch her get out, buttoning her jacket. *Chol*, I'd believe she's on her way to poison an archbishop.

"Now you," she says, closing the door on my hungry face. She retreats to a maintenance cart, leaning against it.

Having received so much instruction, my movements are jerky under her exacting gaze.

"You're like a marionette. Now try it without thinking so hard."

I repeat the process several times, getting smoother each time, looking for her approval. "Stop worrying about what I think," she says. "You're the crown prince of Vorburg, and you've come to solve the housing crisis or weed out corruption in the financial sector. Be sure to turn to greet the crowd." I wave and even that comes under scrutiny. "Dial that down. You're not a puppy looking for attention. You already have it."

She runs me through my paces several more times. More than necessary. Finally, I get it through my thick skull that she's checking me out.

"Alma," I admonish, pushing the button through the hole for the ninth time, "what are you doing?" I turn and give a brief wave, walking to the cones. The process over, I make my way to her. I should stop well away, put my hands in my pockets, and wait for the performance review. I don't. I inch close, crowding

her against the workbench, and placing my hands on either side o
f her.

"Do I need to make a human resources complaint?" I ask.

She looks unrepentant. "What would you tell them?"

"I'd tell them a princess of Sondmark is objectifying me." I
inch closer. I'm playing with fire, flicking the lighter and rolling
my fingers through the orange flame. This is going to end with
third-degree burns.

She bites her lip and runs her finger down my lapel with a
light touch. "You're not the crown prince of Sondmark." *You're
not the boss of me.*

My feelings for her are like a foot planted between my shoulder blades, forcing me into her arms. She would take me. I'm an
idiot to refuse.

I drop my head. "Alma," I groan, "we agreed not to do this."

She runs a hand through my hair, gripping it, a sound of
frustration in her throat as she tugs my head back. "I agreed to
nothing of the sort. There are good reasons to delay announcing
my broken engagement," she says, eyes dipping to my mouth.
"And you can't stop me from hoping you'll change your mind."

I've felt this feeling—an echo of it—on a motorcycle. Pouring
through a turn, hitting gravel, and feeling the control slip, slip,
slip. Surrendering myself to the inevitability of pain. A fool
would know better than to play around with this.

I'm worse than a fool.

I narrow the distance between us. A flush washes over her cheeks, her hand slips out of my hair, and she tips her face up. If I have to suffer this temptation, she'll suffer with me.

"It could be you," I say, lips a breath away from her mouth, "who changes her mind. You could announce that you're done with Pietor and that you've taken up with a man from Vorburg. You could do it today."

I want to give her a taste of my own torment. Instead, I'm caught in the dangerous undertow of how much I want *her*. Her breath hitches, and her eyes drift closed.

I—

I hear a metal door clang open. Alma ducks past me, and I drop my head.

Karl's voice rings across the spacious garage. "His Majesty the King is on the phone, Your Royal Highness. He would like to speak with you."

26

— · —

DILIGENT STUDENT

ALMA

The following week, I gather with Jacob's team in the drawing room for a short stretch of instruction before I have to run off to a family meeting. Seated at the table, I catch my reflection in one of the palace mirrors. Despite a carefully managed diet, regular exercise, and challenging work, my resolve to uncomplainingly carry the burdens of royal life has worn thin. Keeping myself from Jacob is arduous.

I thought I was happy before. I had my father, brother, and sisters. My mother trusted me to support her at every turn. Pietor's infidelity was an obstacle to be surmounted, not stumbled over. Then Jacob happened.

Karl drills the crown prince, going over key dates in the Soviet invasion and eventual fall of Vorburg, and my mind wanders. I've spent all these weeks trying to make Jacob more like me—someone content to sit primly with her hands folded in her lap while the thing she wants most in the world lies within her reach. In some ways I've succeeded. His appearance has sharpened. His grasp on protocol is growing comfortable.

In all other ways, it's been a disaster. I've changed far more than he has.

Karl asks a follow-up question about the rise of the dissident movement, and Jacob's hand brushes mine under the table. I close my eyes. This isn't an accident. We've traded these covert gestures all week, becoming more reckless.

Karl crosses the room to consult a research library for the answer, and Jacob leans over. "Announce the broken engagement," he whispers.

I want to pull a fire alarm and alert everyone to the fact that I haven't been engaged for weeks, but I grip the edges of the table, drawing my hand away. "Have sense."

I'm not that reckless. Not yet. Though I want to find out what these feelings between us will become, I can't publicly cut Pietor loose until after the trade negotiations. Keeping us a secret is a mutually beneficial solution to an attraction that could easily get out of hand, damaging the long-term success of his country and mine.

Karl places materials in front of Jacob. "Memorize the main points, if you will, sir. I'll fetch a book with more details from my room." He excuses himself, leaving Jacob and me alone.

Jacob plucks up a page, and I lean over his shoulder, my hair brushing the side of his neck. He freezes, like one of the carriage horses before a parade.

"Alma." His head tips back and his jaw sets, I see the effort he puts into holding himself back.

I touch his upturned face as we watch each other. "You're not the only one trying to change someone's mind."

An alarm beeps on my phone, and I straighten. "I have to go," I say, reaching for my portfolio, my color high.

Are we just trying to persuade each other when we touch? Maybe it's simply that we can't help it.

I mull over these questions at the family meeting, even as the wheels of Mama's constitutional monarchy grind around me. No one asks about Pavieau and the strange softening Mama exhibited when she sent Freja to meet our family. We know how to be patient while Mama decides what to tell us. At the conclusion of the meeting, she holds me back. "How is His Royal Highness doing?"

I guard the truth that I've never withstood a temptation like the Crown Prince of Vorburg, that we are in a standoff about whether we're going to start kissing at regular intervals, and that I would give anything this minute to forget I'm a princess of Sondmark.

"Have you managed to sew a satin bonnet from the bundle of rags?" she smiles, amused at the folk saying.

I swallow. "He's a diligent student. King Otto will have no cause for complaint."

"That's the most important thing," she says, "to clear us of this debt. We can't be rid of him fast enough." Her chin tips away, and she asks, "When does he return to Vorburg?"

"A fortnight," Caroline supplies. "We just received the itinerary from Djolny."

I knew it was coming, but to have it spelled out so clearly is like a hand on my throat.

"It can't come too soon." Mama touches my cheek and shakes her head. "While your sisters are exploring the novelty of pursuing their own self-interest, I miss having my steady right hand."

Caroline taps a few strokes on her tablet. "His Royal Highness will be receiving little more than a week of Vorburgian court training in conjunction with briefings on their end of the state visit. They don't have much time."

"They should take him now and do a proper job of it," Mama declares. "Perhaps I should mention it to the embassy."

"No," I say. My eyes shift away. "I have more to teach him."

Mama nods and turns to go.

Caroline shoots me the briefest glance. Heaven knows what she sees. "He'll be back before long," she murmurs.

He won't be back in the same way. When King Otto's royal motorcade pulls up to the front entrance of the Summer Palace, a tiny flag affixed to the roof of the car, he won't be arriving with Jacob. He'll be accompanied by His Royal Highness, Crown Prince Jacob of Vorburg. Our roles will be clear, defined, and constricting.

Whether he wants them to or not, his priorities will shift. His allegiance will be to a hostile throne, and these feelings between us might evaporate into nothing. No matter what promises he wants to make, he's a future monarch who may never have any use for a Sondish princess. In the face of so many risks, it's wise to choose discretion.

When I return to my suite, I find him kneeling in front of my dollhouse, a tiny paintbrush in his hand, daubing glue along a loose chair railing. In the weeks since he took up the project, several rooms have returned to their former glory, the staircase in the Great Hall as sturdy and elegant as the real thing.

"Finished?" he asks, intent on his task. "How did it go?"

I dump my portfolio in a chair. "Noah is getting grouchy in his old age. He hates Karl for reasons I can't understand."

Jacob grunts a laugh. "Is your mother going to let Ella come to the state dinner in a trouser suit?"

I kick my shoes off and kneel over the back of the sofa, watching him. Each move he makes is controlled and certain.

"They got into it for twenty minutes. Honestly, Ella would kill in a pair of narrow black pants but it's nearly impossible to pair that kind of thing with a sash, orders, and a tiara."

I don't stop to weigh my words or wonder how he'll use them. What's happened to me?

"I heard Max was coming to a family dinner." He wipes a bead of glue and moves to the next section of paneling. "True?"

"Who are you gossiping with?"

He smiles over his shoulder. This isn't part of persuading each other, but I'm tempted nevertheless. "I built Nils a new filing system for the guard house."

I touch his cheek with the back of my hand. He doesn't pull away but leans into it, closing his eyes and breathing deeply. I need this. He needs this. "It's true. Mama extended an invitation after Freja's housewarming. It looks like Max the Naval Hottie has conquered the Summer Palace."

"Who are you calling a hottie?" His brow lifts.

My hand falls away and I smile. "Clara will be pleased." My little sister is over the moon, but I release a small sigh. Jacob gets to his feet, attuned to my shift in mood.

"I'm not giving in," he says before he settles in the corner of the sofa and gathers me into his arms, wrapping me in an embrace that keeps me from getting fuzzy around the edges.

Clara is a fighter. Freja never consulted anyone before acting to secure her own happiness. These facts trouble the House of Wolffe, but Mama's forbearance of my two siblings doesn't herald a newfound liberality toward the rest of us. She called me her steady right hand. My role is helping her to keep the ship of state on an even keel.

The broken engagement is trouble enough, but I'm sure she has Caroline running up a new list. Perhaps she's already engineering an event to perform a quick, economical series of introductions. Maybe she's planning, this time next year, to begin a series of discreet appearances, rolling him—this invisible suitor's face has no form or substance—out slowly. I will be her great hope.

What would she say if I demanded that a certain Vorburgian prince be placed on the spreadsheet?

I push out all thoughts of Mama and burrow more deeply into Jacob's arms. "I'm not giving in," I echo.

We stay like that for more than an hour. A setting sun reflects off a mirror and travels across my closed eyelid, turning the world to amber.

Jacob's phone pings a notification and I read the text. *See? Nothing to worry about. Test results are on the patient portal if you want to be nosy. When are you coming home?*

"What's that?" I ask.

"It's my mom. She battled cancer when I was a kid." I nod. I know that part of the story. "She still needs regular check-ups, but I prefer to go to appointments with her, if I can."

I lace my fingers through his.

"You agreed to be the crown prince because of her," I say. I wondered for so long, but now I know without asking. It wasn't that she pushed him into it. It wasn't because he wanted it. It wasn't the title or the castle. For all our differences, Jacob is as loyal to his family as I am to mine.

"I was an inconvenient kid. I came along at the wrong time. I was the reason she went back to Blackberry, and I ate like a horse." He pulls me in more tightly.

"None of that was your fault."

"I know." He brushes a thumb along my index finger. "I know. She could have gotten rid of me or dumped me on my grandparents but she—"

"Willingly took up the duties laid at her feet," I finish. "She became a new creature to meet the challenging road before her?"

I understand now. He was formed by a woman who knew how to make a sacrifice. I wonder if King Otto knows how lucky he is that Tiffani Fawn Gardner is the mother of his heir.

"Stop trying to draw parallels, Alma," he says. "The cancer scared her, and she wanted me to know my father."

"And when the judgment came down?"

"We were all surprised. She didn't ask me to do it."

"But she wanted you to."

He breathes deeply. "You were going to tell me why I don't want to be a man of the people," he reminds me, bringing our hands up to kiss. We're acting as though we have settled things between us—as though wanting an agreement is the same as having it.

I lay my head against his heart, feel the steady beat, and answer the old question. "The money and luxuries of royal life aren't what set you apart from your subjects. In a sense, those things are just bribes to make it worth turning your life over to the country and becoming a national symbol. Though there's always bound to be low-level grousing about the cost of running a monarchy, no one really expects a symbol to take the trash out and bring the wash in. To fight traffic or the national healthcare system."

"Being a symbol doesn't seem much fun."

"It isn't."

I hear the smile in his voice. "My father had fun."

I lift my head. "You will *not* have fun like that."

He grins and presses my head against his heart again. I go on, more reasonably. "It was a different time. No social media. No phones in every pocket. He could get away with behavior you'll never be allowed. Also, he was their king when it mattered most."

Jacob grunts. "You'd think he was the one who defeated Communism."

"Stop thinking like an American. We don't have the creeds you do. No, 'We hold these truths to be self-evident, that all men are created equal...' For good and bad, it's bloodier than that. We have land. A tribe. A king."

I roll until I can look him in the eyes, chin against his chest. "The Cold War almost stamped out your national identity. Folk dress and traditional songs were outlawed. Feast days were re-purposed for revolutionary figures. It was your father who kept the light burning."

Jacob frowns. "He kept it burning with a lot of anonymous blondes."

I hold his face between my hands. "His life is proof that Vorburg itself survived. When he dies, you won't come to the funeral as his son. You'll be expected to stand in the place of your people and mourn for *them*—to be the public, uncomplaining, inhuman face of national grief. Strangers will cast themselves into your arms and expect you to comfort them."

"I won't know how to do that."

I smooth the tightness around his mouth with a light touch. "I don't believe that anymore."

Each day we spend together is precious, and as they speed by, I can't surrender myself to the simple enjoyment of being with him. There's too much pain when I think of the future. In order to throw a cloak of protection over him when the time comes to meet the world, I redouble my efforts. I'm merciless, reviewing every scrap of information and demanding mastery.

I wake up one morning to discover there are only three days left, and when I meet him in the drawing room, I want to burst into tears. His greeting is practiced and smooth. He doesn't need me anymore.

"You look beautiful this morning," he whispers over my hand.

I imagine a future and close my eyes against it. "You said that yesterday."

He picks up the agenda. "It was true yesterday," he murmurs, wearing an expression that warms my cheeks. He lifts the page. "It just says staircase. What are we doing?"

"We have to practice our entrance for the state visit." He follows me from the room, and from the top of the grand staircase, I explain the logistics, resting my hand lightly on his arm. The contact is at once comfortable and electric.

"The press will be limited to two journalists—one video feed, and a single photographer," I say, pointing at a corner of the Great Hall. "There is no need to look at them until we hit our mark." He starts off, and I tug at his sleeve. "Too fast. Remember, I'll be in a tiara and ballgown. You will have to adjust your pace. Watch me."

"I'm an expert at that." He shoots me a smoldering look, too comical to hurt. It does anyway.

"Jacob," I hiss, taking refuge in my role. "If the photographer captures that expression, we'll be all over the papers for a month."

His cheek tucks. "What am I supposed to look at you like?"

"Like I'm a cousin."

He grins. "What, am I Moses? You can't expect miracles."

We're halfway down the stairs when Pietor storms through the front door, his face shining and red. The doors shake on their hinges, and the tall mirrors throw dancing light onto the marble tiles.

"Alma." He clips my name like I'm a dog being brought to heel. The muscles under my hand gather, and I grip Jacob's arm.

"Pietor," I clip back. "What brings you?"

"I was at the Grousehof." A look of cold fury seeps into his watery blue eyes. "You said this"—he stabs a finger at me and then Jacob, words tumbling out of him—"was a job, but a reporter came up to me and made other insinuations. Do you know what it makes me look like to have someone as uptight as you choosing a knuckle-dragging American bastard? You *vrou*—"

With lightning speed, Jacob rips out of my grasp and runs down the stairs. He chokes off the obscenity with a fist around Pietor's tie, and yanks the hereditary grand duke high onto his toes, propelling him backward, through the door and onto the front steps. Pietor makes indistinct squealing noises and claws impotently at the rough hand.

Jacob doesn't say a word but releases Pietor with a brutal shake. If the *vailys* is willing to step one foot down, he won't fall, but Pietor refuses to give an inch. His arms windmill, and he skids down three shallow steps, landing on his back in a splash of gravel.

Swiping dust from his trousers, he jerks his clothes into order and smooths his hair. "He's a piece of garbage, Alma. He can't protect you. His title is worthless."

He half turns to go, then charges Jacob, catching him in the midsection, and ripping his hair loose. Jacob grabs him off, lands a punch, and blood gushes from Pietor's nose.

"Bastard," he spits, crimson specks dotting the steps. "Do you know who my father is? You think I can't take you down? You're going to be a laughingstock when I'm through." He delivers this to Jacob, walking backward, and slams into his car.

The engine pings to life, and the threat penetrates my brain. There was malice in Pietor's words, and he has the power to back them up. *Stultes es.* What have I let happen? Stupid pride. All I had to do was swallow Pietor's insults and show him out. Now Jacob is his target.

Pietor's electric sports car whirrs into the distance, and Jacob brushes his sleeves, raking the hair back. This is my fault. I had forgotten how high the stakes are.

"Excuse me," he murmurs with a laugh. "I had to take out the, er, *svet.*"

I want to burst into tears. "You can't do that," I shout. "Ever. You're not a private citizen. This has consequences."

"Even when he called you *vrou*—? Well, I don't know what it was supposed to be, but it can't be nice."

It isn't. "I've been called worse."

His expression darkens, eyes lit with deadly fire. "By who?"

Vede, he's taking names. "Whom."

27

—·—

Roslav Cathedral

JACOB

At first, Alma tries to reason with me.

"You can't engage in behavior like that," she argues, her voice loud and tight. She paces our sitting room, running out of space and striding back.

"He was asking for it. This dirt weasel barges into your palace and calls you—"

"Stop. Stop." She holds a hand up. "I don't care about your reasons. Think about what you owe to your people. Markets are going to go haywire every time you form a grudge. You'll be an embarrassment instead of a diplomatic asset. *Vede*, Jacob, don't throw this away because you can't swallow a few insults."

At this moment, all I want to do is get rid of my title. What has being a crown prince ever given me?

Nothing but my mother's peace. Nothing but knowing Alma.

Chol. Chol nia.

"You can't let people treat you like there's no line you won't let them cross," I counter. Surely her people would understand that. Vorburgian people would. Not sure about soft Handselites.

"He has the power to hurt you," she says, voice shaking.

Who cares? I would have shrugged off anything Pietor said about me. But he attacked Alma. "I've got twenty-five pounds on him that say otherwise."

She bangs a fist into the sofa and growls her frustration. She thinks I'm stupid. I think Pietor shouldn't have started something if he didn't want me to finish it.

"He wasn't bluffing. I don't know what weapon he'll use, but he has one, and you just begged him to use it."

I reach for her fist, working it free with my thumb. It loosens, but she turns her face away. Weak winter sun shines through the mullioned windows, and dust motes dance in the light. I hear her sniff.

"Alma. Don't ask me not to fight for you," I say, my voice rough.

She breathes in and out, a slow cycle, then drags her hand away, slams through her bedroom door, and shoots the bolt home for good measure.

The Cold War is back on.

Karl and Caroline speak only when spoken to. Mr. Tumwater clicks his tongue and shakes his head, doing the final fitting on my tuxedo. Alma gives up on trying to persuade, blasting me instead with an arctic wind. I retreat into a shell of silence and manly pride. I can't understand her, and she won't understand me.

That's it, then. A bastard prince of Vorburg and a princess of Sondmark were always going to be a hard sell.

My father sends an itinerary via Karl. Mom chats via video message as she cycles from the market, showing off her cancer-fighting greens, and reminding me to represent Blackberry well.

"Are you getting sleep?" she asks.

"I'm getting sleep," I say.

I'm not getting any sleep. Everything hurts.

I stare hard at the door of my suite, memorizing the lines as well as I've memorized Alma's face. I text Ella, gaming with her when I need to get out of my head. Every night.

"You're coming back, though," Ella says, her pixelated avatar carrying a pixelated brick to a pixelated castle wall and slotting it into position.

The game isn't destructive enough, and I distract myself by looking around the room. Ella's space has a lot of color and patterns. "When did you all move into your own suites?" I ask, fighting off a sneaker—one of the pixelated marauders who crop up occasionally to tear down the buildings. His pieces spring apart and absorb into the ground as mulch.

"As soon as we moved on to college or the military academy. Mama gave Noah and Alma adjoining suites so they'd feel more independent. They got a kitchen. I got a hotpot." I laugh. "Noah moved to Lily Cottage a few years ago. He has a dog."

"Did she let you decorate?" I've glimpsed enough of the other rooms to know they're all stamped with a personal style. Freja's has the look of a stately English home, Clara's is a mix of antique pieces and ultra-modern accents—pastels and gold. Ella's is three fandoms in a trench coat.

Ella rubs her nose and pushes up her glasses. "She tried to steer us but used words like 'appropriate' and 'classic'. I don't speak that language."

I glance at the stuffed raccoons piled on her bed. "You don't say."

She elbows me hard, and I chase down a sneaker, axing it in the back.

"If we had let her get her way, I'd have brocade wallpaper and Aubusson rugs, matching pillows with no tassels whatsoever."

"You're describing Alma's room."

Ella's mouth drops open. "She actually let you in?"

"Just a peek," I lie. No need to tell her about taking her sister's hair down, of standing in her doorway and having her do my tie, of reading paperbacks late into the night. "It looks like a build-your-own palace bedroom kit."

That's not entirely true. The top of a console table is stuffed with family photos over the years—candid pictures instead of the carefully posed portraits of a royal family or press images from tiara events. These pictures include muddy hands and sandcastles. Rabbit ears and zits. My grandparents have one of those shelves.

"She has plenty of her own personality. Don't make the mistake of thinking she doesn't," Ella warns. "People are always calling her this perfect princess, but there's no such thing."

Ella sounds like she stands next to her sister, armed with a gaming controller, prepared to fend off all attackers.

"She is perfect," I murmur, the controls going slack in my hands. "No one is more terrifyingly prepared than your sister. If I walk into a room without reading the briefing materials ahead of time, she makes me regret it. She's sharp and relentless. If she makes a mistake, she owns up to it. She's smart and funny. I was—"

"Dude. Sneakers wiped out my north wing while you were monologuing."

"Sorry," I say, tapping a few buttons and upgrading my weapon. "I'll clear the area."

I'm creating a pixel-bath of dismembered attackers when Ella clears her throat.

"Alma isn't the kind to bawl her eyes out about a break-up. Is something going on I don't know about?"

My answer comes fast. "Nope."

Yep.

I'm in love with Alma. The truth of it has settled on me during the last months like sawdust falling over my wrist—unnoticed while I worked on other things. But unlike sawdust, these feelings can't be brushed off.

I've tried. I keep telling myself a cute little story about how I just have to make it until Thursday. I'll pack my bags and have a few memories about falling for a girl I was all wrong for and how it didn't matter because we were never going to make it.

The real story is about how I fell completely in love with a woman intent on smoothing away my rough edges. How it hasn't worked. How I want to carry her back to Vorburg over my shoulder and fight every man in Sondmark if I have to. How I will never deserve her. How I would spend the rest of my life making her happy. How I want her next to me when I am king.

No one else. A shudder works up from my spine as I fight against accepting the unalterable fact. My father doesn't have another heir. What happens if I can't have Alma?

"You're still leaving in a few days?" Ella prods.

I imagine the future Alma has painted for me a thousand times. Frigid Djolny Castle. My father pushing me to marry and get myself an heir. Stumbling through thousands of meetings, receptions, and engagements.

I can do it. I can. Alma has taught me well. But a lifetime of doing it without Alma sounds like running a marathon on a belt sander. With every revolution, I'll get smoother and smoother, smaller and smaller. Eventually, I'll have to watch Alma move on. She'll find a brand new Pietor, and every step will be in the news. Parliamentary approval. Roslav Cathedral. Royal babies.

I flinch against the pain. It's still too easy to imagine another future. One in which I'm not a secret and she isn't placing me last on a list of considerations. Thanksgivings in Blackberry with the cousins. Roslav Cathedral. Restoring the castle. Our babies.

I swallow. The House of Wolffe could use some hearty peasant stock.

"The king has ordered me back," I answer.

Ella rolls her eyes as she maneuvers her avatar across a rope bridge. "Idiots."

28

— • —

Little Ceremony

ALMA

No amount of shouting will get Jacob to understand what he owes to his position, to his people, and to the responsibilities he has to take on. So I use the oldest war tactic in the book. I freeze him out.

It's an imperfect strategy. Unlike Napoleon's troops marching into Russia, he seems prepared for winter, digging in across the drawing room from me, his warm gaze thawing me faster than I can summon the cold. The barrier between us is translucent, brittle. It would take nothing to break through it.

On the night before he leaves, I lie in bed and watch the clock, eyes fastened on the second hand racing around its tiny axis. Four minutes until midnight. Three. Two.

The second hand is without mercy, and I want to throw the thing out the window, watching the priceless clockworks shatter against the stones. The minute hand turns over with a tiny click. Today is the day he leaves. I turn off the lamp and screw my eyes closed.

My commitment to Sondmark and my queen provide precious little comfort when I'm standing in the palace forecourt the next day. Though the sun is shining, a chilly wind blows up from the harbor, and I shiver. Karl, shoving a disreputable duffel bag into the boot of the car, holds a conversation with Caroline. I open my mouth to tell him to take care of the 'Johnny *Flamen* Marr' shirts, but Ella emerges from the doors, holding Jacob's arm as she navigates the steps.

They look comfortable together, and I can't stop the bitter thought that he should have fallen in love with her. If he had asked her to throw over every consideration of royal life and damn the consequences, she would have done it. She would have hacked into the security feed, climbed over the palace walls, and phoned for a getaway car.

I look away, into the wind.

"Cold, ma'am?" Caroline asks.

I turn with a set expression—neither pleased nor displeased, neither hopeful nor despairing. Neither happy to speed the parting guest nor wishing he would stuff me into the car and kidnap me to his foreign kingdom to love me forever. I blink rapidly.

Caroline bobs a curtsey. "I hope your stay was pleasant, sir."

Stultes es. That was my line. Jacob turns to me, performing the ceremony as though he was born to this. "Your Royal Highness," he murmurs.

My smile is weak. "We look forward to your return." We. *I.*

In the thin air of early spring, it's a wonder no one can hear the sound of heartbreak. When he comes back, I'll never have him to myself. He'll be the crown prince, and he won't be sleeping in the room next door. I want to scream and throw my shoes, demanding he see reason. None of this shows on my face, which is good. I haven't lost my touch.

But my lip shakes, and I catch it between my teeth. Holding my hand, Jacob leans forward, lips at my ear. "Don't look like that."

My hand tightens on his. *Don't go. Don't go.* But though the words rattle in my chest, the tether doesn't snap.

"Sir," Karl prompts. "We must respect the schedule."

Jacob steps back, taking half of me with him. Brisk spring wind sweeps across the lawn, ruffling the grass as he speeds away.

I sway on my feet. He's gone. He's really gone, but I can't take it in. It's as though I've dropped a penny into a bottomless well, and keep listening for the plink.

"Your mother wishes for a few minutes of your time," Caroline says.

At my mother's door, I brush my cheeks and check my expression. My face is pale and my eyes are hollow, but Mama doesn't see it. She glances from the papers in her dispatch box with a smile. "Has the barbarian finally departed?"

"Yes." But the penny is still dropping.

She hands off the final preparations for the state banquet. "Can you put a few hours into this? I've missed your support."

I nod and go to my formal office, a little-used room that has the benefit of not reminding me of Jacob at all.

For the remainder of the day, I work with half an eye to the queen's interests. The other half watches out for Jacob, making certain that things don't go wrong for his inaugural event.

By late afternoon, Mama summons me to her office again, and I'm brought up short by the sight of my former fiancé.

I've seen his picture in the press. After Jacob threw him out of the palace, he took a skiing holiday at a carbon-neutral resort in Switzerland, tanned skin visible in a band under his helmet, eyes squinting against the sun on snow. A balaclava hid his swollen nose and fat lip.

It's almost back to normal, I note, performing a curtsey to the queen. I can't bring myself to give Pietor the smallest sign of respect.

Hypocrite.

I've been furious at Jacob, raging that he must swallow his pride. Do the correct thing. Bow. Bend. Beg.

I can't.

Mama's brow lifts, but she escorts us to an arrangement of chairs overlooking the lawn and the ocean beyond. Dark clouds gather in the west, but Jacob should be over the mountains by now.

"Pietor," Mama prods, "may I ask—"

Pietor tosses a manilla envelope between us, and the rudeness of it shocks me. "My press secretary received this from *The Daily Missive.* They purchased it from a citizen photographer and want a comment before they run it." The look he gives me is scathing. "One of their journalists made contact several days ago. I denied everything, but they have evidence."

Mama removes a photograph, shaking it out and holding it up. I know how bad it must be when she goes completely still.

Obviously, Pietor and his philanthropic bikini model were caught. Stupid mistake. Stupid man. You never have ready access to a guillotine when you need one.

"What have you done?" I ask. "You know how careful we've had to be this month."

"I've done?" He snatches the photo from Mama and thrusts it into my hands. It takes a second to make sense of the blurry, truncated image, the play of shadows turning two figures into one.

Then I discern the outlines of vintage Sergei San Martin and gasp. No need for a guillotine. The image is of me and Jacob, moments after a kiss. His arm is around my waist and my soft eyes are lit by a streetlamp. *Dominanstid*. Is this how I look at Jacob when I think no one is watching?

Jacob's silhouette makes a bold stamp on a thin, white valance, but his identity is not immediately obvious. Nothing else matters.

"What am I supposed to do with this?" Pietor asks. His voice is petulant and furious. I would have spent my lifetime with him, running around, putting out fires, managing his emotions. "What am I supposed to tell my financiers?"

My lips feel cold. "When do they plan to run the picture?"

Already I've shifted into crisis management mode, but underneath it all I feel panic. I think Jacob—of all our long afternoons of northern European history, our bowing and walking, the security protocols, and the Pankedruss he tried to like. We have to make it count.

"Sunday. My fiancée will parade across the pages of *The Daily Missive* with another man." His eyes narrow and he adds with withering contempt, "I didn't think you'd need reminders about propriety, Alma."

"How dare you?" I accuse, my voice low and menacing. "How *dare* you? The picture shows nothing."

"Nothing?" Pietor counters, snatching the photo and slamming it down on the coffee table. "How much more did the photographer miss? Was the crown prince trying to get an heir? You've been throwing yourself at that consolation prize for months."

"Consolation prize?" I grit out, the words containing a deadly warning.

He ignores it. "Couldn't you have found anyone better?"

My hand snakes out and I slap him across the mouth, the crack loud and satisfying. "That's rich coming from a man whose family tree resembles a stick."

Pietor's skin is red and throbbing, and I ball my hand, but Mama grips my fist. "Enough," she commands, her tone furious. "That will do. The palace has no comment."

"And when they run the photo anyway?" Pietor spits, holding his face.

Mama's terrifying gaze swings between us. "All of us have things we need to protect, and we have a couple of days to work on the optics. Alma, are you willing to take part?"

When have I ever failed to support the monarchy? I loathe Pietor, but I know my duty. "I am."

Mama nods. "Your engagement must appear solid for the sake of Sondmark's trade deals and Himmelstein's investments."

"And Jacob's future," I add.

"And the health of Vorburg's monarchy," she allows, voice trembling with power. She pins Pietor and me with a look. "The two of you have a few days to play the devoted pair. Be as convincing as you can."

She holds my wrist, not my hand. Curbing, not consoling. My throat crowds with thick emotion. She's suggested a good, time-proven strategy. We need to get out in front of the news. Make the whole idea of a polished, firmly engaged princess running around with a rough-hewn giant ridiculous. The lie turns my stomach.

Mama gives Pietor a wintery smile. "*Vrouw* Tiele will send you an itinerary. Now, get out of my palace and never come back."

Pietor stalks from the room, his shoulders rigid, and Mama flings my hand away. Her voice is deadly. "When were you going to tell me about the liaison?"

Liaison. Jacob would laugh at the word. It's too French. Too insubstantial. Too fleeting. But this is how my mother sees it.

Jacob, with his Americanness, blue-collar profession, and vintage concert tees, wasn't ever going to be an option for Queen Helena.

"There's nothing to tell," I say.

She releases a shallow breath and taps the photograph. My mother wasn't born yesterday. "Minimize the damage."

"Of course." I snap a picture of the picture before I go. I'll have to know exactly what lies I'm supposed to be telling.

As soon as I'm in the hall, I text Jacob.

A photograph is about to be run in the papers. Us, in the landing at Freja's party.

There are no emojis, no unnecessary caps, and no overabundance of exclamation points. Still, my hands are shaking. Dots bounce on the bottom of the screen, and I let out a breath. Good. He made it safe to Djolny. I don't have to worry about him stuck in the mountains anymore.

Kissing???

Almost. They can't identify you, yet. The curtain hid your face. Strong silhouette only.

I clip the photograph and send it. His response is immediate.

Northern Europe will put two and two together when we're walking down the grand staircase. I'm ready to go public about us now.

My nose stings with unshed tears. Even after all these days of silence and formality, he hasn't given up. I slip into a supply closet and perch on several boxes of printer paper, tapping my phone against my head before typing a response.

The picture proves nothing. I could be getting an eyelash off your face.

Woman.

I hear his voice when he sends that single word. Woman. Exasperation and frustration in every syllable. Something else, too.

In spite of myself, a smile brushes my mouth as I type. *Don't be dramatic. You look like a cousin, maybe. For legal reasons, the article will likely speculate that you could be.*

And then systematically eliminate all possibilities with a graph. In color. They know.

They think they know. Don't worry. You're safe.

The bouncing dots appear and disappear.

I don't care what they say about me. Alma—we have a chance to set the record straight. Tell them about Pietor. Us. The whole story. Ring up Neer Hjefdal, and you could have this on the news tonight.

I choke out a painful laugh. The press is not our friend. It never is. Talking to them will only make things worse. *They don't know who you are. You don't have to involve yourself.*

The silence between us stretches. I hear the coming and going of palace office workers beyond the door. Finally, he sends a screenshot of the photo, covered in scribbles.

"Me," it reads, pointing at the darkened silhouette of his head. Another arrow points to me. "The girl I'm in love with." Heat pours through my veins, but his caption is brief. "I'm involved."

I want what he's offering so much, but being connected with me, right now, would be a disaster for him. It's too soon.

I tap out a message. *The danger of Pietor. The grand duchy of Himmelstein. The Sondish economy. The Vorburgian economy. A historic trade deal. My mother. This isn't as simple as you and me.*

His answer slices through my excuses. *Will it ever be?*

29

—·—

COMING STORM

ALMA

Are you there? I tap the words out and hit send, watching the phone for any signs of a response.

Jacob???

Why aren't you answering?

I'm ruined for meaningful work for the rest of the day, squeezing in what I can between checking my phone. I turn it off and on again. I look for a software update and ask my sisters to send me texts. Everything is in working order. Jacob has cut me off.

For good reason. What is there to say? I can't apologize. I'm handling things in the best way I know.

A team from the palace and a team from the grand duchy agree on a series of pap walks, strategically positioning Pietor and me in places where we're likely to be photographed. He surprises me with breakfast at La Baiser Chaleureux, but it was Caroline who secured a reservation for the popular bistro. We walk past a line of people who whip out their phones, and I tuck my hair behind my ear, confident that social media will push these posts to thousands. The man behind the gleaming glass display smiles in welcome, even as his confused glance twitches between me and Pietor.

Pietor takes me to a concert in a dress that should have the fashion press talking for weeks. The slit is so high, I fear the wrath of my Lutheran ancestors, and on the ride home I shiver. He never thinks to offer me his coat.

This is a courtesy I wouldn't have had to teach Jacob. As soon as we got into the car, he would have shrugged out of his coat and draped it over my shoulders. But being a prince, I have discovered, is not the same thing as being a gentleman.

I spend my days toting the opal boil from one end of Handsel to the other, giving Pietor meaningful glances in full view of paparazzi and cell phone cameras. When he puts a hand on my waist, I paste a smile on my lips.

The pictures popping up all over the internet, morning news shows, and on the homepages of every gossip site in Sondmark are convincing. We're being talked about. It's no longer about economics and state visits, for me. Over the last few days, my focus has shifted. This is for Jacob. I can't fail him.

I spend Saturday night sitting cross legged in front of the dollhouse, touching a gentle finger against the tiny spindles of the staircase, moving objects around, and staring at my phone.

On Sunday morning, I wait in the breakfast room, prepared to face the worst. The maid lays the newspapers on the table, and I reach for *The Daily Missive*, taking a deep breath before I read the headline.

Headlines.

"Princess Alma Making Sparks with Mysterious Man-bun"

"Don't Break His Heart, Alma: Friends Weigh in on the Hereditary Grand Duke"

"More Scandal Rocks the Royal Family"

Sure enough, page two has the graph of possible Wolffe cousins with percentages under each name, giving the likelihood that the man was a relation—a cousin with a strange mole I needed to inspect. The graph is rendered in color. The conclusions are unscientific but damning.

I pick up my phone, scrolling through my text history.

I can still taste the Pankedruss.

It's been days. That's biologically impossible. For the pride of Vorburg...Suck. It. Up.

Clara rushes in, her hair clipped into fat rollers, with Ella hard on her heels. "What just happened? What is this? Do you want to sue?"

Ella snatches up the newspaper. "Is this the reason why you were doing pap walks with Pietor all weekend? Did Mama make you do it? What happened with Jacob?"

I look up, and something in my face—self-pity or bone-weary exhaustion—silences them. "Mama isn't *making* me do anything."

Ella snorts. "All she had to do was ask."

My lips twist, and I blink.

"Oh, *vede*, don't look like that."

"Like what?" I'm fighting tears.

"Like Superman swallowed kryptonite. You're the steady one." She shakes her head. "This will pass. It always does. We've had eight hundred years of things just passing."

I release a slow breath. I'm the steady one. The queen's right hand. The one who can be counted on. I'm not supposed to need saving. My chin pulls with the strain of self-control.

"I have to see Mama," I say. An excuse. I need to get out of here.

Clara nods and makes way when I pass. "No one blames you for having a rebound," she states, turning the knife in my wound. "We've all done foolish things."

The thought catches in my throat. I get it. The thought of him and me...it's laughable.

The palace elects to make no comment, and we spend the rest of the day pretending six news trucks aren't parked outside the front gates, gathering man-on-the-street reactions to recent headlines, and prepare to receive Freja, Oskar, and Max to dinner.

We are to dine in the old family apartment where Mama lives in solitary splendor since Père moved out, and I help Una select the linens and china. She entrusts me with the ironing and the table settings. The work is simple but precise and keeps my mind away from full-blown panic.

Dinner is delicious, and though our family has its problems, each member of the House of Wolffe knows how to make conversation and avoid tricky subjects. Freja and Oskar give us a diverse range of topics—updates about the museum, citizenship tests, and the weather in Florence. Max doesn't try too hard to fill the silences, and Clara holds his hand under the table. He doesn't bother fighting her off or being awkward about it, but he maintains the bearing of a military officer. Mama will like that, even if she doesn't want to.

As we move into the lounge, Père kisses my forehead and gives me a quick squeeze.

"I like you," he says, apropos of nothing. How can he say so? I've messed up. The prime minister was caught on a hot mic threatening to move up talks over Freja's place in the line of succession, and the country has spent the whole day dissecting my morals—and not in a good way.

Still, my father's easy affection warms me.

When the night grows late and our small talk is exhausted, the party breaks up. Noah holds me back as the others disperse, rolling a small measure of whisky around a heavy glass tumbler and eyeing me from the sofa. Though the weight of the crown is on Mama's head, my brother, as her heir, has the right to take an interest in anything that threatens it.

"Do you blame me?" I ask, leaning against the mantel.

"I would have picked a better time to throw away a lifetime of good press." He takes a drink and smiles into the glass. "Especially for Vorburg."

"For Jacob. Do you blame me?"

He looks at me for a long while. "If it's a matter of the heart, what do I know?" he asks, voice tinged with bitterness. "You have to be careful." He lifts a hand. "I know you will. But still, things are unsettled. Freja. Clara. Even our parents." He stands and stretches, pulling me into a careless hug and kissing the top of my head. "Mama actually gave the go-ahead for Freja to visit family in Pavieau. Heaven only knows what will happen next."

When he takes himself off, I retire. But instead of turning right at the top of the stairs, I find myself outside Ella's door. She buzzes me into a darkened room, and I find her lying on the bed with a Seongan drama projected on the opposite wall, subtitles spooling out above a chair rail. She pats the bed and I crawl in, reaching for a handful of peppermint puffs, watching the flickering lights, and letting them dissolve on my tongue one at a time.

Within minutes, Clara knocks, and Ella presses a button. Our little sister pushes through the door, dragging Freja along behind her.

"We sent our menfolk off. We haven't had sister time in forever," Clara explains, shoving aside the mountain of stuffed raccoons.

Ella glares as they push their way onto the bed, flopping haphazardly as they take in the drama.

It makes no sense. Men with sharp-drawn eyebrows and elaborate up-dos execute a series of gestures in a magical duel. A woman in a contemporary business suit collapses in her cubicle in another dimension. The hero is mortally wounded, falling into some alien, wind-scoured terrain.

"What is this?" Clara asks, scooching me over.

Ella reaches for the black licorice. "It's a classic called *Knight: The Tormented and Forsaken Angel*. He's a thousand-year-old guardian spirit, and she's the national security analyst who inherits him. Hijinks ensue."

The desperate heroine shouts into the void, tears streaking her make-up as her lover, standing invisible and mute at her side, looks on.

"These are hijinks?" I bite back a wail.

Ella emits a soft laugh. "We're way past hijinks. We're in the part where he's been banished to a shadow realm for changing his destiny and daring to fall in love with her."

Vede. I want to grip the edge of a railing and shout across the frozen mountains of Sondmark. Come back. *Come back.* But Jacob is in the dark heart of Vorburg, and he has frozen me out.

"Tissue," I demand. Clara reaches to a side table and slaps one into my hand. I stanch the silent tears, only to have the thing almost disintegrate. "Tissue."

Ella halts the show when I start sobbing. She gathers me into her arms, and I bury my face in her shoulder. Clara wraps an arm around my waist. Freja covers my bare feet while every tear I've ever swallowed works its way out. I want to curl up, knees to forehead, but there is no retreating from my sisters. They would only curl with me.

"Tissue?" I ask.

Ella directs Freja. "There's another box next to my sink."

A sister slides away and returns.

"Alma." It's Clara this time.

"I'm fine."

"These things go in cycles," she tells me. "Eventually, the press will ease up." Clara should know. She's been the target of enough negative coverage to paper over every surface in the Summer Palace. "When you're in it, it feels like a hurricane. But the storm will shift."

"It's not the coverage." I press the balls of my hands into my eyes, easing the tight pressure, rubbing away the grit.

Freja's brow wrinkles and she finds her own answer to the strange sight of seeing her most self-composed sister crack up. "Your engagement is broken, but we haven't been here for you. I've been—"

"It's not that." Honestly, if it weren't for having to look affectionate to Pietor in public and having my name linked with his, I would have forgotten him entirely. When I finished with him, I finished.

Ella stares up at the baroque plasterwork on the ceiling. "This is about Jacob."

She says it like a scientist holding up a petri dish and diagnosing a bacterial bloom. This is about Jacob. Fact.

"He spent the last week on my couch obliterating an alien horde." Fact.

My nose prickles with more unshed tears. No. There is to be no more of such things. I sniff, and a fat tear rolls down my cheek.

Freja shakes her head and points to me. "She would not be overset by a tutoring assignment."

I open my mouth, and the truth comes spilling out, as though bursting through a crumbling embankment, destroying farmland and wiping out thatch-roofed cottages.

"It was New Year's Eve, and he smelled so good...Every day he showed up wearing this awful suit and every day it mattered less and less...Tailored menswear can save the world, I swear...If Freja hadn't told him about Pietor, none of this would have happened...All that training, and he still thinks he can go around beating people up when they call me names," I cry.

"Pietor deserved the fat lip," Ella spits. "My only regret is that I wasn't the one who delivered it."

"Jacob isn't supposed to be hitting anyone," I wail, glossing over my own lapse.

Clara snorts. "Max would have flattened the reporter who stalked us, but I told him it was better to cripple him financially. He only agreed because he likes precision weapons."

Freja pipes up. "I don't understand. You've been all over the papers this week with Pietor. I thought you two were back on. If not, why are you even seeing him so much?"

Ella whacks her. "Keep up. It's because of the picture in the papers today. She had to get ahead of the story and protect her reputation."

I sit up, holding my arms over my stomach. "I don't care about my reputation."

My sisters go completely still, absorbing the words until Ella breaks the silence. "Excuse me?"

I scrub my eyes with the heel of my hand. My mascara disappeared a dozen tissues ago, and I'm too tired to pretend. "The damage to me is done. I can't let Jacob—"

"Oh." Freja reaches for my hand, feeling her way through her thoughts. "You like him."

Freja doesn't grasp interpersonal relationships like the rest of us do. Things have to be an astronomically big deal before she drags her attention away from her pet obsessions. Though it's a massive understatement, my sister has hit the nail on the head. Yes. I like him.

Ella falls back and stares up at the ceiling. "I thought you were making out and flirting. No judgment," she lifts her hands. "You needed an outlet. But a Vorburgian prince—" The lyrics of the drinking song come into my head. *One Sondish princess, but not one more.*

She points at Clara, Freja, then me. "Commoner, Immigrant, Enemy. This is Mama's nightmare timeline."

Clara whacks her. "What are you going to do? Date in secret? Outingen Huis is closer to the border. You could meet—"

Bless my littlest sister for thinking of logistics. In happier circumstances, I would need love nest recommendations for my clandestine romance, but Jacob has given me days of radio silence, and I don't know what to do.

"I don't have a plan." *We* definitely don't have a plan. "I have to keep things quiet through the state visit so he can be in the spotlight without the added pressure of scandal."

I look down, twisting my fingers. My sisters take a position on every side of me, arms tight, warm breath stirring my hair.

As bad as Sunday is, Monday is worse.

Caroline finds me working in my suite. Her mouth is tight when I answer the door. After years of service to the Crown, she's never ventured into the private residential area of the palace, always staying in her place—the admin wing, with her neat, compact office out of which she conducts the affairs of Queen Helena.

"Ma'am, you need to see this," she says, handing me a stack of newspapers comprising every outlet in Sondmark and several more in a language I recognize as Vorburgian.

My heart rate spikes, and sourness rises up my throat. "Come in," I say, making my way to the sitting room and setting the newspapers on the floor. I fish *The Holy Pelican*, the most sedate newspaper in Sondmark, from the pile, and take in the head-line. "Bastard Prince a Heartbeat from Throne of Vorburg". I scan the article, "Tiffani Fawn Gardner of Blackberry, Oregon, U.S.A. was a dancer when she ensnared His Majesty King Otto of Vorburg..."

The story contains salacious elements. A girl running away from a small town and heading to Hollywood. A performer who thought she could catch a king. An unplanned pregnancy. A child raised in exile. A cancer diagnosis. A payoff. *Payoff.* The word pulls me up. That's the word they chose to describe a man taking responsibility for his child's education. The bare details are true, some of them well known in Vorburg, even, but the light shining on them is not the soft glow of positive coverage. This is the harsh illumination of a hit piece.

She doesn't have anything to do with this.

Those were almost Jacob's first words to me. I remember it being the first thing I liked about him—his loyalty to his mother and his desire to protect her, recognizing the same impulse in myself. My hands are stiff and cold as I turn the pages over. The world is being introduced to Crown Prince Jacob of Vorburg, future head of state.

"How could the courtiers in Djolny allow this?"

Caroline shakes her head. "They never would. It can't have come from those loyal to the crown."

My hands shake. "Did my mother leak this?" I have to ask. I hold my breath, waiting on the answer. If she has, I won't forgive her.

Again, Caroline shakes her head. I sense her gentle pity. "She doesn't want unnecessary drama to overshadow the state visit."

"Karl? He looks like a weasel."

Caroline flashes an expression that tells me I am unworthy of that thought and she will pretend she didn't hear it. "He's a loyal servant to His Majesty The King. Vorburg needs things to go well, even more than we do."

Who else even knew Jacob was in Sondmark? My mind spins through the possibilities, a kaleidoscope of faces and names, until it comes to rest.

Of course. "Pietor."

Caroline looks like a teacher, tapping the tip of her nose when I find the right answer. "I have no confirmation of that."

Never trust a reptile. Never turn your back on a snake. I take a breath and allow myself to see the whole picture—the mess of newsprint, the number of words dedicated to tearing into Jacob's heart and ripping the crown from his hands.

What protection will he have from his father? Heaven knows. I can't trust it. Who else will fight for him?

My hand balls into a fist, crushing the limp, gray sheets of the *Daily Worker* ("Newest Royal Set to Overturn Oppressive Trad-Fam Norm"). This is my fault. Like a skyscraper, rigged with explosives, I seem to collapse in on myself in a blast of dust and smoke. I have come, at last, to the truth.

I love Jacob.

These headlines make me want to grab ties and push people down stairs in Jacob's defense, no matter how many cameras are pointed at me.

I wade through the headlines ("Dancer High Kicks Her Way to the Crown" from *The Daily Missive*) and perch on the edge of the sofa. Holding a hand over my mouth, I try to make sense of the change. I have lived for my mother's praise, expecting a bright red ribbon with a portrait of my queen as my reward. It could never love me like he does.

"I was fighting him," I say, the words strained, "the whole time. I was trying to force him to see that the country needed to come first. Not sometimes. Always."

I don't look at Caroline, and she doesn't ask for explanations but stands, ghostlike, on the edge of the room, crowded around with dozens of other shadows—my ancestors, pressing close to hear their child discover a novel idea for the House of Wolffe.

A laugh chokes from my throat. You're not supposed to change for love. That's the idea. Advice from every women's magazine and opinion piece is that love is something you have to walk into after you're fully actualized, killing it at work, and with a year's saved wages or a real estate portfolio. An iced Americano you grab on your way to some other destination.

This isn't like that. I didn't want to love him—I was fighting—but now I have new eyes that can't unsee my government's backroom dealing, my family's shoddy alliances, and the emptiness of living like an arm of the State.

He refused to put me second to anything.

I cover my eyes but still see it. What a mess. I spent all my time worrying about Jacob's introduction to the world being perfect, but if he stepped into this room right now, he would fold me into his arms and kiss my head. He'd say that now is the perfect time to tell Sondmark that he's my man. He'd refuse to come second to a country.

Okay. I nod my head briskly. New plan. I'm going to war.

"Caroline," I say, getting to my feet, "I'm putting out a statement."

She nods. "I'll call your mother."

"No, this will come from the office of Her Royal Highness Princess Alma, Duchess of Lowenwald," I say, using my most formal title. I sound polite. But I also sound like I could sever the heads of my enemies without a drop of regret. "It's nothing to do with my mother. I'm not asking for permission."

She nods and lifts her pen, prepared to take dictation. "Yes, Ma'am."

"No," I repeat. "I don't want to get you into trouble. Just forward a list of email addresses. Oh," I say, holding a finger and darting into my room to return with the opal monstrosity in a small red box, "and send this back to Himmelstein via the diplomatic pouch."

She takes it with a tiny smile. "Right away."

My statement goes out less than an hour later with no input from courtiers or secretaries. It's simple. "Her Royal Highness Princess Alma and Pietor, Hereditary Grand Duke of Himmelstein have mutually decided to go their separate ways. During this difficult time, they ask for privacy as they look forward to the historic visit between Sondmark and Vorburg. No further comments will be given at this time."

I forward the email to several news outlets and Pietor.

Mama is going to explode, but my nation will have to build its economic policy off someone else's back. The trade negotiations will be shoved off the front pages as the press continues to speculate that I've been cheating on Pietor, but so will news of Jacob's past and parentage.

I have no realistic expectations of privacy. The press is going to be vicious, but my finger didn't hesitate to hit the send button. For once, I don't think about all the people I might be disappointing.

I see the storm coming, but I think of the submerged amber forest, waiting to give up its treasure when the waves begin to pound.

30

BRING MARSHMALLOWS

JACOB

A storm chased us from the East Gate to Djolny, dark clouds visible in the rear-view mirror. We arrived at the castle at midday, and as I waited on my father, I received Alma's text messages and the photo.

The first time I saw the image of us standing in the window, wrapped up together, I grinned. She's stuck with me. Further messages complicate the simple idea of that. If we are aboard a sinking ship, she plans to shove me into a safety vest and lash me into a life raft. "Stop being so stubborn," I type, enlarging the photo. "You're not alone."

Before I have a chance to send this message, my father enters a drawing room, breathing heavily.

I bow. Unlike the stilted effort I was capable of almost three months ago, the action is smooth and practiced. He keeps me at a distance, looking me over. I didn't travel over a snowy pass in leather-soled shoes—I'll never be that stupid—but the rubber-soled leather boot is a good compromise. Alma would be pleased I've paired some well-tailored denim with a brown belt, checked shirt, and wool blazer to meet the king.

"She hasn't destroyed your animal spirit," my father says. I lift my brow. "Ideally, a king of Vorburg should look like he could steal your wife but also beat you to death in a bar fight." He winks from a fleshy, red face. "It's the duality."

He turns to Karl. "Confiscate the phone. We'll leave for the *dacha* immediately."

He lumbers from the room. No wonder he has a decent working relationship with Queen Helena. They have the same arrogance. The same assumption of being obeyed.

Karl takes my phone and hands me off to a footman who looks like a bouncer. "This way, sir." He leads me through a series of convoluted passageways to a side entrance of the palace where three rugged vehicles are parked.

We find Karl, stuffing my duffel bag into the boot of one of the utilitarian vehicles. He catches my look. "The king likes to know he has the ability to outrun armed communists, should the need arise."

"Where's my phone?" I say. "Did you pack it?"

He lifts his head. "It's in a vault. His Majesty is taking you on a retreat."

No, no, no. "This is a bad time to be off the grid." *Chol.* I left Alma hanging in the middle of a crisis. I want to drive back over the mountains, drag her off to Max's cottage, and spend the day convincing her to take us seriously. I want to do more than talk.

Karl's brows snap together. "It isn't a request. This is a command from your king."

I release a frustrated breath. "This is my first time camping with Dad. Is he bringing the marshmallows?"

We drive hours into the most remote part of Vorburg, eventually bumping along a narrow, rutted mountain track. The cars are streaked with dirt and old snow when we pull up to an ancient timber-clad cottage, not big enough to be a full-sized house. The siding is weathered gray, and the roofline is capped with a small onion dome that sways out of alignment. Thick icicles hang from the eaves. I don't want to like it. I don't want to like anything about my father.

The grounds are set in a forest clearing, covered in snow and overgrown grass, brittle and brown. Beyond the house, a measure of land is smooth—a frozen pond with a layer of snow. Around the back I see a large, dormant garden, much like the o ne *Oma* tends.

"This is Góra Ulek." *Mountain of Ulek*. "This is our heart," my father says, climbing out of his vehicle. He claps his hands together in large, fur-lined gloves.

For once, his florid language does justice to the feelings I have looking over the snug house, eyes following the bent wood arches framing the doors and windows. He pushes through the gate, but I halt, crouching in front of the carving of a bear topping a post, stroking a hand over the butter-soft carving.

I no longer wish for Max's cottage.

To anyone else, the building might appear dilapidated, but I touch the joinery on the beams with an experienced hand, running deft fingers along carved panels of wood. It's strong.

"Ten days to turn you into a prince of Vorburg," my father says, as Karl brings in the bags. King Otto's are deposited on the ground floor—a dining room converted into a bedroom—and mine are taken up a narrow stairway.

The courtiers are dismissed. Karl whispers that they will be stationed along the road and in outbuildings, where they can secure the perimeter but leave us to ourselves.

Left alone in the silent house, I expect my father to deliver lessons in comportment, similar to the ones Alma shaped me with. Instead, Father has me chop wood and carry it in for the stove. We prepare a simple dinner and make coffee the Vorburgian way—dark and bitter—and sit in wool socks before the fire. I stare into my mug, thinking of Alma, wondering what she would think of my father's methods. Uncivilized.

I go to bed, hugging a hot water bottle, and dream that my hand is caught in a blade. I don't feel pain, but when the hand is long gone, the sensation of having it returns. In my dream, I lean across the table to touch someone out of reach. I keep having to remind myself that what's gone is gone, but I wake up to an aching loss.

Our days at Góra Ulek follow a pattern. We work in the morning, knocking the heavy snow and ice from the roof, clearing the balcony with its ancient slat design. We read books of poetry and philosophy when the sun goes down, our pages lit by the glow of a candle. Occasionally, my father places a finger to keep the page and makes some remark.

"The occupation was like that."

"Pruss caught the spirit of Vorburg. When his heroine burns her house down in the middle of winter rather than turn it over to the enemy—"

"Star-drenched midnights. Vorburgian poets are lucky they had such skies."

But midnights make me think of a Sondish princess and how much I want her in my arms. Alma is with me at every moment.

On the fourth day, he has me chop a hole in the pond with a short-handled ax. We fish for our dinner. On the fifth day, he has me make the hole bigger and walks me to a primitive sauna—hardly more than a shack in the woods—where we strip naked to the waist wrapped in long white towels and hit the hot rocks with dripping branches, grunting in our misery.

"It's time for ice," he says. I've seen this tradition. I knew it was coming. Vorburgians are hardy and proud of it, bundling their babies and leaving them to nap in frigid temperatures—even in the cities where indoor heating isn't a luxury. My father casts off the towel and runs in all his royal glory, white flanks rivaling the snow, and jumps into the water with a splash.

He comes up, sputtering a bellowing, hailing me at a distance. "If a fat old man can do it..." he shouts, waving me on. I drop the towel and run. The first rush of cold air is a relief, then a torment. My feet sting as I sprint across the ground and arctic wind whips over my skin. All those weeks Alma spent turning me into a crown prince, and now I'm ready. My steps grow heavy in the thick snow, but I don't slow my pace. The water is floating with chunks of ice. This is insane. I can't do this.

I jump. The shock slaps me across the back, waking up every nerve and baptizing me in the embrace of Mother Vorburg. The sky is clear and blue, and my eyes are dazzled by the light.

On the sixth day, Father leans from his chair. "Come here, boy." I lean from mine, and he grips me around the back of the neck—the thick nape where a bear carries a cub—and brings my nose almost touching his. "I'm the bastard. I admit it." He exhales heavily, half-drunk. "I don't expect your love."

The tang of heavy liquor colors the air between us and his words fur around the edges. "Give it to Vorburg," he says, pounding his heart with a closed fist. The fist turns, stills between us. "Vorburg." He pounds the fist against my heart.

On the eighth day, I cut my hair with a pocketknife. It's ragged, and Karl nearly passes out when he returns to the dacha with the three vehicles, responding to the flag Father raised in the garden.

"Sir," he says, taking the bags from my grip and stowing them in the car.

"I know, Karl. Have a barber waiting for me when we get back to Djolny."

"Sir." He looks like he's going to cry with joy.

The barber does his work well, leaving me enough to feel like myself but clipping the sides and back, close to the head. I'm never going to look like one of those heads of state Alma wanted me to pattern my appearance after. Father doesn't seem to want it. Let Sondmark be Sondmark. Vorburg is Vorburg. *Chol nia.* I'm hearing his voice in my head now.

The rest of the evening is dense with briefings, meeting with men and women wearing dark bureaucratic suits as they go over the logistics of the state visit, teaching me everything my father hasn't covered. Sondmark has been preparing for this day for months. My father chose to spend more than a week in isolation, throwing the entire royal apparatus into an uproar.

I note the lesson. Government priorities matter, but a king's priorities may differ.

Karl escorts me to my quarters as the evening grows late, going over last-minute instructions while I sit on the bed and remove my tie.

"I've been following the news in Sondmark," he says.

It only takes one mention of Alma, and the crown prince falls away. I push my fists into the mattress. I'm just a man, and I want her here.

"A compromising photo—"

"I saw it before you stole my phone."

"May I ask, sir, if it was you in that picture?" Karl has become deferential in a way he never was in Handsel.

I grunt.

"There's been a firestorm of speculation about who she was with."

I rub the heel of a hand over my heart. She's been in Sond-mark, facing the press alone. I'm not ignorant like I was several months ago when I first stepped foot into the Summer Palace. I know how these things play out in public now.

"Have they blamed her?" I ask, slipping off my shoes.

He nods. "She's holding up."

That's my girl.

"You have not been identified." Karl carries my shoes to the closet. "The primary problem for Vorburg is that your name and personal history have been leaked already—information about your mother, your grandparents, and a cousin who owns a junkyard. Again, papers have been—"

"What has been done about my mother?" I cut him off. I walked into this role hopelessly naïve, thinking I would be able to build a wall between the crown and my life. I thought that if I was firm enough, my mother would escape being insulted in the press. Her son would be a prince. The target would shift. It had to.

But these weeks in Sondmark—around a functional, well-oiled monarchy—have taught me that privacy is hard-won and elusive. Mom has learned that lesson already, I think. I remember how she showed up for court dates with huge sunglasses and a confident, leggy, stride.

"His Majesty flew Your Royal Highness's mother back to America as soon as he was briefed this afternoon," Karl rushes to explain. "Upon her request. She said to tell you no journalist has a prayer of getting past your grandfather and that you aren't to let Blackberry down."

I swallow and nod.

"Speaking of security, we had to scrub your phone. We'll get one reissued in the coming days. Now that you're a public figure…" He trails off.

I close my eyes briefly. "This is the job."

Karl's pale face glows with approval. "Indeed, sir."

He carefully arranges my clothes for tomorrow and turns to go. "One more thing, sir. Her Royal Highness Princess Alma announced that she and His Royal Highness have broken off their engagement," he says.

Karl's words land like old-growth timber falling from the axman's blow, taking out lesser giants, snapping branches in a violent explosion of dirt and debris. I am a forest of stunned silence.

Alma told everyone. Why? For me? It can't be. Sondmark comes first. Always first. But I can't keep back a stirring of hope.

"It was a fortunate development, actually," Karl prattles on. "Your personal biography was no longer front-page news. But, whatever you do, don't mention it when you meet the family tomorrow. I imagine it's still a tender subject. Sleep well, sir," he says, closing the door.

I stare at the ceiling the whole damned night.

31

SURRENDER NOW

JACOB

The following morning, my father and I helicopter into Handsel, separately in case of some freak catastrophe. When I decry the waste of fuel, Karl tells me I have to get used to the idea that my body is precious. I adjust the headphones, dulling the noise of the rotors, and repeat a litany. *She did it for Sondmark. She did it for Sondmark.* I don't know how publicly breaking things off with Pietor benefits the kingdom, but I'm trying to hold back unbridled optimism like a medieval monk in the face of a ferocious Vor attack.

The Vors always won, my mind says. Surrender to it now.

From the helicopter window I see black luxury cars, a military band, and a row of dignitaries lining a red carpet, including the mayor of Handsel, the prime minister, and two members of the royal family. I know from the information recited by Karl before breakfast that the advance delegation will be composed of Crown Prince Noah and Princess Alma. My heart has been beating out of my chest since then.

We touch down, and I wait for Karl's signal to exit the helicopter. I can do this. I can see Alma and not have to kiss her.

I keep this thought in mind as I advance over the tarmac, buttoning my suit jacket and remembering how the sight of it once made Alma go cross-eyed. A smile touches my lips, and I take my place, one step behind my father, while the national anthem of Vorburg plays.

Just as Alma taught me, I make no unnecessary movements. There is no fiddling with my clothes. I note the swarming presence of cameras and journalists, held back by a thin chain strung between two bollards, and feel a weight settle on my shoulders—not unexpected and, to my surprise, not unwelcome.

My father strides to the Sondish delegation, greeting Noah with a hearty kiss on both cheeks, breaking the rules of protocol and getting away with it. He gestures me forward to shake the prince's hand and exchange a few remarks. To the press on the far side of the landing pad, it must look like we're meeting for the first time.

The king has moved on when I step in front of Alma. Mindful of her exacting instruction, I don't let my eyes linger on the way the tips of her toes kiss an invisible mark on the pavement, her strong runner's legs, or the controlled sweep of her hair—just the color to pair with an amber tiara. I don't tell her that I was desperate for her in the mountain cottage where I learned to be my father's heir or that every night I woke up reaching for her.

She squeezes my hand. *Too long.* I quickly release her and move on, greeting several government officials. No one can see that I'm irrevocably in love with a princess of Sondmark. I haven't stepped an inch out of line. She would be proud of that.

The band concludes a prepared piece, and my father waves to the press, heading to a town car with tiny Vorburgian flags fluttering over the headlights. I turn to another car when a pop rings out across the tarmac.

Pop. Pop, pop, pop.

I'm confused for a half second. Then I hear security guards scramble, drawing their weapons and shouting, "Get down! Get down!"

People scream, and the crowd scatters. My father's car roars away, and the entire brass band runs for the terminal as shots keep coming. Two members of palace security grab me by the arms, pulling me in the direction of the car with its open door. *Give into them. Follow orders.* I've memorized every word Alma ever said. If I do what I'm told, I'll be out of harm's way in seconds.

Alma.

I look back to the helicopters and the crumpled red carpet to see Alma on the ground, balled into a small target and waiting for security. The need to protect this woman claws out of my chest, and I throw my shoulders hard against my guards, tearing out of the tight grip. I break into a run, roaring her name.

She screams, but I scoop her into my arms, tucking her head under my chin and covering every inch of her body I can reach.

Security grabs me when I've almost reached the car. They push our heads down and throw us into the backseat, one landing on the other. I hear the slam of the door and the screech of tires when the driver takes off.

The smell of burned rubber wafts through the vents.

"You didn't just do that," she breathes, arms strangling my neck, hand cupping the back of my head. "You could have been killed. You idiot."

She can call me any names she wants. She's alive, and she's in my arms. Nothing else matters.

The car flies over speed bumps, throwing us around the bench seat, and our driver peels onto the motorway, picking up speed in the straightaway. The sound of sirens builds and fades as police cars race by in the other direction.

"You could have been hurt," she says. "Are you hurt?" She scrambles off my lap and begins to pat me down, opening my jacket.

"I've never been better," I insist, but she continues her inspection, trusting nothing until she's touched every limb and canvassed every square inch of chest.

"Are we good?" I ask.

Not a second before she is satisfied that I am unharmed, she sits back. I work my way upright, dragging her close. The knees are blown out of her nylons and a scrape is oozing blood, but she hasn't noticed. "You're all right?" I ask.

She nods, but her whole body is shaking. She never loses her head, but she's losing it now.

"Ma'am," a voice breaks in from the driver's seat. "We've got a security update."

Alma shoves herself out of my arms, arranges the hem of her skirt, and doesn't speak until she's in total control. "Yes?"

"Our team deployed a drone within seconds of the attack, and police were able to apprehend the assailant in short order." He lifts his eyes to the rearview mirror. "The gun was firing blanks."

She sags against the leather seats. The route takes us through the city, and we pass shopping blocks and brightly lit storefronts, making the turn up the hill to the Summer Palace. I reach for Alma's hand and hold it in mine like I have every right to. There were photographers at the airport and, if I'm not mistaken, a live video feed, which I'm sure caught me charging across open ground to reach my princess. That's going to excite some comments.

"Ma'am," the driver says. "Police have his identity now. He's a native of Himmelstein."

Alma curses under her breath and meets my eyes. "Pietor," she whispers.

My brow lifts. *How?*

"Not him," she explains. "He'll have employed someone to do his dirty work. Count on it—we'll find out that the discharge was accidental or that the gun wasn't even pointed in our direction. But this happens to be the first time you stepped onto the public stage, and he made sure to ruin it. He said he would."

Alma runs a quick tongue across dry lips. She's still shaking.

"I'm going to kill him." We say this at the same time, and she breathes a laugh. "My mother will beat us to it." Alma lifts her voice to the driver. "Aren't we going around back?"

"Word from the palace is that the official reception will go forward, ma'am."

"*Stultes es*," she mutters, putting a hand to her temple. "I don't think I can do it."

I know Alma. As angry and upset as she is, she'll be furious at herself if she doesn't.

"Take off your nylons," I say. "They're ruined."

I turn my head while she writhes out of the stockings, and I reach for a bottle of expensive water. Unscrewing the cap, I spill some into my pocket square, handing it to her over my shoulder. "See to your knee."

She lifts it free, and a few seconds later I hear a gasp. Her fingers are in my hair, tugging the short crop back. "What have they done?" Her voice wobbles. "Jacob—"

I lay a hand over her fist and the car slows. Ready or not, we're in the palace forecourt under the watchful eye of courtiers and clicking shutters.

I pull out of her grasp and look her over. There is a tiny gash on her knee, still, but she looks like my Alma. I take a large breath and drink in the sight of her. It has been too long. I brush her face with my fingertips. "It's just a haircut."

Her mouth tightens. "It's not just—"

I buck my chin toward the palace and the long line of waiting dignitaries. "We'll talk about it later," I promise without an inkling of how I'm going to pull that off. Gone are the days when I wandered the palace without an entourage.

I know what Alma would want. She would want to remember her responsibilities. She would want to perform her duty to Sondmark and her queen without weeping through the introductions or keeping the whole delegation waiting.

"You look good," I say, assessing rather than complimenting. "Let's go stun them with perfection."

"This isn't finished." She blinks away her tears and reaches for the door.

Chol. We haven't said anything. Almost two weeks of missing her, and I didn't grab her by the shoulders and speak in a loud and clear voice, "I need you. Let's settle this."

Too late to grab her back now. She steps from the car, swinging her knees in a careful arc, and strides forward.

I play my part as well as she does, laughing when Her Majesty passes off the security nightmare as a little hiccup, easily brushed aside. I recognize the pretense but appreciate the need for it. So much of Vorburg's economic future rests on this historic meeting.

Caroline ushers us into a large reception room to examine a series of artifacts: a gift dating from the reign of Piasa II, one of many peace treaties which failed to halt the War of the Amber Cross, its heavy wax seal as dark as blood, and an original photograph of my father dangling from a helicopter ladder over the crowds at Liberation Square.

Cameras click, and the princes and princesses wander after our parents, drawing near when one of Their Majesties points out some interesting historical fact. Freja, on what must be her first official assignment since her wedding, walks with Alma. I can't be at her side and not want to touch her, so I keep pace with Noah. He pauses by the Amber Cross.

We're beyond the range of microphones, and he makes a good picture as he points at the relic. "Alma is my closest sister," he murmurs. "I don't know what your father asked you to do—"

"My father has nothing to do with this." My tone is level.

I glance up, catching Alma's reflection in a mirror lining the wall. Her head is bent over an antique brooch, highlighting the soft skin of her neck. I must look too long because Noah coughs lightly.

"Anytime you want to return the rest of the jewels in the set," he says, pointing at the Amber Cross, "we've got a place for them at The National Museum."

"No deal." My gaze returns to Alma. "My wife would never forgive me."

32

QUEEN'S PEACE

ALMA

When the delegation from Vorburg departs for their quarters, I watch Jacob's retreating form. He is exactly what I asked for. Reasonable hair, correct manners, and the ability to answer the demands of public conduct. There he is, the man of my dreams.

I don't want it.

The reception room doors boom shut, and my sisters rush to my side, talking over each other and hugging me close. Farther down the room, Mama is in a rage, issuing orders to Caroline to dig up Pietor's financials "yesterday" while Noah is on his phone, his tone blistering. "Destroyed. Do you hear me? We're going to own Himmelstein by Christmas."

It's not a hug, but I'm comforted by their fury.

Père wades through a sea of princesses and cups my face, resting his forehead on mine. For several beats, we breathe the same air and my heart matches his easy rhythm. Gripping his wrists, I let the tears slip down my cheeks.

"Do you feel up to this?" he asks when Caroline reminds us of the schedule. I nod and move to follow my sisters, returning to their suites to prepare.

Mama looks up from her twelve-point plan to annihilate Pietor.

"Follow me to my office for a moment," she calls.

When I stand before her desk, I'm conscious of the scraped knee and scuffed heels.

She's barely spoken to me since I released a statement without running it through official channels, focusing her efforts on Sondmark, trying to stay in the national conversation when the prime minister keeps trying to sideline her. She feels more isolated than ever, and I don't blame her, but the biggest headline in northern Europe was primed to be, "Neanderthal Mouth-Breathing Prince Falls on Face, Future of Vorburg in Doubt" and, in a few short, explosive sentences, I shifted the story. "Princess Alma: Cheater." I don't regret it.

Mama halts in front of me, her mouth set. We have not become accustomed to our new roles. I am not her faithful right hand or the keeper of the queen's peace. I am trouble.

She takes a breath. "The crown prince"—she avoids his name—"saved your life. Though the gun had blanks, he had no way of knowing that. This is his first time in such a situation, and the fear would be incredible. I was watching it live." Her mouth tightens, but her eyes are fixed on me. "What I saw was a man turn from the safety of an armored vehicle to run across open ground under a hail of what he supposed was gunfire to rescue my child."

My child.

The words aren't a commendation or a badge of honor. They're not a title conferred because of my worthiness or merit. I didn't earn them. I *am* her child, and hearing her say the simple words is as soothing as oil applied to a stubborn hinge, restoring it to proper working order.

"Are you going to offer him the Order of the Dragonslayer?" I ask, clearing the tightness in my throat.

The tips of her fingers press together, a light tapping that betrays her discomfort. "I wondered if he might prefer my eldest daughter."

I stand up very straight, shock rippling through my body.

"Surprised?" she asks. Her gaze swings to the window and the ocean beyond. "You think I don't know you? You think that being the firstborn princess under a monarch with high expectations is such a mystery to me?" Her smile is strained, and she releases a short breath. "Kissing on landings. Trashing your reputation in the press. You would never do such things for a man if it wasn't serious."

"Jacob," I say, carrying his name as carefully as a crown jewel on coronation day.

She nods, a nod that says, *Queen Magda never had to do this.* "Jacob. If you're determined to have him, I will approach his father to arrange a match."

My lungs stop functioning. This offer is a stunning admission from a proud queen. King Otto would jump at the chance to borrow legitimacy from Sondmark. It's the perfect solution. A contract marriage. Negotiated intimacy.

"No," I murmur. "No, thank you."

A line forms between Mama's brow. "Alma, I'm giving you my approval to go forward with this relationship."

I recognize the sacrifice Mama is making, and I attempt to be as diplomatic as possible. "This matter is not your concern." Her brows gather and I explain. "I have no wish to time a wedding announcement so that we're not interrupting commodities trading. If there is even one committee meeting about it, I would be tempted to follow Freja's footsteps."

My hand shakes with the effort to be as clear as crystal, and the spinning world slows to a crawl. "I mean this with the greatest respect in the world, Mama," I say, drawing a sharp breath. "I love him, I hope he still loves me, and we will decide the course of our relationship on our own."

Magda the Great would have called this treason and started a war. My mother closes her eyes and takes a breath, but the war is within, raging across her face. She wants to maneuver, make commands, and see that her will is done. She wants to find the next move in a larger game, working for the good of Sondmark. But I've given her no room to negotiate.

When she swallows, I know I've won. "A little discretion will go a long way to smoothing his path as a future monarch and making you, as a couple, more acceptable to both countries. Try to convince him to slow down," she suggests.

I breathe a laugh. If he wants me, it won't be possible.

If. The word is like a hairpin, digging into my scalp.

Mama dismisses me. I return to my suite to surrender myself to the hairdresser, spending a good long time with my make-up and a magnifying mirror to erase the effects of a near-assassination and standing toe-to-toe with the most powerful queen in Europe.

I have chosen the dress I wore on New Year's Eve—cut low and glittering. The fashion press will call wearing one dress for two occasions a sustainable choice. I might get lucky and they'll say I'm a good example. I chose it simply because I hope Jacob will remember kissing me.

Ella puts her head around my door, not bothering to knock. "Have you seen social media?" she asks.

I step away from the mirror and examine the placement of the sash pinned to my bodice. "Not when I can help it."

She rolls her eyes. "You're a new GIF." My heart sinks. Not another one. "It's spawned hashtags such as #pietorwhatpietor, #herfaceisathreeactplay, and #onemoreprincess. It's you on the tarmac today, and if you ask me, it's a little soon for the internet to be doing its thing. Do you feel up for a look?"

Jacob is safe, and Pietor has people queuing up to make him rue this day. I can take anything. She holds up the phone.

The scrambling security guards and lumbering brass band have been cropped out. The camera lens is trained tightly on my face in the seconds before and after Jacob reaches me. I vaguely remember screaming at him to get safe and the GIF plays the tail end of that fury and terror. Then he has me in his arms and the panic drops away, melting into surprise. I'm not looking anywhere else but at him and then our eyes lock. I'm calm. Safe. My face...my cheeks burn. My face is a three-act play.

"It's not that bad," Ella says. "Everyone knows cameras lie."

"It's not lying."

I smooth my skirt and drag her off to the reception room, where Mama inspects us, her exacting gaze sliding over our jewels and our gowns, the sashes and orders secured at our shoulders. Ella fidgets, her glittering tiara a little lost in her bright curly hair.

"We don't jiggle in Sondmark," Mama observes. Ella ceases tapping her feet and lifts her chin.

Mama nods at Freja, offering no criticism. It would sound silly if she did. As long as my sister might be forced out of the line of succession, fussing about her dress is like applying touch-up paint to the wreckage of the Hindenburg.

Mama's gaze slides to me. I wonder if she recognizes her perfect princess anymore. This Alma hates pickled herring. She knits poorly. She dislikes the Lowenwald tiara (which she is wearing right now). She loves a Vorburgian bear who doesn't know how to tie his shoes.

Mama looks like she's searching for something nice to say when Père walks to her side.

"Helena," he says, lifting his arm. Mama stares at it, the Zouvier diamonds swinging from her neck. Then she brings her fingertips to rest lightly on his sleeve. It feels as though nature and heaven and the entire country holds its breath.

He escorts her to her spot and Clara mouths from the end of the line, "What is happening?"

I lift my shoulder as guests begin to file into the room, finding their dinner partners. Caroline escorts Jacob to my side, and my heart lodges in my throat. He didn't say one thing about missing me when we raced through Handsel in the back of the car, and I'm trying to wring every bit of comfort I can from his impeccable manners and first-class hug. It isn't quite enough to quiet my nerves.

"Good evening," I murmur. My eyes lift to his jawline and no higher. This affords me a stunning view of the way his tuxedo skims his broad shoulders, and I offer up a silent message of gratitude to Mr. Tumwater, his fairy godfather of precision tailoring.

The room is a crush of people bristling with orders and merits. Clara scoots past me to reach the Minister of the Exchequer, jostling me lightly, and I overbalance into Jacob, gripping his muscled arm though the material of his jacket.

He sets me on my feet, dipping his head to look me square in the face. His eyes lift to the tiara, and when I put a hand to my hairline, our fingers brush.

"It's fine," he murmurs, mouth tipping in a smile. His eyes drop, skimming along my shoulders and over my curves. "Nice dress. It's my favorite."

The softness in his voice nearly undoes me. To say I missed him would be to say that the earth is round—true but a gross understatement. I haven't thought of anything else in weeks, and the amount of sleep I've lost is beginning to place a heavy burden on my retinol cream.

"Has Miss Pendragon been solving any murders while I was away?" he asks, tucking my hand into the crook of his elbow.

"Not one," I manage. The trumpets begin a fanfare, and the tall doors swing open. Caroline nods and we follow, two by two, in the wake of elegant Mama and imposing King Otto.

Jacob's pace is perfect, his posture formal but relaxed. We're expected to exchange a few words as we go but I can't think of anything to say. He gives me a few smiles as we descend the staircase into the Great Hall, careful to make way for my dress. The press will approve of that.

He pauses before the official photographer, and we smile. I know as I hear the click of the shutter that nothing can be made of this. Not even the grimiest gossipmonger will be able to wring the tiniest bit of juice from two grown adults performing official duties as bloodlessly and impersonally as we are.

I remember the GIF and almost stumble. *Fool.* No matter how professional we look, the stories will be about how he saved a Sondish princess—carried me off like I was his stolen bride—and about how I held onto him like he was my life. Nothing will matter next to that.

When the banquet gets underway, I tell myself the worst is over, but the food tastes like sawdust, and I blindly lift my glass when the monarchs toast one another. During the fish course I raise my eyes to find Jacob's gaze on my hands, a shadow of a smile touching his mouth.

"Is the herring going to be studied under a microscope?" he murmurs, nodding to my plate. I look down, knife and fork in hand. The slices are paper thin.

I slip one into my mouth, controlling my features with superhuman strength. "I hope you enjoy the Pankedruss custard when it comes. I added it to the menu for you."

"Alma," he reproves. My name on his lips is enough to give me hope through the cheese course.

Dancing follows the dinner, and I have to watch Jacob escort the daughter of a Sondish ambassador through a waltz. He moves with strong, sure steps around the floor and I turn my back on it, weaving from group to group, shaking hands and laughing about fishing rights or old wars—whatever it's diplomatically expedient to laugh at. We're in the same room, but protocol keeps us apart. The clock above the band is a mill stone, grinding me into chaff with each passing hour.

At the ragged end of the party, Caroline halts at my side. She's wearing a severe black dress with a nipped in waist and carrying herself with the unmistakable air of a woman who could point any guest to a bathroom.

"Good evening, ma'am," she says. "Are you enjoying your-self?"

I'm in love with the crown prince of a foreign country and see a bleak future bearing down like a freight train. But, other than that, I'm fine, Caroline. And you?

"You've done a wonderful job," I say.

"Please don't linger at the end of the party," she observes. "The logistics are well in hand."

She slips back to her duties, no doubt to organize the catering staff or manage the loading and unloading zone, her steps brisk and efficient. I imagine her donning a reflective pinny and tak-ing up lighted batons to untangle potential parking snarls when everyone else has gone to bed. I'm thankful for it. If I can't be a perfect right hand for my mother, Caroline will. She can always be counted on.

At a quarter to midnight, King Otto is persuaded to retire, and my mother endures his effusive farewells. Jacob follows his father's resolute steps, and I dip a curtsey as they pass. A burden shifts onto my chest, and I almost stagger under its weight. Jacob and I won't speak again for the duration of this visit. Not alone. I know the schedule better than anyone and can account for every minute, from the moment he wakes up tomorrow until the moment he boards that helicopter again.

Caroline has promised to manage the details of the party, and I need rest. I need to figure out how to get through to Jacob, even if he's blocked my number.

I slip out of the ballroom and scurry up the staircase in the Great Hall, nodding to the extra security detail placed at the head of the private wings. The palace exhales with the sounds of a retreating feast, and I halt in my tracks.

I'm in a centuries-old palace. I pick up my pace, almost running down the darkened hall, eyes trained on the carpet.

We have secret passageways.

33

— • —

SECRET PASSAGEWAYS

ALMA

"Your posture," I hear, the voice low and amused, as familiar as my own.

Jacob is leaning up against the wall, still in his tuxedo, the tie loosened, crumpled against his white shirtfront, and I'm hit with a wave of longing. He's waiting for me, just like always.

He clicks his tongue several times against his teeth. "What kind of impression do you hope to make if you can't put your shoulders back?"

I recognize the words as some of my own. Blood races through my veins, too fast for sense, and I push through the door of our suite. He rolls behind me, and I feel the weight of his gaze like a touch. Jacob is back.

"How did you get here?" I ask, continuing to my room, knowing he won't ask permission to follow. Counting on it. Every nerve in my body is sparkling like a firework. "The footmen wouldn't have let a son of Vorburg up the staircase in the Great Hall on a night like this."

I perch on a chair, and he steps behind me. "Does your tiara hurt?" he asks.

I shake my head. "Not much."

He puts his hands to my hair, drawing pins from the complicated knot one by one.

"Caroline was in charge of assigning rooms," he murmurs, fingers brushing the sensitive skin around my ears. "She gave me the Tower Suite and made sure I knew where the amenities were. She even offered up a history lesson about the wars of succession while she was at it."

"Why are we talking about the wars of succession?" I ask, a furrow in my brow. We could be talking about us.

His gray eyes dance, and he gives me his infuriating American grin. I lose my train of thought for a moment but, when it returns, I bolt upright and turn in my chair, mouth agape. "Did she actually show you where the secret passageway was?" The location of every hidden passage in the Summer Palace is almost a state secret. I'm surprised Caroline didn't take the information to her grave.

Hands on my shoulders, warming my skin, he turns me around to face the mirror. "She didn't have to, once I knew it was there. I'm familiar with traditional construction techniques and was"—he gives me another grin—"pretty motivated to work it out."

He removes the last hairpins and lifts the tiara from my head. With careful hands—hands I could trust with my life—he places it into the box along with the earrings. A knock sounds on the outer door. "You'd better do it," he says, leaning down to press a kiss into the crook of my neck. A blush blooms from the spot and blood rushes through my veins. "The Cyclops wouldn't suit you at all."

When I return, Jacob is waiting for me in the sitting room. Late as it is, he's touched a match to the fire, and light spills across the patterned carpet.

He sets the fireguard, and we look at each other for a long while. I wonder how far we've traveled from those first tentative steps on my sister's landing. He wanted a promise I couldn't give. Every minute, I've wished to go back and give it.

It can't be too late. It can't. I close the distance between us, touching the close-cropped hair above his ear. "They cut your hair."

He catches my hand and shakes his head, nuzzling into my palm. "*I* cut my hair."

My chin trembles. "You swore you wouldn't, no matter how much I tried to get you to." Jacob's hair was as much a part of him as Blackberry and concert tees. "I never should have—"

He bites the smile on his lip. "Are you about to admit you were wrong about something?"

"I have a whole presentation," I say.

He kisses my palm, and I catch my breath. Even without the long hair, my heart turns over when he touches me. "You know how I love your monologuing. What's it about?"

"My great aunt wore fashion turbans for thirty years—at least a decade past her prime. Powder blue turbans with brooches jabbed into the center. Queen Magda had tattoos up and down her arms—"

He chuckles, his low laughter warm in the shadows. "Magda the Great? That Magda?"

"King Frederick VI used to braid his beard and tie the ends with red bows. He tried to turn leather shorts into formal court dress, and no one ever accused him of not taking the affairs of state seriously."

Jacob's grin is lopsided. "He was the one with the high body count, so they wouldn't."

I flick his stomach.

"Oof," he says, rubbing the spot, inching closer.

"You could have kept your hair long and still become a great king."

"I'll remember you said that," he promises. "I'll hold you to it for the rest of your life." His look is like the touch of a match to dry tinder.

"Why did you do it?" I ask. "I loved your hair."

"Now she tells me," he murmurs, close enough to breathe in. "I saw that picture you sent. We didn't need the press to start connecting the dots at a time like this."

I nod. "Vorburg doesn't need that kind of publicity."

He tips his chin. "Agree."

He's so close, I can't even think. "You're admitting I'm right about something?"

A smile tucks his cheek. "Sometimes Vorburg will need me to get out of its way," he shakes his head, "but that's not why I did it. You were being chewed up by the press, and I couldn't leave you on your own." He touches a lock of hair, rolling it through his fingers. "Maybe there was a better solution, but I couldn't ask you what to do. Karl took my phone and still hasn't given it back."

At his words, some painful tourniquet unwinds, and blood returns to starved organs, relief coming almost immediately.

"Oh..." Jacob digs into his pocket and places something into my hand. "While I was away, I had time for this."

I hold the object up between us in the low light, picking out the chipped paint and playful curves of a tiny rocking horse, repaired and fitted with a smooth, newly carved forelimb. No one would mistake it for brand new, and the end result isn't perfect. But it isn't broken. I run a finger along the ridge of its back and see a flash of its future. Queen Ageltheld was reputed to be a white witch. Maybe this is her gift—to see curly-haired boys riding on their father's back around the castle nursery, laughing as he growls like Ulek. One of them clutches the horse under his chin when his mama tucks him into bed.

I touch what is left of Jacob's unruly hair, running my fingers through the length. He sacrificed his most precious thing—not the hair but the stubborn insistence that he wouldn't fall in line with everything royal—because it would save me some agony in the press. I take a deep breath and feel every fiber and filament crowded with love.

My dreams used to be modest—to help Mama, to serve well, to behave always—but when I'm with Jacob, he makes every room feel too small and every horizon feel impossibly big.

"You cut it, just like that?" I laugh. I can feel how my eyes shine.

"Just like that." He lifts a brow. "You don't hate it, do you?"

"Don't be silly." I swallow. "I love you no matter what you look like." His smile disappears. I've never told him so, and it deserves more than to be tucked into another conversation like a loose receipt, marking our spot. But we'll come back. I'll say it again and again for as long as I live.

I brush his hair off his forehead. "You're going to grow it again."

"Alma," he says, his voice gruff as he pulls me into his arms. I slip the rocking horse onto the mantel and fit myself against him, reaching up on my tiptoes to kiss his mouth—a warm, clear declaration that I am his. It's not enough. He lifts me until my feet leave the ground, and I hear a roll of laughter before his lips settle on mine, dark-tinged and sweet, leading me off carefully marked paths and into the forest.

Together, we lose our way and forget ourselves, lingering in the magical woods.

"Tell me why you released a statement," he asks when he lifts his head, breath shaking from his lungs.

"You can't turn the people you love into pawns," I say, repeating the words of my aunt. "Not if it's really love." I try to pull away slightly, needing him to understand, but he gathers me into his arms again. "I'm sorry that I treated you like a secondary concern. I'm sorry that I wanted you only at the right time and under the right circumstances. I'm sorry for being so worried about inconveniencing my country or looking bad in the press. I'm sorry that I didn't want to make any sacrifices." I tug at my lip.

He pushes a gentle thumb across my mouth, releasing it.

"I'm sorry I didn't tell everyone that I wanted to date you—" I whisper.

"Date," he grunts, dipping his head, pressing a fierce kiss on my lips. "We're not going to date."

I breathe a laugh. The ancient Vors had a tradition called handfasting. It tied a couple together with promises before a priest cinched them up at an altar—not yet married, but almost as good as. I lace our fingers together until my soft palm is kissing his calloused one. I imagine a cord twining around our wrists, weaving an unbreakable knot to bind us together.

"I don't need you to tell the press about us," he answers. "Not yet. It's enough that you don't have a public fiancé. I don't mind keeping it quiet."

"I'm not keeping you a secret," I counter, ready to dictate a press release.

He smiles. "Then keep us private. There's a difference."

My breath catches. I didn't understand Freja until this moment, how she could know Oskar was for her—enough to stake her life on it. I didn't understand how she could get carried away and forget herself.

I understand now.

Jacob traces rough fingertips along my neck and follows them with kisses. "I don't want to go back to Vorburg."

I know what the rest of the state visit looks like—events planned for every minute of the stay, no chance to run away, no accidental brush of hands that won't be caught by a photographer. Vorburg is going to demand his time and energy, and I see the difficulties ahead as clearly as ever. We belong to hostile countries, our reputations have taken a hit in the press, and I don't know how anyone will accept us. But I remember something I told him when he grumped about losing his right to vote in American elections. Loyalties can't be divided.

Mine aren't.

I rub the short bristles at the back of his neck and guide his lips where I can reach them, loving the way his powerful body surrenders at my lightest touch. "I don't want to stay in Sondmark," I say. I might die if I can't kiss him again.

He pulls me to him, solid muscle banding my waist. "So we're doing this. I'm going to need an itinerary and a timetable of how often we see each other, boss. Locations and logistics."

"I'll have it to Karl by noon," I promise.

I cut off his laugh with a kiss, breathing him in, and with each touch, he tells me that his heart is in my keeping. I finally understand what I have, I think, cupping his face with my unsteady hand. It's far too precious to place in a box and surrender it to the care of anyone else.

Silently, I make a vow. No matter what pressures are brought to bear upon us, I will fight every dragon of Sondmark to safeguard the heart of my prince.

I lead him to the sofa, and we weave more knots between us. The coming days will be difficult. We need to store up reserves against the frustration of being in different countries and the rational arguments to choose anything but this.

His thumb traces along my bare ring finger, up and back, imprinting his touch.

The mantel clock chimes twice.

"It's late," he says, lifting his head. "I should let you sleep."

I groan in protest, slipping into his arms again when he pulls me to my feet. "You don't have to sound like you're doing me a favor."

The fire has turned into glowing coals, and blue moonlight touches the planes of his face. I trace a finger along his lips and he kisses it. "I know I'm not what you planned for," he says, eyes searching my face. "Are you happy?"

I pull his head down for one more kiss, unable to resist smiling against his mouth.

I'm happy.

34

Epilogue

ALMA

Jacob and I shamelessly exploit a loophole in Mama's North Sea Confederation that permits open travel between Sondmark and Vorburg. He has never been stopped by border guards on the way to Max's cottage.

I pull up to the small house and hit the brakes in a wash of gravel, leaping from the car. Mist touches my face as I stow my keys, and before I can knock on the door, I'm yanked under the low-hanging eaves around the corner. I emit a little squeak. The purse drops to the ground, and I have just enough time to throw my arms around his neck before Jacob's mouth settles on mine.

His kisses are starving. "A whole week," he grumps, tipping my chin up, punctuating each thought with a deeper kiss. "Just texting. Video chats. Voice messages. Phone calls. I'm not kissing you anywhere near enough."

My fingernails scrape the back of his head, and a shiver works across his shoulders. We are blind to the fact that anyone could walk by. I work myself more firmly into his arms with a sigh. If we have to spend the whole evening in the company of others, I'm not going to hurry this. I forget everything until the honk of a car horn makes me jump. I peer around Jacob's shoulder, absentmindedly brushing sawdust from his sleeve.

"Who invited Freja and Oskar?" I mutter. Jacob kisses my temple, and a laugh rumbles through his chest.

"I did," Clara says, tipping her head around the door. She looks at the complex tangle of hands and bodies I comprise half of, and clears her throat. "Could you guys keep things tame for company?"

"Genuinely unsure," I answer.

"Come see my progress," Jacob says, dragging me into the cottage. He's been constructing a built-in bookshelf and window seat for Max, and though he's tidied his work away, the smell of fresh-sawn lumber tickles my nose.

"You couldn't get Ella to come?" Freja asks, absently kissing my cheek and handing a bottle of wine off to Max.

Oskar peels her out of her coat and hangs it in a closet. Jacob is hard on his heels with mine, and he exchanges a few words of Sondish with Oskar, proud to show off his unbroken DosParlance streak.

"She's been busy, and said she wasn't ready to face so many couples. Give her time," I tell Freja, wandering into the kitchen.

The food is excellent. Clara tried homemade pasta, and Oskar murmurs an offer to teach her how to do hand-rolled *panze*, a traditional Pavian dish.

Jacob eats with his left hand, anchoring an arm around my waist, and brushing the cleft with the edge of his thumb. I thought we'd managed to be discreet, but at the end of the meal—after talk of naval deployments, museum funding, and Jacob's upcoming investiture—Clara stands. "If you two are going to be nauseating at the dinner table, you're going to do the dishes," she laughs.

"Fine by me," Jacob says, snapping on a pair of sunshine yellow gloves and leaning over to kiss my neck.

We've finished every knife and serving spoon when Clara steps in, her face unreadable. "Alma, you need to check your phone."

I wipe my hands and unsilence the notifications. *Ping. Ping, ping ping.* This is never good news. Did someone catch a video of Jacob crossing the border? Did a forensic photographer identify Jacob on the landing?

Jacob slips an arm around my waist, his hand resting on my hip, and I lean into him. Whatever it is, it's not going to change what I feel. I'm good. This is good.

No, not good. The best.

It scares me how near I was to accepting Pietor's opal ring and his organic baker. These days, my prayers include profound gratitude for Italian Bikini Model Philanthropists.

"There's a link on PAPZ," Clara says, directing me to the notorious gossip site as the others crowd into the room.

My fingers fumble with the search bar, but finally the page pops up. How bad can it be? Another replay of Jacob's daring rescue? A sour drop hits my stomach when I see my name in the headline. The press has had a lot of material from the House of Wolffe, and I'm no longer immune to negative stories and hand-wringing polls.

"Grand Duke's Sexy Beach Clean-up: Cheater in Paradise." The pictures attached to the article are the same ones that fractured my engagement to Pietor.

I murmur aloud, "New photos shared by ReadHe user @trashpandaprincess showing Pietor, Grand Duke of Himmelstein romping with internationally famous philanthropist-model Gabriella Campana, shed new light on the break-up of Princess Alma's royal engagement..."

My mouth drops open. News coverage in the last few weeks has been savage, and I never expected to get my reputation back.

I lift my head. "Mama wouldn't have leaked this, no matter how bad things got."

My sisters nod. Mama's best tactic is frozen silence and this—the pictures, the ReadHe caption that went with them ("It was over in December.")—is steaming hot tea.

Jacob reads aloud over my shoulder. "Citizens of both Vorburg and Sondmark, rooting for a romantic development between Vorburg's Crown Prince Jacob and Sondmark's Princess Alma, have new reason for hope." He gives a low chuckle and pulls me against his chest, arms crossing over my waist.

"Who is @trashpandaprincess?" I ask. "How does she know any of this? And what is a trash panda?"

"It's a social media thing," Freja answers. I still can't wrap my head around the fact that she cares about social media. "They're describing a raccoon."

"Racoon? Who—" I begin.

Jacob beats us to it, his laugh filling the cottage. "You seriously don't know?" He bumps his chin. "That's Ella."

Acknowledgements

My beta readers did some heavy lifting on this one. Afton Nelson, Paula Thacker, Kylene Grell, and Debra West did not roll their eyes to my face when I gave them janky draft after janky draft. For that, I am truly thankful. They are all women of sense and good taste, and these books wouldn't be as wonderful without their feedback.

Kristin Gardner is my Asian drama bestie, and it was such a happy opportunity to use her last name for my hero. I was looking for an occupational surname to indicate Jacob's humble origins, but let me assure you that Kristin is a queen. We bond over poetry and drama. Our DMs include everything from esoteric meditations on the art and purposes of storytelling, aaaaaaaaaalllllll the way down to heart-eyed, kdrama romance fangirling. Get yourself a friend like that.

Leni Kauffman produced such a wonderful cover. I love her. The rise of AI will be a rollercoaster but I want you to know that the human being behind this image is a genius of experience, creativity, and talent.

Emily Poole is my editor at Midnight Owl Editors and you should know that any misplaced commas should be laid at my door. She does a wonderful job cleaning up my manuscripts and I'm like a janitor at an art museum who can't resist adjusting the canvases once everything is in place.

My family is precious to me. This year, three of my five children will be in college and I'll wander the empty houses of Casa Dominguez wondering where all the noise went and why my Scotch tape is so easy to find. It's not been perfect but love is like spackle. It covers all the cracks. I thank Nathan, Jonah, Jane, Spencer, Zac, and Maren for making it possible to be a wife, a mother, a church lady, a kdrama enthusiast, and an author, even when it's sometimes sketchy.

I'd like to thank my readers. I appreciate the reviews and social media posts. I love it when you rope sisters, friends, mothers, cousins, and neighbors into trying these sweet royals books. I am not a marketing genius (alert the presses), but you've helped me enormously. When I'm rewriting a kiss for the seventh time or considering the expenses of being an author, I think, "But my readers are the best and they deserve the best I can give them."

Finally, I'd like to leave you with an Asian drama recommendation. (Can we turn this into a thing? Sure.) Lovely Runner is currently rejiggering my brain chemistry in the best way. You may recognize the image of Byeon Woo-seok on the cover, when Princess Ella gets her love story.

Happy reading, Dearests. Until next time!

ABOUT THE AUTHOR

Keira Dominguez loves her husband.

She has more adult children than children-children, and it's going to take some time for her to come to grips with that.

She writes slowly and reads poetry.

She gets seasonal allergies in the spring and wears warm socks in the fall.

Though many areas of her life might stand to be streamlined or maximized, she does not know how she got to be such a lucky duck.

Also by Keira Dominguez

The Magical Regency Series

Her Caprice

The Telling Touch

The Sweet Rowan

The Royals of Sondmark

The Impossible Princess

The Winter Princess